MIDNIGHT KISSES

a novel by

JEANINE BENNEDICT

*To everyone who wants to be better now.
Give yourself time to grow and heal, and
never let the mistakes of your past impact
your vision of the future.*

Or, as 21 Savage puts it:

i am > i was

NOVEL OVERVIEW
EXPECTATIONS AND WARNINGS

Please do not read this novel if you are not comfortable with graphic, explicit sexual content or if you are still coping with the loss of a loved one. If you are sensitive to references to substance abuse, please be cautious when reading. Discussions of a toxic relationship are present, though not displayed, and there is brief mention of suicide.

This is a grumpy-sunshine, college, sports romance that's centered around a friends-with-benefits relationship. This novel has a lot of detailed sex scenes in it (erotica) and is an emotional, slow-burn romance.

This book was also written prior to the NCAA's revision of the NIL compensation laws regarding college athletes, which is why college athletes are not financially compensated in this universe.

For more detailed content warning, visit itsjeanyb.com and scan code below for the official playlist

GRETA

ORAL FIXATION

I'VE NEVER BEEN one to say no to a party, especially if they serve free booze without a bullshit BYOB policy. But today, I wish I had.

"You didn't tell me this party is hosted by the football team," I gripe to my close friend James. He sways to the music, looking around the room aimlessly as he sips a beer.

"I didn't?" James feigns a gasp of surprise and shrugs. "Whoopsy-daisy."

My right eye twitches and I clench my fist. "I'm about to whoopsy your daisy."

"Kinky." He wiggles his brows and winks. "Me likey."

If I had a propensity for violence, James would be dead meat. Scratch that—he'd already be six feet under. The first time I met him, I'd been in dire need of a caffeine fix but also fearful of being late to class, a fear that turned out to be legitimate when he stole my coffee order at my favorite campus cafe, *195 Extractions*. Upon taking a belated seat in the back row of our government class, I'd caught sight of a small latte with the name GRETA etched on it, and thus reignited my once-dormant instinct to kill.

I was livid, especially when the professor publicly shamed me for being irresponsible with my time.

But as it is, I'm a pacifist. This is to say, though I wish I could pack a fist, I instead embody tranquility, not violence, to guide my life.

"Don't be upset," James urges when I remain stoic to his quip. He winces when my scathing glare persists. "It's not like anyone'll recognize you."

Recognition is the least of my concerns. I don't go to football games or accompany my father, Riverside's head football coach, publicly.

But let's play a game of *Things That Won't Ever Happen* and say I am recognized. It's not as if any of his players would approach me. *Le désir de l'interdit*, but not when it might get them benched for the entire season.

No. What I'm fucking pissed about is that for every fitted jersey I see, all I can think about is *him*, and that makes my stomach drop. My insides ache to where standing in this house, surrounded by men who smell like sweat and cheap Dollar Tree soap, is unbearable.

Though it's less than plausible, I'm convinced I'll suffocate if I remain here. If not from the grotesque odor filling the room, then from the somber memories crawling out of that locked box burrowed deep in my heart and rising up my throat, the repressed emotions threatening to choke me.

Elbowing James, I jerk my head in the direction of the backyard door. "I'm gonna head outside for a bit. I need a breather."

"Need me to join you?" Ever the selfless friend, he peels his eyes away from the person he's been ogling across the room. I shake my head and offer a tight-lipped smile. As I retreat, he's quick to holler, "You better not fuckin' smoke, Tata! I'll snitch if you do."

I wave off his threat, but nostalgia stings my lips. Despite how proud I am to have quit the cancer-inducing habit, I want a cigarette more than anything right now. The only thing stopping me is my lack of supply.

As destiny would have it, the second I open the door, the rusty hinges creak, and I set foot outside, sweet temptation hits me square in the face.

"Shit," a deep voice greets me as I'm quick to flap a hand around my vicinity to disperse the nicotine cloud blown into my face. "My bad."

The impact is immediate, his efforts to dilute the concentrated fumes are futile. My fingertips tingling, mouth itching, and nostrils flaring.

I swallow a lungful of the pungent smoke, savoring the tang of herbs and tar burning my nose and hitting the back of my throat. I don't recoil in disgust. Instead, my nerves tickle sentimentally, and I begin to yearn.

I'm rendered motionless for a brief moment, and when I find myself again, I respond with a choked, "All good."

Smoker Guy shuffles back, angling his cigarette away. His consideration is in vain. Temptation wafts to me, the strong stench permeating every square inch of the backyard. I'm trapped.

Going back inside means I'll be tortured by ghosts of memories past, but staying here means I'll inevitably cave and ruin my smoke-free streak. In a meager attempt at self-preservation, I put some distance between Smoker Guy and me, staying on the porch since the grass is wet from the quick spurt of Mississippi rain this afternoon.

It doesn't help one bit, not when my thoughts revolve around climbing the length of this burly guy's body so I can snatch that glorious tube of death from his lips and suck on it myself.

But alas, I'm not a koala, he's not a eucalyptus tree, and climbing strangers is frowned upon.

The backyard is small and empty, and it's not surprising that another cloud of smoke floats to me. I suppress a groan.

"You know, those things can kill you," I mumble. Though I'm

speaking to him, I mention this more as a reminder to myself. It's one thing to observe vicariously, but it's another to participate.

He takes a quick drag, turning away from me. It's too late. I already saw him roll his eyes. "Yeah?" It's a sarcastic "*yeah*," mild enough to appear glib but not so severe to be rude.

"Mmhmm," I hum, running my tongue over my teeth. I wish I'd brought one of my hard candies with me. My mouth feels dry and empty, making resistance more difficult. Watching him smoke a cigarette doesn't come close to the satisfaction of indulging myself. "It's bad for not just yourself, but anyone else around you."

"Shucks. That means you'll have to keep away from me." He brings the cigarette back to his lips and takes a slow, deliberate hit, his defined cheeks hollowing deeply, releasing the vapors in a single, elongated breath. Desire rumbles in my chest, and my resolve crumbles. When he faces me again, there's a wry smirk on his face. "What a shame."

Fuck it.

"It's not a shame at all, actually," I'm quick to reassure him. I'm aware that what I'm about to do is a bad idea, yet I can't conjure a single reason I ever quit smoking. "I love succumbing to bad habits."

This switch in attitude piques his interest. Smoker Guy tilts his head and arches a brow. "Really?"

I nod eagerly, a sensual smile tugging the corner of my lips up. Holding my hand out, I beckon him by scissoring my index and middle finger. "Care to share?"

He hesitates for a second, confused. Thankfully, he doesn't make me wait long. He settles his half-burnt cigarette between his curled lips and rummages through the pouch of his hoodie to procure a pack and lighter. He smacks the box against his palm a few times to pack in the tobacco. I greedily snatch one when it's offered, and without missing a beat, he leans forward to give me a light, cupping his hand to block the gusts of wind brushing past us.

When he leans away, shivers ripple down my spine. Whether from the breeze that rushes to fill the void he's created or from the sweet taste of my once-curbed addiction saturating my lungs, I'm unsure.

All I know is that I want this to last. I know it's fleeting, this serenity. I know that no matter how many drags I take, this artificial feeling of peace will escape with each vapor particle I exhale.

I know this, and still, I delude myself into thinking I can prolong it. If I close my eyes and pucker my lips over the tube, luxuriating every inhale, I can pretend I'm back in high school, sharing a cigarette with *him* in Dad's convertible, chatting about nothing and existing in a separate bubble that encompasses our everything.

Finally at ease, I check out the guy standing next to me. He's dressed down, his attire unsuitable for any party, casual or otherwise. I'll give him props for matching his sweatpants with his top.

He's tall, and under the dim porch light, his hair appears to be a dusty brown, his eye color indiscernible. He's pretty fucking handsome, that much is clear, and the more I observe him, the more I can't help but notice he looks oddly… familiar.

"Do I know you?" I blurt, tapping the ashes away with my index finger.

"Maybe." He takes one last puff of his smoke, flicks the worn butt onto the deck, and smashes it beneath his slides. I make a face at his blatant littering but say nothing. Clearly, he's not much of a talker, and I've never been one to beg for conversation.

Smoker Guy remains outside with me for a while. I half expect him to run back in once he's done, but he doesn't. This dude just stands in place, hands shoved in his pockets as he rocks on his feet, staring past the fence line as if the barren sky is remotely interesting.

I don't bother making more attempts to pinpoint his familiarity. Instead, I relish this guilty pleasure until the end burns my skin and I'm forced to—properly—discard it. All the toxic molecules entering my body serve two purposes: to kill and comfort me.

It's what a poet would call situational irony.

When it's done, I find myself feeling empty and too aware of the dullness in my gums. I'm back at square one, cursing myself again for not having anything to occupy my agitated mouth. So, I do the next best thing and smack my lips, chew on the inside of cheeks and suck on my bottom lip to displace any additional cravings.

This lapse is meant to be a onetime only thing. Asking for another light is unacceptable. Unless...

Smoker Guy notices my obnoxious behavior. "You good?"

It's obvious that he's not actually concerned. "Yeah. I know I sound like a camel, but I just..." I pinch my lips. They're desperate for some pressure or heat—anything to distract me. "I just have an oral-fixation problem."

Smoker Guy's irritation softens. His eyes flicker to my lips and he doesn't look away. Instead, he stares, his lids growing heavier.

When he looks back up at me, he's transformed, and his expression... Well, let's just say I've used it on many men before pushing them into an empty club bathroom. "Oral fixation, you say?"

I nod. Immediately, there's a shift between us as we channel into the same frequency.

"I could help with that," he drawls. The smile he wears is coy, his eyebrows raised suggestively. Mischief twinkles in his eyes, complementing the way he licks his lips. He moves toward me.

I want to comment on the one-eighty in his attitude, but I don't. Because this guy looks like his very purpose on this Earth is to be a wonderful diversion for people like me, one I'm more than happy to be a part of.

He's just what my lips need.

"Could you now?" I lean a shoulder against the wall. "You were struggling to use your mouth earlier."

"It was busy before, but it's free now."

"So it seems."

He slopes forward until I'm pressed flat on the rough brick of the house's exterior. I angle my head back, tilting my chin in an invitation, my eyes twinkling in reciprocated wickedness.

This is all he needs to bridge the gap between us and press his chest to mine. He cages me in, his forearm fixed above my head. Slanting over me, his nose brushes my cheek. I wait, suspended, fists clenched in anticipation.

I don't even know his name, but instead of deterring me, this fact serves to excite me.

"I'm thinking about occupying my mouth again," he whispers, his strong breath fanning over my face. My eyes flutter as a shiver rolls down my spine for the second time tonight. "Care to help?"

He's prolonging the moment to build excitement. The random guys I normally hook up with at parties are a lot less patient and a lot more grope-y, so this is interesting.

"Absolutely," I reply, a thrill shooting to the soles of my feet. I place my hand at his nape, and he chuckles.

"Good girl."

Just like that, he ends the torture and kisses me.

And when I say he kisses me, I mean this motherfucker *kisses* me.

the sluts + a virgin
Sat 11:02 PM

lisey

MAYDAY MAYDAY MAYDAY

I LOST HANSON

I'M FREAKING OUT GUYS!!!

james

i swear it doesn't get any dumber than you

y tf would you bring a dog to a football party?

SO YOU KNEW THIS WAS A FOOTBALL PARTY?

AND YOU STILL MADE ME COME?

YOU STUPID LYING ASS HOE

james

cry me a river w the fuckton of free booze you knocked back bitch

i didn't drink you fuckwad

lisey

hello my dog??????

tata help ME :(

can't

my stupid ONS is staying

apparently i run a bnb

if you don't find hanny tomorrow morning ill help you

james

ooh lala

tata is letting a guy stay over?

must be love

OTIS

DIRTY THOUGHTS

PARTIES AREN'T MY thing. Like, at all.

Given my low tolerance for alcohol and mild claustrophobia, I always attend my team's postgame parties long enough to be noticed, but not for so long to give me a raging headache for the rest of the evening.

Tonight, however, I have no social capacity to engage in vapid small talk and gingerly nurse a lukewarm beer. Coach Sahnoun's spontaneous decision to bench me, despite reassuring me I would play the first quarter for our Week Zero game the day before, has me ready to snap a person's neck if they glance at me wrong.

"You're still recovering. You need to take it easy," had been Coach's justification when he announced in the locker room that Tuckerson would be the game's starting quarterback.

His logic was bullshit. Our team doctor *and* the athletic trainer had both signed off for me to resume my position on the field, my rehabilitation complete, my condition up-to-par. Coach saying otherwise was another example of what a neurotic power-tripping ass he is.

I'd been inconsolable the entire game. Our offensive coordinator, Duger, and our defensive coordinator, Princeton, tried to assuage me by delivering empty promises.

We'll talk to Coach, Duger said.

We'll make sure you start next week, Princeton added.

But the truth is, there's nothing they can do about it. Farid Sahnoun might be one of the best collegiate coaches in the United States, but he's a wishy-washy, genius bastard, and to him, I'm damaged goods. I'd received the kiss of death, and my ACL tear is a blemish on my otherwise perfect record. It doesn't matter that I regained my abilities and was performing as well as I had prior to my injuries—after only eight months, I might add—or that I'd worked harder than anyone else on the team with an intense, rigorous, vomit-inducing physical therapy regimen. To him, I'm still considered a risk on the field, stating that not enough time has lapsed to properly ascertain my athletic aptitude, and thus his decision to toss me to the wayside.

When we walked across the field to our technical area just before the start of the game, I didn't wear a smile. Not when I saw the cheerleaders going hard. Not when I could hear the crowd roaring and cheering on for Riverside's Three Hopefuls, which comprised of me, the quarterback, Francis Quinn, the halfback, and Jefferson Rodney, the fullback. Not even when I read the signs saying:

OUR HEISMAN IS BACK!
WE LOVE U MORGAN
HELP US SCORE & I'LL FLASH MY TITS, HEISMAN

On any other game day, I would have laughed and waved at the crowd, relishing in the confidence their cheers and posters gave me. But not today.

Today, I'd glanced around in animosity before glaring at the ground, wearing a deep scowl on my face. Smiling at them would have been misleading. In seven minutes, they'd be sorely disappointed when a second-rate quarterback took the field instead of me.

That isn't fair for me to say, I know. I need to be nicer. And it's not as if Tuckerson is bad. Coach would never have let him on the team if he were. But he's not *me*. Even with an injury, I can still whoop the guy's ass in terms of dexterity, precision, and depth. The only difference between us is that sometimes, I make a good play, while other times...

Let's just say that, as of late, Milton Tuckerson has a more consistent track record, even if his off-the-cusp plays aren't brilliant.

Coach might have been warranted in making a safe bet with Tuckerson, but that still didn't change how he broke a promise. He shouldn't have said shit and given me hope if he didn't intend to follow through. It's like the man doesn't understand the value of his words. Or worse, he does, and if that's the case, he's genuinely evil.

The frustrating disappointment of the day brings me outside for a smoke. Normally, I wouldn't be so stupid as to light up around my teammates. Coach has a stern zero-tolerance policy—which is laughable, given the abundance of performance-enhancing drugs used in the professional league—but some of the fuckers I ball with are rats.

The fact that I'm taking the risk goes to show how pissed I am. The backyard is vacant, though; the weather too cold for anyone to have a good time out here. There's no way someone would come out here to chill, so I assess the risk as minimal.

I'm proven wrong when some chick walks through the door.

At first, I pay no attention to her. She comments about my bad habit, but I'm not in the mood to entertain or explain how infrequently I partake in this vice of mine.

But then she asks for one, throwing me for a loop. My natural reaction is to ask her if she's playing the role of the pot, given that she'd unwittingly cast me as the kettle.

However, before I get snarky, I take a better look at her. Call me shallow, but fuck, she's good-looking. Pretty, curly brown hair complements the smooth, light-fawn shade of her skin. Pretty hazel eyes. And those lips—calling them pretty doesn't do justice to how fucking incredible they are.

The compulsion to kiss her takes hold after she puts the cigarette to her mouth and dwindles only a little after she claims I look familiar. I do my best to ignore the comment in favor of watching the way those plump red lips enclose the thin tube. The action inspires dirty thoughts of how those very pretty lips would look stretched around a flesh that's thicker and longer. Thoughts about the flutter of those pretty lashes, her pretty eyes on me, the sound of her pretty moans vibrating around my cock when I hit the back of her pretty throat.

Pretty, pretty, pretty. God, I would love to fuck the pretty out of her.

At first, I resign myself to these feelings. As I said before, I'm in no mood for small talk, and flirting is all about small talk. It takes so much effort and energy, two things I do not have in me. But there's playfulness in her expression, a softness in her gaze, and brazenness in her demeanor that has me marveling... *What if?*

What if it was easy? What if I flirt with her a little and she reciprocates? What if I ask to kiss her, and she agrees? More than that, what if I kiss her, and she enjoys it? What if I invite her upstairs to my bed, and she accepts?

Living in ambiguity isn't in the nature of Morgan men and women. Leaving things inconclusive is unacceptable. Our life motto is, "The worst they can say is no."

Missed turning in an assignment? Turn it in late. *Worst they can say is no.* Want a raise? Ask. *Worst they can say is no.* Want to kiss the pretty girl making comments about her oral fixation and looking at you like you're the answer to the problem? Ask. *Worst they can say is no.*

Except, I'm not the fuck 'em and leave 'em type. I don't normally engage in casual sex. This has nothing to do with my lack of desire for it and everything to do with how little time I have—and what a serial monogamist I usually am, but that's irrelevant now. Between practices, classes, and rehab, there's not enough time for me to breathe, much less scout around and fuck someone for fun. Since my last relationship ended a couple of months ago, I've expended all my extra energy on fully recovering, getting back to playing condition, and even superseding my performance, leaving me with no time for a relationship.

But this girl is so gorgeous, and I'm tense, in need of letting off steam. All I want is one night of blissful relief from something other than my hands, and this intriguing, attractive person beside me looks like she can wring every iota of stress from me.

And that was all it took. Now here I am, towering over this girl who's at least five-foot-ten or five-foot-eleven, curious about what she'll taste like.

So I ask, because she's just admitted to having an oral fixation, and I'm sure I can offer some assistance.

"I'm thinking about preoccupying my mouth again. Care to help?" I whisper, settling my forearms on either side of her to hold off my weight. The swell of her breasts brushes against my chest each time she exhales, her lips twitching in a barely concealed smile.

Fuck. I want her, and if she says she doesn't want to have sex tonight, I'll respect her decision, even if a part of me might die.

"Absolutely," she responds. Her eyes twinkle, her tone thick, and she's reaching for me, bringing me toward her.

In that instant, I'm certain I've made the best decision of my life, coming on to this strange girl. And after complimenting her eager behavior, I finally satisfy us both and kiss her.

At first, it's soft pecking. It's meant to test the water, to gauge her instincts, but she responds immediately, parting her lips and tilting her head to find a better angle.

The tentative touch of her tongue is all I need to go for it. My hand moves to grip the front of her neck, my palm flat against the pulse of her jugular. Thumb extended, I caress her cheek and chin, brushing against our joined lips. I pull away for the briefest of moments, angling my head in the way she'd implied earlier. Capturing her mouth again in a gentle kiss, I draw back before going back in. I do this again and again until her breathing quickens and her hands slide along the lengths of my arms to settle on my shoulders. Her back curves and she presses deeper into me, rubbing against my groin.

Yes.

Her mouth opens when mine comes down for another fleeting kiss, her impatience evident by the way her fingers tangle into my scalp, commanding control of me. I can't hold back the small chortle rumbling in my chest as I capture her bottom lip, sucking and scraping my teeth along it at a painstaking pace, allowing the tip of my tongue to skim the surface. A sound of approval hums through her, and the grip she has on my hair tightens. It would be painful if my masochistic ass didn't find it fucking hot.

"You like to tease, don't you?" she asks. I task myself in kissing her jaw, my hand on her chin to guide the tilt of her head and give me more room. My other hand travels lower to trace her collarbone. I smile against her skin and lean back a little.

"Tease? Me?" I shake my head and pout. "Never. I'm simply"—I bend to press a soft kiss on her suprasternal notch—"meticulous."

She couples her hum of approval with a snort. "Meticulous. Sounds unnecessary."

"It's very necessary." I suck the submental surface beneath her chin, enjoying the taste of her.

"To you, maybe, but I get bored easily."

I gasp, my expression suddenly serious. "Well, we can't have that." Now I really fucking kiss her.

To me, kissing isn't just about what you do with your mouth. Anyone can shove their tongue down a person's throat and call it game. But *really fucking kissing* takes patience and practice. It's an art form—a study in drawing sensation.

Not all at once, of course. It's a process. Deliberate. Seductive.

My study of her is far more playful, teasing shivers and lively hair tugs. It's only when one of her chilly hands sneaks beneath my hoodie to settle between us, eager fingers brushing against the warm skin of my abdomen, that I stop being frisky and start getting *frisky*.

Grabbing ahold of her hip, I rub circles against the soft, exposed skin above her shorts. I take a small step forward, effectively eliminating any room for Jesus. My thigh separates her legs, rubbing at the apex. Naturally, she hooks one over my hip, and I bite back a bellied moan. Even through my sweatpants, I notice how hot her pussy is.

And goddamn, my body can't help but react. I gyrate against her, my dick twitching to life.

"Fuck," she pants, tearing away to swallow gulps of air. She tosses her head back.

My good leg presses firmly between her thighs, my knee touching the wall behind us, giving her nowhere to go.

I press a chaste kiss on the center of her neck. "You're burning up. *Fuck.* I just know you're dripping."

"And if I was? What would you do about it?"

Putting my mouth on her again, this time above the swell of her breast, I punctuate my reply with a suggestive thrust. "What do you want me to do?" The hand on her hip creeps up to her ribcage to skim the clothed underside of her breast.

There's a prolonged silence from her as I task myself with kissing as much of her skin as I can reach. A twinge of panic settles in me, and for the first time in a while, I invoke on a higher power and my mom's favorite entity: God.

Yo, I dunno if you're really out there, but if you are, please let her want to have sex with me tonight. I know I haven't talked to you in a while, and sure, I don't go to church anymore since Mom isn't here to drag my ass there, but if I've ever done anything right in life, please do me this solid. Sincerely, your somewhat follower, Otis.

When she finally speaks, it's with a question. One that's so off-topic, I have to pause in my ministration to answer her.

"Are you good at multitasking?"

"Uhm, yeah. Why?"

"What about cats? Do you like cats?" The fingers tunneled in my hair massage my scalp, as if we aren't in the middle of dry humping.

"Yeah." My childhood home back in Texas had been a strict cat-only one, given both my sisters' severe allergies to dogs.

I'm seconds away from asking her to get to the point when she whispers into my ear, "That's good. Cats are great. I have one."

How is this relevant?

"That's cool."

"*Mmhmm.* And I was wondering," she begins slowly, gnawing on the tip of my earlobe, "if you would like to go back to my place and play with two? What with you being good at multitasking and all."

Is it weird that I've just been propositioned by a girl with the use of her cat? Indubitably. But my response is a resounding, unhesitant, "Fuck yeah."

Within five minutes, I have confirmation that she's not drunk and definitely understands and wants what's about to happen. I have to leave her side for a moment to grab my keys. It takes forever to fend off eager partygoers who want to have a conversation about what a bummer the game had been for me. By the time I make it back outside, she's waiting beside my truck, as I'd instructed before I went inside.

We don't talk for the entire ten-minute car ride, but I watch her wriggle in her seat, legs bouncing in anticipation. The heady scent of desire lingers in the air, and when I catch her eyes lusting on me, I bite my lip. *Me too, baby.*

I shift the gear into park before the car even stops and hop out, following quickly behind her as she navigates us through the maze that is her apartment complex, tugging me along. It's only when we get through the threshold of her house that I realize I have yet to ask for her name.

And I don't get the chance to ask before she's giving me instructions and introducing me to her cat.

"Let's clear some shit up so we can hurry and fuck, yeah? One, I live alone. Don't worry about any interruptions and feel free to be as loud as you want. Two, that's Raven." She points at the black tabby who's come to greet us at the door. I'm bending to pet the gorgeous feline when the girl whose apartment I'm in commands, "Three, you need to strip. Now."

3 hopefuls (and jenner)

Jenner

There's a random ass dog loose in the house

The carpet is a mess

Help me find the owner

Rodney

is it the pit? i saw him w a fine Black girl earlier

when i tell u guys this girl is a BABE...

almost ditched meg for her

Jenner

And?? I don't care how hot she is

Help me find her you useless, half-penny whore

Quinn

Keep the dog away from my room plz

Mickey is allergic and I dont want him sneezing all night

Rodney

you two better not be loud

or im telling ur gma u like to kiss boys

Quinn

don't hate the playa hate the game bb xoxo

Jenner

Did you guys find the owner? I ain't taking care of him all night

Jenner

His name is Tinkle, and he is my son now

GRETA

EAT THE CAKE

I LOVE A man who follows instructions on command.

Smoker Guy doesn't hesitate to strip when I order him to, obliging with boyish enthusiasm, haphazardly tossing his clothes aside. All the while, I silently marvel at his well-maintained physique, tilting my head in quiet amusement.

But it's when he's in the buff that I can't help but react. He smiles, blasé and cocky when I give a faint whistle.

His body is a work of art, chiseled and carved to perfection, a study of precise geometric proportions. He's cut, his biceps bulging, his skin stretched taut over the muscles. Flexing his core for me, he wears a cheeky grin while I map the prominent ridges of his abs and the contour of his obliques.

I reluctantly tear my eyes away from his ripped torso to travel lower. I skim past his massive thighs, lingering on the ugly scar above his left knee before trailing back up to the main object of my affection. I bite my lip to keep from moaning when I get to the junction between his legs. My gaze zeroes in on his dick, the wheels in my mind turning in equal parts worry and hope.

One thing is certain. By the time he dabs me up and leaves my place, never to be seen again, I'm going to be limping, my back out of alignment, my guts rearranged. Whether this is from pleasure or pain will depend entirely on how skilled he is in the art of fucking.

Even Raven, pupils dilated, ears perked, can't help but stare at him.

My focus redirects to the naked man standing in my living room. My mouth waters at his slight erection. If he turns out to be bad at sex, that's fine. I'll get my fix another way: orally. His dick is perfect for a nice, slobbery blow job, and nothing turns me on more than watching someone unravel from my mouth alone.

My imagination runs wild, my pussy pulsing in delight at the mere prospect of getting him hard and swallowing him whole.

The silence lingering in the room is long, the air between us charged. He cuts the tension with a guttural, "Like what you see?"

Smoker Guy motions toward his body with one elegant swoop of his hand, the other resting on his hip, his stance open like he hasn't an iota of modesty, like he trained himself out of such a virtue, proud of the masterpiece he's carved. I lift a single eyebrow. His grin widens.

"Absolutely." I unbutton my shorts, tugging the zipper to expose the see-through lace of my panties. I've never been patient, and I have no plans to start practicing it now. "Now it's your turn to like what you see."

"It gets better than this?" he replies with a grunt, attentive to my every movement. He stalks across my living room as I slip off my bottoms and peel my top off. Unlike him, I neatly pool my clothes at my feet. Raven scolds my promiscuity with a meow and walks away, disgusted.

Prude.

I hook my thumb under the thin material of my thong, pausing long enough for him to lick his lips expectantly. "Do you want to take these off, or should I?" I pose. He's standing in front of me, leaving enough room to make my skin burn.

"Depends," he murmurs, reaching over to trace his knuckles

below my navel. "You attached to this thong?"

"Not particularly."

That's all the permission he needs to rip them off. In the next instance, we collide together. It's skin against skin, every inch of me touched by his warmth. My hands find purchase on his pert ass, pressing him further into me, the thick column of his dick wedged against my abdomen. My pussy flexes at the thrill of our physical proximity.

How we navigated to the bed, I'll never know. All I know is that the second our bare flesh rubs together, there's an explosion of sorts.

The kisses we share differ from before. When we kissed at the party, it had been a game of enticing, a display of what we have to offer, pecks designed to tempt.

But now, it is about consuming, overwhelming ourselves in each other, honing our senses so everything else in the world falls away.

Fuck, fuck, fuck. I want it. I want it now. He's already shown me just how much desire he can exact from me. And now I want—*need*—more. If his goal is to have me beg, he need only ask. I have little to no dignity when it comes to getting some and would beg at the top of my lungs once he rammed his dick in me—that's a Greta guarantee.

Wanting to expedite this experience, I wedge my hands between us and caress his torso, dragging my nails to elicit shivers. He hisses and stops kissing me. His head hangs in silent amazement when I brush my palm over the head of his cock. The hand massaging my breast pauses, and he mouths, "Shit."

I smirk. "Do you have plans to fuck me anytime soon? Or do I need to take care of myself?"

Before he can respond, I tease my fingers over his balls, reaching lower to skim his perineum, and he closes his eyes, the apple of his cheeks stained red, another violent shiver wracking him. He has yet to settle himself between my legs, instead slating his body diagonally, hovering.

"Someone is impatient. Don't you know good things happen to those who wait?" A strangled groan breaks from him when I dance my fingers over his chest. "*Jesus fuck*, that feels so good."

I glow with satisfaction at discovering this is an erogenous zone for him and continue to play him top to bottom, orchestrating a symphony from his moans.

"Do I look like the type to practice patience?" I spread my legs to capture him between them, lifting my hips to rub over him. "Besides, I prefer great over good."

"I'll fucking give you great," he growls, his deep voice raspy and tight.

My hips still in his grasp, the harsh press of his mouth cuts the chortle I let out from his quasi-ferocious display. He kisses me hard, his tongue slipping between my teeth to rub against mine, tracing salacious promises before retreating. He drags the tip of his nose down my neck to the valley between my breasts, tending to them in devotion.

It's while he's sucking on my nipple that he brings his hand between my legs and touches my slick cunt. The contact is unexpected but no less wonderful, his touch certain.

"Oh, fuck," I choke out, rearing up. "Yes, please."

I feel his laughter more than I hear it, the amusement jostling both our bodies. He slides two skilled fingers along the seam of my pussy, collecting the moisture that pools there. My back arches off the bed, excitement furling at the pit of my stomach. My neglected clit throbs, and just when I think he's about to touch it, he withdraws.

I could crush this sniveling little shit to pulp between my knees. "What the…" I begin, outraged. I use my forearms to sit up and glare, my cheeks blistering.

Smoker Guy shoots a level look back. "Relax, sweetheart. No need to rush." He quirks an eyebrow mockingly. "Unless, of course, you have better plans than this." He touches me again.

"No, but—"

"But nothing." He wraps a hand around my ankle, and with a firm yank, drags me down along the mattress. "I'm going to take my fucking time to make this last as long as possible. Can you handle that?"

The condescending tone has me indignant, and he's quick to realize it.

My muscles are tense, less pliant than before. Frowning, he trails kisses from the side of my knee to past my inner thigh, stopping where my pelvis and femur meet. He looks at me through his gorgeous curly black lashes, a corner of his lip curved down.

"Was that too mean? Did I upset you?" I don't respond, and he sighs. I suppress a shiver of delight. He clicks his tongue, shaking his head as if disappointed. Pressing another kiss to my skin, he murmurs, "I'm sorry. Can I make it up to you?"

Call me a sucker, but I refuse to pass on getting what I want. "How?"

"However you want." His comment is suggestive as he pecks along my mound. "Tell me." When I say nothing, he nips lightly, insistent. "What do you like?"

"Patience," I purr. But as playful as I may appear, my heart can't help but skip a beat at the eagerness shining in his eyes, my body reacting accordingly.

He smiles against me. Another kiss, but this time it's lower, close to my clit but not on it.

I'm dying.

"What do you want? What do you like?"

The question is intimate, and I'm not comfortable responding. Divulging sexual kinks is like exposing a raw flesh wound and requires vulnerability and trust. And I'm not about to do that with a stranger who might not know the difference between *choking* me and choking me.

"Eat me out," I command, staring at him with unabashed desire. He chuckles and nips at my inner thigh. "Your wish is my command."

Tapping my legs, he beckons me to lift. I abide, digging my heels into the mattress to arch so he can place a hand under my ass. He directs one leg to split aside, hanging off the mattress, the other resting over his shoulder, settling at the base of his spine. The adjustment has me completely open. I hold my breath, tense, one hand on the metal bed frame, the other clutching the sheet.

"Do you normally get this wet for people you don't know?" He circles a finger around my entrance. "Or am I special?"

"You have to make me come to be special," I choke out, straining my neck as I stare at my ceiling as though the scattered patterns will alleviate the pressure inside me. A breathy moan follows my words when he bites my labia, and without needing to be instructed twice, he gives me what I wanted and more.

I told him to eat, and this ravenous man takes it one step further and fucking *feasts*. Kissing, touching, licking, sucking. He's good. So fucking good. No—great. He's *great*.

He's not the tongue-and-done type; he uses everything at his disposal to stimulate. What's even better is how he leverages his grasp on my ass to guide how he wants me positioned. He alternates between rubbing my clit and pressing on my pubic mound. Normally, I would hate to have my mobility restricted like this, but he's attuned to my responses and knows exactly where and how I want him, so I forgive this fact.

It begins with the tongue, as it usually does. He places the flat surface at the bottom of my cunt and slowly drags it to my clit, drawing it firm when he reaches the bundle of nerves to flick it back and forth before spanning down.

I'd like nothing more than for him to focus his attention there, but he doesn't, opting to repeat the motion another time, teasing his tongue into the opening of my pussy with a few shallow thrusts, a precursor to what he'll to do with his cock later. My hips twist in delight at the cresting ache expanding inside me as his tongue fucks me faster.

The entire time, he's staring at me, watching shades of pleasure flit across my face, compelling me to whine and twist and pant in his grasp.

And I watch him too. Not the entire time, but for a little while, because he gazes at me like I'm his last supper, moving his mouth over me like this is his only means of sustenance.

Bless James for dragging me to that house party.

He moves away briefly, supplementing his fingers in lieu of his mouth, rubbing tepid circles over me. The glossy sheen over his face makes me clench in need. "You like that?"

Obviously. What girl wouldn't? This guy might be as good as a seasoned lesbian. I respond with a soft whine, and he hums in approval.

"Good. Enjoy that. But just know you're about to fucking love this."

He sucks on my clit, applying soft pressure, and I strain into his mouth. He moans, and the sound echoes inside me like a strike of lightning, my pebbled nipples growing harder still. I grasp at them to ground myself. Repositioning himself, he arches me off the bed almost entirely, smothering his face against me even more. I stamp my heel into his spine. Rather than protest, he's spurned on.

At this new angle, he focuses on licking my clit in a rapid, circular motion that sends raw arousal through my veins as he creates a pulsating sensation by flattening his tongue before elongating it with each radial turn. He alternates between that and sucking, creating a loud, wet vacuum, and lets his teeth gently raze over me as I fight to breathe.

The knot of pleasure that's been tightening inside me has almost hit its peak. Without pause, he removes his hand from my mound and brings it against my folds.

He pushes two digits inside me, taking slow care to let my walls stretch against the invasion. When he's knuckle deep, he curls his fingers, the pads of them brushing against my walls, and I cinch around him, stifling an obnoxious moan. He laves his tongue everywhere else as he pistons in me.

"Damn. I didn't expect you to taste so fucking delicious." He groans into me, sliding his mouth off to offer his veneration.

I want to tell him to prove it, to let me have a taste, too, but I can't. Coherence eludes me as he brings me closer and closer to a bliss point, his fingers twisting and scissoring, furling and unfurling as he plays them inside me, tuning me to the rhythm of his choosing. The sound it makes, compounded with his pants and hums of approval, has me swooning, my heart threatening to escape the confines of my chest. His head dips down to savor me again. "So amazing—you taste so fucking amazing—I'm thinking of making you my new obsession."

Do it. If I could be dined on like this again, I'd be more than happy to concede to him.

Coupling his pistoning motion with the lewd ministration of his mouth, there's no wonder I'm getting teary-eyed. I'm ready to burst, to come undone and let the tantalizing relief flood me, and he knows this—knows how ready I am by how tight my slick walls close around him with each stroke.

"Such a pretty girl. Are you going to come?" A noise pitches from the back of my throat. "That's right, come," he encourages. "Come, so I can hear if your scream is as pretty as you."

That's all it takes for me to let go. A compliment.

My eyelids flutter as blinding white stars appear in my line of vision. My toes curl, my stomach tightens, and *whoosh*, a torrent of heat pounds through me. My pussy squeezes snugly around his fingers as I explode, and he works me through it.

Ripples of pleasure wash over me in inexplicable ebbs. A tide of euphoria rolls beneath the surface of my skin. It's wonderful, so

I let out that pretty scream he'd asked for, showing gratitude with the high pitch, my throat strained from my effort to please him as he'd pleased me.

All the while, he whispers, "So good. You did so good, sweetheart," into me, and I'm so over-sensitive that a tear drips from the corner of my eye as molten sensation threatens to burn me to crisps, that his new compliment causes me to let go again. It doesn't matter that I don't know this guy and can't be his sweetheart—in this moment, we'll pretend I am.

When I'm done, when I'm no longer imprisoned by the pleasure, I open my eyes to see a proud gleam in his smoldering eyes. He's careful as he withdraws his fingers from me and motions to touch them to his mouth. But I'm already opening mine, and when I draw him into my mouth and suck, inverting my cheeks and flicking my tongue along the thick digits, I'm enthusiastic about my filthy display, gratified by the way he watches me, his pupils blown with lust. I'm fascinated by my own flavor and even more by how much enjoyment he exacts from his display.

"You're so good at this." He gulps, his eyes comically wide. I give my best lopsided smile despite my mouth being preoccupied. The perks of having an oral fixation.

Once satisfied with my efforts, I pull back and stare critically at him. His lips are sleek, and for the sake of consistency, I bring them to mine to clean him off. He moans in response, placing a gentle hand around my neck to dip me into the mattress, the kiss growing sloppier, more fervent.

Fuck, I want him to grip harder.

When I've licked away the traces of myself from him, he wrenches away. Rising onto his knees, he looks down at me in heady need.

"Condom?"

Dragging myself back to the head of the bed, I awkwardly reach for the nightstand but fall short, my movements inhibited by his body. He acts on my behalf under my instruction, and when he does, I notice his cock bobbing in the air, begging for attention. It's entirely hard, straining and beating with life. A trickle of pre-cum leaks from the top, and I can't help myself when I suckle on it, pleased by the thought of him being this aroused by eating me out.

When the soft suction of my mouth meets the bulbous tip of his dick, I hear the drawer slam, and I giggle at his reaction.

The quicker he tries to be, the slower the process becomes. It's a battle with the condom as he attempts to tear the packet open, first with his hands and then with his teeth, and I'm sure my playful fondling isn't helping him.

"You have got to stop doing that before I nut all over your face," he warns, but he caresses my cheeks while I swallow more of him, my mouth buzzing with satisfaction. I twirl my tongue along the tip, giddy from the tangy drops of cum leaking out of him and mixing with the saliva collecting in my mouth.

He hooks a finger under my chin right as he thrusts forward and I break away, a string of spit hanging between us before I lick my lips, still working him with my hands. "I wouldn't mind. I'm due for a facial, anyway."

He chokes on an inhale and grows even more frantic. When he finally gets the packet undone, I'm stroking his length in a ploy to test his readiness, when in reality, I'm relishing in the weight of him in my palm. I try and put my mouth back on him again, but he evades me with a desperate, "Please."

I might like to make men beg, but I enjoy getting fucked more.

Despite how much he enjoys my handiwork, Smoker Guy tears my hold away to roll on the condom then directs me to lie flat on the bed, my limbs pliant and eager to do his bidding.

"You're flexible, right?" he asks, bending a leg back against my chest.

I snort and kiss the center of his chin. "After what you just did, I can be whatever you need me to be."

REMINDERS
shit to do

- ○ non-scented litter
- ○ new chew toy (mouse & snake)
- ○ find mom's cartier bracelet
- ○ schedule annual vet appt
- ○ buy new carrier cage
- ○ new jimmy choos for NOLA concert
- ○ confirm lisey bought NOLA tickets
- ○ bring group yellow chocolates
- ○ econ homework :(

OTIS

HIS NAME IS BUSTA, BIG BUSTA

MY PLANS TO last five minutes are shot straight to hell when the girl beneath me settles a leg over my shoulder.

I'd merely wanted to stretch her limbs out some more or maybe tuck one close to her chest, not have her demonstrate the malleability of the human body.

"Damn," I murmur in respect.

She appears smug and effortlessly hooks her other leg around me, the top of her foot resting between my shoulder blades. It's a splendid position to be in for what we're about to do. She's aware of this, her eyes sparkling with delight at my suspended disbelief. "Whatever you need, remember?"

The fuck she is. She's more than what I need right now.

"You a gymnast or something?"

She rubs her hand up and down my lats, capriciously tracing patterns. The muscles there twitch as the effort to keep my weight off her grows more difficult with every caress.

"Cheerleader." Her marauding touches travel lower to play with the curve of my ass. Thank God Duger has me squatting more lately, giving my backside a juicy plumpness that she appreciates.

I would have never pegged her as a cheerleader. Volleyball or basketball player, sure, given her vertical advantage. Not that I'm judging or care. I'm happily surprised. In fact, my dick twitches at the idea of her in one of those tight little uniforms. "Glad to see you haven't lost any of your skills," I grumble, my voice strained.

Leaning forward, I grab my dick and tease it against her folds. She hisses and squirms, and I bite my gum to keep from letting out a howl of relief at the molten wetness enveloping me when I touch myself to her.

She's ready. I'd been the one to ensure said readiness, enjoying the task on a visceral level. There is something gratifying about giving head and how reactive it makes people—this specific person, splendidly so. In fact, I wouldn't mind having a second go-around.

She grunts an objection when I make a show of rubbing against her, purposefully glossing past her entrance. I know it might seem like I'm trying to tease her into a state of incoherence, but in truth, I'm employing a self-preservation tactic.

Metaphorically speaking, I'm dipping into the pool of moisture to grow accustomed so I don't lose myself when I take the first plunge. She doesn't care about my stamina, though, wriggling beneath me as scattered whimpers fall from her lips like she wants me to nut right then and there. It's a good thing it's dark in the room—dark enough to conceal the intricate details of her body and her expressions—or I'd have been a goner by now.

I try to appease her by massaging my tip against her clit, but this serves to excite her further and she curves into me, indicating it's not enough.

And she's fucking right. It isn't enough. But by God, if I let go too fast, I'll disintegrate right on the spot.

"Patience," I usher, rubbing a little faster, a little harder. Beads of sweat collect at my neck and drizzle down my back.

The girl beneath me makes a face and snaps, "No."

If she were mine, I'd reprimand her for being so bratty. But she's not, so all I can do is try not to be reduced to a pitiful mess.

"You've got to give me time," I plead when she defiantly thrashes. The haphazard movement rubs my dick in all the right ways, but I don't need this right now. I lean down until my face is millimeters from her. "I need to make this last, and you feel too good."

She doesn't settle down right away, but my honesty—as embarrassing as it might be—causes a shadow of surrender to cross over her face. A satisfied smile makes the corners of her mouth twitch, hinting at adorable dimples. Warmth unravels in my gut.

Of all the people I could have hooked up with tonight, I picked someone sensual and excitable one. Maybe my luck is turning around after all.

With a wistful sigh, she stops moving altogether. I let out a quiet whimper of relief and almost thank her.

When I'm sufficiently accustomed to her dampness, I grumble a word of warning and drive into her, closing my eyes as my tip notches past the tight opening. She lets out a small moan from the intrusion, her leg constricting around me. When I muster the sense of mind to open my eyes again, I see hers blazing like I'm doing her a favor.

News flash: I might be doing *her*, but she's the one doing *me* the favor. Especially when she clamps around me like that, dousing me with unadulterated pleasure.

"Fuck me. Your pussy feels so…" I trail off as I gradually work myself inside her. She laughs. The sound of her amusement causes her body to shake, her pussy clenching wonderfully with it. It takes every ounce of self-control to not savagely ram into her.

"I *am* trying to fuck you. You're the one taking it slow." Despite the control I have over her overactive hips, she undulates beneath me, sliding me in even farther. I inhale sharply through my nose at the suddenness while she digs her nails into my skin, a scattered mewl pushing out of her as she presses her forehead against my clavicle.

Slow. I need to take this slow. Stretch her out. Not plow her six ways to Sunday. I'm a Southern gentleman, and no woman should reduce me to anything less respectable.

I twist my hips and grab behind her knee to force her legs back against her chest, sliding in deeper but not entirely sheathed. She's snug and damp, her walls working to expand and bear down as she takes me. I don't move, tossing my head back in wonder.

The pleasure is still blinding, the thin layer of protection hardly detracting from the sensations. It's all stillness, and yet I'm lightheaded from the rush of tingles jolting down my spine.

Needing this unusual Cat Girl to know how good this feels for me—how fucking amazing her cunt is—I tell her, doing my best to sound coherent given how delirious I feel. "You're so fucking tight. So wet. Shit, I'm pretty sure this is heaven."

She grazes her hands from my ass to my chest, admiring the cords of muscles years of football have molded. When she traces along it, I tense, my forearms and biceps trembling beside her head. Cat Girl turns her head to see this, smug as ever. She intertwines her arms around my neck, her nails scratching soothing patterns against the nape. My head tosses back in unadulterated delight.

She better stop playing before I ask her to marry me.

"You feel so good inside me, too." She licks my chin. My heart skips a beat, and I move to kiss her. She dodges me, nipping at my Adam's apple instead. I tilt my hips again, easing in deeper still, and she accepts me with a gasp.

Oh, I've started something bad. The talking—what a terrible fucking idea. I find being vocal in bed a turn-on—not only for myself, but for my partners, as well.

But this girl, she's not rendered speechless by my prowess. She reciprocates instead, which is simultaneously torturous and charming. Because upon hearing those words, the otherworldly spirit known as Big Busta almost anointed me with the nut, and I have to fight for my life to kick this unwelcomed visitor out, mentally reciting every preceding Heisman winner and their stats.

When I regain control, I trudge onward like a battered man marching into battle—less reluctant, of course. I'm almost completely inside her when she says, "You're so big. So thick. Filling me up. Mm."

"No more talking," I practically sob. I don't care if I sound pathetic. I'm so close to losing it, it's not even funny.

Hanging my head, I pant, avidly working to not let go. But she's scratching my neck and bowing her spine off the bed so our sweaty chests are flush together, her nipples hard.

Those swollen lips—the pretty ones that started this descent into madness—press to my ear. "Make me." She nips playfully at the sensitive shell, and my cock, buried to the hilt in her beating cunt, leaks zealously into the pocket of the condom.

Call it a man's pride, call it childish, call it whatever the fuck you want, but her kinky challenge sets something off in me. And without pretense, I'm pulling out of her entirely, grabbing a pillow to set under her before adjusting the fit of our bodies so her lower half is twisted to the side, one leg still on my shoulder, sliding back in with a swift thrust.

Her eyes widen, her smile fading when I repeat the motion, her body jolting against the bed frame from the force of my movement.

And it feels good, the way she accepts me. The sounds make it even better: the breathy, pitched moans escaping us, the sloppy beat of our joined bodies, and the harsh smack of my balls against the bottom of her ass as I fuck her hard—then harder, then softer before driving in even harder.

But I don't let myself get lost in it or hyper-focus on all the ways my body is being stimulated. That would make me a one-pump-chump, and I would rather be castrated than be remembered as that.

Instead, I focus on her, memorizing the erotic softness etched on her face as I give her what she wants. She's positioned just right that a silver of moonlight illuminates her fucked-out face.

She squints, her mouth agape and her head craned up, exposing the vulnerable column of her neck. Her breasts jiggle with the movement, and one of her hands comes up to grab one, squeezing and pinching like that'll ground her.

Turning my head, I look away for a second to banish the flutters in my chest. I kiss and nip at her ankle, her toes curling with each brush of my lips.

I maintain this unvarying momentum with ease, my entire body drenched from the effort I'm putting forth from both the refrain and the exertion. All the while, she's encouraging me, mewing out pleas—"faster—yeah, just like that—please—make me come—I know you want to hear me scream again"—when I screw my hips at a downward stroke, intentionally bumping her clit.

"No more talking, remember?" I tut.

She chokes out a laugh before the sound morphs into a short scream when I grab her perched leg and force it as far back as possible, her toes grazing the headboard as I sink into her with such sharp precision, I swear I feel her heart beating.

A knot twists at the bottom of my spine, a warning. Or maybe it's not a warning. Maybe it's her nails biting into my skin, wishing to rip it apart in the same way I'm ripping her apart.

Either way, I carefully register the other telltale signs of my imminent orgasm, and I know I can't keep this up if I want to make it last, to have this be a moment of infinity she and I can fondly look back on. I want to leave a mind-blowing impression on her so that one day, when she's married and having the same boring sex with her significant other for the ten-thousandth time, she can think back on tonight and wish it was me—that nameless stranger from the party who gave her a light—fucking her.

So I pull out, and she's about to protest until I usher her upright and push her against the bedframe. Wrapping an arm around her waist, I run my palm over her perky cheerleader backside.

Fuck. I grab my dick and slot it between her cheeks, and she pushes back. "*Fuck* yeah," she groans, rutting back even more. I bite my lips and my eyes roll back into my head yet again.

Jesus, her reactions. I need to keep this girl on retainer. Make her more than a one-night fuck.

"Grab the headboard," I bite out. She looks back and blinks, eyes glazed. When she doesn't follow my order, I wrap my hand around her neck and tilt her head back, placing my lips to her ear, punctuating my words carefully. "Be a good girl, and grab"—I bite the side of her neck—"the"—I tease my cock against her— "fucking"—I tighten my hold around her throat—"headboard."

Now it's her eyes rolling. She extends a moan and complies, wheezing in joy. When I run my dick over her ass again, she inhales sharply and shifts back.

"Seriously?" she chokes out. But it doesn't sound like she's opposed to what I'd inadvertently implied. My surprise manifests itself in a hesitant chuckle.

"I was just admiring the view. Now, spread your legs and stick that perfect ass of yours out for me, sweetheart."

I grab her and bend to sink back inside the plush heat she's put on display for me. There's no resistance, and I can't articulate how fucking exquisite it feels. The view of my cock disappearing into her has me moaning, the coil of anticipation traveling below my navel. I test my movements like this, relishing in the way my cock fades in and out of her. One of my hands is resting on the swell of her cheeks and I squeeze, even if what I really want is to slap it to see a big red handprint there. And the best part about all this? She's not passive. She's so active in all this, circling her hips with every thrust.

I literally can't comprehend how this chick is real.

I'm getting close to the point of no return, so I hold her still and bend forward to press a kiss on her shoulder blade, blowing a chill breath over her bare skin. "I'm going to split you apart, and you're going to be good and take it, right?"

And she is a good girl. The best of girls. Because she knows actions are worth a thousand words, and she's writing a fucking dissertation with hers.

She gives her body to me, moving in tandem with mine. I'm trying to not just be fast but hard, driving into her purposefully. It's difficult maintaining this exact pace not only because she feels so fucking good, but because she's reaching behind to help control the force of my thrusts. Those smooth, drenched walls flutter around my cock with every inch she takes, trying to hold me in even when I'm pulling away. The friction it creates is unbelievable.

Even the soft noises she makes are phenomenal. Especially when she tasks herself with rubbing her clit, trying to get *there* with me, babbling incoherently all the while.

Fuck, I love a woman who takes charge.

I know she's close when she grumbles words of encouragement against the headboard, and I reply with a breathless, "I know, baby. I know. Just come for me again and let me feel it. Let me hear it." Because I do. I do know. I'm experiencing the exact same thing she is, and I *know*.

As I'm about to finish, I place my hand over hers and help apply more pressure. Then, I dive back in again and again—shallow, rough, and persistent. My face is on fire, my heart pumping out of control, trying to keep up with the strain and vigor of our fucking. If we go any longer, I'm pretty sure the bed is going to break or I'm going to collapse. And then—

My orgasm punches through me. My mouth clamps onto her shoulder, hard and violent as an actual scream tears from my throat, my body convulsing. The haze of arousal gives way, and the carnal rush of pleasure washes through me like a storm. Ecstasy douses me as my strokes stutter out of beat and my cock throbs with the charge of my release, emptying into the condom.

Her release chases her a few seconds later. Cat Girl screams,

"Yes," and I swear, I'd sacrifice my left nut to hear her hold that note again. Her pussy contracts around me, as if it's trying to wring every last drop of pleasure from me, and she succeeds, prolonging the jarring surge of euphoria flooding me as she rides the waves of her orgasm.

When it's over, all the energy in my body seeps out, and I'm incapable of holding myself up. I splay back on the mattress, my dick sliding out of her with ease. I hiss when it slaps against my abs, sensitive. She remains on her knees, still clutching the headboard for dear life, her knuckles white.

Cat Girl looks beautiful painted in the dim lamplight, and so I admire her with lazy focus. Her sweaty skin gleams with glitter. The faint glow accentuates her figure, the dancing shadows paying homage to the dips and curves of her lush body. My hands tickle, yearning to reach up to caress the shape of her.

When she regains composure, she turns to look at me. I lick my lips, desire sweeping over me again.

But alas, I'm fucking wrecked. Exhausted. Rendered physically useless. My dick can twitch all it wants, but there's no way I could go another round anytime soon.

"Thanks for lasting more than two minutes," my one-night stand says finally, sounding parched.

I nod and smile, a little glad her standards are so low. I must have been a grade-A fuck for her, huh? "You're super fuckin' welcome."

REMINDERS
task list

- ○ respond to the Bear's GM Bernard
- ○ call insurance for icka's inhaler
- ○ finish stats paper outline
- ○ study for midterm 1 NIS 3325
- ○ hit new PR for DL
- ○ buy flowers for mom's bday
- ○ budget for next month w/ katia

GRETA

PILLOW TALK: TAKE ONE

"**WHERE DO YOU** keep the extra bedsheets?"

"Closet. Top shelf on the right. Grab the yellow ones."

Smoker Guy struts past where I stand in front of the bathroom vanity and to my walk-in closet. He hesitates for a second, his eyes lingering on my reflection. When I meet his gaze through the mirror, he winks and moves along.

Regretful as I am to admit it, I'm beginning to like Smoker Guy a little more than I should. From the way he aptly follows instructions to the way he successfully conducted a one-way express to pound town, the idea of this guy is nearly too good to be true.

To add to his generous list of qualities, he strips my bedsheets, tosses them in the wash, then goes to put on a fresh pair, all without being asked. There's a mother out there who needs a fruit basket delivered to her doorstep.

Even as I attempt to remain vigilant about my nighttime routine, I can't help but teeter back on my heels to covertly watch him through the door, absentmindedly massaging serum into my skin for longer than necessary.

I bite my tongue and suppress a groan at the way he places

the fitted sheet on my mattress. And when he folds the loose ends perfectly along the edges, creating immaculate hospital corners? I'm frothing at the mouth, pressing my legs together to keep an iota of sanity intact.

Is it wrong to be turned on by someone making the bed? Maybe. But the pussy wants what it wants, and the way his biceps and shoulder blades move, the contours of his bare, intricately-inked back flexing as he undertakes this mundane chore, has my well-fucked muscles quaking.

Smoker Guy leaps upright when he finishes the task. I nearly get whiplash from how quickly I jerk out of sight, busying myself.

No matter how attractive a man might be, I'll never be caught slacking and fawning.

"Should I let Raven in?" he calls. "He's meowing outside the door."

"Nah, that's okay. He's just hungry. I forgot to refill his bowl for a midnight snack. Let me finish up here, and I'll   "

"Don't worry about it," Smoker Guy interjects, popping his head through the doorway. "Keep doin' what you're doin' and take your time. I'll feed him. I'm assuming your cat food is somewhere in the pantry?" He doesn't wait for a response and bolts out of sight.

"No. I mean, yeah, it is, but I can—" I start, flustered. I cap my moisturizer and go to catch him. Grabbing his arm, I hold him back from rounding the corner, my face creased in annoyance. "You don't need to feed *my* cat. I'll do it. I only needed a minute to finish up. Don't trouble yourself."

But he doesn't get it—or maybe he does and doesn't care—and insists, like he's fucking Lancelot, cursed with knightly chivalry until he dies. Gently, he pries my grip off him and curls his mouth in a reassuring smile. "It's okay, really. It's no trouble. I was supposed to play with both your cats tonight, remember?"

Just like that, I'm left flabbergasted in the middle of my own damn hallway.

Is this guy stupid? Did he replace his brain with a cloud full of smoke? I swear, he couldn't pour water out of a shoe if the instructions were written on the soles. How does he not get it?

It's not about the trouble. It's about the domesticity of all this. About the overt familiarity and niceness. About the ease of us rolling out of bed and beginning post-sex habits like this is a regular occurrence between us rather than a novel experience.

It's the fact that we didn't need to communicate our tendencies and still fell into step with each other. He asked for a towel and hopped into the shower while I went to pee, tending to my notifications on the toilet before wiping off my smudged makeup. And when he finished washing off, we swapped places. But instead of tending to his personal hygiene, he busied himself by tidying up my room like I hadn't given him ample time to make an escape during my shower.

Did this situation not strike him as unusual and unnecessary? Or is he so oblivious that he needs shit to be spelled out? Maybe he's a serial killer. But then again, what serial killer voluntarily makes beds and feeds the cat?

I bet I'm going to have to play the bitch and kick him out. Not that I mind playing the bitch. Of all the roles I undertake—daughter, friend, and bitch—the latter is allegedly my most natural form.

Maybe I should let him do a few things around the house before I give him the boot...

I'm French braiding my hair when Smoker Guy walks in with two glasses of water, Raven trailing close behind, hind legs sashaying from side to side, his tail extended high in delight. My overstayed guest dons his hoodie from earlier, depriving me of the delicious view of his muscles.

The least he could have done is offer me eye candy since he's so determined to irritate me.

"I thought you might need some water after working your vocal cords so hard earlier."

Fingers twisting around my strands, I gesture at the counter. "You can set it down. Thanks."

He's too considerate. So considerate that he keeps his arm extended until I'm done braiding my hair and finally grab the glass from him. Mouth pressed to the brim, I take ginger sips, inspecting him from between my lashes. It's hard to gauge how dangerous he is when he flashes me a deep, dimpled smile, a glimmer of innocent joy shining in his bright blue eyes.

Okay, so maybe he's not a criminal. But he definitely has a few screws loose up there.

The power of sex is marvelous, I realize, thinking of the difference between the perky man standing before me and the broody one I met earlier.

Damn, I must've fucked the attitude right out of him. Another skill I can add to my CV.

"So, uh," he starts carefully.

My body tenses, apprehensive of his tone.

"I know this is a little weird to ask since we don't know each other, but would it be cool if I spent the night?" He scratches the back of his head when I don't reply, his gaze averted. "I wouldn't be asking if I didn't, like, really need a place to crash."

A scoff rumbles in the back of my throat. *And... that's not my problem.* I invited him to fuck, not to sleep over. I hadn't been explicit in those terms, but they're implied as per guideline sixty-nine in *The College Hookup Guide.*

I'm on the cusp of singing *sayonara* to Smoker Guy, apathetic to his request, when he shifts to finally look at me again, the corner of his lips turned down, his eyes glazed in need. Pity bubbles through me.

Well, shit. It's a little hard to be a bitch when you're feeling suddenly empathetic. I've been in his situation before, where I'd hooked up with someone and one reason or another required me to stay the night with them rather than go home. And having to explain myself had been the worst.

I don't owe him anything. I know that. Still, a part of me feels inclined to relent to pay back the kindness afforded to me in the past. Plus, he'd asked so nicely and has been so helpful that I feel I should reward him. I'm not sure whether his kindness is a ploy, but I don't have the mental capacity to psycho-analyze. So, I yield.

"Fine, but you're sleeping on the couch."

THERE'S A KNOCK at my door. I purse my lips to keep from groaning. "Yes?"

The metal knob clangs and twists. The door to my room creaks open. Smoker Guy pokes his head through the slight crack he's created, the soft glow of the hallway's light creating a halo around him.

"Can I sleep in here with you?"

Say "psych" right now. I sit up to peer at him properly, unblinking. "Seriously?"

He nods and widens the door gap, a pout set on his lips. If I wasn't so aggravated, I'd find it adorable. He clutches the spare pillow I'd graciously given him. "Raven keeps jumping on me, so I can't sleep."

As if to testify, my pet meows and struts into the bedroom. He leaps onto the bed with unparalleled grace, makes bread over my duvet-covered legs, then curls his body to rest against me. The guy at the door regards my cat in obvious envy.

I fight back a smirk. Intimacy avoided. "There. Problem solved. Raven'll sleep here. Night."

MORE QUIETLY THIS time, three quick raps sound at the door.

"Are you awake?" He doesn't whisper so much as quietly shout.

I'm ready to snore my way through this lie, but the video I'm watching on my phone is loud, and when I try to turn the volume down, I do the opposite, outing myself.

Damn me. Damn me straight to hell.

"Yes," I drawl, reluctant.

He pops his head into my room again, his expression even more pathetic than before.

"Can I help you?"

Gaze intent, he nods. If he wasn't so hot or hadn't been such a good lay, I swear I would have him sleeping on the streets right now.

"The couch is really uncomfortable. Are you sure I can't sleep beside you? I mean, we've already had sex, and I promise not to, like, fuck you. I'm not into somnophilia."

At this point, I'm willing to max out my dad's credit card and buy him an entire room of beds if it means he'll stop bugging me. Besides, I'm sure nothing will come of this. It's just sleeping.

"Fine." I'm already stealing most of the covers from his side, burritoing myself in the heavy fabric. Biting my tongue, I repress a scathing retort about not bothering me. I don't want to cancel out the good karma I'm accruing from being kind. I need it.

"Thanks."

I hope he goes back to being moody. I don't want to hear a peep from that pretty-boy mouth.

"ARE YOU ASLEEP?"

We've been lying in bed for all of three minutes, backs to each other, his body heat emanating like a furnace.

There's a shift on the other side of the bed. I feel him hovering, looking at me. Much to my dismay, I'm awake. Too awake. My mind drifts between a state of exhaustion and awareness. Despite the dry sting in my eyes, they're wide open. And this truth is once again presented to him against my will.

"No," I drawl, my weariness partially muffled by the pillow.

"Neither am I."

"And here I thought I was talking to a ghost."

"You're funny. A little mean, but funny."

Mean? Because I don't entertain chit-chat or welcome random people I've met at a college party into my bed with enthusiasm? Twisting to face him, I flash a sardonic smile, my tone tempered. "Really? I'm mean? Do you *want* to go back to the couch?"

Better yet: outside.

He swallows audibly. "Can I do a take-backsies? I want to take-backsies."

He's lucky I'm feeling generous. Exacting torture, I pretend to think about it, his eyes growing wide until I sigh sanctimoniously and relent. "Fine, I guess. But only this one time."

We both sit up. Placing one hand on his chest, he raises his other in an oath. "I solemnly swear to take all the backsies."

"That's what she said."

Smoker Guy doesn't hesitate to retort, immature as his rebuttal might be. "She might have said it, but you were definitely screaming about it."

Amused, I wear a genuine smile. The corner of his eyes crinkle, too, though his lips remain in a flat, solemn line. His cheeks twitch, unsuccessfully fighting that same smile, revealing his crescent dimples.

Thirty seconds later, the bedside lamp on his side turns on, and we're talking.

I tell myself it's because I can't sleep, and the drone of mindless chatter always helps me sleep. It doesn't matter if this breaks the set of rules I co-authored in *The College Hookup Guide*. I convince myself that conversation is conversation, and I'm only using him for personal gain, not for a connection or sentiment. It's more entertaining than counting sheep.

But if that's the case, why do I fight each rush of weariness that catapults through me?

"DON'T YOU THINK it's weird that we haven't exchanged names?"

Smoker Guy sits crisscross on the bed, our bodies turned toward each other. He fiddles with the trim of my blanket, seeming almost bashful as he asks, as though he hadn't dirty-talked me to orgasm earlier. His shirt is off, but sadly, he keeps his sweats on.

I'm lying on my side, cheek perched in my palm. "No."

Disappointment overlays his reply. "'*No?*' Why not?"

For a heartbeat, I consider explaining my motives. Do I tell him about how anytime I get close to someone that I might have a potential romantic interest in, I easily grow bored in a month—maybe two if they have an interesting enough backstory? Or how the unknown makes him more exciting and me more interested, and that eradicating this thrill would dissolve the short-lived connection we're engaging in at present?

More than anything, I don't know how to explain that I don't want to know who he is. He was good at sex, but so are a bunch of other guys I've fucked, and they're not around. I don't know their last names. I'm not attached to them, and that means their absence can't hurt me. Besides, I'm not in the market for establishing more relationships, platonic or romantic.

I have more than enough people in my life. It won't matter how well we get along tonight, which, based on the last twenty minutes, would be swimmingly—we've been debating the NCAA's bogus rules and whether football or rugby is more physical. I'm most likely going to cut all ties with him and ensure we have nothing to do with each other the second I wake up tomorrow, both for self-preservation and out of my whorish principal.

"It will ruin this," I surmise.

"'This' being..."

"The mysterious fun of a one-time hook up."

"Ah." He puckers his lips and nods, crossing his arms over his chest.

So dreamy, I think, admiring the way his biceps flex from the motion.

"What if we exchange middle names instead?" he suggests.

Another lull of silence falls over us, the gears in my mind turning to confer if this is acceptable. Smoker Guy opens his mouth as if to redact the request when I speak up. "Miriam."

He perks up, the pitch of his voice high. "Mariam? That's your middle name?"

"Not mare-ee-um. *Meer*-ee-um. Like meercat."

"Miriam," he repeats, whispering it under his breath. My stomach turns from the way each syllable flutters past his lips. He's attentive in contorting his tongue to properly enunciate the unfamiliar name. I've never had anyone treat my name with such delicacy and respect. "I like it. Miriam."

"It's decent." I shrug to exemplify false humility. "What's yours?"

"Mine is—" he wavers, his face creasing. "Wait. Before I say anything, you've gotta swear you won't make fun of me."

There's no way I'm swearing. I maintain a placid façade. The anxiety he displays tells me this is going to be good. For me, obviously. Not for him. "It's that bad, huh?"

He rubs his forehead. "It's not bad, per se. Just… antiquated."

When he doesn't resume speaking, I usher him along with a wave of my hand. "Well, c'mon. Get on with it, old chap."

He shakes his head. Covering the lower half of his face, he mumbles unintelligibly behind his hands, and when I ask him to speak up, he does, repeating himself, incrementally increasing in volume each time until he clearly shouts, "Rutherford!"

I swear, I try to keep my composure, to not be surprised, and to act as if the name doesn't inspire images of old, smelly aristocratic men. I try but fail tremendously.

"Rutherford," I repeat, slack-jawed. "You're telling me I had sex with a dude named Rutherford?"

"My name isn't Rutherford, it's O—Rutherford is my middle name, not my name." He purses his lips and pauses while I struggle not to roll on the floor in hilarious disbelief. "It could have been Demetrio, but my pawpaw won the rock-paper-scissors match at the hospital against my *abuelo*, apparently. But I swear, my first name is much better."

"Uh-huh. Sure. Whatever you say, Fordy."

"Don't call me Fordy."

"YOU CAN'T LIKE chocolate ice cream but hate raw chocolate."

"I can and will," I assert.

He sputters, arms flailing in the air, doubling down. "But they both taste like chocolate."

"No. Chocolate ice cream has the diluted flavor of chocolate, so it's not too sweet. Chocolate tastes like—wait for it, this is going to blow your mind—chocolate."

"Fine. Whatever. Let's say we take your explanation." It's obvious he doesn't want to take my explanation. "Then that means you also like chocolate milk."

I snap into a finger gun. A hopeful look lights his face and disappears when I speak. "False. I only like plain milk. Two-percent. Don't give me that whole-milk shit."

There's no disguising his disgust. He scoots away as if my preferences are contagious. I suck my bottom lip to maintain a poker face. "You're the type of monster to like mint chocolate chip, aren't you?"

"Absolutely. I love my toothpaste with a hint of cocoa."

Rutherford shivers in revulsion. "Heathen."

I cackle manically, drumming the tips of my fingers together like a perfect villain.

IT'S LATE.

It's late and I should be asleep, ignoring this guy that claims only to smoke when he's stressed and has a Southern twang when he's upset. But I don't. I engage in the conversations he starts and even assist in maintaining them, intrigued by every silly story he divulges and each irrelevant, yet shocking, opinion he shares.

It's late, so I blame my vested interest on that and the exhaustion. It affects my cognitive abilities and has me behaving in ways that are out of the ordinary. And if that's not a good enough excuse, then let's say I'm expediting my boredom. The faster it comes, the better. Cause those arms are looking real good right now, and if he asks to cuddle, I don't think I'd put up a fight.

"You're not in a relationship, right?" Rutherford asks, petting a sleeping Raven. My cat purrs in his dreams and unfurls his paws.

"Why? You don't enjoy being a side piece?"

He makes a face and levels a grave look. "You shouldn't joke about cheating. You've got to know how serious it is."

"But I don't actually know," I deadpan.

He stills, blinking rapidly.

I promptly elaborate to clear any misconceptions. "I've never been in a committed relationship to cheat. So, yeah, I might *know* cheating is serious and wrong, but I don't actually *know* know. Y'know?"

He places a hand over his mouth, disbelief gleaming in his eyes. "Never? You've *never* been in a relationship?"

I shake my head. "Never," I mouth, mirroring his expression with mock horror. He remains stunned for a while. I'm feeling myself a little. It's always nice to render a guy speechless. "What about you?"

"What about me?"

Drop it. Say, "Never mind." Except, I'm sleepy—that's the excuse I'm using tonight, right?—and sleepy people care about things they normally wouldn't. So, I persist.

"Have you ever been in a relationship?" He looks like the type of guy who had three girlfriends by the end of lunch on the first day of middle school.

He throws his head back and laughs. "Tons!"

Am I psychic or what? "I see, I see." I wiggle my brows and chuckle with him.

"What can I say? Man gets passed around." He brushes his hands over each shoulder and smirks. Then, in earnest, he explains, "I just like being in love."

Can't relate, but it's cute that he's so upbeat and optimistic about this type of shit. A little psychotic and needy, but cute. "Were you in love with everyone you've been with?"

Rutherford thinks for a moment, then shrugs. "Kind of. Like, while I was with them, I was so sure it was love. But my pawpaw used to say that it's not love if it doesn't hurt when it ends."

"And you never felt hurt when it ended?"

He shakes his head. Guilt quickly overcomes his features, his gaze unfocused. He speaks softly, absentmindedly, rambling as though he's scavenging for something in his words. "Never. Not even in my last relationship, and that one had been pretty serious. But then... I was such a... And it was so hard for me after all the shit I went through with... and she... But I didn't feel bad. I mean, I did, cause I'm not, like, a total tool, but then I got over it. I've been single since.

"But yeah. I don't know. I don't know if I've ever been in love, since I'm always the one that's usually doing the hurting, not the one... hurting."

There's a stillness as his sincerity blankets us, demanding reflection. I'm barely concealing my astonishment. A flinch of awareness convulses through his long limbs, making him mindful again. Shame stains his cheeks.

It's clear he didn't mean to say it. That of all the things we've divulged tonight, all the menial little secrets about our dietary preferences, how good our morning shits are, or whether we prefer Wolverine or Deadpool, this isn't one of those things to just *say*.

The confession is jarring. Even so, for some reason, I'm intrigued enough that I don't know whether I want to throw him out my window or slip him some truth serum to induce more confessions.

He covers his blunder by clearing his throat and tossing the question back at me. "How about you? Have you ever been in love? I mean, I know you haven't had a serious relationship, but that doesn't mean you can't fall in love."

"Nope. Never." I've loved, but I've never been *in* love. I've never wanted to. Loving my family and friends is enough. The most painful of heartbreaks has precluded me from being a fan of the emotion—or any excessive notion of attachment, for that matter.

"That's a little sad."

"I don't think it's sad." I stare at the wall behind him. The poignant thought that pops into my head is meant solely for me, but the synapses between my mind and my mouth have short-circuited, and I speak aloud, unwittingly discovering a desire I hadn't realized I harbored—a desire I thought I'd extinguished years ago, after *him*. "It's actually a little exciting. I get to look forward to falling in love for the first time, y'know?"

A private smile rounds his countenance, the register of his voice crispy, deep, and kind. "That is exciting."

I rip my gaze from him to scrutinize my bedding. An unfamiliar sensation brews in my gut. It's envy. He's easy to talk to, has a nice body, is good at sex, and can make a bed. I get how falling in love is easy for a guy like him.

But the feeling of heartbreak afterwards must have sucked.

Good thing it's not something I'll have to worry about anytime soon.

"HOW DID YOU lose your virginity?"

We're learning everything about each other tonight. Just one night. An exception to my rules. Tomorrow morning, he'll be gone, and I'll resume life as usual. I'll pick up my hookup handbook and swear to uphold its guidelines again. But for tonight, I'll be deviant.

Rutherford's droopy lids fling open. "What the—wow. Asking the hard-hitting question. Christ, I wasn't expecting that."

"I can go first if you're uncomfortable."

"Be my guest."

"All right, well," I begin, getting up to turn on my bedside lamp and lean against the bed frame. "I was fourteen, his parents were out, and we didn't expect them to be back 'til midnight. We were watching *Shrek Forever After* and... yeah. It was wham-bam, thank you, ma'am."

"Shrek?" he balks. "You got your back blown out for the first time to Shrek?"

I grimace. "My back wasn't blown out so much as it was tickled."

"Even so... Shrek? Those movies should be watched with the utmost attention."

"Oh, trust me, I was paying attention. I had no reason *not* to pay close attention."

"That bad, huh?" He shuffles to sit upright again.

"It was too short to be bad."

"Oof." Rutherford pats my knee sympathetically.

"It's not a big deal. It happened. What about you, though?" I lick my lips, tasting the berry flavor of my night balm. "When did you lose your virginity?"

"In the back of my truck. My high school sweetheart and I were stargazing when they told me they wanted to have sex. It was super fucking awkward, and I didn't last long either, but I'm sure I wasn't as quick as your guy."

"Oh, trust. No one can be as bad as Darryl." Even after the first time, it had been terrible and short. It wasn't until Nick that my sexual encounters became really good, and it was Jamal who'd ignited some of my more... *unique* preferences.

Our conversation goes off on different tangents as we flit through topics at a rapid-fire pace. It's dumb, the shit we're talking about. Time runs away with little warning. I hardly realize how much I'm enjoying myself until we're sprawled lazily on top of the covers, snickering over a prank he pulled on his roommate. That's when I realize Raven has moved from lounging beside me to sitting on his lap.

I feel betrayed, even if there's a little flutter in my heart.

RUTHERFORD HAS A mosaic of tattoos on his back. The entire expanse of it is decorated in charred black nickel. There's scarcely a stretch of skin there that isn't marked, and I'm baffled that I've only just noticed how intricate and beautiful the artwork is.

"Damn. You must really like tattoos."

"Yeah." The muscles on his back tense when my hand hovers above the skin. My mouth parts in surprise as I try to delineate the art canvased on him. His physique alone is a masterpiece, and to have another set of abstract work etched onto his skin... I mean, could this guy get any sexier?

I'm just about to ask him what the tattoos mean, given how poorly I can make sense of the patterns collaged together, when he speaks up, eyes on me. "Do you have a tattoo?"

The hand floating a hairbreadth over his skin immediately draws back—had I really been that close to touching him?—and I roll away from him until I'm at the other edge of the bed. The scrawled name printed beneath my left breast, stained above my heart, tingles. "Yup."

Still facing down, he shimmies closer. "Where?"

"It's a secret," I say quietly, placing a finger on my lip.

He makes a sound in the back of his throat and reaches over to push it away, then shoves the hand beneath the pillow again, his face appearing in front of me suddenly. The tips of our noses brush, our heavy breaths mingling. "A secret? I like secrets." He matches my hushed volume. His proximity is electric and my fatigue-addled mind struggles to discern who he is to me.

"So do I."

"Do you also like to share?"

"Not particularly."

"But sharing is caring."

"Are you under the impression that I care?" He doesn't respond, but it's clear he was. I click my cheek in mock concern. "Oh... Oh, Fordy. You naïve, adorable, little boy." I reach over to pinch his cheeks and he suavely avoids me.

"I could just..." One of his hands slides out from beneath the pillow and across the mattress. His touch crawls up the curve of my waist and slips beneath my shirt. My pulse slows, thumping out of beat. My breathing hitches. The calloused pads of his fingers feel so good against my skin.

"Seduce me?" I finish for him when the flat of his palm skims between the valley of my breast until he's reached the wing of my shoulders, my voice cracking in anticipation.

He nods and blinks slowly, deliberately. If Rutherford was close before, there's no way to describe the proximity now. His lips are brushing over mine, not pressed but lingering. The rest of our bodies are angled away from each other, but that doesn't matter because I still can feel him everywhere. My mouth waters, and the Jolly Rancher I've been sucking on dissolves.

Thankfully, I have enough sense to not lose myself in his sex appeal and charm. "It's cute that you think you have an effect on me, *Fordy*."

"**CAN I ASK** you something incredibly cheesy?"

He looks at me curiously, but his gaze glimmers in good humor. Or maybe they're watery with sleep. "Go for it."

There's something inside me that wants more from our conversation. Maybe I want it to end on a note more substantial than which Teletubby could have gotten away with murder. He says Po. I say Tinky-Winky.

No motherfucker would live their life crime-free when the universe did them so dirty with a name like Tinky-Winky.

"What's something you've, like, always wanted to do but never have?"

Rutherford doesn't hesitate in his response. "Easy. I wanna be pampered like a pretty little princess."

I level him with a blank stare. "Be serious, Fordy."

"I am." He perches his cheek onto his palm. "I've never been spoiled or taken care of like that. And dangnabbit, I want it." He says the last part like an old southern man.

A blasé comment sits at the tip of my tongue, but he's looking at me with those eyes again—the same eyes that compelled me to let him stay—and I know there's more to his confession. So, I swallow it down and nod approvingly. "That's fair. Unrealistic and probably never going to happen, but the heart wants what it wants."

"Please, hold back your encouragement. I can't take the overwhelming enthusiasm."

I wave my hand in the air in a bow-like motion.

"What about you? What's something you've always wanted to do but never have?"

I think for a moment, wracking my brain for an answer that isn't the one blaring at the forefront of my mind. But when a dozen seconds pass and no other thought comes to mind, I respond honestly. "Camping."

"You've never gone camping?"

I shake my head.

He checks me out and smirks. "You should. You'd look good in hiking boots."

"I'd look good in anything."

"Or nothing."

My stomach flips from the look he's giving me, his eyes lingering on all the parts of me he's already memorized.

He's quick to snap out of it, banishing the sultry ambiance by following up on my response. "Why do you wanna go?"

"I was supposed to go, uh, right after my high school graduation, but things came up, and I didn't." I don't expand. Don't want to. Don't think I can. The hollow ache that carved itself in me earlier at the party comes back, and I press my hand against my chest, over my tattoo, as if that'll soothe the sting.

It doesn't, and I'm left thinking, *Fuck, this was a stupid idea. Why couldn't I just end the night on Teletubbies?*

"Hopefully you can go camping someday," is all Rutherford says. The resonance of his voice is gentle, nearly whimsical, as if he knows. As if he's privy to the inner workings of my mind and heart.

But he's not, and I'm imagining things, attempting to find depth in a connection that exists but is shallow at best. "Hopefully you can be pampered."

It's then that we decide to go to bed. Neither of us says anything—we just shuffle back onto our sides, back into the positions we were in at first.

"You know, you're a cool guy," I tell him. I want him to know that. When we part ways tomorrow and never see each other again, I want him to know that this girl named Miriam he had sex with once, who has a black cat named Raven and an assorted stash of Fruit Roll-ups and hard candies under her bed, thought he was cool.

"A cool guy?"

"Yeah."

"Seriously? That's it? Cool guy?" I hum, and he huffs. "Am I supposed to take that as a compliment?"

"How else should I describe you?"

"I don't know. Fucking hot? Sexy? Amazing? Riveting? Thought-provoking? A goddamn princess? But not just a plain old cool guy. As one of the best dick downs you've ever had—"

"I didn't say you were the best." Implied it, sure. But I never said it.

"—I feel like I'm worthy of a more distinguished title."

"Fine. Let's settle this and say you're a princess. Now turn off your bedside lamp. I'm tired, and you need your beauty sleep."

VOICEMAIL

lisey
Columbus, Mississippi
August 28, 2022 at 1:59 AM

Transcription

"Oh my god Tata you would not believe the day I've had I lost Hanny-Han and I need your help call me back I know you're doing the hanky panky with some guy you've never met and I hope you made him wear a condom because its icky to not wear one with a guy you don't know even if you like to do it without one I'm happy you're satisfying your hoo-ha after all these months but I need you to call me back and be safe"

OTIS
KIBBLE TIME

SINCE I STARTED playing football, I've always woken up at the ass crack of dawn. I'm awake right as the devil retires, my pawpaw would say. It's a habit that I can't shake.

It began because of my dad. Construction work started early, and before he left each day, he would stop at my and Katia's room, and whisper, "I'm off to work. I love you."

And every day, I would be awake to receive his greeting. He didn't know this—or maybe he did and that's why he stopped by every day.

After he died, there was no reason to wake up, but I still did. I would lie still, very awake, staring at the door and waiting, almost like I was expecting him to show up one day and say those words again.

When I got older, waking up early became an obligation. It started in middle school when I was tasked with making the girls' lunches while Mom whipped up breakfast before her twelve-hour shift at the hospital. Right as I entered high school, it was ensuring Pawpaw took his medication first thing in the morning. And once I made varsity, it was doing drills before football practice, all while performing the aforementioned tasks.

The routine has stuck with me. The hardwiring from those formative years has made it such that even on days off, like today, I'm awake right as the sun breaks the horizon. It doesn't matter that I only got two hours of sleep—*God, had we talked for that long?*—I'm wide awake.

My current morning regimen is typical of any D1 athlete and has changed only slightly since my injury. Rather than leaving my bed the moment I wake up like I used to, my post-injury routine calls for five minutes of stretching each morning. Which, since Miriam is sleeping peacefully beside me, drool pooling onto her pillowcase, is something I can't do today.

Aside from the study session with Herik two weeks ago where we fell asleep in each other's arms, it's been a while since I've woken up to a person by my side. Not a long, long time, but enough that, when I woke up with my arms wrapped around Miriam, her nose pressed into my neck and her freezing feet sandwiched between mine, I nearly jumped out of my skin in surprise.

I remain like this for another five minutes, finding comfort in the steady pattern of her breathing. Then, when my muscles strain, I unravel myself carefully from her hold and motion to Raven, who observes me from the foot of the bed.

The cat readily follows, meowing excitedly all the while. We both pause at the door to watch the woman face down on the bed sleep soundly. The cat is probably thinking, *Wow, my owner is a lazy shit*, while I'm thinking, *Wow, her ass looks good.*

I admire her for so long, her cat admonishes me by scratching my ankle.

"I get it. You're hungry. Jeez," I mumble, trekking through her apartment with ease. It's odd how familiar this girl's place feels.

"It's kibble time, kibble time, won't you share some kibble of mine," I sing softly as I pour the feline's food into his bowl. It's the song Monica, my kid sister, would sing when she fed Chairwoman Meow, the family cat. Raven likes the song, his tail swaying to the tune before he directs his attention to the food.

I sit beside him and stretch, suppressing the obnoxious moans of relief bubbling up my throat as my muscle fibers decompress and expand. When I feel sufficiently lax, I spring up and head toward the kitchen to make breakfast. It's the kind thing to do. She offered me her home to stay in, no questions asked, and now I thank her with a baller breakfast. People like gestures like these, right?

I'm no Gordon Ramsey, but I wouldn't be surprised if Chef Boyardee and I went neck and neck and I whooped that old Italian man's ass.

I like to cook. Back home, secret smoking was what I did with Pawpaw, but cooking was what I did with Mom. Being a single mother of three children—two of whom were demons—and a scrub nurse at St. Jude's meant she had little leisure time. The three days she had off from work during the week were usually spent doing chores around the house, and since I'm the oldest, I would help. Cooking was the only thing I genuinely enjoyed doing with Mom, and I often looked forward to it because I knew, come dinnertime, she and I would dance around the kitchen to Tejano songs and gossip about my shitty football team and her passive aggressive co-workers, all while whipping up a delicious meal together.

So, when I open Miriam's fridge to find it empty, I'm appalled, immediately grabbing my keys to head to the grocery store two streets down. I feel a little guilty about leaving the house with the door unlocked, but I can't find her key, and time is of the essence. I make the journey quickly, purchasing only the breakfast supplies I need and a toothbrush, because there's no way I'm going to walk around her house with musty morning breath. There's a flower shop across the street that's about to open. I deliberate getting her some but stop myself when I see the price.

Who the fuck has five dollars for a damn flower?

I'm back in no time and rush to brush my teeth. I chortle at the display afforded to me by her open bathroom door. Miriam is lying on her back now, snoring like a chainsaw. I admire this hilarious scene for a while before working on breakfast, though I do stop at her desk to jot down a note for her, stuffing it in my pocket to present later.

In the house I share with three other offensive players on the team, we take turns making breakfast for each other on Sunday, each of us proficient at our own things.

Me? I'm amazing at omelets and French toast.

Today just so happens to be Sunday, and since I'm not home, I thought I'd christen Miriam's house with this ritual. My teammates must have known about my treachery, and midway through making the raspberry *coulis* for the French toast, my phone rings. I answer it, not caring that I've gotten sauce all over the screen.

"Frosted Oats!" Rodney greets, animated for a guy that's hungover. "Where the fuck you at?"

"A girl's place." I suck on my thumb and nod enthusiastically at the well-balanced flavors in the sauce. Sweet with a hint of bitter citrus. Add a little syrup to taste, and it will be decadent. Damn, I'm good.

"A *girl's* place." Loud chatter erupts in the background from Quinn and Jenner. "What the fuck? When did you get a new girlfriend? I thought you were going to start dating guys again."

"She's not a girlfriend. Just a random chick I met at the party." Is it bad that when I say this, I grin like a sleazy bastard?

The tight end whistles, impressed with my promiscuity. "Well, well, well. If it isn't Otis Morgan, the slut. Man-whore extraordinaire."

"What can I say? I learned from the best." I dip a diagonally sliced piece of bread in egg batter before placing it onto the frying pan.

"Of course you did." He cackles, amused by my lapse in conduct. "And we're proud you're finally in your slut era or whatever, but what the fuck? Why aren't you home yet?"

"Aw, you guys miss me that bad?"

"That's right. Now come back home and take care of us." In the background, I hear Jenner groan an elongated, "Please."

"Why? Cause you're all too hungover and don't want to make breakfast for yourselves?"

"That, and the house is fucking filthy. Did you see the group chat? We found this stray dog that's barking too damn loud."

I'm about to make a smart-ass remark when I hear a door open. A second later, Miriam waddles toward me, chin pressed to her chest, hair curtaining her features, her steps sluggish and zombie-like.

"I gotta go, Roddy." I immediately hang up with no elaboration and take a moment to look at her. As she approaches the counter, her posture straightens. She flinches when her eyes fall on me.

"What the—what are you still doing here?" The ties of her pink robe are loose, and I can see the oversized shirt-and-panties ensemble she put on for bed. She's not wearing a bra, and her breasts move freely with each step she takes. Her legs are smooth, her thighs wonderfully thick. They're a dusty, golden hue that reminds me of a long stretch of barren country road, and fuck, I want to take a road trip through them. If only I'd paid them more attention last night.

Who's to say you can't do that another night? Ask. The worst she can say is no.

I hold up the fork I've been using—she doesn't have a spatula, which is a culinary travesty—and grin. "I'm making breakfast."

"Breakfast," she repeats gingerly.

"Breakfast. Y'know, the meal you eat to break the fast you did all night while you were sleeping. Also known as the most important meal of the day."

The grogginess in her eyes dwindles. She gives me a flat look. "Is your name Merriam, too? Oh, wait, don't tell me—your last name is actually Webster. Is that why you looked so familiar, Mr. Dictionary?"

I whistle. "I'm impressed. The leggy brunette has jokes." I wag the utensil at her approvingly and flip the toast.

Miriam cracks a tired smile as she approaches me, her arms crossed over her chest, her neck craned for a better view of what I'm doing. Raven follows suit. "If you think my legs are impressive, you should see what's between them."

She's too much. I grip the silverware in my hand tighter and narrow my eyes at her. "Then how about you hop on the counter and spread them apart so I can get another peek." She snickers and shakes her head dismissively. Her nearness makes me giddy, and with little thought, almost like a reflex, I bend down to give her a sound smooch. It's meant to be quick and familiar, but it's not.

The moment my mouth presses against hers, I demand possession, which she readily cedes, intoxicating me further. I'm drunk on the *liqueur de Miriam*, and if I have it my way, I won't be sobering up soon.

Grabbing the ends of my hoodie strings, she stands on her tiptoes to press firmly against me, her back arched to eliminate any gaps. Taking my upper lip between her teeth, she tugs. I make a sound, somewhere between an objection and a hum of desire. She apologizes with gentle flicks of her tongue, coaxing my mouth open so she can conduct a study on the structure of my mouth. I'm only too eager to assist her in the task. Her rack isn't one to inspire devote R&B songs, but she could definitely get an indie band to slip a line or two about them in theirs.

Still holding onto the fork, I use my free hand to trace her body. I dip my fingers through her robe and under her shirt, tracing them up the side of her waist until I reach a breast, her nipples growing hard. She likes this. I brush my thumb over a taut peak and cup her completely, giving her tit a nice squeeze, loving the way she fits into my palm.

She takes advantage of both her hands and tasks herself with exploring me, tracing the ridges of my abs. I flex, protruding the muscles in that swoon-worthy way guys and gals seem to love. She giggles against my mouth, and I can't help but smile back, breaking the heady tempo of our kiss for a moment. We get right back to it, and when she's moved on from caressing my torso, she rubs her palms up and down my arms, admiring the strength there instead.

Just when I'm about to delve my hands into her panties to test the waters, Raven hisses and swats at my feet ferociously, effectively ending the kiss. I yelp and pull away from his owner and look down at the jealous cat, aiming all my ire at him for interrupting us. Miriam takes two steps away and reaches behind her to grab the counter.

Her lips are swollen, red, and wet, her eyes glazed, her breathing labored. I'm reminded of the debauched look on her face when she came against my mouth, and my dick twitches in my sweats, eager at the prospect of maybe having her again.

Wait, she's too sore. That's what she'd said last night. The admission had been both a blessing and a curse—a blessing for my pride and a curse for my sex drive, which is howling for more after an abstinence spell.

"Damn," is all she says.

I clear my throat and fix the uneven lengths of my hoodie strings. "Yeah. Sorry about that." To keep from pawing her again, I busy myself with putting the finished slice on a plate and preparing the other one. "Just wanted to kiss you good morning."

"It's all good. No need to apologize. That was"—she brushes a finger over her mouth, the corners of which curve up slightly, her expression set in muted ardor—"nice."

I make a face. "Nice?"

Miriam shrugs, mischievous as ever, and entices me by sucking on her bottom lip. I'm not one to take action based on perceived gestures, but the one she makes has my fingertips tingling. I swallow, a little timid, a little excited, and all too willing to act on what appears to be a mutual desire.

"Semantics are important here," I say, keeping my eyes on the pan. "So what I want to know is, when you say 'nice,' do you mean *nice*, or do you mean fucking spectacular?"

She doesn't reply right away, torturing my curiosity. When she relieves me, it's done in playful provocation. "I'm pretty sure I mean *just* nice."

I drop the fork and face her. She's leaning back against the counter, her tantalizing eyes dancing playfully. My hands find purchase on her full hips. "Oh, dear. That's not good. Not at all."

"It isn't?"

I shake my head solemnly and take a step. "Nope. I mean, what type of man would I be to leave a girl with the impression that I'm *just* nice?"

"You'd be a cool guy. That's what you would be."

Another step. "Didn't we establish I'm a princess last night?"

Miriam shakes her head, her playful gaze transfixed on me. "You're right. You are a princess. And that makes me... What? The frog?"

A chuckle gets stuck in my throat. One final shuffle and we're exchanging the same air. "Not just any frog. A gorgeous, leggy frog." I bridge the space between us and lift her onto the granite countertop. She makes a satiated noise and pulls me between her legs, digging her knees into my side, her hands cupping my face with gusto.

I'm not trying to toot my own horn here, but I pulled out my A-game for this kiss. I mean, fourth-quarter, seven-seconds-left-to-make-a-touchdown type of game.

I keep my eyes partially open, scrutinizing the way hers flutter and disappear beneath their lids as I play with her. I switch between soft brushes of our lips to deep open-mouth kisses to navigating around her jaw before going back to light pecks. By the third time I've done this, my body cuts painfully into the counter as she actively tries to crush me between her legs.

Only when she tugs at the hair on the nape of my neck do I give in to the depths of my desire. Only then do I give her what she wants—what *I* want.

I glide my palms over her legs to the small of her back, then grip the swell of her ass. I open my mouth just a little to give her a taste, to hint at what's to come. She releases a breathy moan, touching our tongues together and skimming the inside of her bottom lip with a swipe.

It goes on like this for a while. She holds me firmer, tighter, wanting more, and I give it to her, little by little, until our tongues slide ceaselessly against each other, taking turns to submerge and retreat, speaking a language only we can understand. Sucking on the top lip means *lick my bottom one*, a light flick of the tongue against the left side of the mouth means *follow me back to mine*, and a hot, brief open-mouth kiss means *let me taste you again*.

Contentment fills me as we kiss endlessly, losing ourselves. The embrace isn't obsessive or lust-filled. It's wistful and serene, unadulterated perfection.

The entire scene is a study in closeness. Nothing exists but us. It's cinematic, the way this moment unravels. My eyes are closed at this point, and I can practically imagine us as if I'm a third-party observer. The background blurs before it fades, and all that remains in focus is Miriam and me, intertwined.

I know, I know. I'm cheesy. Corny. Cringe in a sweatsuit. But it's not like I can control how I feel, nor am I saying I love this chick. All I'm saying is that if she wanted to holla' at me, I'd definitely be down to holla' back.

When our kisses grow softer, lighter, like the tickle of a feather, a knot of longing wrenches in my stomach, tingling down to the soles of my feet. By the time we part and press our foreheads together, our breathing has evened. I know that I have to let go of her, that this moment will end all too soon, but I try to fight it, to prolong it until the very last second.

"Fucking spectacular?"

"Fucking spectacular," she confirms. A brief silence passes. Then, she *ribbits.*

I choke on a laugh and nuzzle her neck. This is only meant to be a one-night stand—that much she made clear last night—but fuck, I want more of her.

"The food is burning," she whispers, pushing at my shoulders.

I don't register what she's said, reluctant to let her go until the smell of burnt crust overwhelms my nostrils and I tear away from her to tend to it. "Damn." I toss the slice away.

She crosses her legs, swinging them faintly as she watches me, amused.

I flash her a sheepish grin. "Give me, like, fifteen more minutes, and breakfast will be ready."

She appears hesitant, her lips parting as if there's something she wants to say. But she doesn't. Miriam nods, hops off the counter, then opens the fridge. I focus on preparing the meal, determined to make it as spectacular as the kiss. I'm starving, and the way the cheese melts on the omelet makes my stomach growl.

I arrange the food on plates. "Are you ready to be blown away?" In all the cooking shows, presentation matters, and I'm not one to cut corners.

She's placed our cups of coffee on the table. "Hell yeah."

I carry our plates to the table and hum Beethoven's fifth symphony.

She hops in her seat, expectant and eager, quite the opposite of the way Raven looks at me as if he wants to scratch me into smithereens for pawing his mother earlier.

"Tada," I sing, flourishing the plate under her nose. "Your meal, *mademoiselle.*"

"*Merci beaucoup.*" She rubs her hands together and stares at the food before digging in. She eats with zeal, making satisfied noises and nodding.

"You like?" The answer is obvious, but I want verbal validation.

She groans and rolls her eyes into the back of her head. Her words mirror her expression when, between mouthfuls, she says, "Absolutely. This is *orgasmic*."

I grip my utensils tighter and give a pleased, tight-lipped smile. She's got to stop being so outrageously salacious when there's nothing I can do about it. It's not funny anymore, not when my dick is practically wagging like a dog's tail.

Conversation is a bust throughout the meal. I don't have the capacity to talk to her when she's making noises like that, and she doesn't bother to talk since she's too busy making said noises.

And everything is fine. Everything is good, and I'm excited for the meal to end because that's when I plan to hand her the note. When the meal is done and the kitchen is clean and all that's left is the conversation about where to go from here.

Everything is fine until I offer to clean the dishes, and she objects fervently.

"You made breakfast in *my* house. There's no way I'm letting you clean, too." She blocks the sink.

"But I like to clean." I clutch the plate we're playing tug-of-war with.

This is when it changes. It's immediate, the look that falls on her face—once polite, now not. Miriam jerks the plate from me and practically throws the dish into the sink with reckless abandon. A loud *clang* reverberates as metal and porcelain clash. I flinch and look up.

She does not look at all happy. In fact, she looks genuinely annoyed—livid—her nostrils flared, her face red. "This is…" She pauses and takes a deep breath, rubbing her palm against her forehead.

I'm too afraid to say something and provoke her further, so I wait patiently for her to speak, knowing full well that whatever she's about to say will end this. "This is too much, and I really think you should leave now."

There it is. I might have expected it a split second ago, but still, my blood runs cold. I blink at her several times, trying to process how the mood suddenly shifted.

I pushed the invisible boundaries she'd established, boundaries I'd been vaguely aware of before. I pushed, and she snapped, and how or why asking to wash the dishes became her breaking point, I may never know. What I do know is that there's no way for me to retreat, rewind time, eat my words, and act like nothing ever happened.

I did nothing wrong—asking to wash the dishes is *not* wrong, it's fucking polite, a quality my mom engrained in me—and yet I feel like shit. How fucking wonderful.

"I have friends coming over soon, so I need you to leave," she says briskly, growing colder when I don't react. Her expression somehow becomes more unpleasant. Her tone is calm, but the severity it delivers isn't any less dismissive. "Like, right now. Leave."

The bitter astonishment I experience is replaced by offense— not just because she's kicking me out, but because she's lying. I can't confirm it's a lie, but fuck, it reeks of it. And she's doing that to… What? Banish me from her presence like I'm some corner wench who's overstayed their visit?

I'm pissed. Fucking pissed.

She doesn't owe me anything, and I don't think she does, but the fact that she's looking at me with cold, dead eyes, her lips still swollen from the kiss we shared not half an hour ago, enrages me. The world before me turns into a canvas with different shades of my fury.

Did she forget last night—not just the bombastic sex, but what happened after? We sat on her bed and exchanged thoughts like we were two kindred souls rather than mere strangers. We might have started the night by knowing nothing of each other, but we ended it by sharing every stupid belief we each have.

"Will do," I snap, my expression and tone matching her hostility. She doesn't react, though, but turns and opens the faucet. She doesn't bother grabbing a sponge to pretend to do the dishes, and that adds insult to injury.

I leave her apartment without saying another word, my fists clenched tightly around my keys, my mind trying to properly process what happened in the last minute.

When I get into the car, I rummage for the note I'd written. I barely glance over the words I'd scrawled and crumble it, tossing it into the back of my dad's truck. I stare out the window, thinking about everything that happened between us from the moment she stepped into my backyard. Nothing particularly special happened, just moments that were so enjoyable, so ordinarily wonderful, that I deluded myself into thinking we were more than strangers.

"This is too much," she'd said. The fuck was too much? Cooking or the dishes? The sex or the conversation? Where is the line between too much and just enough? Because I swear if it's the dishes, I might lose it.

God, this is fucked. The memory of what we did together is tarnished, tainted by her irate dismissal. I wish I had never made her breakfast. Better yet, I wish I hadn't spent the night—that way, I wouldn't know how funny, how chill, how cool she is. I should have suffered back at my place. I intended to stay at hers to get some sleep, and that didn't even happen.

No amount of scrutiny helps me understand, and I'm left feeling whiplashed. Knowing I'll never be able to decipher this—decipher her—I decide to stop dwelling on it.

When I peel out of the parking lot, I don't look back. I don't let myself feel disappointed over what could have been. I don't even allow myself the comfort of having the windows down. I focus my thoughts on one thing and one thing only: *Thank fuck I didn't ask to see her again.*

Because Miriam, the girl that lives on the corner of Lexus and Luther in apartment 420C, she's a fucking bitch.

VOICEMAIL

katty batty katia
Dayton, Texas
August 27, 2022 at 10:10 PM

Transcription

"You fucking loser answer the phone God I'm so sick of being such a good sister when you don't deserve me I saw that you didn't play today and I know you're probably super fucking bummed but don't be okay you better not be smoking or on my life I will tell mom and she'll kill you cause you know she hated it when dad or pawpaw smoked so for once in your life don't be a tool also make sure to buy flowers for mom's birthday I already scheduled the edible bouquet to go to her work tomorrow so Venmo me 20 bucks bye uggo"

baby mon-icka
Dayton, Texas
August 28, 2022 at 1:22 AM

Transcription

"Answer your stupid texts and send me money you ugly idiot I need to buy homecoming tickets and mom is being a stingy bitch"

GRETA

ELISE LET THE DOG OUT

"**ARE YOU SERIOUSLY** telling me you don't know his name?" James asks.

I roll my eyes and repeat myself for the umpteenth time. "I already told you that I don't."

"And you're sure you didn't, like, have sex with a ghost or something?" He dodges the kick I aim at him by doing a cute ballerina twirl, laughing all the while. "What? I'm being serious here. I looked up the name Rutherford in our school's registry, and nothing popped up except this old alum from the 1880s. All I'm saying is, if my mom was able to see into the great beyond and predict that I would be a disappointment to my family, then you can have hot sex with a hundred-and-forty-year-old ghost."

"Your mom didn't need the great beyond to know you'd be a disappointment. One conversation with you would tip anyone off."

James brushes my insult aside with a wave and taps his foot against the pavement, hands stuffed into his pockets, his expression twisted in concentration. "I just don't get how you could have enjoyed sex with a dude named Rutherford."

"Me neither," I grumble. "For the rest of my life, I'll be grateful of the fact that we exchanged middle names *after* I finished."

"Yes, because when meeting someone for the first time, we all exchange our middle names and not our first."

"You know I don't like to get personal with my trysts."

James gives me a knowing look, eyebrows raised to his hairline.

"*Anymore*. I don't like to get personal with my trysts *anymore*."

"That's right, Sahnoun. After you had—and lost—me, you decided you couldn't stand having your heart broken again."

"I neither had nor lost you." I whack his abdomen in reprimand, and he laughs, rubbing the offended area. But he's not entirely wrong.

Our liaison happened a couple of times, a week after I confronted this coffee-stealing barbarian. It was at a party, and we were both drunk. A game of beer pong and two body shots later, we were fucking like rabbits, and the next morning, I woke up entirely debauched and satiated on his bed. We started a no-strings-attached relationship that lasted less than a month. When we hit that impasse, wherein he got too invested while I remained detached though interested, I decided that the best thing to do was to remain friends with none of the added benefits since he and I got along really well. It was perhaps one of the smartest decisions I've ever made, and I don't regret it one bit.

Actually, that's not entirely true. I do regret it at times. Like now, when he throws our liaison back in my face.

"Are you really not going to try and look for him? Maybe have another tussle in the sheets since he was so amazing?"

I shake my head. "Nah. It was one night. It was good, but it's not like he's the only one who's good."

"You say that," James begins, precautious, "but you've talked about him more than any other guy you've slept with."

I choke out a defensive scoff. "I haven't talked about him that much. And if I have, it's because you asked."

"I asked how your night was, not why you're waddling."

"I am not waddling." Indignation turns my face bright red. I spin to point in his face. "And you know damn well you were asking me how my night was to get the details."

"Still doesn't change the fact that you spent fifteen minutes telling me everything that happened." He points a finger back at me and narrows his eyes. "Don't you think there are some things you should keep to yourself?"

I have no rebuttal, so I back down and fold my arms over my chest, looking away with a scowl. The accusation wounds my pride.

I actively try not to have many regrets in my life. This is difficult, mostly because I'm a walking fuckup, as my father so lovingly likes to remind me every so often.

But just because I'm trying not to have regrets doesn't mean I don't. In fact, regret was the most pervasive emotion that slammed into me the second Rutherford stormed out of my apartment. It wasn't his absence that I regretted—in fact, it was quite the opposite.

His presence gnawed my insides in that nauseating way. Because if he hadn't asked to stay and sleep at my place—if we hadn't spent a good chunk of the night talking about nothing—then he wouldn't have been there in the morning. And if he hadn't been there in the morning, presuming we were closer than we actually were because of the conversation we had the night prior, he wouldn't have made me breakfast. And if he hadn't made me breakfast, he wouldn't have kissed me and made me think about breaking my one-night-stand rule because it was so good.

And if he hadn't asked to wash those fucking dishes…

I never should have let him stay. No matter how good it was, or how badly I needed to replenish my good karma, I should have done what I always do and ended it after the bust. Because I've had good, even phenomenal, before, and I've ended those in all the same, unaffected ways, but this time… I don't know.

Maybe I'd been jarred by going to the party and being around all those football players. It had thrown my chakras off balance, so I gave allowances to this particular guy. Or perhaps it's because I hadn't had sex with an actual human in a while, relying mostly on vibrators or my own nimble fingers and overactive imagination to do the job. Or it was the smoking—the toxic vapors had stained my lungs, infiltrated my mind, and disengaged my cerebrum.

No matter the reason, I had regrets. And I'm not happy that James is reminding me about them.

A long bout of silence enshrouds us. James has never been comfortable with extended periods of quietness and decides to break the tension, ever the people pleaser. "Did he really say he was going to split you apart?"

"Yeah."

"And he kept his promise?"

"Yeah."

"And he asked for round two and you said no?"

"Yeah."

"Did he—"

"Either change the subject, or I'll tell Veronica that you have a big fat crush on her."

He's quick to oblige. We talk for another couple of minutes, topics ranging from my terrible grades to whether or not we want Barton's or Ricky's for lunch, waiting patiently on the sidewalk for Elise to come out of her sorority house. I'm sucking on my fourth Caramel Delight to occupy my vacant mouth. It's another five minutes before we see a familiar, gorgeous Black woman skittering out the front door, her eyes puffy and red, her nose dripping with snot.

"They found him!" she wails, sprinting toward us before nearly knocking me down in a bear hug. I wrap my arms around her as she continues to sob, rubbing her back soothingly.

James takes half a dozen steps back. He hates criers, guy or girl. Natural, human emotion is his kryptonite. Like me, except he's worse. "What's she saying?" he mouths.

"She found her dog. Or someone did," I translate, tightening my hold on Elise, who's blubbering all over my shoulder. I don't like criers, either, and I'm not a super touchy-feely gal, but the girl is delicate, and I'd rather have her crying muffled against me than yodeling like a banshee on the street.

It's hard to exact more intelligible words from the devastated dog mom. But after a lot of gentle encouragement, both James and I manage to get the address for where her missing canine is.

"I'm pretty sure we've been there before," James says as he starts Elise's Mercedes. She's too frazzled to drive.

It is sexist, having him drive instead of me. Sexist and entirely unfounded to state that I'm a bad driver simply because I'm collecting speeding tickets like I'm trying to get a loyalty card punched by the Mississippi state police. Two more and apparently my license will get suspended, but it's not suspended *now*, so I don't see why I shouldn't be driving her new GLE.

"We have? For what?"

"A party. The one last night, remember?"

Elise blows her nose and gasps. "*Oh my ga-wd*, that's when I lost Hanson!"

"Why'd you bring him to the party?" I lean over the console to pass her another tissue. I grab her used one with the tips of my index and thumb finger, discarding it in the bin by my feet.

"I don't know. I was really drunk. The only thing I remember was the game and…" She looked expectantly at me and then James. "And then what? What did I do?"

"Don't look at me. I don't go to games." But I do know all the stats. In fact, I texted my dad throughout, insulting the piss-poor formation of his team's D-line. Mom chimed in on criticizing his O-line. She and I make a good team.

It's James's turn. "Don't look at me. I was at the top deck with Veronica and Will. Weren't you sitting in the box seats with your dad?" He switches to the left lane without checking his blind spot. And *I'm* considered the bad driver.

"Yeah, but I drank too much Chardonnay."

James and I exchange a look in the rearview mirror. *How the fuck do you get drunk off Chardonnay?*

"I don't remember anything after halftime."

"Not even what you did later?"

Elise shakes her head, her doe eyes glossy, her lips set in a pout. James reaches over and pats her shoulder. I lean back and shake my head in dismay. Of course Elise doesn't remember. She'll remember every outfit she wore this month as to avoid repeats, but she can't remember last night.

"Don't worry yourself over it, Lisey." Panic grips me when crocodile tears pool in her ducts, threatening to streak down her face and further ruin her makeup. "Someone found Hanson, and we're going to pick him up right now," I add.

"But what if he doesn't love me anymore? What if he thinks I abandoned him? What do I do then, Tata?" she whimpers. She's so theatrical, I want to flick her forehead. But I don't like weeping either, so I hand her another tissue instead, praying her emotions away.

"I mean, technically, you—" James begins, but I kick the back of his seat so hard that he slams on the brake. "Jesus H. Christ, woman, I'm driving."

I ignore his exclamation to pat her shoulder in reassurance. "He's not going to think that. He knows you love him. Why else would you have bought him a collar from Tiffany's?"

With the way Elise spoils Hanson, even I would be willing to bark a few times and hump her legs. It's materialistic of me, but what's so bad about being a vapid, shallow bitch when it gets you pretty, shiny things?

Another five minutes go by of frantic whining over her poor maternal skills and me lying out of my ass to reassure her.

We arrive at the house where I met Rutherford. At the house that has… Rutherford's truck? Wait—what? Why the hell is his truck here? Does he live here? If he lives here, and the party was hosted by football players, does that mean he's a football player?

And if he's not a football player, then what's his car doing here? Do I have to see him again? I mean, I was kind of rude there at the end, and I'm not too sure he'll be happy to see me.

Oh, fuck. Fuckity, fuck, fuck. This right here is why I don't let people warm my bed.

If I were a lesser person, one with a weak resolve, I'd act like a petulant child and refuse to leave the security of the car. But that would make me a little bitch, and I'm only willing to be a vapid, shallow bitch.

As all three of us walk to the door, James and me on either side of Elise, I tell myself it doesn't matter. And no matter how hard I try to pretend like I'm unaffected and aloof to all of it, my jaw is clenched, my fists are balled, and my heart is fluttering faster than a hummingbird's wings.

The bell is rung. The wait is long. Then the front door swings open.

Inbox - hanselngreta@rsu.org

4,009 MESSAGES, 3 UNREAD

✉ Dr. Muneer Asab

Hi Greta, Though I empathize with your situation, you will not be able to make up the quiz you missed during class on Friday. As I have stated in the syllabus...

✉ Prichard Marbury

Ms. Sahnoun, Thank you so much for joining our team here at Hillcroft Elementary. As your academic advisor has already informed you, the students your working with have speech...

✉ Ticket Me!

Order confirmation for (3) Fall Out Boy tickets in the name of Greta Sahnoun...

OTIS

WHO'S YOUR DADDY?

HERIK IS DISTRACTED, and when our team's biggest player, the center offensive tackle, is distracted, casualties ensue. This very concept is demonstrated when he calls the wrong play to the other offensive linemen and Davidson zips through a gap created by my blockers and tackles me to the ground, having enough sense to not maul me with the full brunt of his power like he would in an actual game.

"I'm going to kill you," I moan as I drag myself to where Millie, our on-hand personal trainer, is waiting for me. This is the fourth time in the last hour I've been toppled, all because my childhood best friend has something on his mind. "I'm going to shove my fist so far up your ass, I'll look like a ventriloquist, and you my personal dummy."

Plopping on the bench, I extend my bad leg, and without saying a thing, Millie crouches on the turf and massages the sore muscles. I help her, taking on my thigh as she endeavors to soothe the spasm on and around my calves. Herik drops down beside me with a goofy smile on his face, shaking his sweat away, his dreads flying around his head. When I click my gums in annoyance, he shrugs apathetically and rubs his sweaty arm against mine to get my attention, and I give him an unimpressed look. His smile turns apologetic.

"My bad. I didn't realize Rodriguez was switched to cover safety."

"Cause I didn't say it about a million times," Coach Sahnoun snaps sarcastically, wearing an ugly scowl as he approaches.

Herik straightens his posture, and his expression morphs from sheepish to vigilant.

"You deaf or something? Or am I not talking pretty enough? If I giggle and flirt, will you fucking listen, Herik? Huh?"

Herik opens his mouth to respond.

Coach is already cutting him off. "Don't bother answering. I don't give a fuck. Get your goddamn act together, Herik, or I'll put you on that bench so fast, your ass will feel raw."

"I'm sure he wouldn't mind that. He enjoys keeping his boyfriend company during games," Rodney chortles. Duger smacks the back of his head with a clipboard and makes his way toward us. Rodney scowls and brushes his hand behind his head to make sure our assistant coach didn't fuck up his waves.

"Shut it, Rodney, or I'll have you doing laps with *your* boyfriend." The assistant offensive coach points to the other side of the field, where Kelper is jogging. Cupping his hand over his mouth, Duger shouts, "Pick up the pace, Kelper, or it's another three laps." Miraculously, the tailback's legs move faster.

"And you." Coach points his clipboard at me, mean-mugging me, disappointment dripping in his eyes. My heart plummets to my gut. "I don't know why the fuck you keep bitching about starting when you can't even fucking throw for your goddamn life. How the fuck you got a Heisman is beyond me. Clearly, it went to your head and pushed out the rest of your mental skills. Fucking incompetent, I swear."

Placing the tablet under his armpit, he demonstrates his next words. "You get the fucking ball, you know the play, you read the field to confirm it, and *bam*! You throw it." The invisible ball he tosses into the air flies flawlessly out of his grip. I can see it. He turns back to scowl at me, shouting, the tendons on his neck straining from the effort to shatter my both my eardrums and my will to live. "That easy! It shouldn't take you but three seconds tops to do that and find your fucking receiver. Tell me why you're averaging four and half?"

At this point, most of the team, including Tuckerson, have congregated around us to witness the annihilation of whatever vestige of pride I have left. My backup quarterback looks alert and eager, clearly satisfied by the humiliation I'm being served. I actively keep myself from looking at him, in fear that I might punch his stupid fucking face.

"You've been so focused on getting back into shape, you forgot how to be a fucking quarterback."

"I haven't," I bite out. "Herik didn't realize Rodriguez moved to safety, and Pratt was supposed to—"

"Who told you to speak? Huh? Who? Tell me, so I can smack them after I staple your lips together."

My mouth snaps shut audibly, my face on fire. Millie pauses her work on my leg, the sting of his words resounding.

"Don't give me a goddamn excuse when I didn't ask for it. I don't want to hear squat," Coach growls. He bends down, coming face to face with me. The motion is jarring, not because of the proximity but because of the potent smell of his woodsy cologne. "You either get your shit together before practice is over, or you're not playing Saturday."

I'm quiet, holding my breath to keep my rage in check. He gives me one last lingering look of contempt before walking away. "Better show that you're worthy of that Heisman, or I might ask the DAC to rescind it."

Of all the things he's said to me, from the moment he recruited me to now, that hurts the most. It slams into my chest, nearly knocking me off balance. No matter how hard I try to breathe, I'm only able to take in short, unsteady sips of air. Coach calls for a fifteen-minute break. When Duger makes a motion to approach me, Coach Sahnoun stops him and snaps, "Don't you dare fucking baby that kid. Let him cry like the pansy-ass he is. Maybe that'll make him a better player."

Mortification thrums through my veins from both his words and the pity on everyone's faces as they disperse. Coach and Princeton call on Jabbar to take one of the random drug tests they assign. The only people remaining are Millie, Herik, and Tuckerson.

"Pratt was deep, left field. He bypassed Morris right after the hut," the little blond shit says.

I don't look at him, keeping my eyes downcast. I haven't been able to look Tuckerson in the eyes since he's the only one who might actually know what happened between Autumn and me, and I can't... And the fact that he's meant to be my substitute? Fuck. The guy grates my nerves. "Cool."

He shuffles closer. "Don't beat yourself up, Morgan. It's hard to get back after an injury like yours. Give yourself some time and maybe—"

"Tuckerson"—the register of my voice is deceptively tranquil despite the coil of hatred that rattles deep in my bones—"either get out of my fucking face in the next two seconds, or I'll have you sporting a Halloween costume early this year."

My notorious temper isn't to be fucked with, and that hasn't changed with my injury. He mumbles something under his breath and scampers away.

"I'm sorry," Herik whispers after a minute.

I grunt and try to keep from projecting the rage rushing inside me. When I don't acknowledge him, he puts a hand on my shoulder and repeats himself. "For-realzy, Oats. I'm sorry I didn't block Davidson."

And I'm sorry Coach is such a dick, he doesn't say, but the message is there, subliminal. I also see it in his eyes. He just can't say it aloud in fear of being overheard.

"It's fine." My vocal cords stretch in fraught indignation. My words come out gruff, giving way to how mentally and emotionally afflicted I am. "It's not your fault I can't throw the fucking ball in time."

And though I'm angry about his negligence, I'm more livid about Coach's words. They're warranted if my performances were observed in a vacuum. But they're excessive and cruel when put into perspective. The lack of understanding or inkling of empathy for the nuances of my situation makes it all the more difficult to cage the frenzy that simmers in my veins.

Herik doesn't respond, knowing full well that his consolation holds no value to me. Still, he maintains his hold on my shoulder. His proximity alone is reassuring. I take my feelings out on my leg, rubbing and pressing with bruising intent until the fog of distress clears from my mind. The pain gives me the mental focus I need, and after a minute or two, I dismiss Millic with a *thank you* and relax.

"So… You gonna tell me who's got you smiling like that or what?" I ask Herik, willing a distraction from the topic of football as I try to build my psyche back up.

He looks up from his phone, hides it in his lap, and cups his cheek, eyebrows shooting up in surprise like he can't believe his lips have been curved up the entire time. He winces. "Shit. Didn't even realize I was smiling."

"Uh-huh." I snort then wiggle my brows. "Who's the chick? Is it that girl you've been hooking up with from your econ class?"

Herik shakes his head and bites his lip. "It's actually this girl I just met, and I didn't want to say anything about it after you told me about… Y'know."

I keep my expression blank in false ignorance. "Told you about what?"

"That Mariam chick."

"Miriam, like meercat," I reply automatically. The urge to kick myself is overwhelming as Herik wears a smug look. "And what do you mean, you didn't want to tell me anything because of her? What does she have to do with anything?"

"I didn't want to rub it in your face that I got a girl while you lost one." I used to appreciate his bluntness, but right now, I wish he'd beaten around the bush.

"I didn't lose her," I correct. "I didn't even want her to begin with. We just fucked. That's it. Nothing more."

"Sure."

"I didn't—I don't." I clench my teeth. This conversation is definitely not helping with my mental state.

"And so you talking about her every time you think you see her on campus is just... What?"

I respond slowly, racking my brain for an explanation. "It's venting."

"Your venting sounds a lot like obsessing."

I nudge him a little too aggressively with my shoulder, but he pushes right back. I bite my tongue to keep from mentioning how much I don't care about Miriam or how jerking off to her two nights ago was simply because the memory of what we did that night is fresh on my mind. Nor will I admit to enjoying the personal servicing a little too much, only to lie in my bed, still horny, still angry, and even more bitter than before.

"Stop stalling and quickly tell me about this girl you're fucking with."

"I'm not fucking with her—well, not yet at least. I met her Sunday."

"Sunday?" I balk. "You met her three days ago, and you're already acting pussy-whipped? And you guys call me a simp."

He doesn't even deny it. "Bro, she's fucking amazing. Gorgeous, with a Barbie body. And she's all cute and innocent and so fucking nice. A little, uh, naïve, but that's whatever. I've never had a problem with corrupting girls."

"Anyone can be nice." I snort. *Not Miriam, though.* I stop that train of thought right away, afraid it will run out of control. "Where did you meet this girl? I was with you most of Sunday."

He takes a deep breath. When he speaks, it's all blurred words, everything coming out like quickfire. "No, you weren't. That was Monday. Sunday was when I was studying while you guys went to lunch, remember? I saw that tweet about the dog Jenner found at the party, so I called the chick to come get it. She came by with two of her friends a few hours later, and it was love at first sight."

That dog... The pit bull had thought our green living room carpet was grass and shat all over it. We'd all laughed in surprise by this comically intelligent mishap and cleaned it without too much fuss. Of course, afterward, when the stench continued to permeate the bottom floor of the house, I felt peeved. That didn't stop me from playing with the pup, whom Jenner had aptly named Tinkle, since his piss kept coming out in small tinkles.

"Shit. You're saying you're hooking up with Tinkle's owner?"

Herik nods exuberantly, the look of elation coming back. "Her name is Elise, and I swear to fucking God, she's perfect. I've never met anyone more beautiful, more sweet, more—fucking everything. She's *everything*."

"Show me a pic." Coach is walking back to the center of the field, and I know in about thirty seconds to a minute he's going to blow the whistle to resume practice. So does Herik, and with speedy fingers, he taps at his screen and shows me a picture of her.

"She asked me to take this when I returned the dog. Isn't she fucking beautiful?"

The picture takes me by surprise. For one, he's completely right. In fact, the word beautiful undermines how gorgeous she is. Her face is wonderfully arranged: wide eyes, high cheekbones, thick eyebrows, plush lips, and straight, gleaming teeth. Her hair is artfully twisted into intricate braids, her deep-brown skin clear and smooth.

She's fucking stunning. That, I'll easily admit. Make-you-act-silly type of stunning.

But that explains a small portion of my shock. The girl in the foreground, though eye-catching, isn't the reason my heart stops.

No. It's the person in the background, a girl with an equal magnitude of beauty, though hers is less obvious, more delicate. It's quiet, requiring inspection to truly appreciate the unique lines blending together to create her magnificent features. A girl who appears tall despite her shrunken proportions, with brown hair, fuckable lips, golden skin, exquisitely long legs, and bright eyes. She's talking, partially turned toward a guy beside her, her mouth open and her eyes crinkled in good humor.

"Who's that?" I point at the girl in question.

"The girl behind Elise?" He squints in concentration for another dozen seconds. "I know the guy's name was James, but the other girl's name was... Fuck, I don't remember. She didn't introduce herself to me."

The whistle blows, and Princeton makes the call for practice to restart.

"Don't fuck up, Morgan," Coach snaps at me when Herik and I jog to the line of scrimmage. Then, to the rest of the team, he announces what plays we're doing, describes all the mistakes we shouldn't make, and offers compliments to the chosen few—Quinn, Rodriguez, and Davidson—before walking off.

We're meant to get into position, but instead, I seek out Herik. My teammates glance urgently at me, but I don't care.

"Can you find out for me?"

"Find out what?" He pauses before realization dawns on him. "Oh. About the girl you were asking about?" He narrows his eyes. "Why?"

Thanks to my shame, I choose not to be forthcoming—a first in our friendship. "I think she's pretty."

"Not as pretty as Elise, I'll tell you that."

Objectively speaking, he's not wrong. If there were a competition over who was more conventionally attractive, Elise would take the cake. But as true as that might be, as much as I can appreciate the visuals she provides, it's the out-of-focus girl standing behind her, the one who could talk at length about the multitude of storylines and universes for Batman and who used various sex toys in her drawer to outline different offensive plays, that I find more stunning. "Whatever. Just find out who this other chick is."

Herik nods and fits his mouthguard in. "I'll be the best damn FBI agent you've ever had," he lisps.

I slap his ass in gratitude, then crouch into position. Behind my helmet, I'm wearing a smile. Then I call our play.

One point three seconds later, the ball tears through the air in a perfect spiral, spinning flawlessly on its axis, it's retrieval successful. Coach is staring at me when I turn to face him. He doesn't look happy, but he doesn't look mad, either.

I'll take it.

IT'S ELEVEN AT night, and I'm two problems away from finishing my stats homework, which is due in fifty-nine minutes, when Herik barges into my room and cheers, "Who's your daddy?"

I stop working on my problem and push my glasses higher up my nose, furrowing my brows. "Otis Morgan Senior. But he's dead."

Herik rolls his eyes, unfazed by my recurring joke. "I mean your other daddy."

Tilting my head, I close my laptop and look at him expectantly. "Who? You? You think *you* can handle being my daddy?"

"That's right, baby boy," he coos, stopping at the foot of my bed and pumping a fist into the air. "I'm your daddy. And your daddy has found her."

I toss my textbook aside and scoot over, beckoning for him to sit beside me. My muscles are still weeping after our night workout, the ice bath afterwards having done nothing to cool the burn, which is the only reason why I'm doing homework in bed instead of downstairs at the kitchen table with the rest of the boys.

He hands me his phone and lounges beside me, wearing a million-dollar smile.

I look at the screen in excitement, though it instantly plummets when I glance at the Instagram profile he's presented to me. "This is a guy."

"Yeah, but scroll down on his profile. She's everywhere."

He's right. The second I swipe, I see photos of Miriam with the guy and Elise. The more I scroll, the more I see of her, like a gradient with its highest concentration at the bottom.

I tap at every single photo she appears in. Which is a lot, if you ask me. Enough to make me think that this J.HMONG user is her boyfriend. Not that I'm jealous. Jealousy is for people who care, which I don't. I'm curious, which is totally different. Besides, I just want to know whether a girl I boned was in a relationship or not. It's a matter of principle—I'm willing to be referred to as many things, but homewrecker isn't one of them.

"Does she not have her own account?" I ask, swiping through the photos. I pause when I come to one where she and James are kissing, trying my best to keep a scowl off my face. The date reads nearly two years ago. The caption: *New Year, Old Me.*

He should definitely revise that cliché shit.

"Nah, bro. Not that I could find."

"That's a little sus." What person doesn't have social media? "Were you at least able to figure out her name?"

Herik shakes his head. "Nope."

I stop scrolling and toss his phone back to him with a glare. "Then how the fuck could you have found her, asshat?"

He scowls at me. "I found pictures of her, fuckface."

I pull my textbook back onto my lap. "On someone else's account. That's not finding her." Opening it back up to the page I was on, I add a flippant, "FBI agent, my ass."

"Hey," he barks. "Don't talk to your daddy like that!"

"I never said you were my daddy." I point at the phone in his hand. "And after this, you're definitely not."

Slapping him across the face would have been kinder. He looks at me in utter betrayal, a hand placed over his heart. "You did not just say that."

I focus on my stats problem and point at the door. "Get out."

"Fine, I will." The mattress rises when he removes his weight from it. "But I want you to know that I was going to ask Elise about her during Midnight Kiss tomorrow, but since you're being a bitch, I don't think I'm gonna."

I look at him, holding my breath. He lingers knowingly at the door, a *gotcha* grin on his face. I hate him. I know what he's going to make me do, and it's worse than groveling.

"I'm sorry," I grit out between clenched teeth. "Will you ask Elise? Please."

"Only if you tell me who your daddy is," he whispers suggestively.

Honestly, it doesn't surprise or bother me that half the team thinks we're pegging each other. I inhale sharply and swallow every ounce of dignity I've managed to retain during my twenty-one years. "You're my daddy."

He smirks and coos, "That's right, baby boy. I'm your daddy."

Herik slips out the room and shuts the door before the pillow I toss in his direction can hit him.

So he can block that but not a three-hundred-pound white guy? I ought to kick my daddy's ass.

Inbox - otis17morgan@rsu.org

✉ **Emerson Loyn**
Morgan, I've spoken with Coach Sahnoun, and we're good for dinner on the 23rd. Please confirm that you're able to make it, or we will have to reschedule for...

✉ **Riverside University FAO & Otis (13)**
The following application has been rejected. Please resubmit a signed copy of your mother's W2 along with a signed affidavit. We cannot grant you any more financial aid without confirmation of her...

GRETA
CLOSING THE GODDAMN DOOR

"**MAMAN! PAPA! JE** *suis là*! And guess what? I brought you guys a present," I sing off-key as I walk through the front door carrying my heavy hamper.

"*Dégage. Je suis claquée.* Is it considered a present if I don't want it?" Mom hollers back.

I follow the voice to the kitchen and beam at the sight of her in front of the stove. In mock excitement, I hold up the bin of dirty clothes. I'm already out of breath, a sheen of perspiration layered over my skin from the short trip between my car and the house. Lord, I'm out shape.

"Absolutely. You taught me a gift is anything given from the heart." I jostle my laundry. "So take it. Take my heart." With that, I drop it onto the granite countertop.

Mom rolls her eyes, flawlessly dicing the onions without tearing up. "You're a grown woman, Greta. You need to do your laundry at home." *By yourself*, she implies.

"My washer and dryer are broken." I'm lying. We both know the real reason, but neither of us feels the need to speak upon it. I'm here, and that's all that matters.

"Still? It's been five weeks, no? Sounds like I need to call your apartment and ask what on Earth I'm paying two grand a month for."

I grab the hamper again, waddle toward the laundry room, then deposit my clothes into the gigantic machine, too lazy to separate by color. "That 'I' is misplaced. You're not paying. Dad is."

"If you think Papa controls the money in this house, you're out of your mind." She lets out a maniacal cackle as I enter the kitchen again.

"If that's the case, d'ya want to go shopping Sunday? We haven't gone in a while, and I'm in need of a fix." When she doesn't take the bait. I add, "I saw Celine released a new tote, and I know you've wanted a new one since your Bottega got torn."

Her face lights up, and she points her knife at me. "That sounds like a wonderful plan, darling. But let's also stop at some jewelry stores. I have so many outfits that don't have matching accessories, and it's making me go crazy."

I nod. "As long as I can buy some more perfume, I'm down."

"Perfume. Yes, I need that too. Your papa loves it when I wear perfume while we—" She stops, realizing who she's speaking to. But it's too late. I'm already willing my existence away. Mom clears her throat. "But let me pick a fight with him first so he doesn't get too suspicious about the charges on the card."

Still disgusted, I throw a silent thumbs-up and go start my laundry. Even after I'm done, I linger in the room until the grotesque image of my parents screwing fades from my mind. Four gags and two shivers in horror later, I'm strutting back toward her.

"*Où est Papa*? Out?" I grab a gala apple from the fruit basket. There's only one there, and I know my dad bought it today in preparation for my arrival. I hadn't told him I was coming today, but his paternal intuition was always good. Everyone else in the Sahnoun family loves green, sour apples, and only I like gala— specifically gala. And because of that, there's always at least one available for me to snack on.

"*Ici.*" She looks down the hall. "In a meeting with one of his players."

I click my tongue and shake my head empathetically. "I bet that poor guy came in for some advice but ended up getting chewed out." And because I'm nosey, I crane my neck in the general direction of his home office, hoping I'll hear something. I'm met with silence.

"You better fold your clothes the second they're finished in the dryer," Mom chides once I've given up eavesdropping. I take a big bite of my apple and let the juice dribble down my chin then collect it with a deft swipe of my tongue. She pours the prepped veggies into her frying pan while I, ever the handy helper, lean against the counter, doing my part by pointing out the two pieces of spinach that fall onto the stove.

"I'll do it when I get home."

"Don't lie to me, Greta. I know your closet is a mess."

Damn. I'd forgotten about my trip to Louisiana three weeks ago when I forgot to feed Raven and had her go over to my place to do it. She probably Sherlock-ed the entire apartment, and rather than yell at me about it right then, she chose to keep it to herself so she could use it against me later. Clever woman.

"After dinner, you'll fold the clothes and we'll watch a movie, since Papa said he's in no mood to play any board games."

She fails to mention that him not being in the mood has to do with how often Mom and I collude and cheat to win. He doesn't appreciate how resourceful we can be. "Fine, but I can't stay for too long."

"Greta." My name holds a warning, and chills crawl up my skin. Céline Goodeau Sahnoun is normally calm, but when she's about to snap, she always gives warning so the perpetrator can tread lightly and avoid getting attacked by her viper-like tongue.

"Fine," I mumble half-heartedly. "I'll fold them while we watch a movie."

"*Très bien.*" She points at the bowl of seasoned shrimp and signals for me to bring it over.

I linger behind her as I do so, placing my chin on the top of her head, towering over her.

"*Recule.*" When I don't step back, she bumps her hips against me and snaps, "*L'espace vital tu connais?*"

I pout and blink innocently at her, shuffling to the side to get out of her way. "Not to, like, put pressure on you or anything, but when is dinner going to be ready?" Mom clicks her tongue in reproach, and I quickly add, "Again, no pressure. Seriously. Just curious since, y'know, I'm starving and all."

"You're always starving."

"It's why they call me a hungry, hungry, hippo." I grab my gut. It's not big, and I'm not complaining about my weight, but the pudge and my thighs definitely give away my extremely comfortable—and only slightly addictive—relationship with food.

"If you would just go to the gym with me twice a week…"

I roll my eyes. "Not all of us can look like a MILF. Especially not when your parents refused to give you any of the good genes, choosing instead to give it all to their youngest child."

"Julien was always so handsome." She pauses.

An all-too-familiar pang of longing squeezes my heart at the thought of him, a feeling I'm certain my mother is experiencing tenfold. When she breaks out of her daze, she looks at me. And whatever doubt or annoyance I might have about these visits to my parents' place dissolves with that look, the one that shines in her eyes and is filled with gratitude because even if *he's* not here, I am, and that's good enough for her to stay together instead of fall apart.

Reaching over, she pinches my cheek with an idle hand, grabbing hold of the skin there in a vise-like grip despite my endeavors to move away. "But you're just as beautiful, *mon chat.*" The compliment is an afterthought. That doesn't diminish its sincerity, but it definitely lessens the impact.

"Yeah, yeah, yeah." I swat her touch away. I finish my apple, both of us silent as I try to stop thinking about Julien.

My dad's voice echoes throughout the house a couple minutes later, interrupting Mom and me talking about shoes. "I see Greta's car in the driveway. Is she with you, Lina?"

Rather than respond, Mom waits for him to walk into the kitchen. When he sees me, he simpers joyfully, his strides widening as he makes his way toward me, arms outstretched. I move away from the counter to accept his warm gesture, reciprocating with a single-arm hug. It's brief, and he lets me go after a quick kiss on my forehead.

"*Coucou*," I say, but he cuts me off.

"You forgot to close your passenger-side door." He shakes his head, hands on his hips, his stance wide and intimidating. "Do you do this often? That's dangerous, Greta."

You'd have a heart attack if you knew how often I keep my front door unlocked.

"No," I quickly reply. "I just forgot today because I was bringing in a load of laundry."

"Your washer and dryer are broken again? What is this bullshit?" He turns to Mom and speaks in French, deliberating over whether they should go to my apartment manager and get the issue resolved or if a call would suffice.

Resigning himself, Dad beckons me to sit at the counter while he follows my mother's orders and chops the assorted vegetables.

"How are classes?" he asks. "Are you failing any?"

Fuck. Not this again. Not now.

"Oh, ye of little faith," I respond vaguely.

He passes me a bowl of parsley, and I immediately begin picking the leaves away from the stem.

"Allow me to manage my expectations, please." He looks up and pretends to count on his fingers. "Expectations you've failed to meet four semesters in a row."

"Should I make it five? That's your favorite number, isn't it?"

Dad obviously doesn't appreciate my flippant attitude and stops chopping to shoot me his coach look. "Greta."

Did I mention my mom learned the warning voice from my dad? I carefully consider my words before continuing, "I'm only doing *poorly* in one class." The word choice is deliberate, but I still can't save myself from his lethal scrutiny.

"Which is?"

"Economics."

Dad sighs.

"How hard can it be?" Mom chirps. "Supply and demand. There, you're done."

"Can you be my professor instead?" I mumble.

Dad folds his arms over his chest, the look of disdain on his face deepening. I can't decipher whether he's speaking to me as a coach or a dad. "Greta, it is unacceptable for you to fail another class. Not after you've promised me over and over again that you'd pick up your grades. You're barely sitting at a passing grade point average."

I opt for silence, and he persists, incapable of withholding his disappointment. A downside of being the coach's daughter is that he has no filter at work, and that translates to having no filter at home.

"This isn't a matter you can ignore. This is serious. All you do is spend my money on useless things. You barely study. You're embarrassing me, being so academically reckless. I can barely look at the dean or chancellor, knowing how poorly you're doing. And if you think I'm going to keep tolerating this negligence, you're out of your mind." His hand motions illustrate how furious he truly is. "I have rules, Greta, and you've consistently—and very blatantly—disregarded them, thinking you're somehow entitled to everything with no effort on your part."

A smacking sound resonates against the high ceilings when

he slaps the tabletop hard, his cheeks turning red. The edges of a Kabyle accent bleed into his words. It doesn't matter if he's not entirely fluent in the language, this thick elocution always makes an appearance when he's angry.

I'm too used to it, though, so I don't even flinch.

"I mean, how can I have my players following my rules, but my own daughter does not?" He shakes his head, takes a few deep breaths, then resumes chopping. "This is my last warning, Greta. Your mother and I are sick and tired of always being disappointed by your mediocrity and refusal to challenge yourself. If I see one more failing grade on your transcript after this semester, I'm terminating your lease, and you're moving back here with your mother and me."

Even when I got good grades, you had nothing good to say. No one can ever please you. What's the point in trying? There are so many retaliatory words poised at the tip of my tongue. One being *fuck* and the other being *you*, in that specific order. But around my dad, I've learned to curb my innate desire to speak my mind.

And when I say learned, I mean in the hard way. So, I bite my tongue, willing to draw blood if it means I can prevent an explosive fight. I don't want to ruin my mood for clubbing later.

"Yes, sir," I answer robotically, mockery evident in my delivery. I'm certain he'll pick up on it and maybe comment on how I need to learn to respect him when discussing serious matters, but he doesn't.

When I'm lying in bed and waiting for sleep to come later tonight, I'm sure I'll think of all the other things I could have said to him. But for now, I won't let him win. I won't let him affect me. I will remain detached and unaffected, because that's how to win with a Sahnoun. That's how you stay alive.

There's a duality to my father, one that can be switched on and off seemingly at will. Very few people have witnessed both sides of him, given how astutely he compartmentalizes the people in his work and personal life. I think I'm the only one that has even registered these two sides.

The family side cares for his children and wife and does everything in his power to ensure their safety, well-being, and satisfaction. This side can be goofy and cool, and it is only in these types of environments that anyone sees my father relaxed and smiling.

Then there is the coach who thinks he's always right and wants everything and everyone involved in it to do his bidding exactly the way he envisions it. Failure is an option only if that person can withstand the onslaught of torture and ridicule that accompanies it. Excellence is expected, and mediocrity is shunned.

Julien had always seemed good at coping with both sides, while I tolerated only the former, rebelling against the latter, forcing my younger brother to take most of the heat.

If only I'd helped him bear the burden a bit…

All this is to say that my dad isn't a bad guy. He has his flaws, but what parent is perfect? If they were, therapists would be out of their jobs.

A spell of uncomfortable silence falls over the kitchen, the sounds of clanging cutlery and rhythmic chops piercing the air in an orchestra of unease. I'm done with the parsley and give Dad the plate without looking, the strain between us still palpable.

"What did Otis need, Farid? Why did he stop by?" Mom asks, effectively changing the subject. The tension dissipates, and we all visibly relax. My mom has always been the peacekeeper, even when she behaves like the aggressor. Someone has to do it, and since Julien isn't with us anymore and my dad and I are too similar in temper, it's her.

"He just wanted a guarantee he would start tomorrow. He's pissed about that article Micah Green wrote in *Sports Exclusive* about washed-up college athletes."

"Otis? Otis who?" The name strikes me as oddly familiar.

"Otis Morgan. He was my starting quarterback the last two years. Remember the freshman that scored seven rushing touchdowns his first year? That's him."

"Oh, yeah." I clap my hands. A blurred apparition of him flits into my mind. I remember my father speaking about recruiting him during his senior year, traveling to Dayton, Texas for a week to scout him, and giving him a verbal offer after witnessing a single game.

I'd never met the guy, but I've seen enough shots of him on ESPN that if I ran into him on the street, I'm sure I would recognize him.

"What happened to him this year? He won the Heisman last December, and then *poof*, he disappeared. Milton Tuckerson has been your starter since the beginning of the season, right?"

Tuckerson isn't bad, but he is the definition of an average player. Since Morgan, the powerhouse quarterback on his way to the NFL, has been out due to an injury, Tuckerson has had more time to display his skills.

But he's only college-football good, and there's nothing special about that.

"Tuckerson and White. As for Morgan... He got the kiss of death in February." A shadow of sadness dims over my father. No matter how much of a massive dick he is to his players, he loves them. Does he have a depraved, convoluted, borderline-abusive way of showing it? Absolutely. Does love make that acceptable? Hell no. But it's love all the same.

I thought that would change after Julien, but I guess not.

I suck in a deep breath and wince empathetically. "Yeesh, that sucks. But he must be okay now if you plan to start him?"

"Physically, he's there. He's been killing himself in therapy and practice. But mentally... no. The kid keeps messing up on me, as if all his natural talents and all those strategies we taught him went to shit after his injury. Yesterday's practice was terrible. He picked up a bit during the last hour, but not enough to make me feel confident in his abilities."

"Just put him in during the first quarter," Mom suggests, coming to the sink to wash her hands. "If he doesn't do well, bench him again."

"Then I'll have the media all over me. They'll think he's injured still. They'll question his skills, and make fucked-up comments about his viability in the league. If he gets up and plays and does a poor job, they'll blame me, and then they'll harass him. There's no winning." My dad shakes his head. "Duger and I were talking, and we think it might be good just to let him wing it. Have him play the entire game, and if he sucks, then fuck it. That's on him. It's game one against UMass, and it's more important to have our football team's star player play than to win. University morale and all."

"Wing it?" I repeat, surprised. "Since when have you been the type to wing anything?"

"I don't want to, but I think because he didn't play game zero, he's doubting himself and it's messing with him. He used to make a play in about one-point-three seconds, and now, it's taking him over three-point-two. Hell, he's getting tackled by his teammates so often, his practice jersey is green."

I frown. "That's a little disappointing. It must upset you, having one of the most promising players of the decade turn into a flop."

"He's not a flop, Greta," Dad growls defensively. "He's just having a hard time."

And I bet you being a total asshole to him during practice isn't helping him, either. He might defend and advocate for his player in front of me and my mom, maybe even in private with his assistant coaches, Duger and Princeton, but I know full well Dad—more aptly referred to as Coach Sahnoun in this situation—ripped Morgan a new one yesterday. I might not ever have witnessed a single college practice led by my father, but based on what I know from high school and Julien, I'm positive my father has torn Otis

Morgan to shreds.

"Hey, Dad," I begin slowly, a thought suddenly appearing in my mind, what with all this football talk. I swallow, keeping my tone neutral, almost disinterested. "I actually have a football question for you."

"*Shnou bghiitii?*" Of both my parents, my dad is least likely to speak his mother tongue and that's because he never actually lived in Algeria. His dad, my *jedi,* immigrated to the United States as a war refugee, right before my dad was born, making dad a first generation Algerian-American. Being raised here had him fully assimilating to the culture, fighting his heritage in a bid to fit in. Amongst his family, he's the outsider, being the one that never wanted to go back home after things settled, and he stayed for a career in The States.

The only time he doesn't speak English is when he's stressed or not thinking, and even then, his Kabyle is rough given how little he speaks it day to day. And when he and my mom talk, it's mostly in French. The only time I've heard my father speak Kabyle for an extended period of time—brokenly, I might add—is when he speaks with family back home, or when we visited those few times, and even then, his elocution would rally criticisms. It's funny how good Dad is at French. The day my *jedi* found out his son had learned the colonizer's language for a girl, all hell broke loose.

When Mom tells the story, she laughs, but Dad always looks pale. I would also find it hilarious if the whole situation wasn't deeply traumatizing and serious.

"Actually, it's not really a football question so much as it's a question about your football team." Popping my knuckles, I build myself up and quickly get on with it. "Do you have a kid on your team named Rutherford? Middle name, not first." *Stupid, stupid, stupid.* I hate myself the second the words fly out of my mouth.

"Rutherford? No, I don't… I don't think so? But then again, I don't really know my players' middle names. I barely remember their first names." He looks suspicious. I've never, not once, concerned myself with one of his players. "Why?"

Before I have a chance to respond, the doorbell rings—once, twice, three times—insistently.

"Greta, get the door," Dad commands.

I look at Mom, hoping she'll offer instead.

Dad doesn't like that one bit. "You, Greta. Get the door right now."

Begrudgingly, I hop off the stool and make my way toward the foyer. Had I known my life was going to change the second I opened it, I would have walked slower. Maybe I would have put up a fight and insisted Mom do it. But I didn't know.

I twist the knob and swing the door open with reckless abandon and come face to face with a man I promised myself to not think of again unless it was in fond, sultry, detached recollection.

He exhales audibly. "Miri—"

He doesn't even get the last syllable out of my middle name before I close the goddamn door in his face.

let's go for a drive ⛅ juju

greteleatsbread · 13 songs, 48 min 49 sec

👤 ⏮ ⏸ ⏭ 🔀

I'm Not Okay (I Promise) My Chemical Romance	♥		3:06
Numb Linkin Park	♥		3:05
The Diary of Jane Breaking Benjamin	♥		3:21
Iris The Goo Goo Dolls	♥		4:50
It Ends Tonight The All-American Rejects	♥		3:39
Chasing Cars Snow Patrol	♥		4:28
Somewhere Only We Know Keane	♥		3:56
Riot Three Days Grace	♥		3:37
Apologize OneRepublic	♥		3:38
Yellow Coldplay	♥		4:26
How to Save a Life The Fray	♥		4:23
Basket Case Green Day	♥		3:02
I'm Just a Kid Simple Plan	♥		3:18

OTIS

A DINNER FROM HELL (FEAT. SAHNOUNS)

I'VE HAD A door slammed in my face before. I was eleven, selling popcorn to the neighbors for the Boy Scouts. Mean old Ms. Heckles battered the door in my face upon seeing me with an open box of delightful treats. I wasn't able to say our slogan before she shouted, "Stupid, ugly kids," and swung the door shut.

Despite being a big boy, I cried in dejection. Pawpaw wasn't having it and harangued the woman, pounding on her door with fists and feet, cursing like a hellion. All the bad words in my arsenal were acquired that day.

At the present, I'm too old to cry, but I do groan in pain— excruciating pain—because unlike then, I taste the iron of my blood. Miriam had packed tremendous force in that swing, and I'd been far too close to the large wooden slab upon impact.

I'm clutching the front of my face in agony, placing a hand on the doorframe to stabilize myself and keep from doubling over. The tang of blood grows more evident, and not a second later, I feel it oozing from my nose.

"Greta," Coach's muffled voice booms from the other side of the door. "Who's there?"

I don't hear her if she responds, and when a rush of pain hits me again, I groan loudly, and the door opens again.

"What in God's name?" Coach sputters at the scene before him. "Morgan, what the hell is going on?" He's by my side and helping me stand upright immediately. I grunt at the motion, hand still covering my face to keep the blood from dribbling onto his doormat. He presses on the back of my neck to crane my head forward. "What happened?"

Despite the weird, hunched position I'm in, I do my best to look at Miriam—or is it Greta? "Nothing," I mutter, swallowing the blood that's traveled to my mouth and cringe. I'd never make it as a vampire.

"This didn't happen from nothing." When my neck bobbles backward, he shoves it down, more aggressively this time. I know he's trying to be helpful, but *oh my God*, that hurts. "Greta, go grab the first aid kit."

Wordlessly, Miriam—Greta, her name is Greta—does Coach's bidding, scampering out of sight. My anxiety is amplified, and I do my best to hold onto the hope that her being inside of my coach's house doesn't mean she's who I think she is.

Coach guides me inside his house and directs me to sit. I can hear another woman's voice traveling through the hall, getting closer as she approaches us.

"Farid, *c'était quoi ce bruit?*" The concern on the French woman's face fades briefly when she spots me, greeting me with a nod and a warm smile.

"Nothing, apparently." Coach snorts. "Where's Greta? She's supposed to bring the first aid kit."

"She is. She's in the garage looking for it right now. Be patient, and do not yell."

Coach grunts and hands me a wad of tissues. "Use this."

I press it to my nose with as much pressure as I can bear, keeping the bridge compressed. The flood of blood slows. My nose and upper lip still throb, but it's duller than before.

"I found it," the familiar, feminine voice calls out after a lingering silence. The very same voice that talked me through the concept of cat heaven.

"In here," Coach calls. He says something else in another language—French, maybe, or Arabic. I'm not sure—and that feeling of doom intensifies as I remember the French Miriam flawlessly pronounced at breakfast. She'd uttered only two words but enunciated them with such ease that it was only natural to assume she's fluent.

But maybe that's unrelated. She and Coach bear very little resemblance to each other—his skin is two shades darker, his eyes smaller, his nose sharper. And yet…

Removing my hand, Coach makes a big fuss about cleaning my face. It's actually disarming, him being all concerned and shit, even if it's aggressive.

The only time he's been this attentive was when I was lying on the field, immobile, shouting in agony from my injury. The sheer panic in his voice that day will forever remain with me. It was the first time I truly understood that despite being Satan's better half, he cares. When it comes down to it, though he may not show it, Coach Sahnoun actually cherishes me.

Or at least, that's what I'm telling myself.

I'm finally able to look forward again after what seems like forever, and I swear my neck creaks in protest. Mrs. Sahnoun studies me with so much distress, I honestly wonder if I have horns growing out of my head. "Should we take him to the emergency room?"

"Don't be dramatic, Mom," Miriam dismisses. "He's barely hurt."

My head jerks to face her, my eyes narrow. Coach grabs my chin, and for a split second, I think he's going to yell at me for laying eyes on Greta. Instead, he inspects me, rolling my head around to get a good look at every angle.

"I'm fine," I add, not because the throbbing in my face has alleviated, but because it should be me, not Greta, making the declaration. "Really."

Mrs. Sahnoun nods solemnly before mumbling an excuse to go back to the kitchen. Before she departs, however, she turns to look at me again. "Okay, then you must stay for dinner. It's no good to drive right away with an injury like that."

"Oh no, it's okay. I just came back for my phone. I left it in Coach's office."

"Greta, go grab his phone." When Greta doesn't move, she speaks quickly and quietly in French. Then Mrs. Sahnoun addresses me, softening her disposition. "And Otis, I really insist you stay for dinner. We have more than enough food for a big healthy boy like you."

I'm about to decline again politely when Coach gives me this look that screams, *Say no to my wife one more time and I'll kill you.*

"That sounds lovely, Mrs. Sahnoun. Thank you for the invitation. I'd love to have dinner here." Anxiety shoots through me. I glance at Miriam, who's already walking away.

Coach is patient and attentive as he helps me. Thankfully, he doesn't fill the time with conversation. Still, I can practically hear him thinking, *Are you really stupid enough to get your face fucked up before a game?*

By the time he finishes tending to me, Greta has returned and tosses me the phone, maintaining a distance. She stares at me like she doesn't even know me, her eyes dead, her expression void.

Not going to lie, it hurts. I'm not saying I should inspire poetry, but I know my worth. I remember the way she gawked at me when I took my shirt off. In fact, if we were to hook up again, I could probably coax that same high-pitched scream she made when she came from both my mouth and my cock.

And yet here she stands, Miriam—no, wait, Greta. *Greta, Greta, Greta,* I repeat to myself—with a look of detached casualness, but all I want to do is shake her until she acknowledges me properly. But I can't, so I just stand a little straighter, my body visibly tensing.

Coach notices. "You okay? You hurt still?"

No duh, I'm still hurt. And I'm not just talking about my wounded pride. My physical injury is still fresh.

I shake my head, a little put off by how overtly kind he's being. Is it all for show? And if it is, how do I manufacture an environment to invoke such considerate behavior during practices or games? There are only so many times you can be called a walking fuckstick through the headset without taking it personally.

He inspects me one last time and nods when he's satisfied with his handiwork. "Greta," Coach says when he gets up from his seat beside me, gathering the supplies he's taken out. "Keep our guest company. I'm going to help your mom finish making dinner. We'll call you guys into the dining room as soon as it's done. Shouldn't be long."

He leaves. We say nothing and just look at each other.

I'm the first to speak, my throat burning with unease. "Please tell me you're his niece."

"Nope."

I swallow a whimper. "Cousin?"

"Nuh-uh."

"Maid?"

A smile breaks past her aloofness. "I've put a cup in the sink. Does that count?"

I swallow thickly and touch my nose to occupy myself. Still, my eyes wander, my focus gravitating to her, checking her out, comparing the vision in front of me with the memory I've stored. She stands there, wearing an oversized t-shirt and tight biker shorts. Casual and cute is what she's going for, apparently. She's tied her hair up, her crazy curls tamed with only a few scattered strands left loose to frame her full face. It's the type of hairstyle that'd be perfect for getting on her knees or for being pulled if I took her from behind.

Oh, fuck. I can't be thinking about this at Coach's house when she might be his d—

"So," Miriam drawls, extending the vowel lazily. "Your name is Otis. Otis Morgan."

Does she know me? Is this how she knew so much about football? It isn't because she's a self-proclaimed avid fan, but because she's Coach's—

"And yours is Greta." *Just Greta, with no last name that starts with an "S".*

"You're a football player," she continues.

Is she playing a game of facts?

"And you're…" Well, fuck. I know so little about her that I fill the latter half of my statement with an observation, "tall."

Shit, that's stupid. I should have gone with "cheerleader."

"Not as tall as you."

"True." I'm six-five. If I didn't have such a good arm, I'd probably be a lineman or even a basketball player.

"And you're a quarterback." Her look of impassivity deepens, projecting a dislike I don't understand.

Part of me wants to deny this label, to see if that will melt her frigid disposition, but lying is futile. A quick Google search, and I'll be found out. "That I am."

She finally peels her eyes off me. The constriction in my chest remains, and I know there's no way to alleviate the pressure that's plaguing me unless she admits to having no affiliation with Coach.

Don't think about it. I'm going to have to sit through a whole-ass dinner with Coach, Mrs. Sahnoun and Miri—Greta, and if I keep thinking about it, I'm going to either throw up, run through the wall like the Kool-Aid man, or drown myself in their toilet.

I use the breathing technique my rehab therapist taught me when we worked on any exercise I found near impossible to do, my mind refusing to exert any effort in fear of suffering or failure.

"You can take a seat," I mumble when I notice the way she shifts her weight from one foot to the other.

"I know."

A resurgence of panic zaps through me, breathing exercise be damned, so I go for a distraction. Conversation. Before I'd asked to wash the dishes, we'd been good at that. And even if her body language is telling me she wants nothing to do with me, I go for it.

"So, Greta... What's your major?" That's a question she had refused to answer as Miriam, thinking it too personal.

She responds without looking at me, the wall overhead much more enthralling than my face. "Education with an emphasis in social science."

"You want to be a teacher." The notion brings about a wonderful mental interlude. If she'd been my teacher, I'd have failed every single class, spending the entire period daydreaming instead of paying attention. Better yet, I'd misbehave so she'd be the one to discipline me. Shit. Not the thing to think of right now. I'll put a pin in it and save it for a desperate shower or sleepless night.

"Yup."

I wait for her to reciprocate and inquire about what I'm studying. But she doesn't.

I allow the awkwardness to linger for a heartbeat longer before I break. "You're welcome to ask me anything in return." I do my best to be lighthearted. "I'm more than happy to quench your curiosity."

She snorts through her nose and shrugs. "Nah, I'm good. I've got no thirst to quench."

A second later, she contradicts this claim by offering to grab us both glasses of water, which I graciously accept because I need some time to collect my thoughts.

Alone, I begin to develop crazy theories.

Maybe she's a succubus and her *modus operandi* is to fuck men and make them feel valued and smile all throughout the night with fun, stupid conversation, all while offering nothing about herself, just the pleasure she can give. And just when the men decide they want more, she withdraws, relishing in the torment she brings her victims.

I'm so oblivious to my surroundings as I concoct this crazy theory that I hardly notice when she comes back.

"VOSS," I comment when she hands me the heavy glass bottle. I take a careful sip, my face still tender. "I didn't know Coach drinks VOSS."

"He doesn't. He drinks tap. Guests of the Sahnouns drink VOSS."

I take another refreshing gulp then crack an upbeat grin. "Wow. Coach considers me a guest? I was so sure he thought of me as a doormat."

"Don't get it twisted. You're still a doormat. Just a doormat that gets nice things sometimes." She twists the cap onto her drink and sets it on the coffee table between us. "See, with Coach Sahnoun, it's all about psychology. He has a master's degree in it. He knows how to build you up and break you down over and over again until you're nothing but an empty vessel obsessed with pleasing him."

"Are you one of his players, too?" I joke.

Greta shakes her head. "Not me. Someone I know." She tilts her head and gives an arrogant smile. "I'm not such an easy target."

That succubus theory is becoming more plausible.

Just as I'm about to ask her to clarify, Mrs. Sahnoun walks into the open room and smiles sweetly. "*A table.* Dinner is ready."

COACH IS PUSSY-whipped, and I can't wait to tell the rest of the team.

"Lina, I don't think you understand how beneficial this car would be in our life," he pleads. "Not only is the driving experience flawless, but it fits a kayak."

"We don't have a kayak." Mrs. Sahnoun takes a sip of her wine. The meal ended five minutes ago, but no one has moved.

Greta is staring at her phone, texting and smiling, absent from this conversation.

I, however, am completely attentive to the discussion— dumbfounded, really. It's like watching a train wreck. I want to look away, to preserve the big-bad-wolf image Coach has flawlessly curated, but the beautiful disaster holds my attention.

"But if we got a kayak, it would hold it."

Mrs. Sahnoun scowls and points a stern finger in his direction. "I said no, Farid. Don't argue with me. We're not getting that stupid car."

"Céline," he whines.

"No! Bring it up one more time, and I swear I'll…" She speaks the rest in French. I stare in awe as the reproach on Mrs. Sahnoun's face deepens his demure pout.

"Are you guys done fighting over the stupid Rolls-Royce?" Greta gripes, finally putting her phone down. She rests her elbow on the table and cushions her cheek with her palm, her face turned toward them.

"It's not stupid," Coach grumbles, but Mrs. Sahnoun sucks in a hiss. He purses his lips and glares at his empty plate.

"Whatever." Greta checks her smart watch. "It's almost eight-thirty, and I kind of have an appointment to get to."

"No, you don't," Mrs. Sahnoun replies without hesitation. "You're here until ten. And don't think I forgot about your clothes that are still in the dryer. I'm not folding them for you."

Her left eye twitches. "I'll come back later. I have a thing to go to soon and need to get ready."

"What? Clubbing?" Coach snorts and shakes his head, wagging his spoon at her. "Just because you're twenty-one doesn't mean you need to develop an addiction to alcohol."

"It's not the alcohol I like," Greta retorts with a roll of her eyes. "It's the—"

"Attention and boys," Mrs. Sahnoun finishes, interrupting Greta with a smirk. "Don't worry, darling. You are just like me when I was younger."

"This woman right here was a vixen, I'll tell you that," Coach mumbles, shaking his head in fond dismay. "I was practically on my knees, begging for her to have me with twenty other men lined up to take my place the second she got bored of me."

Greta arches a perfect brow and gives a coy grin, addressing the gorgeous French woman. "Why you said yes to him is beyond me."

"Me too." The women clink their glasses.

There's no way they're her parents, I think. They're too cavalier about her sex life.

"You can leave at ten," Coach says. "No sooner."

"But—"

"And you better use your own money for the drinks," he adds with a glare. "Don't make James pay for all of them. He's not an ATM."

James. The picture of them kissing pops in my head, and without realizing it, I'm glowering, unintentionally aiming my scathing gaze at Mrs. Sahnoun.

"Are you all right, Otis?" She pushes out of her seat and moves toward me.

I wave to stop her. "I'm okay. Sorry. I'm just a little tired."

"Tired?" Coach booms. "You can't be tired. Midnight Kiss starts in four hours."

Damn Midnight Kiss and my geriatric sleep schedule. It's a long-standing tradition of Riverside University's football team. It happens every game week during the season, either on Thursday or Friday nights, depending whether the game is away or home. It's always hosted at Ender's Field, where there's an adjacent forest clearing. The starting football players are obligated to ask for dates. At ten minutes to midnight, the dates hide in the woods and the players are required to find them. The first one to find their date and haul them to the center of the field gets a victory lap around the field, carried on the shoulders of the losers, while the date gets a bucket of ice water dumped on them. It's an omen of good luck if all the players find their dates before midnight strikes.

Afterward, alcohol-induced shenanigans typically ensue, with chants, cheer performances, scarce bonfires, and other dumbass pastimes college students like to do.

Mrs. Sahnoun gushes at me when I don't reply right away. "This will be your first Midnight Kiss this year, yes?"

I nod.

"You must be so happy! Will you be taking your girlfriend?"

The question feels targeted—she asks in the same way I might ask a person I'm interested in if they're involved. I'm taken aback, but that's not a problem because Coach speaks for me.

"What girlfriend? He's as single as a Pringle." He chuckles lightly at his own joke.

Greta rolls her eyes.

"What about the girl that—you know who I'm talking about Farid, the one who was at the hospital after his injury." My heart stalls at the reminder, and I do everything in my power to suppress whatever memories and emotions arise from the comment.

Coach claps his hands and points at his wife in realization. "That girl! They broke up right before finals last spring." I gape at Coach who stares right back, a brash glint in his eyes. "What? You think I don't listen to what you boys talk about?"

"You always tell us to shut up, so I thought you didn't want to hear it."

I chance a glance at Greta to see her peel her eyes away from me, making her expression blank again. She'd been looking.

Not thirsty, my ass.

"I *don't* want to, but you boys are so bitchy"—his wife slaps him—"that it's impossible not to listen."

It must have been fucking Tuckerson who blabbed about Autumn and me. He's her cousin, and they're close—a fact I didn't know until after we broke up. There's no way Herik or my roommates would talk about it so openly. They're pretty tight-lipped.

Actually, I take that back. Rodney could have talked shit. That motherfucker has the self-awareness of a squirrel and gossips more than a dried-up housewife after church.

Mrs. Sahnoun shakes her head at her husband. "Don't be so rude, Farid. It's healthy for young men to show emotion. If they don't have an outlet, then…" She trails off with a sad, far-off look in her eyes. Even Coach's cockiness humbles.

The entire dinner, I've put a concerted effort into treating Greta the same way she treats me: Like she doesn't exist.

There are small moments here or there where I struggle to maintain an air of disinterest, light brushes of skin when we pass each other a bowl or a condiment. Even when she fishes a lollipop from her purse to suck on, I don't pay her any mind or think of how she briefly sucked me that night, giving me a dose of the heaven her mouth could provide.

We don't stare. We don't talk. We hardly even acknowledge the other is there. In fact, I behave more like a fly on the wall than an invited guest.

Thankfully, Mrs. Sahnoun breaks the somber energy that's lingered from her comment and forces a smile as she speaks to me. "If you have no one to take to Midnight Kiss, then you should ask Greta." The older woman brushes Miriam's bangs away from her face aggressively while the younger attempts to crane away from the touch. "She's as single as two Pringles, and I'd like to see her in a relationship before I die."

Greta couldn't have looked more repulsed if she tried. "First off, the saying 'single as two Pringles' doesn't even make sense. Second, I like being single. And third, did you not just hear about my plans to go out?"

"You go clubbing all the time, but when have you ever gone to a Midnight Kiss?"

"Never, and that's by design," she responds without hesitation. "Do you really think I haven't had the opportunity before?"

"One of my players asked you to Midnight Kiss? Who? When?" Coach growls, flaring his nostrils.

I clench my fist on my thigh, tensed and ready.

"Stop being so dramatic, Farid. You should encourage her to participate in school activities."

"She does lack school spirit," Coach says disapprovingly.

"Yes, and this would be fun." Mrs. Sahnoun looks excitedly at Greta. "You should go!"

"Pass."

The rugged edges of contempt etched on her face make my stomach drop. My face heats, but I do my best to appear impervious to her attitude. When I speak, I make sure to sound resolved and severe.

"Thanks for the offer, but I already asked someone out." *Someone who isn't an ice queen.*

"Good. I'm not fond of the idea of one of my players pawing at my daughter." Coach Sahnoun looks between us and shivers. I'm frozen by the comment—the blood in my veins feels like ice.

There it is, my suspicions confirmed. Definitive. Irrefutable. Out there. I'd fucked Greta Miriam *Sahnoun*, the coach's daughter.

I'm going to be sick.

THE SECOND I step out of Coach's house, I throw up. I try to wait until I'm near Herik's car—I had to borrow it since mine is in the shop—but I don't make it halfway to the driveway before I'm hurling all over the cobblestone.

"Jesus Christ," someone calls behind me.

I close my eyes and groan, clutching my stomach as another wave of nausea rolls through me.

"That's disgusting."

"You need to get away from me," I say. What if her dad is watching through the window? Does he have a shotgun in the house? Will he shoot me right here and now for standing too close?

She sighs. "Too bad. We need to talk."

I cough and wipe my mouth, partially turning my face to give her a sour look. "Please, sound more disappointed."

I can practically hear her eyes rolling. "Just... meet me at my apartment at, like, ten-thirty."

"Your apartment?"

"Yeah. Do you remember where it is?"

Corner of Lexus and Luther, apartment 420C.

"No."

She tells me her address. And right before she leaves, she gives me a pat on the back that makes me jolt. "Don't worry. My dad won't kill you for sleeping with me if he finds out."

Maybe not, but there are a million other things he can do. And her words, which were presumably meant to reassure me, only escalate my anxiety, causing me to throw up again.

yee-to-the-haw

frosted0ats · 10 songs, 38 min 51 sec

👤⁺ I◄ ❚❚ ►I ⤭

Down To The Honkytonk
Jake Owen   ♥   3:06

Before He Cheats
Carrie Underwood   ♥   3:19

Mama's Broken Heart
Miranda Lambert   ♥   2:57

Forever And For Always
Shania Twain   ♥   4:43

Do I
Luke Bryan   ♥   3:59

Life is a Highway
Rascal Flatts   ♥   4:35

Brand New Girlfriend
Steve Holy   ♥   3:40

When the Sun Goes Down
Kenny Chesney & Uncle Kracker   ♥   4:50

Brokenheartsville
Joe Nichols   ♥   3:50

Mississippi Girl
Faith Hill   ♥   3:52

GRETA

WHY'D YOU HAVE TO BE SO CUTE

MAKING GOOD DECISIONS has never been part of my repertoire. Thus far, my whole existence has exclusively involved *bad* decisions, which is why I thoughtlessly invited Otis up to my apartment to talk rather than having a quick, assertive conversation outside to put whatever is between us to rest.

Given my infamous lack of self-control, it's a terrible idea, but I'm already late to meet up with my friends, and if I want to pregame with them, I need to hustle.

He follows me wordlessly. I'm storming up the stairs to my place like a bat out of hell and I ignore Raven when I walk through the front door, tossing my folded clothes onto the sofa. When we get to my room, I instruct Otis to sit on the bed while I rush to the bathroom. I tell him to give me a second while I wash my face, since I won't hear him over the water anyway.

Which isn't entirely true. He could talk and I could just listen, but I need to think. I need to clear my head and figure out how we're both going to dissolve any familiarity between us for good. To go back to being strangers.

Since seeing him at my parents' house, I've been in survival mode. At the sight of his chiseled, handsome face, the reins on my self-possession give way. I had to shut him out of my mind to maintain a modicum of composure in front of my parents and prevent them from seeing anything more than mild disinterest.

This son of a bitch made it damn near impossible, every subconscious movement from him a test.

He raised his arms to stretch, exposing a strip of his abdomen, giving me a glimpse of the dark flecks of hair just below his belly button, leading to his crotch. He leaned forward to grab more *felfla*, giving me a close-up of those thick, veiny arms, as if I haven't been imagining them caged around my head during my more recent self-care moments. He let out a fake laugh from something my dad said, his eyes squinting with delight.

It's just lust, I reminded myself repeatedly. Even as I conversed with my parents, giving my best damned performance of "I Don't Know This Guy, and I Don't Care About Him," I was thinking about how much better he'd look if his shirt was drenched and his pants were off.

What makes it even worse is who Otis is. Even if I was interested in being in a relationship, his current aspirations and potential occupation are deterrents.

He isn't just a football player. No, he's a football player who plays for my father. And if those two qualities aren't bad enough—trust me, they are—he's also the quarterback, and my God, I couldn't have gotten into a more fucked-up situation if I'd tried.

It aggravates me that I knew it. I mean, I didn't *know* know, but I knew.

Like the scar I'd seen on his knee and ignored in favor of ogling his solid chest and impressive shlong. Or the fact that I saw his truck parked at the football house where we picked up Hanson, Elise's dog, even though he hadn't been the one to open the door. Or the irate manner in which he spoke about the NCAA's bogus monetization rules for college athletes, speaking so passionately that I thought, *Wait, is he a university athlete?* in passing, the notion fleeting and unexplored. Even the way he's built, his muscles trained and toned from repetitive, strenuous activities and not just machines, were indication enough.

But I'd brushed off these hints, evading the truth it pointed toward in favor of... What? Why had I done something so reckless? For a good lay? A fabricated sense of peace since I didn't actually *know* he was a football player, so fucking him didn't go against any of my rules?

It was horny and pathetic. I'm horny and pathetic.

With a fresh face, I pat my skin dry and take a deep breath, prepared to face Otis. Except the words I've just come up with, ready at the tip of my tongue, elude me when a cozy warmth thrums through me when I catch a glimpse of Otis sitting on my bed, wearing that generic white T-shirt from our university's athletics department.

His silky hair is rumpled, his dark jeans worn at the knees, giving him a rugged, dirty handyman vibe. And to make the entire ensemble all the more heart-throbbing, Raven, the treacherous little bastard, is perched on his lap, endeavoring to make bread on the football player's toned thigh. Otis looks down at the feline with a small smile on his lips as he pets him gently, his mouth moving to speak softly to the kitty.

It is so freaking cute, I have to swallow an elongated, "Aw."

Stop it, Greta. Stay focused. Don't get distracted. He's always going to be hot, and you're used to hot. I mean, look at yourself. You're the progeny of the one and only Céline Goodeau Sahnoun. Get a grip and power through, you horny little slut.

"Otis," I begin slowly. Those expressive blue eyes, framed by gorgeous, thick, curly lashes, immediately zero in on me. He blinks slowly. Can I just say that I hate him? For no reason other than the fact that he has eyelashes that I—my parents—pay good money every month to imitate.

"Greta," he replies, his tone mild.

"I would like to apologize," I begin slowly, deliberately, doing my best to sound sincere rather than annoyed. Seriously, how can someone be so effortlessly attractive? It's sickening.

"For what?" he asks as if I've wronged him in more than one way.

I gesture at my face. "For smashing your nose into the door. But for the record—"

He holds a hand up and tuts at me. "Stop right there. You can't apologize and then say 'but.' It literally defeats the purpose of the apology if you're going to excuse your actions."

Biting the inside of my cheek, I count to three. "Yes, well, I'm trying to explain my behavior, not excuse it."

"Did I ask for an explanation?"

I gape at him.

He nods knowingly and arrogantly announces, "That's right, I didn't. Still, I'm a gracious man, so I'll accept your apology."

"I'm rescinding it, asshole," I snap.

"You can't take back a sorry. Sorries are permanent. Once they're out there, they're out there."

I flail my arm around, grab at the air five times, then pretend to stuff each letter back into my mouth. "I'm taking all the backsies, Princess." I sound petulant, but I don't care. I snatch one of my serums from the sink, aggressively pump some into a palm, then rub my hands together before applying it. "Apologies can be rescinded when the recipient is being a total tool, as I've just demonstrated."

"*I'm* the tool? *I'm the tool?*" Otis shrills, his pitch causing Raven to meow in distress. "You're the one who acted like I didn't exist the entire night!"

I turn to give him a pointed look and scoff. "What did you want me to do? Throw myself at you? Mount you right then and there? I'm sure my dad would have loved to see me give you a lap dance."

His eyebrows pinch together, and he purses his lips. I could swear I almost see a flush stain his cheeks. Is he imagining it?

Cause I sure as hell am.

"The leggy brunette has jokes. Hardee-har-har." He shakes his hair out of his face and gestures aimlessly at the air, eyes set in a harsh glare. "On the real, a little warning would have been nice."

I rummage through my makeup bag and apply products with quick precision. "Warning?"

"Yeah, that you were Coach's, y'know"—he gags on the next word—"daughter."

"And you should have told me you're a quarterback." I'm just as derisive, if not more so.

"Normally, I don't have to." Translation: People recognize him because he's just that famous. I'd consider him cocky if the assertion didn't have grounds. "Besides, what would that have changed? Would you have let me stay over? Or would I at least have gotten a kiss goodbye at the door?"

"Please, I'd have kicked you out faster." I sneak a peek to see him scowling and can't help but titter.

"Excuse me, but anyone should be so lucky to be in my presence. I mean, people love me. I've won the only Heisman this school has ever had."

"My, my, my, someone sure has a big head."

"You know perfectly well how big my head is," he hums.

I pause in my task to regard him impassively. The only crack in my façade is the way I lick my lips, my mouth remembering the way he fit so well inside it.

He's obvious about not looking at me, staring at Raven as he speaks louder, more clearly. "Besides, what's so wrong with being a quarterback?"

"I could ask you the same thing. What's so wrong about being the coach's daughter?"

He sputters and throws his arms up. "Other than the fact that I'm going to be benched for the rest of my college career?"

"That's if my dad finds out. Which he won't, because why would he?" I don't mention that my dad also probably wouldn't care. He might get annoyed at first, but then he'd get over it and hide a pack of condoms in my dresser, fearful of another pregnancy scare.

"But that's what we're here to talk about. If we continue to see each other—"

A squalling ring interrupts Otis's explanation. Raven jumps in surprise and hops off his lap, fed up with the excessive noise. Otis tilts his head in apology as he answers his phone.

I'm still baffled, my mouth wide open in shock at his unfinished sentence. It's lucky I'm not putting on eyeliner when he says that out-of-pocket shit or I definitely would have messed up.

"Monica? Wh-what happened? Why are you crying? I can't understand you when you yodel. Can you take a deep breath and calm down, please?" He pauses. "Okay, you've got to get it together. Mom isn't being a bitch, and if I ever hear you call her that again, I'm going to—"

Another pause, and he's tugging at his hair in annoyance. I'd bet a lot of money that Monica is his younger sister. "Monica, if— Monica, I swear—Shut up and listen to me. How are you going to call me and then not listen? If mom says you can't go out, then you can't go out. Period. What do you want me to do?" After a two-second delay, he barks out a laugh. "You're out of your mind if you think I'm going to do that." Realizing just how personable he's being in front of an audience, Otis glances at me and releases a sigh. "Look, Icka, I gotta go. I'm busy. But just chill out. When I come home for Christmas, me, you, and Katia will go out and have a blast until two in the morning if that's what'll make you happy. Just sit tight for now, and stop making shit so difficult for me and Katty. And for the love of all that's holy, be nicer to Mom, jeez." There's no exchange of endearments as he ends the call, finally affording me the opportunity to explode on him, delayed as it might be.

"*Continue to see each other?*" I sneer. "Do you have a memory lag? Are you prone to forgetting things?"

"I could ask you the same thing. I know you had a good time last Saturday. You told me so yourself, and if you try to deny it, I'll go door to door and ask for testimonials from your neighbors."

"Don't be obnoxious." I clutch my beauty sponge tighter. "You know that's not what I'm talking about."

Otis appears at the bathroom door and leans against the frame. I'm put off by what he said, but mostly, I'm livid at how hyperaware he makes me. When I turn to face the mirror to shun him, my curious eyes betray me, flickering to his reflection, noticing new things about his physique each time.

"Actually, I don't," he drawls, unrushed, suggestive.

I can't stay still. Can't keep staring at him. I make myself busy by going into my closet and picking an outfit. "What part of me kicking you out of my apartment did you not get?"

"So you admit it. You lied. You didn't have friends coming over?" He sounds entitled and defensive.

"And?" I grunt, embarrassed at my inadvertent slip. I finally settle on the skankiest top I have, pairing it with a tight, short skirt that makes my ass look absolutely stunning. "I wanted you out of my house. Which means…"

He doesn't fill in the blanks but parrots in confusion. "Which means?"

I zip my skirt then walk out of the closet and glower at him. I know that football players—and athletes in general—aren't the *crème de la crème* of academia, but I also know they're not huge dolts, given how strategic sports are. There has to be an iota of intelligence in those concussed brains of theirs.

It irritates me that he plays dumb. So when I respond, I'm not nice. Not in the slightest. "Which means I want nothing else to happen between us. I don't want to play house. I don't want to be wooed with breakfast in the morning. I don't want any sort of obligation or regular commitment to exist between us. We fucked as strangers, and we part ways as strangers."

He doesn't hear me, staring at me like he wants to devour me whole. His eyes are wide, his mouth parted, his breathing quick. He maps my body with his gaze, lingering on the swell of my breasts, the exposed skin of my abdomen, and the thick curvature of my thighs.

With all my heart, I wish I could say I'm unaffected and that the hunger clouding his features isn't at all reciprocated. I wish I was disgusted by how he strips me bare with his stare.

I can't say that, though, because when he licks his lips and finally meets my eyes, I'm struck by desire that travels from the top of my head to the apex of my thighs. I already feel myself beating with slick need, moments from our night together flashing theatrically in my mind.

It really had been a good fuck. Great, even.

"You look good," Otis murmurs, admiration bleeding out of every syllable.

An unfamiliar sense of bashfulness crawls up my skin. I overcompensate to hide it. "I know."

He bites his bottom lip and angles his head like he's trying to get a better view of me. "I mean, like, really good."

Play it off. His compliments shouldn't affect me like this. Shouldn't make my heart pound in my neck like I'm about to burst a vessel. "That's the goal."

"Your goal is to look really good?"

I shrug.

"That's it? You sure it wasn't to look fucking delicious?"

I suppress a shiver at the recollection of that night, at the thought of his praises, and how he'd promised to make me his new obsession. The fervent compliment ricochets through me. It's this very reaction that gives me enough sense to whirl away from him and resume getting ready. I can't get caught up in whatever sensual spell he's putting me under, so I lean over the sink to get close to the mirror. When I lift my concealer brush, my hand moves with a subtle tremble, and I have to clench twice to steady it.

Damn my libido. Damn it straight to hell.

"Did you hear what I just said?" I snap with contempt, hoping to sever this haze of desire that clouds us.

"Uh." He was staring at my ass, but my exclamation brings his attention back to my face. He shakes his head, letting his rambunctious thoughts fall away. Flashing me a sheepish grin, he licks his lips again. "No. Sorry."

I blend another creamy product into my face, more determined than ever to get him out of my house.

"I said I don't want a relationship." At least that's the gist.

"You don't want a relationship." He's pensive for a drawn-out moment, then grins. I'm stunned once again by how adorable he is. Why does he have to be so fucking cute? Why couldn't he just be glib and unapproachable like that first time I met him? It's impossible to ignore him—dislike him—when he's looking and acting like this. "Well, shit, that's great to hear. Fantastic, actually! Cause I don't want a relationship, either! I don't have time. I have football, and I gotta focus on getting an invitation to the Combine this spring and my classes this semester are fucking hard. So instead of a relationship, we could engage in a… mutually beneficial friendship, y'know?"

"Like fuck buddies?"

Otis nods, overzealous.

I shake my head immediately, not giving myself time to consider it, my intent clear from the start. "No, thanks."

My rejection is lost on him. That much is clear from the way his forehead wrinkles, his eyes narrowing in concentration. Rubbing a hand over his mouth, he articulates himself plainly, "You don't want to have sex again?"

"No." *Yes*. God, I can still remember the way my toes curled when he dined on me.

"Even if it was good?"

Good? That's what we're classifying it as? Plain ol' good? What a fucking travesty. "No." *Absolutely. Take me right here, right now, daddy.*

"Damn. All right, I… uh—well I feel real fucking stupid right now." He laughs, the sound hollow and cynical. Raven, who's relaxing on my bed, raises his head from his paws to stare at Otis, clearly telling the big guy to shut the fuck up. When he's done crowing like a villain, he flashes a facetious smile. "So if you want nothing to do with me, what was the point of having me come over just now?"

I open my mouth to explain, but my mind blanks. He has a point. Fuck. This is on me.

Why had I brought him here? We could have settled this on my dad's lawn with a, "We fucked. Our sexual compatibility is off the chains. But that's it. It's never going to happen again."

But no, I'd asked him to come to my place. To what? Figure out what we would do? But what is there to figure out if we weren't even doing each other? Everything between us ended Sunday morning and could have been laid to rest earlier. Later this week, I'm going to drag Elise with me to a fortune teller. Maybe they'll explain why I tend to make bad decisions.

He takes my silence as an invitation to speak for me. "Because what I think is that you do want me. You wanna fuck me just as badly as I wanna fuck you, but for some reason, you think you have to play hard to get." He stretches his arms out wide like he's about to go for a bear hug but remains in place, a presumptuous smirk stretched over his lips. "But baby, you don't gotta play that way. Trust. I want you. Like fuck-you-all-night-till-I'm-shooting-blanks type of want you. And I've been looking for you everywhere since Sunday, so just…" He doesn't need to finish his sentence, his request clear enough.

Did he really just… My heart does a somersault in my chest.

His unabashed admission rings in my mind. I drop my mascara and jostle my hands to disperse the fuzzy sensations collecting in my palm.

Otis takes a step toward me, and I remain motionless, my mind reeling, trying to come up with one good reason why I should make him the exception to my rules.

"We can just have fun when we have the time," he whispers, soft and seductive in the way he entices me. Doesn't he know how captivating he is without even trying? He should take pity on my poor soul because all the reasons why I shouldn't let him fuck me right here and now on my bathroom sink are eluding me. "How does that sound?"

"Fun," I repeat like I'm in a trance. *But he's a football player. You don't do football players.* "We can just have fun."

Another step. The air between us is thick with the smell of his cologne and my chocolate eyeshadow palette. He's so close that I feel his breath wash over my face. "So much *fucking* fun."

I don't know what specifically breaks me out of the trance he's put us both in. Maybe it's the sound of my brushes spilling on the counter when I knock them over in my attempt to get closer to him. Or perhaps it's the way I catch our reflection in the mirror and see how perfectly ordinary this all is.

Either way, I'm just centimeters from touching him when I'm tossed back to reality, my principles regaining control of me. I can't do it. I can't risk catching feelings, not when there's a chance it could hurt so badly again.

"No." There's a quiver in my voice, but I look at him with an unbreakable resolve that renders his proposition a failure. "No, I don't want to have fun with you. Not again. Once was enough."

It has to be. I don't do attachments. I *can't.*

I push him away from me. He stumbles a bit, righting himself before he can fall, disbelief on his face. Then, it hardens as he replicates the anger he wore on Sunday morning when I told him to leave. "Why?"

"I don't have to justify myself."

"No, but I would appreciate it if you did. Honestly, I just want to understand *why*." He's trying to be polite, but the way his nostrils flare, the way he speaks between clenched teeth, the muscles of his jaws ticking haphazardly, tells me he wishes he didn't have to be.

If he wants honesty, fine. I'll give him unfiltered honesty.

"Because I'm not interested in a friendship, even if it's just for fucking. I don't want to have expectations from another person, even if it's just sex. I'm at a point in my life where I just want to get mine and be done with it. Besides, you're a football player." I tilt my head at him and flash a look of sympathy. "I don't do football players. Don't even like them much. You just happened to be an exception since I didn't recognize you." *Liar. You had a feeling. You just didn't care.* "And even if I were to make an exception for you on both counts, aren't you worried about my dad? The coach?" It's a red herring. Not that he needs to know that.

There are questions in Otis's eyes, and I don't need to be clairvoyant to know what they are. *Why don't you want a relationship? Why don't you do football players? Why did you have to bring up your dad?*

I've already offered enough of an explanation of what I want, and I owe him nothing else. So I let myself stare at him just a little while longer—for just a few heartbeats more—before turning to look away, making a point to focus solely on myself in the mirror. The desire to go out and have fun with my friends has diminished. I'm no longer in the mood. "You should—"

"Leave now," he interrupts, his voice gruff. "Yeah, I know."

It's a scene I've witnessed before, one I don't care to watch again. I busy myself with the task at hand, banishing any regret that comes my way.

"Lock your door," he shouts from the living room. A second later, the door slams, and I'm left with a bitter taste in my mouth.

Making good decisions has never been part of my repertoire, and though I would consider this particular moment the right call for both of us, a part of me feels like it isn't.

Fuck, I want a smoke.

Coach Farid Sahnoun has kids?

I've never seen our coach with anyone but his wife but I have a friend that went to Baulman High School where Sahnoun taught before he came to RSU and apparently he has two kids. An older daughter and a younger son. My friend said he didn't know much but that his son died or committed suicide and apparently that's when Sahnoun agreed to commit to RSU early since rumors about his contract had him starting here in 2022 but he started in 2019 with Duger and Princeton as his assistant coaches. But also, his daughter supposedly goes here too but I've never seen her?

Anyone else have more information? I'm curious

3 comments   78%

orangetatters91210 · 11 hr. ago
mind ur business dude wtf is wrong with you posting and asking about shit like this?

limabeens00 · 6 hr. ago
I went to BHS. Can confirm Sahnoun did have a son. We didn't hear much about what happened but that he died. But I can confirm he has a daughter and apparently she's a complete slut lol. Gave 3 different guys head at prom and fucked a teacher on graduation day. She was nice this one time I talked to her in class though

qqbbpp · 1 hr. ago
kid died of od im p sure. there used to be articles about it online but they somehow "disappeared". rsu is paying coach s fuk u money so its not a stretch to assume hes pulled articles about his kid (who was a minor at the time) from publication since there are nosy dickwads like u that care more than they should

12 OTIS

THE DEVIL DRINKS VANILLA LATTES

MY BODY IS not my own. That's what Duger and Princeton demonstrate today during afternoon workout, pushing my endurance to its absolute limit with calisthenics, which I despise. For over an hour, they put my physical and mental agility to the test, escalating each circuit of exercise like they want to see me break. Apparently, my subpar performance in the last game demands this excruciating regimen.

We won the fucking game, but that doesn't matter. Winning with an unexceptional performance warrants no celebration or congratulations. In fact, it upsets my coaches and trainers even more that a team of our prestige, ranked at the top of collegiate football, would win with such pitiful margins against a bottom-rung team. If I had lost but performed my absolute best, they wouldn't have been as pissed. But doing my almost best and barely winning against the worst? A nightmare.

I was familiar with the expectation, but it still stung when no one offered me their congratulations. No one spoke of my performance or gave me kind words. It was my first real game since my injury, and all I got were blank stares and half-assed nods. It didn't matter that the stands cheered wildly at every successful pass I made.

Their opinions don't count. And when Herik tried to cheer me up by listing all my good plays—he barely even used one hand for that list—I'd felt even more shitty.

"Rodney's mom made us dinner, so don't eat out," Jenner says when he sees me waiting outside the locker room. I nod and half-heartedly slap his ass in goodbye when he demands that I perk up.

I'm left waiting for another five minutes before Herik pops out, appearing in the nick of time. My patience had just about worn thin, and I was going to ditch him and our plans to get coffee.

"Jesus Christ!" he yelps upon seeing me. "You scared the shit out of me, you Grinch-looking motherfucker. If you keep fucking up your face like that, you're gonna get wrinkles early." He places his index fingers on the corners of my mouth to turn my frown upside down. It doesn't work, and it earns him a well-deserved shove, making him fall backwards.

"Were you jacking off in there? What the fuck took you so long?" I snap, pushing off the brick wall to help him up. My muscles cry in protest as I haul his dead weight to his feet.

"I wish. I just got roasted and toasted like a fucking samosa by Duger for failing my Econ midterm."

We walk out of our personalized gym, passing the other weight rooms for the different athletic departments. Our university's sports complex is a maze. "Didn't you just take it this morning?"

We both had exams earlier today. I'd pulled an all-nighter studying for mine, determined to make at least a B+ on it. I'm pretty sure Herik fell asleep early and didn't study for his. We were supposed to study over a video call, but he'd been with Elise and stopped texting me at nine.

"Yeah, and apparently, Professor Moron graded it already and gave me a fucking forty-two," Herik spits. The scowl he has on his face is uglier than the one I wore earlier.

"At least it's a good number." He doesn't react. "The number forty-two." When he still doesn't catch my meaning, I expand, waiting for the bells to go off in his head. "Like from *The Hitchhiker's Guide to the Galaxy?*" Another pause, and this time, I'm wondering why I keep company with someone so incompetent. "The meaning of life, the universe, and everything that exists? C'mon! Forty-fucking-two!"

My best friend blinks at me slowly before shrugging. "Oh."

I rub my forehead and shake my head in dismay. "How the fuck do you not know one of the most famous quotes from pop culture?"

"Cause I have sex?"

Despite my urge to beat this sniveling fucker to a pulp, I let his words roll off me.

It's Wednesday, and this past Monday, I'd come to terms with everything that'd happened between Greta and me. I've accepted it, moved past it. In fact, last night, when I was yoinking my meat, I didn't even think of her once. Granted, I had to use porn. But still, it was the lush, blond porn star preoccupying my thoughts and not her.

I refuse to discuss it anymore. My mom always had a saying about worries and troubled thoughts, and its rough translation from Spanish to English goes something like: "To speak about it is to will it into existence. And to will it into existence is to let it occupy your thoughts more. And to let it occupy your thoughts more is to enhance your anxiety."

That's why on Sundays, right after church, she'd have us all sit down on the kitchen table and scrawl all our worries from the week on a sheet of paper. Then we'd stuff them in a jar, and once a year, in the summer, we'd make a fire and burn all those thoughts and feelings. It was liberating. The metaphysical weight of our troubles was lifted off us as the scraps burned to ashes. We'd always walk away from that fire taller, more comfortable.

While we partook in this activity with gusto, my dad always left his strips of paper blank. One day, after both Katia and I had exhausted our musing over what made him do such a thing and why Mom didn't get mad at him, we asked.

"What worries do I have when all my peace is right here?" he'd said before kissing my mom lovingly on the forehead. She'd melted into him and smile with so much wonder, so much love, that at such a young age, they became my inspiration.

It was only after my dad passed away that I realized why all those problems I'd recorded didn't trouble me. It wasn't the fire or whatever psychological crap that went along with literally watching our concerns go up in flames.

My dad, ever the sneaky bastard, would read our worries right after we wrote them and, throughout the year, address each and every one of them in subtle, clever ways, offering solutions or perspective. That way, when we arrived at the bonfire and actually reflected on the problems that once affected us, we'd realize they didn't matter as much anymore.

When Monica grew older, Katia and I did that for her. It wasn't the same, we knew—especially since she barely remembers our dad—but it was enough to give her a sense of what it might have been like to have him growing up.

"Speaking of sex," Herik says, interrupting my thoughts. We've already made it outside and are trekking toward main campus. "Did you know Elise is a virgin?"

"Why the fuck would I know that? I've only ever met the girl once, and she was a little drunk." Midnight Kiss hadn't been as fun as it usually is. My conversation with Miria—Greta fucked me up.

"Well, it's true. She's a twenty-one-year-old virgin who plans to wait until marriage," he replies matter-of-factly. There's no solemn affliction in his tone.

My brows pinch together. "So that's it? You're not gonna see her anymore?"

We pass a group of swimmers we party with sometimes and nod in greeting. One of them shakes my hand and offers a quick, "Good game last week. Good luck against Clorenson Saturday," before passing by.

Good game, they'd said. If only Coach or Duger could say that to me…

"Why would I stop seeing her?" Herik snorts, looking at me like the very idea is insane.

"Because you're a"—what's a nice way to call someone a slut?—"fucking whore."

"I'm not denying that fact, but I do resent it."

"My point is that you're a sex fiend, whereas she's a sex novice." I steer us toward our favorite on-campus coffee shop. *195 Extractions* is the air I breathe, and the fact that my meal plan, which is a stipend by my athletic scholarship, covers a drink at this establishment makes me almost not regret choosing to play at Riverside.

"Which is why we'll get married and run off into the sunset, and right when we reach the top of the hill—wham. She's Jasmine, I'm Aladdin, and I'm introducing her to a whole new world of endless sexual pleasure." He brushes his hands over his short hair, pretending to sweep it out of his face.

"I thought you liked Elise for her personality?"

"I do," he declares. "She's actually so amazing. The whole night, she was telling me all about this volunteering she does with foster kids. She wants to be a social worker, to give back to the community. She and her best friend even work at elementary schools as teaching assistants for their degree plan. They help kids with speech impediments. Isn't that fucking sweet? And she's so passionate about it. It's so fucking cute, I just want to…" He pauses and grapples the air in excitement, the smile on his face reaching his eyes, words eluding him.

I can't help but envy him for what he's feeling right now.

I miss that, the rush of endorphins that would strike me when I liked someone and the frantic patter of my heart when I would hear my phone ding with a text notification. More than anything, I miss having someone I can talk to about anything and everything, engaging in dumb, meaningless conversations that provide nothing but the comfort of having someone there.

When the giddy rush of exhilaration wanes and he drops his hands, he winks at me. "Don't get it twisted. I can like who she is as a person, sure. But as a woman, I'll desire her for the sexual being she'll definitely blossom into." That same goofy grin he's worn all week resurges. "Not going to lie, I'm looking forward to the chitty-chitty-bang-bang."

"Who's doing the chittying, and who's doing the banging?"

Herik thinks for a second, opening the doors to the café for me before responding with a resolved, "Y'know, I think we'll subvert gender roles. I'll let her do the banging, and I'll take the chittying."

"It's always fun to take the chittying," I say with longing, keeping my volume down. "I miss being chittied."

"Didn't Miriam chitty you last weekend?"

I cross my arms and glare at him. "What part of 'I don't want to talk about Miriam' do you not get?"

"The 'don't' part."

"Then let me say it in a way you'll understand." I wrap my arm around his shoulder. The grip I have around him and the low, menacing intonation of my voice belies the friendliness in the gesture. "Mention her one more time, and I'll smack you so hard upside the head, people will mistake you for a bobble head."

Herik slips away from me and gives me a mean mug. "Do you really want to play the insecurity game, Otis? Cause I know all your sweet spots, starting with those Dumbo ears."

I make a concerted effort not to touch my ears. Rolling my eyes, I nudge him forward as the line moves. I'm acutely aware of my surroundings and the eyes that are on us. Even before coming to this university, I was always stared at due to my stature. It just got worse once I committed to a football-obsessed college, and now it's almost unbearable since I won the Heisman. Thankfully, I know how to cope with the attention, given the media training the university forced us Three Hopefuls to get due to the airtime we receive from broadcasting stations and on-field newscasters.

Still, it's difficult to absorb at times and perpetually uncomfortable to have people notice me and want to talk to me. And ignoring isn't as easy as people make it out to be.

Everyone at this joint is trying to pretend that they're not staring at us, but they are. Even people who don't know exactly who we are can tell that there's something special about us. It's both gratifying and annoying.

We're doing a great job at ignoring the looks by immersing ourselves in an age-old debate over whether Jenna Mitchell, our girlfriend in the ninth grade, two-timed me or him. While we're duking this out, however, we barely notice two girls that sidle right next to us, waiting for an opportune time to interrupt our conversation. But then they grow impatient, and right when I'm about to deliver my most damning piece of evidence—Jenna had asked *me* to homecoming, and *him* to the small afterparty—they go for it.

They're nice girls. Honestly, they are. They're pretty, too. But I'm in no mood to exchange flattery or flirt, and I'm infinitely grateful that Herik is.

The girls look hurt by my dismissiveness and clock the way I barely glance in their direction. At one point, I even hear one of them whisper, "Did I do something wrong?" to her friend. A pit of regret settles in the bottom of my stomach, and just as I'm about to apologize for my standoffish behavior, they mumble a goodbye, leaving me to feel like the biggest asshole alive while everyone around me witnesses it.

"You're a tactless piece of shit," Herik hisses at me, his tone stern. It's not common for him to scold me, but when he does, it's usually deserved. "You can't be like this anymore, Oats. We talked about this. You can't pick and choose who you want to be nice to and who you're going to be a dick to."

"I know," I grunt and articulate a half-hearted apology. I can't be fucked to care too much, though, no matter how many people side-eye me and mumble beneath their breath. I already have a bad rap on campus—my nickname at times is Motherfucker Morgan—so what's another incident going to do?

He releases a loud sigh and places a hand on my shoulder. "This is why you have no game—why Miriam didn't want to sleep with you again. You've got to be nicer, Oats."

I don't know why I say what I say next. Maybe it's because I *was* nice for once and it got me nowhere. Or because I feel emasculated for having confessed to Greta how badly I wanted her, only to have her reject me anyway. A man's ego is very fragile, as Katia likes to remind me when she's venting about how 'men ain't shit.' Or maybe it's because I'm sick and tired of being seen by my friends as some dude with no game.

A part of me registers that there's no shame in not having an excessive number of sexual partners, but another part of me feels exceptionally inadequate in comparison to them. Either way, the next words out of my mouth are from me—yes—but they're not representative of me.

"Are you kidding? I'm the one that rejected her, not the other way around."

Herik raises a doubtful brow.

My pulse accelerates, my body pounding with adrenaline from the lie. I persist, wanting so badly to wipe the suspicion off his face, no matter how founded it is. "I was trying to be a gentleman when I told you she rejected me. That's why I left, like, immediately after she invited me up to her place for round two. And the only reason I said otherwise was because I wanted to be chivalrous since you asked me about it in front of the boys. I didn't want her to look bad."

"Is that so?"

The words aren't Herik's. In fact, the pitch is higher, feminine, sultry. At first, I'm puzzled, but then the individual in front of us turns around, and my heart lurches then stops. Blood drains from my face, my veins freezing to the point that it burns. I blink rapidly in disbelief.

This is a joke, right? A big, fat, cosmic fucking joke. The type of joke God manufactures because He's having a bad day and needs a good laugh.

Since starting at this university over two years ago, I've never once seen Greta on campus. Granted, I didn't know who she was, so maybe I had seen her and just didn't register it. Still, that's over three hundred days of walking around this massive campus, and not once have I interacted with her.

And now, in the span of two-and-a-half weeks, not only have I met her and slept with her, but I've run into her at her house, and now—

Now, I've just been caught in the biggest lie of the century.

Choke me with a baguette and rail me with a pogo stick. She heard everything. I'm about to get wrecked.

This is why I don't lie. Not because I have some sort of moral compass that inhibits me. I consider myself a good person, but I'm not a fucking saint. The reason I don't lie is that always, since I was a kid, all my lies have come back to bite me in the ass. Be it immediate or distant, in time, Otis Rutherford Morgan, Jr. is always left to face the consequences of his dishonesty.

And what do you know? If it isn't the repercussions of my own actions, standing before me with a serene expression on her face.

While I gape at Greta in complete shock, Herik regards her in careful observation. Then he claps his hands. "Are you—you're Elise's friend, aren't you?"

I want to kiss him for the inadvertent distraction he's just offered.

"And you're the guy Hanson peed on."

My best friend grins sheepishly and nods. "It's easy to mistake me for a tree or fire hydrant."

"You don't say."

He holds his hand out. "My name is Andres. I also go by Herik, but not Andres Herik, or I'll think I'm in trouble."

She shakes it, and I'm spiraling as I predict all the things that can go wrong in the next twenty-seconds. "I'm Greta, but I'm pretty sure you know me better as Miriam." She gives me a look like she knows she's been on my mind, and I see and hear it in slow motion, as if I'm in a movie and this is the scene that foreshadows my demise.

Scratch that. There's no foreshadowing—not when she's looking at me like she'd like to have my head on a pitchfork and my body burned on the stake.

"Are you also in Econ 321 with Professor Moron?" Herik suddenly asks. Save number two. This means his coffee is on me today. "I think I've seen you sit in the back."

The knowing look she gives me is replaced with a smile when she turns to Herik and says, "Professor Myron, yeah."

"Moron, Myron, same difference. No matter how you pronounce the guy's name, he's a dickhead through and through." He runs a hand over his hair and frowns. "Guy freaking failed me on the exam we took this morning."

"You already got your grade back?"

Herik nods sadly.

She bites her bottom lip, her eyebrows pinching together in worry. "Damn, I should probably check my grade, then, too." She pulls out her phone.

Herik looks at me and obnoxiously mouths, "This is the girl from the photo!" as if I'm fucking blind.

I glance at the door and contemplate just how cowardly it would be to make up some excuse to walk out now. I won't do it, but God, the idea is tempting.

To get away from her—from the cruel girl who rejected me not just once when she kicked me out the morning after but again when she invited me to her apartment, apparently to inform me of how much she didn't want to be with me but only after I told her how much I want to be with her and admitted to somewhat stalking her. We'll gloss over that part since the memory of it makes me want to scream in personal cringe and horror.

"Damn," Greta mutters, and both Herik and I draw our attention back to her. She has a deep-set frown on her face, her fingers worrying her bottom lip as she stares dismally at her phone screen. Then she glances up at Herik and mumbles, "I failed, too."

"I've got to do better next time," Herik sighs. "If I don't, your dad is gonna wear me around his neck."

"He doesn't wear scarves, so you might be safe." But she gives me a pointed look as if to say, *You told him who I am and who my dad is, you snitch?*

I glance away, my heart beating in my throat.

"Good to know."

There's a pause where none of us speaks, and I'm on edge as I just wait for her to call me out.

I've yet to say a single word to her, and I'm not sure if that's what she's waiting for—for me to say something so she can completely annihilate me—but if it is, then she will not receive the satisfaction. Not from me. No, siree, Bob. My lips are sealed, and there's no way in hell I'm going to—

"So, Greta," Herik begins slowly. He can sense the tension between us, and he's not having it. "Did you come to the game Saturday? Otis was looking for you in the stands, and we couldn't see you."

I'm going to drop dead right after I decapitate, dismember, and disintegrate Andres Bartholomew Herik.

"I wasn't looking for you," I rush to correct, my words strangled with hysteria. When I realize I'm shouting at her, I police my volume. "I just asked Coach if you came, since your mom was there."

"Oh, really?" she drawls slowly, batting her lashes prettily at me. "Even after you rejected me, you were looking for me? You're just too sweet."

Herik glances at the both of us then takes a step back, removing himself as the middleman. It's just the two of us now, confronting one another after the clear-cut way it ended.

"I've been told I give people toothaches."

Greta raises a delicate brow and turns to move forward in line. Apparently, there had been an enormous group of friends ahead of us, and they just ordered. We're three people away from the register, not including Greta. I'm just about ready to *skrt-skrt* the fuck out of here.

Craning her neck to acknowledge Herik, she finally answers his question. "I wasn't at the game." Her gaze flickers to me before she continues. "And I'm glad I wasn't. It was a disappointment, don't you think?"

"Um, we won," he replies dumbly, clearly offended.

She nods. "By two points to a team that's consistently been ranked bottom three in the SMC for the last eight years." Greta winces, pity laced in her unsolicited commentary. "If I were the quarterback, I'd be embarrassed by how many safe plays I made just because I didn't want to challenge myself."

I fold my arms over my chest and keep my tone calm, cool, and collected, holding the volume just above a whisper. I don't need to draw more attention than I already have. "That's because their defense kept on taking down my running backs."

"But your wide receivers were always there to compensate. That's how South Harmony is. Their linemen will tackle one person and call it a day. Francis Quinn—I think that's his name. The short, light-skinned running back that's part of the Hopefuls?—knew this and would always go deep."

I have no argument. Absolutely none. She's right. I'd missed that play three times, and Coach had called a timeout after the third to inform my "blind, incompetent ass" of what was happening, only to have the other team's defense switch up their tactic. And because I have nothing substantial to say, I just stare at her dumbly. "You watched the game?"

"I said I didn't go, not that I didn't watch." She narrows her eyes at me and licks her lips before adding, "I am the coach's daughter, after all."

Damn, I want to fuck those lips. I want to hear her speak some more. Louder. To elongate her words until they're faded whimpers. Standing right here, looking at her, I'm transported. I can't get the sound of her screaming in ecstasy out of my mind.

You know how, normally, when you briefly meet someone and you kind of like them, be it in a sexual or romantic capacity, you build them up in your head? The way they look, their personality—all of it is embellished.

My thoughts hadn't done justice to just how gorgeous she is. They had, however, stayed true to her personality. Downplayed it, even.

"You should come to next week's," Herik chimes in. We've moved forward once more. How can freedom be so close, and yet so far away? "We're playing Clorenson, and it's said to be a good-ass game."

"I'm going to hard pass on that offer. I don't do football games." There's a lingering pause before she adds, "Besides, why would I go to a game whose outcome I already know? I mean, y'all aren't going to win anyway."

"Excuse me?" I bite out, unable to keep to myself anymore.

"You're excused, Fordy." She is definitely her father's child. That attitude...

Fuck, she's triggering my fight or flight, and it's partial to the former. "What makes you say we're going to lose? Haven't you seen our defense? Clorenson has played against shit teams, like

JUM and Albridge, who can't take on their offense. You could line toddlers up, and they'd make better defensive players than those idiots have."

"And you think your guys are any better?"

Is it bad that the remark, meant to demean and belittle us into a state of self-mistrust, makes me excited?

Herik, a proud lineman, scowls. "Yes."

"Then let's make a bet." The queue moves forward again. Just one more person before it's Greta's turn. A second ago, I'd wanted this interaction to end. Now, I want to stand here and debate how shitty our team is. Her passion and certainty are addictive.

"What type of bet?" Herik asks.

Greta shakes her head. "Not with you." She raises her index finger and aims it at me, a glint in her eyes. The bottoms of my feet tingle, and I shift my weight to try and squash the feeling. "I want to make a bet with our favorite, sweet little quarterback."

I make a bet with the devil. She has beautiful, perceptive, hazel eyes, spectacularly shaped lips, and mischief teasing the edge of her smile.

And what else? The devil has the same coffee order as me.

motherfucker morgan!!!!!!!!!!!!!!!!!!!

i'm just gonna vent bc i'm so angry and all my friends don't get it since they will kiss celebrity's ass but oh my god otis (who the fuck names their kid that?? like actually??) morgan is the biggest dickhead alive

my friend and i were on east side and went to 195 and saw him and hottie herik and literally all we did was try to talk to them and tell them what a good job they did at the game cuz everyone thought we were going to lose when coach didn't bench morgan after he fucked up the first half and the guy literally has the audacity to ignore us??? and look at us like we're filth??? like we're dying for his attention and he's just too fucking good for us? please. herik was so nice but not our LiL hEiSmAn.

he thinks we fucking care about him. who is blowing smoke up this guy's ass cause he needs to be humbled. we were just taking pity on his injured ass. literally no one thinks he's a good player anymore. he's peaked and if he thinks he's going into the NFL then he has another thing coming.

pathetic fucking loser. so rude. i'm livid.

5 comments   85% ⬆ ⬇

> **fadecomfort** · 1 day ago
> I met him once after a game and he was rude but then turned sweet when a hot chick walked by. Two faced fucker

> **11shrugsizzling** · 22 hr. ago
> Saw him at a party. He would only talk to other athletes. He's such a fucking elitist. It's gross

> **ilikecorn6969** · 17 hr. ago
> He bought me a coffee once when I forgot my wallet. Didn't say anything. Got really uncomfortable when I asked him to sign my cup and straight up walked away. So I'm torn between thinking he's a jackass and he's nice

> **24wizzle** · 42 min. ago
> Ignore him. Jefferson Rodney is so much better and there's already rumors he's signing with the Coyotes next year. Stan 33!

> **chipscaustic** · 21 min. ago
> i got class with the guy. he's super quiet almost shy? if anyone tries to talk to him he just ends the conversation. idk. it's weird. and kind of annoying cause i think he's the one busting our curve

GRETA
ALL BETS ARE OFF

"DRUGS AND FOOD have arrived, m'lady." I saunter across the cozy living-room-turned-makeshift-salon, to where Elise sits on a high-rise seat, her posture terrible and her expression twisted into a semi-permanent wince. My arrival allows a glimmer of joy to break through the tired pain she wears, and I have to chuckle at how animated it is. She closes the laptop on her lap, extending her arms and clenching her fingers in an overzealous *gimme* motion.

I set down the takeout bag from Ricky's Burgers, and shake two Tylenol capsules into her palm. She's quick to dry swallow, a skill I've always been baffled by, but I'm already holding up the cup of Diet Coke she'd asked for. She chugs half of it in a couple of seconds before smacking her lips and sighing. Aunt Myra stares at us apprehensively, her fingers moving in a blur as she braids Elise's hair. I wink at her.

"Don't worry, Aunt My. I brought some food for you, too."

She purses her lips and nods, dipping her calloused fingers into styling gel and smearing it with a light hand onto Lisey's scalp. "Good, cause I was 'bout to say…"

She doesn't need to finish her quasi-reprimand. I know what would have happened if I had forgotten to bring her something.

"I needed that," Elise announces in an unladylike manner, mouth half-full, as I plop onto the edge of the coffee table across from her. If her sorority sisters could see her now, they'd balk.

"I told you you would," the warm and inviting older woman chides, shaking her head. She yanks out the rat-tail comb she'd stuck in Elise's hair to grab another section. Elise winces as her aunt tightly braids the extensions onto her roots. If she wasn't so accustomed to the pain, she would be in tears by now.

"I guess this makes me your hero." I chortle, rattling the bottle of pain medication like it's my weapon of choice. "I'll collect on my kiss later."

"It'll be a big one, so you better be ready," she replies. The lighthearted tone turns into a groan as quick fingers continue to work on her head.

I set Aunt Myra's food aside and put Elise's on her lap. She's quick to dive in.

I chat with Aunt Myra for a bit and catch up with the older woman, since we last saw her two months ago at Elise's last visit. Usually, when I come to see Lisey, it's to bring her food, but today, she'd forgotten her medicine, which forced me to stop at the drugstore on my way here. I hadn't minded too much, glad to have any excuse not to study today.

When the conversation runs dry, Aunt Myra kindly tells me to shut up and presses play on the television remote to continue watching her Turkish drama. I tentatively pick at the carton of large fries I'd ordered to share with Elise.

"So," I begin, turning my attention to my friend, baffled by how heartbreakingly stunning she is despite how disheveled she looks with half her hair done and the other half not. "How was your date last night?"

Elise swallows the bite she's been working on, eager to speak. "Good. So good. He took me to this salsa club, and we danced and laughed, and then we got ice cream when I mentioned I wanted something sweet, and we kissed in the car after driving me to the Delta house, and oh my friggin' God, Tata. He's—Wow, he's a good kisser. Like really good. I turned into a butterfly and soared amongst the stars... That's how good."

Being a good kisser is a big deal for Elise, given how limited her intimate activities are.

"A man that knows how to use his tongue. We have a keeper."

Elise giggles, her eyes glimmering in excitement.

"How long were you out for? You never sent me a text saying you were home."

"Oh. Shoot. Sorry. But it was, like, seven hours?"

My jaw drops. I can't even stand being around myself for seven hours, hence why I always have the TV on at home. "*Seven* hours? What the hell did y'all talk about for *seven* fucking hours?"

"Our favorite movies. Music. Life. Dreams. Oh my God, wait! Did you know he wants to be a chef? He's just doing football right now cause it's paying for college, and he said he'd go into the NFL if they offered him a position, which is likely. He's supposed to go to the Combine this year. But honestly, his real passion is cooking." She goes starry-eyed, her pearly-white teeth gleaming as her grin grows wider. "Isn't that the sweetest thing you've ever heard? I mean, what guy not only knows how to cook, but genuinely enjoys and wants to?"

Aunt Myra makes a sound of derision and looks away from her show for a second. "God damn, you're lucky. The only thing my husband knows how to cook is my damn nerves."

I snort and snap my fingers in hearty agreement before turning my attention to Elise. "That's nice, Lisey. Men who know how to cook are super rare and super fucking hot." It doesn't escape me that Rutherford had demonstrated this very same unique quality, which I admit made him all the more attractive. That French toast he served was delicious. Not that that matters. Or that I care.

It doesn't, and I don't.

"Guess what else we talked about?" She gives me no time to guess. "*You.*"

Tickle me surprised. "Can't keep my name out of your mouth, huh?"

"Tata..."

I still fight away the serious conversation she's trying to have. "Look, if it's regarding a threesome, just know that I need five business days to consider the offer."

She narrows her eyes and clenches her teeth when her head is yanked particularly hard. "Ha-ha-ha. Stop. You're too funny." Her delivery is monotone. "But no, you nasty little girl. We talked about you, Otis, and the coffee shop."

It's my turn to wince and frown. "Oh, right. The bet." I'd forgotten that Elise's Andres is also Otis's friend and my dad's offensive tackle, Herik.

"'*Oh, right. The bet,*'" she mocks in a piss-poor imitation of me, scowling. "Yes, the bet, you stupid head. Why didn't you tell me anything?" She chucks a bobby pin at me.

I catch it. "I told you that I ran into them at the coffee shop."

"Yeah, and that Otis lied about how things went down between you two. But you didn't mention the bet."

I lean back and press my palm against the top of the glass table. "I didn't think it was important."

"Or maybe," she begins slowly, treading carefully, knowing that whatever it is she is about to say, I'm not going to be happy about it, "you don't want to talk about your feelings."

Here we go again. "What feelings?"

"Your feelings... for him."

"Who? Rutherford?"

"You got feelings for a boy named Rutherford?" Aunt Myra pipes in. "Girl, you cannot be falling for boys with ugly names. How do you even moan that in bed?"

Elise bites her cheeks to keep from laughing. She doesn't like being mean.

"I'm not falling for boys with ugly names. In fact," I add between guffaws, "I am not falling for boys, period."

"Oh. So you're into girls? That's cool. I'm down with the rainbow. My daughter likes the ladies, too. Maybe I can set y'all up."

"I'm—That's really sweet, Auntie My." I awkwardly scratch the back of my head. "But, uh, I'm good for now. Thanks."

Elise holds back a giggle and shakes her head, which is the wrong thing to do. She cringes at the motion, hissing. Aunt Myra places a hand atop her head to keep it still, chiding her to not move if she's so sensitive.

"Back to what I was saying." Elise closes her eyes as she sinks deeper into the cushion of her seat. "I think you would, y'know, benefit a lot from opening yourself up to more people."

"I thought you wanted me to close myself up."

"I wanted you to close your legs, but that had everything to do with the yeast infection you had earlier this summer and nothing to do with feelings."

"What feelings?" I need to get that phrase printed on a shirt.

She claps her hands. "Exactly. That's the problem. This cynicism you have toward emotions... It's not good, Tata. Not good, and definitely not healthy."

I swear, if she goes into another lecture about how much I need a therapist, I'll put glitter in her edge gel.

"Yeah, well..." I look away, not wanting to talk or think about it. Because if I talk about it, if I even think about it, then I'll feel it again, the residual pain that pinches my heart. The pain I've worked so hard to mitigate and control. The one that washes over me so seldomly now that it's like I can have a normal life.

And that's what I want. A normal life.

"C'mon. Just... talk about it. You've never talked about it."

"I've talked about it," I mumble somewhat unintelligibly.

Mostly to a grave, but still, I've talked about it.

"Once. When you were high and super weepy."

"So technically, it's not never. I have talked about it."

Elise gives me a look and her lips screw up in that way they do when she's about to give me an earful.

Quick to stop what will surely be a never-ending speech, I rush to explain myself. "I just… I don't want to. I know it seems stupid and childish to you. I know you think enough time has passed and I should be over it. But I just… I can't. He plays football, Lisey—quarterback, just like Julien—and he told me that he likes to fall in love. He's everything I should stay away from. If I were to get involved with him—even if just as friends with benefits— something can happen, and I don't want that. I think about Juju and how bad it hurt, and all I want to do is carve out my own amygdala so I don't ever have to feel again."

"That's a little dramatic." Elise licks her lips, but she's subdued. Defeat has never looked so gorgeous on someone before. Then again, Elise could make murderous outrage look designer chic. "But I get it."

I flash her a pointed look, suspicious. "Do you really? Or are you just saying that to give yourself more time to plot the next intervention?"

If she colludes with James, I'm doomed. That duo is annoying and so undefeatable that I would give them whatever they want just to shut them up.

"I do. We might not have become friends until college, but I saw how hard your senior year of high school was. I know it wasn't…" She pauses and takes a deep breath, her brows furrowed. "I know we all deal with things in our own ways, but I wanted you to know that even when love hurts, it's so friggin' flabbin' worth it."

"Says the girl that fell in love at first sight." I snort.

Elise doesn't even deny it, and just like that, the mood shifts and my feelings are once again stowed far and deep in my heart, ready to collect dust in hiding.

I stay with her for another half hour, giving her company as Aunt My finishes another section of her hair. We're going over Elise's outfit for the charity gala her sorority, and their respective fraternity, are throwing. That causes Aunt My to go on a tangent about how it's ridiculous that Elise's sorority has just recently lifted the ban on "unconventional" hairstyles this semester.

I listen attentively as they both express their shock about the previous rules. Elise is more annoyed than baffled, accustomed to such regulations given her previous experience as a Southern belle and debutante.

The seriousness that accrues during their discussion is severed once Aunt My playfully smacks Elise with the comb and snaps at the younger woman to learn how to cornrow her own hair. The topic shifts, and we discuss volunteering at the elementary school and about her plans to see her dad, the senator, during Thanksgiving, a treat she's been looking forward to since the start of the semester. Given her dad's important position, Elise doesn't get to see him much, but the love she has for him is everlasting.

It makes me envious, even if I would never admit it.

"All right," I announce with a heavy sigh, collecting the discarded wrappers. "Time for me to go. James and I are watching the football game at my place, and I gotta get there before he does or I'll be hearing him bitch and moan about me never being on time."

Elise pouts. "Aw, man. All right, well, I have another, like, four hours here. I have to stop by the Delta house to grab some things, but I'll be at your place in time for our study session."

"Ugh, don't remind me. I don't want to study." But at the risk of being homeless, I must.

"Your grades are doing a great job of demonstrating that."

"Says the girl failing with me."

"We're all in this together, amirite?"

WE'VE RUN OUT of alcohol. This wouldn't be a big deal if James wasn't about to die. A morsel of sobriety is entirely unacceptable to him, given that he's required to tolerate both Elise and me while we're hyper, having downed too much caffeine in such a short span of time which has only escalated our academic rage.

Elise has already had three breakdowns over her paper, while I've received a noise complaint from my downstairs neighbors over my screaming, stomping rampage two hours ago. All the while, James nursed beer after beer and got sloshed to the point where when I accidentally kicked him instead of the couch, he didn't even bat an eye.

Now, the inebriation has worn off, and all that's left is a light buzz that doesn't have any consequential effect. And he can't help us through our assignments in this state. I mean, technically, he could, but he'd go bald from pulling his hair out.

"Should we ask your neighbor for some?" he suggests, polishing off the last beer with a bittersweet sigh. He gets up from the kitchen table and tosses the empty bottle into the recycling. "Not the sophomore who knows how to roll a blunt, but the chick two doors down. Hot, with blue highlights. Always wears a Gemini anklet."

"That's Fae," I supply. I like her. We made out at the pool once on a dare, and she often lends me cat food when I run out.

"If you're thinking of hitting on her, think again. She has a girlfriend," Elise comments distractedly. Never once does she look away from her laptop, her fingers flying over the keyboard in unstoppable ferocity.

James narrows his eyes at her, skeptical. "How do you know that?"

"She's dating a girl in Delta."

Makes sense. Fae had copped a feel on my tits, and damn, did she massage those bad boys well.

Elise remains preoccupied until she registers her own words.

With the finesse of a Telenovela star, she gasps, tears her eyes from her laptop screen, and places a hand over her mouth, her eyes wide. "Oh no. Oh, fudge-sickles. I didn't just say that. I promised I wouldn't tell anyone. Gosh darn it!" Twisting around, she implores James with her innocent doe eyes. "Promise you won't say anything about this."

What a shocker. Elise has never been one to keep a secret, though it's not intentional. The filter between her brain and her mouth is damaged beyond repair. It's why I don't usually divulge sensitive matters to her.

Or anyone living, for that matter.

James is somewhat similar in that respect, but he has this awesome ability to forget nearly everything anyone tells him. He's conceited, so unless the topic directly affects him, he doesn't bother filing any inside scoops in the permanent recollection cabinet of his mind.

I don't confide in him much, but if the compulsion arose and I was incapable of shaking it off, he'd be my go-to guy.

But that's only if I really needed to let it out and was craving a reciprocal response of understanding and validation from the person I'm speaking with. My monthly routine is usually sufficient. Those are my visits with Julien, where I pack a picnic—compliments of my mother, given my poor culinary abilities—and detail, at monotonous length, my life as of late.

He always listens. And in my head, he replies, saying exactly what I want.

"Yeah, because I talk to your sorority sisters all the damn time." James snorts. "Hold up. I need to speed dial your chapter president. While I'm at it, lemme call up your senator *daddy* and tell him all about the new boyfriend you've failed to inform him of."

Elise appears skeptically panicked until she processes that he's being sarcastic. Then, the two begin to bicker over James's insistence on being a bitter, stubbed-toe donkey and Elise's annoying habit of not cursing, a trait James—and I—find deplorable. We've tried in vain to corrupt her, but the girl is steadfast in her morals. It'd be disgusting if I didn't admire her resolve so much.

I, on the other hand, am at my wit's end as I endeavor to tackle this homework problem for the fourth time. Had I paid attention in class, the assignment would have been easy. But who wants to listen to a decrepit man talk about fucking inflation metrics for an hour and fifteen minutes? Not me.

Besides, what's the point of calculating this shit when a quick tippy-tappy on Google's search bar will, *alakazam!* have the answer appear seemingly out of nowhere.

It's Saturday, and rather than indulge in the quintessential college experience of getting hammered this weekend, Elise, James, and I chose to congregate at my apartment for a much-needed study session. Actually, James doesn't need it much, given what a genius he is, but Elise and I definitely do. We're dying. We're taking many of the same classes, what with the overlaps between our majors. But having a comrade doesn't really help, since apparently we're both fucking stupid, given that our average grade for midterms turned out to be a C.

Sacrificing our Saturday night for education isn't typical behavior for us. All three of us have impulse-control problems, and we're definitely not used to depriving ourselves, always willing to accept the consequences of our actions if it means having a bit o' fun.

And man, are our Saturdays fun. There's always a party to be had, always a club to hit up, always a person to fawn over us. Every time some awful, inconvenient shit happens during the week, I can withstand it with the expectation that on Friday and Saturday nights, I'll be able to paint the town with the screams of my unbridled joy while I blow off steam.

But alas, today, the town will be painted by my silence.

There's something about my dad's threat, the one he made again yesterday during family dinner, his solemn reiteration that he will revoke financial support if I don't buckle up, that has me certain he's not bluffing this time.

It's not the first time he's warned me about my academics or used fear to get his way, but it is the first time that I'm genuinely nervous he'll follow through.

Attempt number four of my problem concludes, and with a press of a button, I find that I've arrived at the wrong answer yet again. Fed up and desperately needing a change in scenery, I cut into Elise and James's argument to propose a diversion.

"Let's go grab some wine for James so he'll stop being so whiny and shut the fuck up," I announce, heading to where Raven is. I pet him, and he gets up to walk away, haughty from the unwelcomed physical contact.

That's fine. I just won't pick up his favorite snacks. Ungrateful, sniveling little—who am I kidding? He could scratch my eyes out, and I would still dote on him.

James bounces excitedly in place, a wide grin on his face. If my parents think I'm an alcoholic, then I don't know what the fuck they'd classify him as.

"Do you even have money for wine?" Elise asks, standing. She'd mentioned wanting to go to the store earlier to grab a box of Lunchables. I've known her since grade school, and she's always been obsessed with those malnourishing boxed meals.

Sadly, her sorority house has strict rules about what types of food can be brought in. All their home meals, of which they have to attend at least one a day, are curated by their private chef, and since the processed cheese in those things is barely considered edible, they're not allowed.

"No, but James does."

He grabs his wallet from the table and snatches his keys before mumbling, "For having such a rich dad, you sure are broke."

"You're telling me. The man would rather recede his hair line than give me money." Then I turn to point an accusatory finger at Elise, who blinks at me innocently. "This chick is the one with the really rich dad."

She giggles and shrugs. "Daddy loves to spoil me."

Both James and I gag, and he aggressively snarls, "What did we say about calling your father 'daddy' unironically?"

"You guys are so gross. Don't even." She rolls her eyes then turns to me. "Does this mean we're getting the good wine or the bad kind?"

"Define 'bad.'"

"The boxed kind."

James and I look at each other, and she knows immediately what's going to happen. Throwing her hands in the air, she groans, stomps toward her purse, and snatches her wallet. "Fine. I'm buying, you cheap little muffins. But I swear, if you guys finish my rosé like last time, I'm going to…"

THERE'S A RANDOM-ass person sitting in front of my door.

One moment, Elise is griping and regaling the long, exhaustive process of getting her new box braids in—James had asked to touch them one too many times for her liking—and in the next, we're stopped dead in our tracks at the sight before us.

"What the hell?" I yelp in surprise. Instinctively, I take two steps back and bump into James, who lets out a small "oof," echoing my exclamation before realizing what has me spooked.

James and I fight over who will be the human meat shield, both of us pushing the other forward, while Elise takes a pragmatic approach and skitters back. The stranger must have realized our paranoia, and before any altercation ensues, they stand up. Under the dim lamplight decorating my apartment hallways and the faint cast of moonlight illuminating the right half of their face, I recognize who it is.

My reaction to the sight of him is entirely involuntary and

subconscious.

Just like it has the last three times I've seen Otis out of the blue, my heart lurches in my chest, my body wired with awareness. All I want is for him to smack my ass like a drum—that's how fucking hot he looks right now with his disheveled hair, polo shirt, and beige slacks. He looks like he's ready to take a nice trip around the bay in his yacht, and fuck, I want to ride with him—or just ride him.

"Rutherford?" The grip James has on me falls away as I move toward my unexpected guest. A flutter of excitement brushes through me with every step I take until I'm standing just a few feet away with my keys in one hand and an unopened bottle of SVEDKA in the other.

How long has he been waiting? Goddamn state liquor laws forced us to go to an actual liquor store to get our stock. That's why it took us nearly two hours to get everything we needed, instead of the usual one-hour grocery trip.

"Hey," he simpers in response. He glances over my shoulder at Elise and James, who are observing the both of us from a distance like we're an interesting exhibit of primates, and waves before greeting them with the same placated, "Hey" he'd given me.

It's half-past nine, and he's here, standing outside my apartment instead of celebrating the mind-blowing victory against Clorenson. At first, I'm flattered, a little cocky that he's come to my place right after a game instead of going to a party. That's when I remember the bet.

After learning that Otis had lied to his friend about what went down between us, I'd made a bet with him. I'd wanted to publicly humiliate him for the false narrative he'd created, but it was more entertaining to watch him squirm, which happily led us to the bargain.

It went like this. He, i.e., Riverside's football team, had to beat Clorenson by a minimum of four points, with at least one touchdown made by a pass that's over twenty-five yards, and another from a rush. If he won, he got to be my princess for a day. But if I won, he would have to run around campus in the middle of December stark naked and with bedazzled nipples.

I'll be honest: I was fully convinced I would win. True, he'd been an outstanding player last year, winning one of the most prestigious football awards on the collegiate level, but that was last year. I'd observed his performance during games one and two. Not bad, but definitely not the old him.

In fact, I was so sure I'd win the bet, I was one click away from purchasing the Bedazzler.

And then he proved me wrong. Number seventeen, Otis Morgan, did a complete one-eighty in his performance, baffling not just me but the commentators and the crowd. I thought I'd be horrified to have lost, but in all honesty, I'm glad.

"Did I interrupt something?" he asks, pointing to the drink in my hand. I hold up the bottle and grin, shaking my head.

"Nah. My friends and I just came back from shopping and were just about to start studying again."

"While drinking?" I nod, and he clicks his tongue. "Those two don't go well together, y'know. Studying and drinking."

"You're sorely mistaken. With the handy-dandy help of alcohol, I actually read the textbook instead of bashing my head with it."

"But do you retain any of the information?"

I dismiss the question with a wave. "That's irrelevant."

He chuckles and shakes his head. "You and Herik are made for each other."

Elise makes a sound. James slaps a hand over her mouth. I grin and nod in their direction. "I'm sure there's someone that would disagree with that sentiment wholeheartedly."

"Ah yes, Elise. The girl I know way too much about," he murmurs. He gestures apologetically.

She turns her nose to the sky.

We say nothing for another couple of seconds. He stares at me intently, his eyes traveling up and down my form several times. I'm acutely aware of the shabby outfit I have on and immediately regret not listening to Elise when she told me to change. I'm pretty sure I still have a ketchup stain on this shirt. Fuck.

"Did you see the game?" Otis asks, cutting the air with his deep voice. The slight grin he was wearing has cleared from his lips but remains prominent in his eyes.

"I did."

"So you know why I'm here." He places his hands behind his back and leans against the wall. I step closer, but the gap between us is still substantial.

"You're stalking me?" Otis rolls his eyes, but I insist. "What? It's a reasonable conclusion to make. You're the one that admitted to looking for me everywhere, remember?"

A light blush stains his cheeks, and he exhales deeply, his lips flapping together. "Sometimes I need to shut the fuck up."

"Especially when you get the urge to lie," I say, hushed enough for neither James nor Elise to hear.

That same look of shame he wore in *195 Extractions* returns, and Otis pushes off the wall and reaches for me. I don't flinch, but he stops himself before he can touch me, shoving his hands into the pockets of his pants. Head downcast, he whispers a guttural, "Sorry about that."

I cross my arms over my chest and hum noncommittally.

He rubs the back of his neck remorsefully and licks his lips. "I appreciate you not saying anything at *195*. Wasn't my proudest moment, but I told Herik the truth after you left."

Upon hearing her beau's name, Elise lets out a small sound. Otis and I look at them, then back at each other.

"And I'm also sorry for coming here out of nowhere. I didn't mean to scare you. I just wanted to apologize for what happened."

"Instead of going out to party? You must have been feeling

really guilty." I wipe my palms on my pants. "Usually, you guys go ham after a win like this."

"I don't like to party. Besides"—he nods toward the other side of the hall—"I have my ma and sister waiting for me in the car."

He's not here to stay. Why does that thought sting me with disappointment? "Oh, okay. Well"—I extend my arm out to him—"apology accepted."

Otis is slow to remove his hand from his pocket and shake. I'm hypnotized by the way his grip engulfs mine. My mouth goes dry as I stare at those dexterous fingers, my ears heating from the memory of how they felt inside—skimming over—me.

We shake for longer than we should. I'm certain that if I were to turn to look at Elise and James, I would see them dancing in circles as they silently chant, "Greta and Otis, sitting in a tree, K-I-S-S-I-N-G," so I resolve to look straight at Otis, not acknowledging the duo that's probably going to get a neck cramp from how bad they're straining to hear what we're saying.

"That's not all that I came here for." His hands clench and unclench when he withdraws from my touch. There are remnants of that first night I met him in his expression. Cold, distant, and determined. "I also wanted to absolve you from our bet."

"What? Why?"

"Because you want nothing to do with me," he deadpans. There's no self-indulgent pity in his delivery, just candor. "I don't need any sort of consolation prize from you when it was your doubt that pushed me into the right state of mind."

That's going to leave me pompous for days. *I was right. I helped.*

My victory is short-lived when he rubs his chin and quickly adds, "Well, that, and the fact that my family surprised me at the game."

"That's nice of them." Dismay turns my skin warm and makes the surrounding air thick. "But a bet is a bet."

He shakes his head. "It's okay. Really. Don't sweat about it. You already told me you don't like being around football players, and I'm not one to stick around where I'm not wanted."

I open my mouth to say something... Agree? Disagree? I don't know what.

This is bullshit. I'm annoyed, but I try to keep from showing it. "We had a deal, and if I would have won, then you would have followed through with your end of the bargain, right?"

"That's what you were banking on, though, wasn't it?" He rubs the back of his neck and looks away, a sad, half-hearted smile on his lips. Despite his attempts to downplay how offended he is, it's evident in the calm, almost chilling way, he speaks. "You're kind of like your dad. I know you didn't think we could do it, and that's why you made the bet and set the terms up in that way."

"No, I—" I stop speaking, my face red. I hate it when people speak for me—man or woman. But I'm rendered speechless for a moment because, well... He's right. I'd lied to him once before, and after being so sanctimonious about his own fib, I couldn't do it again. So, I bite my tongue, and he shrugs sheepishly. A shiver of awareness creeps down my spine, defeat burning my throat. I look down, sucking in my bottom lip before admitting, "You're right. I did. I doubted you completely. But"—*honesty is the best policy*—"I'm glad you proved me wrong."

He doesn't hide his surprise. "Yeah?" he says, so faint, so hushed, that I barely catch the utterance, each letter flying away in the wind.

Fuck, this is a bad idea. Terrible. "Yeah. I'm glad I lost the bet."

He releases a deep breath and cranes his neck to look at where James and Elise, those nosey little shits, remain. They're pretending to be deep in conversation, facing one another with their phones out, but their eyes flicker our way too often.

Otis's gaze lingers on them for a while, and I swallow as I wait. I will not beg him to do anything with me. I will not insist more than I already have. But a secret part of me wants to.

When he looks at me, he appears less agitated. "We can't do anything today, but how about I come over sometime next week?"

I'm about to ask for his number to coordinate this meet up when he turns to walk away. He's just at the other end of the hallway before he shouts, "I gotta go. See you next week, Miriam."

As I watch him leave, I'm gripped by anticipation. Not dread. Not reluctance. Just pure, unadulterated excitement. It leaves me feeling wonderfully skittish. A dopey smile perks my lips, my cheeks straining from holding the expression.

I stay like this for a solid minute, looking at where he's disappeared. But when I catch myself doing this, my heart drops, a sensation of frosty dread snaking through me as James and Elise finally make their way toward me again.

"What's wrong?" Elise asks, concern on her face. I continue to gape in horror as I wait for sensation to come back to my limbs.

James scrutinizes me for a dozen seconds before nodding, a look of understanding on his face. He addresses Elise when he says, "I think she just realized she might like him as a person instead of a living, breathing sex toy."

"Really?" Elise gushes with a brilliant smile. "That's a good thing! Why does she look like she's just been stabbed?"

"Because I might as well have been," I groan, covering my face. The cool glass bottle in my grip feels good against my heated skin. "I can't like him." I say it more for me than for them.

They ask for an explanation, but I'm too disgruntled to respond. Instead, I open the door with the grace of a hippopotamus, kicking a single leg in to ensure Raven doesn't get out. Once the coast is clear, I beeline to the couch. We'd bought the vodka for a pregame I'm hosting on Friday, but given the terrible revelation I've stumbled upon, I'll be drowning myself rotten from now until I pass out.

Who the fuck wants to feel, anyway?

2:56

Saturday, September 3

NOTIFICATIONS

Venmo
James charged you $20 - you're a leech and i hate you

mamounette
You are not allowed to steal from your mother you terrible girl...
Give me back my Dior saddle bag...

GroupMe
You have 212 new GroupMe notifications

Amazon
8 Packages Delivered Today - Tell us how we did

lisey
i need you to pick me up my head still hurts :(((

lisey
HELP ME

james
the sluts + a virgin
I'm bringing some of my mom's buuz and y'all better not finish it all by yourself like last time

james
the sluts + a virgin
You better buy Modelo and not Corona this time

lisey
the sluts + a virgin
tata can you pick up my laptop from the delta house. i forgot to bring it w me and i dont wanna go all the way there since it's not on the way to ur place

OTIS

BETTER THAN NICOTINE

"**ARE YOU GOING** to knock on the door?"

I let out a loud, undignified screech, slapping a hand over my heart to keep the muscle confined in my chest. Looking around, I attempt to locate the source of the voice and am even more baffled when I see no one around and no speaker in sight.

"God?" I whisper. Did I get a concussion during my workout today?

"No, genius. It's the video doorbell," Greta says, her voice static through the intercom. I scrutinize the black button. Hot diggity. Technology is wild.

Wait. Oh… Oh no. If she can see and hear me now, does that mean she witnessed my pep talk earlier? My gaze flickers to the sky, and my lips twist in a scowl. I'd shake my fist up at the Big Guy if I wasn't on camera. He has got to use someone else as a source of entertainment. This is getting to be too much. I nominate Kelper or Rodney. They are definitely more deserving of an unfortunate cosmic event.

"That's cool. Quick question… How… um…" I clear my throat and try to talk again, my nerves battered. "How long have you been watching me?"

"I don't know what you're talking about, you hot, Heisman-winning quarterback, with a fatty for an ass." Greta maintains a steady tone until the end, her words disrupted by snickers, using the very same descriptions I'd used seconds ago to hype myself up.

If I throw myself down the stairs, will I at least get amnesia and forget this ever happened? I'd worked so hard to appear cool the last time I was here, trying my best to redeem my tough-guy persona. And now it's all down the drain. "And you said nothing this entire time?"

"It looked like you needed it, and I didn't want to interrupt."

"Thanks," I remark dryly, doing my best to keep my blush at bay. She says nothing on her end, and I wait, hands in my pockets, for her to let me in. A few moments pass. "So... Any plans to open the door, or is this your way of telling me to fuck off?"

"Chill, Princess. The door's unlocked. Come in whenever you're ready."

I'm appalled by her carelessness. The second I step foot into her one-bedroom apartment, I'm hit by the smell of her, a rich aroma of sweet jasmine, mixed with sultry cedar. The scents contradict in the auras they capture, but they complement well.

The first thing I do when I walk in is search for Raven. Sadly, he's asleep in his cat tree. I walk to him and scratch my index finger lightly against his skull. His ear twitches, and he repositions his head to burrow into his nose beneath his paws.

Is it illegal to kidnap a cat? Frowned upon, yes. But illegal? I don't think so, but I should look into it more.

"I'm making dinner," Greta calls.

I head back to the door and shake my head in dismay. "You really shouldn't leave your door unlocked like that." I make it a point to twist the deadlock in place.

"It's fine," she says breezily. "This is a safe-ish neighborhood."

I'm stunned. All I can think about right now is my mom and my sisters in this situation, and sheer panic ricochets through me. The overt aggression birthed from my fear threatens to take hold of me, but I'm able to squash it. I head to the kitchen, griping. *"Ish?* Safe-*ish?* Are you kidding me? You shouldn't take stuff like this lightly. You need to be careful. You never know what could happen."

My concerned outrage falls to the wayside at the sight of her. Her back is to me, but when she senses my presence, she flashes me a look over her shoulder, the corner of her mouth twisted in lopsided smile, her eyes glazed in challenge.

Right then, I'm struck, once again, by just how beautiful she is. Not in an over-the-top-and-totally-perfect type of way. Natural flaws mar her prominent features, but rather than detract, they enhance her appearance, directing attention to the unique lines of her composition. She's stunning. The allure she holds is entirely intangible, metaphysical—a concept that manifests itself in her material form to help bridge the cognitive dissonance.

Shit. Did I just turn into Shakespeare? Well, fuck. Who knew being horny could inspire poetry?

While she rummages through the fridge, I take a seat at the island and stare at the marble countertop, mentally fortifying myself. *You don't want her. You don't want her. You don't want her.*

Greta takes her time to give me a once over, tilting her head. I dab at my face, wondering if there's some residual food on it. "You're wearing glasses."

Immediately, I reach to tap the rim of my specs to confirm her statement and silently curse. Shit.

Quinn and I had been doing weighted-lunges-into-burpees earlier, and he'd tripped and knocked me over during our last set. It caused one of my contacts to fall out, and rather than walk around half-blind for the rest of the day, I donned the extra pair of glasses I keep in my car.

I hate the way I look in them, and if I wasn't so blind without them, I'd take them off right now.

Nudging them farther up my nose, I joke, "Yeah. I can't see

very well."

"Clearly. They look like Coke bottles." I make a face and am about to condemn the remark when she soothes me. "But I like them. A lot. They look good on you."

I snort dismissively. "Sure."

"Really." The pan of water she has on the stove bubbles into a rolling boil, and she walks toward it with a bag of frozen ravioli in hand. "It gives off a hot nerdy-boy aesthetic. It's sexy."

It wasn't sexy when I was younger, I'll tell you that. Before I got big and knew how to defend myself, I was picked on relentlessly. But I tend not to look back on that time in my life, going so far as to retroactively forget it.

"That's good to know." I'm entirely too aware of the thin metal frames perched on my face now, and I fight the compulsion to take them off. I don't hate them half as much as I enjoy staring at her.

She hums in approval, looking at me one more time before focusing on the task at hand.

"Before we get started with anything tonight, I just wanted to apologize," I begin sheepishly. "I'm sorry if I made you feel unsafe, popping up out of nowhere. It wasn't my intention, so… Sorry." I rub my hands together, and when she simply stares at me and doesn't reply right away, my anxiety gets the best of me and I find myself over-explaining. "I won't do it again. Show up at your place without prior notice and explicit permission. Well, after today I won't. I totally get how creepy it must have been for you to see me waiting outside the other night when you were with your friends. And I don't want you to think I'm creepy, cause I'm seriously not. I'm super un-creepy and super safe. Like, *Ocean's Eleven* couldn't even break into me, that's how safe I am."

Greta glances up at me, unwavering and indiscernible, holding up her spatula, an eyebrow arched. Every second that ticks by has my resolve crumbing, and I'm ready to fumble and further humiliate myself in front of a girl who's already humiliated me enough.

"All right, Safe Boy."

The constriction in my chest clears, and my body sags in relief. "It's Princess to you. Now, hurry up with dinner. Princess needs some pampering."

MY ROYAL TREATMENT is coming to a close, and boy, am I upset.

"Can you massage me forever?" I moan as her nimble fingers rub soothing circles on my jaws. I'm lying pretty in her lap, my eyebrows freshly plucked—yes, I cried. Yes, she took a picture. Yes, she might blackmail me—my beard freshly shaved, my lips exfoliated, my face soft and gleaming.

We've been at this for about two hours. And it's nice. Pleasant. My schedule this semester is backbreaking, and though it had been difficult to make time for this, it has totally been worth it.

I'd expected to face difficulty in coming here—not just in swallowing my pride to apologize, but because of how unpleasant our conversation had been after dinner at her parents' and then the whole coffee-shop incident.

But instead, I'm welcomed with unfamiliar warmth. Every now and then, I can't help but feel tense, wondering if she'll snap out of it and be standoffish.

She doesn't, and after half an hour, I relax completely.

Our conversation is good. Insightful and playful. On the verge of being deep enough to manufacture substance between us, kind of like our first night, but put to a screeching halt at the first sign of meaning or vulnerability.

"Absolutely not. After today, I plan to never do two things ever again: Pamper someone and bet."

"I say you bet again. With me, especially."

She narrows her eyes and shakes her head. When I open my mouth again, she snaps it shut under the guise of needing to massage my jaw. I pout but give in.

Greta leans back, the curly threads of her hair no longer curtaining me. But she continues to knead my scalp as the hydrating sheet mask refreshes my face. At first, I keep my eyes on her. I look at the planes of her face and wonder how she can look so soft and so ferocious at the same time. Of course, my eyes can't help but flicker to her boobs now and then, redirecting only when I recognize I've been staring at her nipples for too long, willing them to grow perky by my mental fortitude alone. I'm actively forcing myself to forget the fact that I'm lying on her lap, so close to her pussy.

The one that had been so wet and rich in taste. It had clenched around my cock, hugging it in its warm, soppy heat. It had—

Nope, not thinking of that. What I am going to think about is how good this scalp massage feels. And how pretty she looks. Right. Yes, she's pretty. So fucking pretty. I stare at her face. Her eyes. Look at that. Focus on that instead of her jugs. My eyes narrow in concentration. She alternates between smirking down at me and watching TV, the volume set to a faint buzz.

Every now and then, I notice that her hold lingers for a bit longer than it should, not massaging, just holding still. When she finally releases me, her knuckles skim against the column of my neck. I swear the gesture is intentional, even if she plays it off as accidental.

It's not like that. You can't think like that. She's just fulfilling her end of the bargain.

"You know, I'm actually a junior," I rasp. The leisure state she's lulling me into is not good for me. My thoughts are wandering to places they shouldn't.

"Yeah, I know. We both are."

"I mean my name. My suffix is junior."

"So… What you're saying is that there's another poor soul out there with the name Otis Rutherford Morgan?"

Out there, six feet under. Same difference. "Just Otis Morgan. He didn't get a middle name since my Pawpaw and Meemaw couldn't agree on one."

"And you said your"—she switches to a fake Southern twang to enunciate—"pawpaw"—then back to her regular accent—"is Rutherford?"

I nod.

She fights a smile and loses. "That's sweet. Your family seems close."

"We are." Adjusting myself, I tilt my head at an angle so that I'm looking at her. "You and your family seem really close, too."

"Yeah. Sure."

There's so much to dissect from the intonation of those two words. And if our situation was different, if she was someone I was genuinely pursuing, I would dig in. "Since you got to ask me a lot of questions about the game earlier, how about I ask you questions about your weekend?"

Though they might not look alike, Greta and her father are way too similar in their manners. How the fuck they give backhanded compliments so effortlessly is baffling.

"Like what? I was studying the entire time." Disdain darkens her features.

"Because of the F you got on your Econ midterm?"

"Econ and stats."

That surprises me. "You're taking stats?"

"Yeah. Stats 221."

"That's my major. I took it second semester freshmen year and aced the fuck out of it. I had Professor Gupta."

"I have Middleton." She exhales, clearly exasperated. "Damn. So, not only are you hot, athletic, and nice, but smart, too?" She titters in dry accusation. "God, you're disgusting."

I smirk and give a thumbs up. "Perfect. What you mean to say is that I'm perfect."

"You say tomato, I say potato."

"Uh, what? That's not the saying."

"Tomato, potato," she confidently sings off-key as if it serves as a perfect explanation.

My shoulders shake in hushed amusement. And that's when it strikes me how odd this moment between us is. The air turns sweet and cool. The tension that festered between us before—the unbidden animosity that laid waste after I'd offered to do the dishes and compounded after I'd requested a fucklationship and got rejected then lied about it—has thinned to the point where it's nonexistent.

"You know, for someone who doesn't like football players, you sure are nice to one," I observe cautiously.

"I like football players." Her nose inadvertently scrunches up like she doesn't believe herself, either.

"Uh, no, you don't," I persist. Though I'm too proud to admit it blatantly, her rejection of me based on my football-player status had stung. "I distinctly remember you saying, and I quote, 'I don't do football players.'"

"Exactly, but that doesn't mean I don't like them."

The face mask creases as I twist my muscles into a sour expression. "Right after you said you don't do football players, you said you didn't like them much."

She's saved from a response when my phone rings. I quickly rummage in my pockets, answering it without hesitation before pressing it to my ears. "Hello?"

"Otty? Did you pick up? It's me. I know I've been out of the country, but—"

The person on the other line doesn't have time to finish their sentence. I've hung up in a panic. I shouldn't have done that. My breathing quickens, and I swallow, a sharp, blood-chilling ache rattling through me at the sound of her voice.

"Who was that?" Greta asks, confused by my reaction.

Just my ex. The one I thought I was deeply and madly in love with until it turned out that wasn't the case and I ended up fucking shit up for the both of us. "No one. Is it about time to take this off?" I ask, my voice brusque with barely masked emotions. "I actually forgot that I have to do something."

She doesn't believe me. Whatever. I don't care. The call has put me in a mood. Faking pleasantries is the last thing I want to do right now. Besides, Miriam should get a taste of her own medicine, right? I'm just doing karma's work.

"Um, yeah. Sure. You can take it off right now. Just—"

I'm already getting up from the sofa and walking to the bathroom.

Once my face is cleared, I stare at myself in the mirror. The water drips down my chin and splatters around the edges of her sink. Despite my reflection appearing blurred, I loathe myself.

I close my eyes for a moment and let the image of my ex materialize before me, with Greta making a surprise, unwelcome appearance a heartbeat later. My throat burns as I swallow a shout of frustration. Fuck. I want her. Want to drown in her. Want the minutes and hours of mindlessness to blur together and deplete my consciousness. She's a distraction I very much wish to indulge in—but I can't.

When I exit the restroom, I've already decided that I will smoke tonight. I'll have to go to a gas station and buy a pack since I tossed out my old one after winning the game against Clorenson.

I stop at the threshold of the living room, right at the end of the hall. Rubbing my hand under my jaw, I do my best to put on a mildly amiable disposition. The strain in my voice contradicts what I say. "Well, this was nice. And I really appreciate you seeing through your end of the bet."

"Yeah. Of course. And for what it's worth, I, y'know, actually enjoyed this." She licks her lips and sucks on the bottom one for a second. "You're nice to talk to."

"I'm glad you think that. Maybe you'll start liking football players after all," I tease, half-hearted in my own attempt to make a joke because even if I'm mad, I don't want to end this on an awkward note. I always end things badly, and for once, that's not on my agenda. Not this time.

Before I can slip away and brood in solitude, Greta speaks, rendering me mute. She looks at me in earnest, her gaze penetrating my physical form to reach my soul. "Maybe I already do."

I command my legs to move, to make the harrowing journey to her doorway, but they disobey. Instead, my entire being bristles in awe, scrutinizing that look she's giving me right now. It's the same one she'd given me in the kitchen that morning when she'd called my kiss nice. A look that tells me just what she wants.

Kiss me.

So rather than walk to the door, I stalk toward Greta, each footstep adding an extra beat to my already racing heart until I'm standing in front of her, millimeters away. She remains motionless, holding her breath, her eyes never once leaving mine.

Do it! Those dazzling eyes usher. And I want to, so badly. She's so much better than a cigarette. So much more fulfilling, distracting, comforting than nicotine.

But first, I need to make sure this is what she wants. There's no way I'm going to kiss her then get rejected again because, at that point, I won't have a damn reason to show myself in public. "I read somewhere," I whisper, my lips barely moving as they hover above hers, "that an exception can be made a minimum of two times before being considered a rule."

Greta exhales sharply before replying. "If you read it somewhere, then it must be true." Then she closes the gap between us.

Like I said, so much fucking better than nicotine.

Friday, September 2

NOTIFICATIONS

dr. dre-ik
Damn youre not home :(I wanted to bro cuddle

Instagram
emmajinn messaged: "r u looking for a MK date?"

dr. dre-ik
Sleeping over. Kelper pissed me off and its a bad day

ma
Don't use the credit card. Maxed out. I sent you money. Buy your flight for Thanksgiving

katty batty katia
give her a good dad talk cuz mom is fixin to shave her hair off

katty batty katia
called icka. bitch is nuts. how tf is she related to us?

Quinn
3 hopefuls (and jenner)
@oats U joining us?

Jenner
3 hopefuls (and jenner)
Bet. Kelper and O-Line said they're joining

Quinn
3 hopefuls (and jenner)
Mickey and the hockey boys are going to barton's if yall wanna join us

Jenner
3 hopefuls (and jenner)
I am genuinely concerned for you

Rodney
3 hopefuls (and jenner)
at yo mommmas

Jenner
3 hopefuls (and jenner)
Where we eating dinner tonight?

Kelper
Andres is so fucking sensitive he makes for the worst roommate on god

GRETA

BE A DOLL

IT WAS THE glasses. Those goddamn glasses. They were the catalyst—the straw that broke the camel's back.

The way those spectacles rested on the bridge of his nose, slipping lower every time he made a face. The way they softened his strong, rugged features, drawing more attention to his devilish eyes. Every now and then, he'd nudge them back up, absentmindedly using the knuckle of his index finger, and I would be compelled to stop whatever I was doing and watch.

Before I'd even seen him wearing what can only be described as sex-focals, I was weak willed. Prior to his arrival, I'd toyed with the idea of having him again. Apparently concern is sexy now, because after he chastised me about my security, my body thrummed with arousal by his authoritative concern. Add the glasses, and I'm barely hanging onto my sanity.

What is it about Otis that makes him so... *Otis*? That was my question all week. The answer eluded me until I saw him, and then it became obvious. There's just something so freaking charming about him. He's an amalgamation of sports-bro and puppy, the two personalities haphazard in their appearance.

He's puppy-ish now. As we kiss feverishly, our hands roaming over each other's bodies to re-familiarize ourselves, he stops, ripping his mouth from mine to ask, "We're about to have sex, right?"

I press my lips to his clean-shaven jaw, a pinch of adoration causing me to smile against his skin. "Would you rather we play *Scrabble*?"

He chuckles and tilts his neck back, offering me better access. I gladly take advantage and nose the skin there before digging my teeth in, tugging, sucking, and kissing until he directs my ministrations back to his mouth. A sigh escapes me, bleeding into the kiss. He absorbs this contented sound while I strive to drink him in, licking my way inside, sliding my tongue languidly against his. I hold him captive, intoxicated by the way he relinquishes control, giving me free rein to plunder his mouth as roughly or gently as I want. All the while, he's attentive to me. His hands snake under my shirt, skimming my torso, up my waist, until settling below my breasts, the pads of his thumb teasing under the wire of my bra.

Just as he starts to venture beneath the material to finally touch the sensitive skin of my bare breasts, Otis tears himself away again. This time, however, he establishes a most unappreciated distance between us. And he does all this just to add, "Actually, if we're going to play a game, I vote *Settlers of Catan*. But we're gonna need more players."

I gape at him. He blinks back innocently, and I try to keep calm as I carefully respond, "Did you really stop kissing me to say that?"

He licks his puffy lips nervously and opens his mouth to explain, only to close it again. "Sorry," he hums warily, looking away as he scratches his head. "It's my favorite board game."

My heart hiccups at the silly grin he offers with his apology and the timid way he avoids eye contact. To make this all the more heart-throbbing, he adjusts his glasses and gives a helpless shrug, effectively shattering any flicker of annoyance I might have had before.

A cozy billow of warmth sweeps through me, making the distance he's put between us unbearable. I immediately remedy this.

Hooking a finger through his belt loop, I draw Otis forward. Surprised, he stumbles, righting himself with a hand on my shoulder. I stand on my tiptoes and kiss him, straining my body into his, fusing our skin together.

Assuming the lead, my hands twist in his hair, guiding his movements to fit my demands. *Oh, he'll challenge me*, I think, even looking forward to the push-and-pull we'll have. But he doesn't, and somehow, that's even hotter. Acute waves of excitement thrum between my thighs.

His palms find purchase on my hips, grinding our lower bodies together, and I groan in delight at the feel of his crotch against me. Releasing the hold I have on his waistband, I cup him over the material of his jeans.

Otis groans, the sound resonating through me, the frequency chattering my bones in a delectable way. His arms lock around me and crush me into him.

"Are you clean?" I wheeze as he kisses along the side of my face, my hair falling away to give him unencumbered access to my lips. I'm winded and entirely out of my mind from how empty I feel. I need this—him.

He pauses to flash a quizzical look. "Yeah, I took a shower after my workout."

I simultaneously want to smack him upside the head and pinch his cheeks. "No. Not—I mean, it's good to know you care about personal hygiene, but I'm asking if you're clear of any STD."

"Oh!" He nods, his frames slipping low on his nose from the motion. "Yeah. Super-duper clean."

"Good." I squeeze his length, and he thrusts into my palm. "I am, too."

He looks at me, bewildered as strands of his curly brown hair fall to his forehead. "So, are you like... Are we going to—y'know, with no condom?"

I respond with a kiss, and he whimpers. Mouth frantic, I continue to work him, each squeeze and slide of my hand encouraging his dick to grow harder. And he loves it, frequently expressing his delight as he shifts into my palm by letting out short, helpless noises.

When I grow so impatient as to unbutton his pants, dragging down his zipper slowly, Otis captures my bottom lip between his teeth and clamps down painfully, a growl rumbling from him while I frantically grope him over his boxers. Delight shudders through me, and I'm growing even more wet.

He's burning through the thin cotton material, and I can only salivate at just how scorching his bare cock will feel in my hand. My wandering fingers slither between the slot of his underwear, and I purr as I grab hold of him, the texture heavy and silky. His body slumps forward like he's about to lose footing. For a while, he lets me do what I want, his hands sculpting my waist while mine molds his cock.

"Enough," he reprimands with a snarl when my thumb brushes over his slit, his body jerking in response. He kisses me passionately and bends me back to grab at my ass, squeezing it harshly before delivering a gentle smack in emphasis. "Wrap your legs around me right now."

The gruff timbre of his voice does things to me, and if I were less of a woman, I'd come on the spot. I'm ecstatic to oblige. Hopping up, I lock both my ankles and arm around him, clinging onto him in what can only be categorized as a death grip. He lets out a huff from the force of my leap, adjusting his weight. "You good there?"

"Of course. Who do you take me for?" To prove himself, he hauls me even higher against him until my head nearly grazes the light fixture of my ceiling fan. With my breasts directly in front of him, he pushes his face between them. It tickles, and I can't suppress the girlish squeal that escapes me.

"Stop playing," I admonish between fits of laughter. He does and beams up at me.

Fuck... That smile. That's a smile that could destroy me.

I nudge his glasses higher up his nose. "All right, big guy. Giddy up. To the bedroom." I kick my heels against his back, rubbing against his shirt for a brief moment of friction between my legs. He chuckles sardonically, and before I can even think, I'm tossed onto the couch. A gust of air is knocked out of my lungs. I barely sit up amongst the cushions when he stands in front of me, barricading me in.

"We're not going to make it to the bedroom, sweetheart." He tears his shirt off in one fluid motion. Giddiness jolts through me as I become privy to the chiseled artwork of his muscular body. He continues to undress, and without missing a beat, I reach for him, my mouth watering with every new inch he exposes of himself. When his cock springs free, I reach for it.

Insatiable desire clambers through me, my lips tingling with need. I lick them about a million times, and Otis notices. He brushes a hand through my hair, tucking the strands behind my ears. His thumb traces the circumference of my swollen lips. "How's that oral-fixation of yours?"

I barely suck the tip of his finger into my mouth, swirling my tongue over it, earning a scattered exhale. "Not so good. My mouth has felt neglected lately." There's an accusation in my tone, one that I'm hoping he'll take to heart.

His gaze goes cloudy, dilating in darkened lust. With gentle pressure, he forces his thumb into my mouth properly, wrenching my jaw apart. I let him press my tongue down, staring at him all the while, before closing around it. I bob to test his reaction, then coast my hand up his thigh and grab hold of his dick, relishing in the way it beats.

Out of nowhere, he withdraws his finger to grab hold of my

chin, nudging my head up, my mouth still parted. Voracious appetite darkens his expression, the high rise of his cheekbones and his neck stained red in arousal, his breathing erratic.

"If you're a good girl tonight," he whispers, his voice gruff, leaning down to ghost this delicious promise over me, "I'll help fill your mouth."

Fuck. An addictive beat of pleasure laces into my veins. My pussy throbs, and I stroke his length, squeezing the base of him. With my pulse hammering against my throat, I adjust the position of my head so it's right in front of his cock and stick my tongue out to hold the tip of him there. I don't close my mouth around him, but I let my tongue wriggle side to side, stimulating the underside. He moans, and his hips surge forward only to have me move away, falling back onto the cushions with me still holding his length.

"And if *you're* a good boy tonight," I level, mesmerized by how he looks at me, "I might *let* you fill my mouth."

I release him then. I can't take it anymore—this hollow ache I feel. Being so untouched. I abruptly stand and move him back. Placing both hands on his biceps—*God bless America, and God bless his workout regimen. Yeesh, these guns are nice*—I spin him around and push him down. He lands elegantly on the couch, his arms outstretched along the backrest to catch himself.

I'm a little too overdressed. In one effortless motion, I strip down to my thong and bra. His hands are on my body before I can finish tearing my shirt over my head, and he pleads, "Please. I swear I'll be the best boy you've ever fucking met," only to settle me on his lap.

Clothes forgotten, I perch comfortably atop him, my legs resting on either side of his body, knees pressed tightly against his muscular ass. Despite his best efforts, I refuse to rest my weight on him, hovering instead, the heaviness of his dick brushing my thigh. With a dallying touch, I stroke his pecs and move up the column of his neck before weaving the hair at his nape around my fingers. I tug, just to see how he'll react.

His eyes roll into the back of his head, his Adam's apple bobbing.

I grin. "That's what I'm hoping for." I lick from his collarbone to his lips. He coerces my mouth open and sucks on my tongue. I exhale dreamily through my nose.

Otis shifts beneath me and again nudges me to relax completely over him. I refuse still, and he grunts and moves his fingers up my inner thigh, beneath the band of my panties, until he's touching the searing heat of me. I nearly topple from the touch, my moan echoing throughout the room.

"Fuck, Miriam," he groans in reverence, tossing his head to the side in disbelief as he strums his fingers over me, coating his touch in my wetness. "You're dripping, and I haven't even done anything yet. When did you get so wet?" I don't respond, too distracted, and he withdraws. I pull ferociously at his hair again, more painful than kinky, but he doesn't flinch, steadfast in his inquiry. "Answer me. When did you get so wet?"

"Earlier," I bite out. I lift myself higher and gyrate against his torso, hoping this will help cool the building tension. It doesn't. The pressure feels too good on my mound, yet it serves to kindle rather than soothe.

"Earlier when? *Hm*? When did this gorgeous pussy become such a fucking mess for me?" My head hangs forward, my abdomen tensing. "Was it when you were playing with my cock?"

I shake my head and move to touch myself when he doesn't.

Otis impedes this, restraining my wrist. "I told you to answer me, Miriam. When did you get so needy for me?"

I try to squirm out of his hold, my efforts futile. He's firm in confining my movements, being so fucking stubborn about this.

"Nothing is going to happen unless you tell me." Still, he releases my wrist to curve his hand over my ass again. I spread my legs farther. He doesn't rest there, journeying lower until the pads of his fingers impress over my swollen folds. Not touching, just levitating, mocking, torturing. Alluding to all he could do but won't until I've given him what he wants.

Fuck embarrassment. I'll toss my pride in the fucking dumpster if it means he'll touch me. Hell, I'll even throw in my dignity. That's how badly I want to get some from him. "When you put your head on my lap."

Otis smirks at my admission. He opens his mouth to say something, tease me most likely, but I won't have it, not when I feel so tawdry and small and high strung. It's unbecoming of a Sahnoun, and to compensate, I assert dominance.

Clapping a hand over his mouth to silence him, I reach behind me, grabbing hold of his cock. I drag my fingers over him slowly, his girth impressive, his length punishing. His eyes close, and I feel the vibrations of his pleasure on my hand when he moans. He trembles, hands crushing my waist. He knows exactly what I'm about to do, and he can't wait.

I'm so excited, I just might shove him in me right now. That, however, would be unwise.

"You want to be a good boy for me, yes?" I taunt, leaning forward to move the stringy material of my thong aside. Otis nods, and I press an endearing kiss on his lips, a deceptively sweet smile on my lips. "Then you're going to keep your hands to yourself." I test his readiness with a stroke, collecting the cum that's dripped out the slit to coat him. "And if you make me come with just your cock"—I trace the tip of him along the dripping folds of my pussy before aligning it into my opening, my walls clenching in anticipation—"you'll get to come in my mouth."

He tears his hands off me and grips the back of the couch, his muscles flexing. "I told you, I'm going to be the best boy you've ever met," he whimpers, his pants shallow, his words minced in an exhaustive effort to hold perfectly still as I barely slot him into me. When the bulbous tip breaches me, the tendons on his neck jump, and he bites back a scream, eyes shut tight. "The absolute fucking best. You'll see why I got Boy Scout of the Year twice in a row."

I punctuate my bubbly laughter with another kiss before satisfying us both. With careful precision, I begin to lower myself on him, fidgeting as I bide my time and familiarize myself with the burning stretch. My walls clamp wildly, trying to force out the intrusion, but that only makes it better when I'm successful in descending even farther along him. I haven't been using my vibrator recently—which I usually use with a generous amount of lube—so the biggest thing inside me as of late has been a finger or two.

Beads of sweat trickle down my back, the lace of my bra soaking in the moisture. "You're going too slow," Otis wheezes in agony when I'm not even halfway down his length. Still, his head slants back in a haze of pleasure.

"I'm being meticulous," I mew mockingly. I accidentally shift, his cock nestling in deeper at this new, delicious angle. It's easier to take him this way, my pussy distending and beating as it embraces him. He wears an expression that's somewhere between satisfaction and pain. My free hand goes to his chest, rubbing comforting circles there, dragging my nails over the ridges of his muscles.

He shivers and snaps. "Fuck meticulous." He almost reaches for me but stops himself at the warning that flashes on my face. Balling his hands, he jams a fist into his mouth, biting his knuckles when I swirl my hips, accepting more of him. He's nearly sheathed within me, and though it would take little effort on my part to just drop down that last inch to fully seat myself, I don't.

Let me rephrase that: I can't. I've reached my limit. If I take anymore, I'll be ripped in two—that much, I'm sure of. It's been a while since my lazy ass has ridden a guy—which is just a travesty, but that's a whole other discussion.

I struggle to express my concerns, the words tumbling out of my mouth tentatively. "You're too big. I don't think I can—"

But he's shaking his head in denial, interrupting me with coarse determination.

"You can. You can take it, baby. You're almost there."

It's my turn to shake my head. I'm already lifting off when he stops me with a plea.

"What if I help, hm? And when we're done, you can say thank you by riding me until you come, okay? Doesn't that sound good?"

I cling to his shoulder, stunned. His knuckles are white from how hard he's restraining himself. Maybe I wanted too much too fast. I like being on top, but right now, I don't mind being beneath him, especially if it helps disperse the mass of pleasure that's coiled in me.

He reads my mind. "Don't be scared, you can do it," he encourages, demonstrating his point with a small thrust.

I choke on a ragged inhale.

"You took me so well last time—got fucked so good. You can do it again. I'll even help you."

I let out a distorted sound but don't reject his assistance. Otis is right. I can do it. It's just a matter of working for it. But for some reason, today, I'm nervous and oversensitive. Every nerve ending in my body is on fire, and I can taste charcoaled bliss on my tongue.

He's careful about how he handles me, his eyes imploring me to trust him. I have no reason to—no real one, at least—but I do. It makes no sense, and yet, my entire being surrenders to him.

When I begin to lower myself back down, he bucks up into me twice more, still tempered, and just like that, it's done. My head lolls back from the sensation. I swear he's pressing against a part of me that's never been touched before. The angle—the depth—is so painful that it's fucking spectacular. Vicious sensation consumes me.

"Just like that. Such a good girl," he praises. When I lift then glide down in a swift motion, our groans of relief mingle together. "Look at you. So fucking perfect when you're thanking me."

I do it again and bristle from the sloppy sounds our joined bodies make when I settle to the root, my bottom bouncing on his powerful thighs. Pleasure overshadows the tinge of pain that comes with taking him in so deep, and I'm crazed.

The quickness of it, the friction, the fullness, the extent he reaches… It's so wonderful, and soon, I'm rocking over him a little recklessly, my movement no longer measured. All I care about is impaling myself over and over again. All I want to do is diffuse the sharp tension that's collecting between my legs and traveling up to my head.

I've mostly been keeping my eyes closed, completely lost to the lust, but when I open them again, I'm at a loss for words from the sight beneath me.

He's magnificently wrecked. He's tipping his head back, the metal frames of his glasses slipping even lower, threatening to fall off. He faces the ceiling, offering his unintelligible praises to it, his lashes fluttering, the corded muscles of his neck flexing in tandem with the ripples of pleasure that dance over his abdomen.

And what makes this portrait all the more stunning is the fact that I know he's relinquished control to me. This moment we're immersed in is of my own making. I have the power to bring or withhold the pleasure mounting inside him.

A tsunami of satisfaction crashes through me at the understanding.

"Fuck yes. Just like that," he hisses when I lift myself off him completely, lick my hand, and stroke his slick length before appeasing the fleeting vacancy I've created. As I circle my hips down on him, he arches up, fulfilling our union. When he is buried to the hilt, I swear I hear the wooden skeleton of the couch crack under his strength. A conceited smile flirts over his mouth. "Aren't you glad I helped?"

"Mmhm," I murmur. I stop moving and lean forward, stimulating my clit against him. I hiss, and my pussy sinches around him. He looks as if he's about to kiss me, but I push him away and lean back, a devilish smile on my face. He glares in contempt.

"Fucking kiss me or ride, G. I'll only take so much before I lose it."

I arch a challenging brow at him. He's already leaking inside me, giving way to the imminence of his orgasm. He's not going to last. But fine. Whatever. If that's what he wants, then okay.

He glances down at where we're joined, at the way I lift off him before falling back down. My movements are fast, the strain on my knees and legs ignored in favor of the overall thrill. Each stroke is hard and purposeful. I'm precise about how he'll fill me when I slam onto his cock. It's fucking magnificent, the way my pussy accommodates him. Not a minute ago, it had tried to force him out, and now, my walls pulse and throb to hold him within me, clasping tightly around him so that every lift off is difficult, almost bittersweet.

Over and over again, I do this, balancing myself atop him with a hand on his chest and the other reaching back to grasp his knee. When I close my eyes to bask in the glory of this moment, he watches, his eyes transfixed on where we're joined, awe glimmering behind his frames as he marvels at the way I take him.

It's not enough. It's wonderful. It's great. It feels good, a spiral of delight collecting at the base of my spine, hinting at a promising finish, but still, it's not enough.

And without hesitation or fear of judgment, with the trust I'd bestowed on him earlier, I take his hand, the one that's clutching onto my furniture for dear life, and finally give myself what I secretly want, yielding another facet of myself to him.

I guide his grip to my neck, and his eyes open in realization, his body frozen. Fear strikes me. For just a split second, self-conscious angst hums through me, and I wonder if I've crossed the line. If I've just done something he's not entirely comfortable with. I don't think he'd be uncomfortable, but I worry about the off chance that he is... Then again, we haven't had a conversation about limits. Or safe words. Oh God, did I just—

"Please tell me this isn't a dream," he whispers. He remains immobile, as if a single movement will shatter this illusion we've manufactured. "Please."

A newfound confidence glows in my chest. I sit up straighter, bringing my other hand to his elbow, urging him to hold my neck tighter. "Be a doll and choke me."

His restraint fractures at my request. The light hold intensifies, and the previous power dynamic we'd abided to disseminates. I readily concede control in favor of what he can give me—what I want him to give me.

Under my authority, he takes charge, and I'm so goddamn okay with that.

A blade of moonlight slices through my curtains and casts shadows on his side profile. The expression of indulgence flits away, and in its place is a stony blaze of arousal. To say I'm pumped is an understatement.

"I'm going to fuck you now," he taunts, speaking carefully, his voice deep, auspicious. Flipping us over, he situates himself on top of me, our lower halves flush but no longer connected. I'm too distracted to focus on the emptiness. He tickles patterns into my inner thighs, inducing my legs to part wider, settling himself between them. He leans over to grab his shirt and after a quick fumble, he lays it beneath us. Then he grabs his cock and rubs it against my slick folds, punctuating his next statement. "And you're going to be *my* doll and take it." He slams into me with a harsh snap of his hip, my body eager in accepting him.

"Yes," I croon, arching my body into him, straining my neck upwards. He pulls out again before hammering back in, the force of his punishing thrust so jarring and powerful that I've shifted up the sofa, the furniture knocking into the wall.

Otis doesn't say another word, doesn't offer dirty words or tantalizing praises, and that's okay. I don't need anything more to enjoy this. Not when his face is warped in so much concentration, his body working hard over me, his sweat trickling onto me. He's wrecking me, inside out, and I want more of him. More of his weight. More of this friction. More.

I want to be at his mercy for the rest of my life if that means feeling like this again. Nothing could be better. Nothing could make me happier.

He fucks me just right, finding that perfect angle where his dick touches the overwrought bundle of nerves deep within me, making my entire body bow. It's brutal in delivery, and twinges of discomfort buzz through me immediately, but the afterglow fizzles into an exquisite satisfaction, the rough stimulation poignant in the rapture it brings. The cycle continues, and I'm oscillating in this mindless state. My toes tingle with the vow of blissful carnage.

He places his hand back on my neck, and used his fingers to pinch the sides, keeping the burden away from the front of my throat. The force he exerts is faint, cautious, and that's okay for now. He doesn't know my limits, doesn't know what I can take, but at least he's still indulging me, doing what I asked—what I want.

He's dominating me. That's what the gesture signifies. And that's what matters.

And though his hold on my throat is vague and not as firm as I want, I still struggle to breathe from the overwhelming stimulation. Sparks blur my line of vision. This pseudo-asphyxiation manufactures a stunning light-headed sensation that has me writhing beneath him in desperation.

I'm reaching for my clit, ready to let go as he drives into me with savage intent, rough in the way he fills me to a painful brink only to rear away, nearly slipping out, before surging back in. Again and again, over and over, he does this, his pace bruising, thorough in how he wants me to dissolve in his arms.

Eyes closed, my senses are heightened and I can hear everything as we get closer to that breaking point. Our ragged breathing, the smack of his Adonis-molded body against mine, his balls furiously slapping against the low swell of my ass, of my eager pussy taking him in with a wet streak.

Fuck, I'm close.

He knows this, attuned to my every need. And the fucker weaponizes this insight against me. Pressing his lower body more firmly against me, he leaves no room for me to wedge a hand between us so I can rub myself to completion, needing that extra layer of friction to go off.

A scream of frustration rattles in my chest but is cut short when he speaks.

"D'you want to come?" he snarls, holding himself still inside me. Mobility limited, voice robbed, I open my eyes, willing him to read the desperation and anger there. A smirk dons his lips, and he tightens his hold deliciously around my neck, holding me down more. The edge of my orgasm grows closer. "Then beg me."

If I were in my right mind, I'd push him off me and give him the finger for being such an ass about this. But I'm not. I'm on some dumb shit, hypnotized by his dick, and without even hesitating, the second he loosens his hold around my throat, maintaining the grip with none of the pressure, I'm blubbering for release, fulfilling my role as the biddable partner.

"Please let me come. Please. You feel so good and I can't— *fuck*—more. Harder. Please. Yes. *Yes*. Deeper. Fuck. Just like that. Fuck me like I'm your slut," I babble. And then he's drilling into me, robbing me of breath and autonomy as flames lick my veins.

He's panting. I'm moaning. He's fucking, and I'm taking. He's whispering sweet nothings, and I'm feeling sharp pinches of everything.

"Now, slut," he commands, emphasizing the syllable with a deep, hard, fluid thrust. He holds himself there and leans forward to apply pressure on my mound. "Come around me now."

There it is.

And just like that, I'm ignited, my soul ablaze. "Rutherford," I screech, breaking through the sound barrier. Every cell in my body splits to two. My soul tears out of me and makes its way beyond the stratosphere and to another dimension, bathing itself in the light of this new realm, as my body back home attempts to remain intact. I've lost sensation yet I feel everything everywhere at the same time, my body torn between the contradiction.

All I know is that I never want this to end. I never want the rush of ecstasy to stop crashing into me. My leg has lifted up in the air, my toes pointed to the ceiling. My body curves off the couch, convulsing as I attempt to contain my finish.

He's pounding me through it, removing his hand from my neck. He touches between us to feel the way he's invading me. I'm barely aware of all this, barely aware of how he says urgently, "You feel so fucking good, baby. I'm close. So fucking close, just keep squeezing me like that."

But the part of me that's determined, the one that manages to overshadow the mind-numbing euphoria that's purging through me, takes action.

Without warning, I shove against his chest, using my legs to push him off me. The motion startles him, and he loses balance, toppling to the ground. I know I should be concerned, what with how I've just committed one of the worst crimes known to man—*coitus interruptus* sans the climax—but I'm exhausted and take a moment of reprieve to breathe and regain cognizance.

"What the fuck?" he howls from the floor. There's a shuffle and a pitiful cry of outrage. "Shit, I just broke my glasses."

They'd slipped off when we'd switch positions and he'd gotten on top of me. I'd tossed them aside after they'd fallen on my chest, uncaring to what would happen to them in the heat of the moment.

I felt a little bad, though. I am quite fond of them.

"Did you land on them?" I gasp, my words coming out fragmented.

"No duh. You fucking kicked me to the ground." I turn my head and give him an apologetic smile. With a groan, I raise up on my elbows. I feel like Jell-O.

"Sorry." Another grunt, and I manage to sit up, my feet sinking into the soft carpet. I press my legs together, my pussy is so sensitive. "I just didn't want you to come that way."

"You didn't want me to come? Are you kidding me? You get yours but I can't get mine? This is a hate crime," he whimpers bitterly. He looks down at his penis, a scowl on his face. "I actually feel like my dick is about to fall off."

It takes a lot of effort, but I get up and bend down to help him to his feet. Otis mean-mugs me the entire time. "Stop complaining and start begging."

He's lost. "What—"

But I've already pushed him down on the couch for the second time that day. Kicking his legs apart, I stand between them, hands on my hips, eyes fixed on his straining dick. I lick my lips as saliva floods my mouth in giddy delight.

"I said"—bending, I place my hands on his knees and drag my hands up his leg, hovering next to his thick, inflamed cock, my lips brushing over his mouth—"start begging like a good boy."

🔒 September 1, 2022 at 12:53 AM

Super Secrets Smutty Book Club

The Princess and Her Many Vicars
★★★★☆

historical romances are my new things. i claim Leo as my new book boyfriend

Billionaires and Babies
★★★☆☆

idgy he growled all the time but it was hot also there's no plot in here so don't bother looking for one just enjoy it for what it is

Kill Me Softly with your C***
★★★☆☆

porn that's all

Frozen Worlds and Beasts
★★★★★

i will not be explaining myself or lending you my copy you probably wouldn't be able to read anything over the pink marks anyway

Faeries and Their Wolves
★★☆☆☆

i don't think i'm a wolfy girl :(

My Mate, My Love
★★☆☆☆

never want to read the word mate again also knotting??? ick but hot kinda?

The Honey of Your Nectar
★★★★★

oh. my. god. the angst. the feels. black cowboy romance stay the best. i cried so much it's not even funny. i hope andres can love me the way dax loved sheila

The Vows We Never Made
★★★★☆

another historical i'm feral over this author she's a master

Broken Hearted City Girls
★★☆☆☆

i hated this but i feel like you'll like it and the only reason i'm giving it 2* is because i know the author put a lot into this

OTIS

MAKE ME

"**YOU NEED HELP** back there, big guy?"

Mortification crawls up my neck and stains my cheeks as I double down on my effort to rid Greta of her bra. I'm ready to spontaneously combust when a half-dozen fumbling seconds later, that shit is still very much intact. I'm cursing myself for ushering her onto my lap after she got on her knees in front of me, ready to service me right away.

"Are there locks back there? Why won't this thing come off?" I huff. Bitter from the amused look she wears, I focus my attention on the swell of her breasts, envying the material that hugs them.

"No locks. Just a standard clasp." Reaching behind, her fingers graze mine, ready to assist. Indignant, I brush them away, and she chuckles. "There's no shame in needing help."

Eat me. I'm done. I'm pretty sure I look like a fucking cherub from how red I've turned. "I don't need help. I've taken off plenty of bras, okay? I got this. I just need to—" Except, in my state of indignant frenzy, I've become a little too annoyed, a little too aggravated, and my words are cut off by the sound of tearing when I wrench a little too hard.

My eyes go wide, and I freeze. *Whoops.*

Greta's jaw drops. She cranes her head back to confirm what I've done. I titter apprehensively, letting my fingers trail down her spine to settle under the stringy elastic of her thong.

"Did you…" She pauses to face me and looks down at her chest. With the lack of support, her bra straps have slid halfway down her arms, revealing the edge of her kobicha-colored nipples. "Did you just rip my bra?"

"What can I say? I'm innovative with my solutions." My fingers clench the top of her ass in apology.

"But I really liked this bra."

I liked it, too. It's ornate and nude colored, blending into her skin, her perky nipples making occasional appearances based on how the sheer lace shifts.

But no matter how much I might have liked it, no matter how pretty or sexy I think she looked in it, I know its rightful place is anywhere off her.

"I'll buy you a new one." *Fuck, I'm going to eat air for a week. Those boulder holders are expensive as shit.* This I know from various heart-attack-inducing shopping trips with my sisters. Taking Monica bra shopping is one of my layers of hell.

Greta glares at me and shakes her head ruefully. The hand she has on my jaw moves to curl behind my ears, playing with my hair there. "So much for having taken off plenty of bras before, huh," she mocks.

"I have! Yours was just impossible. It's like a fucking chastity belt back there."

"Given how un-chaste our fucking was, I'd beg to differ." I open my mouth to argue back but she places a finger on my lip. "A chastity belt prohibits access, and I've definitely given you lots of access to me."

"Yeah, well…" I purse my lips and choose not to expand. For the record, I am phenomenal at ridding people of their undergarments. Absolutely spectacular. A connoisseur. Today just happens to be an off day of sorts. An anomaly that should not be held against me or my record. Still, needing to divert her attention from picking on my poor bra-removing skill, I thus occupy her.

First, I lick my way into her mouth, evading her eager tongue. When she's sufficiently exasperated, her nails cutting my skin painfully—wonderfully—Greta settles herself properly onto my lap, straddling a single thigh, grinding her cunt there. My kisses turn fervent, matching the way her wet, slippery heat rubs against my skin.

I tear away and drag my lips to her breasts. Sucking her nipple into my mouth, a sound of satisfaction rises in my throat. Using my hand to knead the other, I ensure her chest is sufficiently cherished and tended to.

Fuck, she has nice tits. They're not melon big, but they're also not ping-pong small. They're decent, nice, my hand engulfing them entirely.

When I tug her nipple between my teeth, she groans, the sound rattling the both of us. I bite down harder, wanting to test her limits. Greta responds by swiveling her hips against me, rocking forward. Hands on my shoulder, head tilted back to afford me better access, she's lost in my ministrations.

With the space she's just provided me, I put as much of her in my mouth as I can, my tongue teasing all along the circumference, my cheeks closing in to create a nice suction to couple with the biting.

It's when I move to her right breast, switching my hands to cup her left one, that I open my eyes for a moment and notice a delicately scrawled tattoo on the underside of it. I only see the first letter, a "J".

I know your secret, I think, my heart racing in excitement at the unexpected finding.

"Is this your way of begging?" she interrupts my thoughts, nosing herself into the crook of my shoulder. She cradles my head in her hand and bucks against me when I squeeze her again. "Cause you're good at it."

"Told you. I'm the best fucking boy out there," I grunt. "You'll never find anyone better than me."

Greta hums in approval, cupping my cheeks to smack our lips together. It's too quick, and she hops off me. My muscles go taut when she drops to her knees again, opening my legs even more to crawl between them. I place a hand in her hair and brush strands away from her face so I can get a nice, clear view of her.

"All right, good boy," she begins, licking her lips as she stares at me with so much hunger that I'm actually a little concerned for my well-being. "How badly do you want my mouth on you?" Kissing around my knees, her hands massage up and down the side of my thigh, drawing ellipses along its span, getting just close enough to my dick that I can sense the touch but not so close that I can feel it.

Evil, sexy woman.

"I'll give you anything. Whatever the fuck you want, I'll—" My words falter and become lost, my breath hitching in surprise. She lifts my dick to run her tongue down the length, her lips grazing the sensitive skin of my balls, her nose pressed against the base. The grin she wears is wicked, eyes hooded.

She pulls back and whistles, the sharp exhale of air fanning over me. I shiver, muscles flexing. "Anything, you say? I do like the sound of that."

I'm about to make a quip, indulge in this verbal sparring, when she does it.

Upper lip curled over her teeth, she descends along my length, carrying the weight of me on her tongue, wiggling the slippery muscle back and forth to massage the foreskin there as she'd done before. The sensation, coupled with the knowledge that she's tasting herself on my cock, makes it impossible for me to remain motionless. I can't help but thrust, desperate to surround myself in the delicious, melting sensation her mouth provides.

She restrains my movement with an anchored hold on my hip. Hollowing her cheeks, she sucks in the tip of me, French kissing the head, careful of her molars. I'm mesmerized, enthralled by the crease in her forehead as she concentrates on sucking me in, bobbing her head in short, exact motions. One hand grips me, keeping my dick up, while the other, once confining me, roams over my chest, exploring the expanse of my taut abdomen, nails scratching over my skin to draw encoded messages as goose bumps creep across my flesh.

I watch, beyond aroused by the view I'm afforded. But then Greta's bangs fall over her face, obstructing my view of her.

"Tie your hair up," I say, the command turning into a hiss when her tongue is digging into my slit, collecting the cum leaking out.

At my request, Greta slides her mouth off me, pumping me still. "If that's what you want, do it yourself."

Fuck. The suggestion has my dick twitching. She smirks at this reaction.

She holds her free wrist out to me, and I grab the hair tie there. All the while, she places her mouth back on me, her fist palming in tandem with her mouth. I jolt forward and place a hand on the back of her head to both stabilize myself and stuff more of my cock in the heaven of her mouth. She keeps still, her breathing heavy, her tongue still working me. Only when I regain control of myself do I release my hold, and she moves.

By the time her hair is drawn away from her face, I'm only too happy to fall back on the sofa and relax. I lay a hand flat on my forehead and abdomen to keep from grabbing her head and directing her movement the way I really want. This is just the beginning, and I need to behave if I want it to last.

For a while, I'm content with what she's doing. The slide of her mouth along my dick, albeit short, is nice, making a tickle of warmth course through my veins, inspiring haphazard tremors of delight. Her hands, talented and soft, play over me with precise pressure and speed.

It's a good buildup and would be a nice distraction if I were doing something else as well, like watching a football game or catching up on my favorite TV shows. But with this being the focal point of the moment, it's not enough. Not when every second that ticks by extends itself into never-ending moments. The feelings inside me are too much, but at the same time, nowhere near enough.

The coil in my stomach is an unsatiated hollow ache. I can't take it anymore, and I'm trying not to be a fucking pig about it, but it's difficult. And when I look down at her after trying to thrust up into her mouth, I notice the way she stares up at me. It's the same look she gave me when she'd asked me to choke her.

Like she *knows*. She knows what she's doing to me. And that's when *I* know what needs to be done to expedite my escape from this purgatory.

"Suck my cock," I command. I don't hesitate to press her face down. She's a fucking brat and lifts off me, a string of saliva stretching between us before she licks her lips and snaps it, swallowing the excess. My pulse drums loudly in my chest at the sight of myself in her dainty grip.

"Isn't that what I'm doing?" She noses the underside, pecking my balls while stroking me off leisurely, her grip growing more lax.

My eyes narrow, and I push her head closer to my dick, bumping it against her slightly parted lip. Rubbing the top over her bottom lip, I paint them in a sheen of cum. "Quit fucking talking and work that slutty mouth of yours over my cock."

Greta's eyes roll into the back of her head, and she hums, opening her mouth again. Her eyes are glassy like she's in a daze, and she lewdly licks the head before slapping it against the flat of her tongue a couple of times.

"Fuck," I moan then trail off into a whine. Jolting forward, my treacherous gaze tears away from her as she swallows half of my length in one steady plunge forward. Her cheeks collapse around it as she traces her tongue along my vein. A swirl of pleasure rushes toward my head, causing my toes to curl. She holds herself there for a good couple of seconds, enrapturing me in sensation. When she pulls up, she does so noisily, moaning all around me so that I can feel the echoes of her eagerness. She spits out the cum and saliva in her mouth over the top and drops back down, her mouth and chin a mess. She repeats this motion again. And then again and again. She goes just a little farther down each time but still not all the way.

I'm beside myself, doing my best to behave and keep my hips still so I don't choke her. I'm unsure what is driving me crazier: her slobbery cock-sucking skills or the enjoyment she demonstrates while blowing me.

Popping me out of her mouth, Greta takes a moment to breath and clear her throat, her strokes lubricated by the wet mess she's left on my cock. I flit my eyes back onto her and observe the way her face blushes and chest heaves. Her lips glisten, and her eyes are bright. What's more, I see one of her clever little hands settled between her legs.

I'm struck by a poignant pleasure at the sight before me. Her wet lips enclose me, her mouth stuffed, my dick denting her semi-hollowed cheeks, eyes bright. She has her fist just below her lips, the one between her thighs rubbing vigorously. Coupling these visuals with the sensation of her gentle suckling and tongue teasing out to collect the pre-cum she's drawing out, and I'm seconds away from going feral.

"You fucking love this," I announce in awe, reaching for her. She cradles her face in my palm and nods, licking her saliva-and-cum-coated lips, fisting me a little faster, a little tighter, her head jerking in a short nod. I groan, speaking my amazement aloud. "You fucking love sucking my dick and taking my cum."

This sets her back in motion. She's swallowing me again,

teasing the head a little with her tongue before curling it around my girth. It's nearly perfect, how stretched out her lips are, how vocal she's being, how sloppy it all is, how eager she appears. But she's not doing what I want, and I'm out of patience, done playing her little games.

"I know you can take more," I urge, my raspy voice strained. My heart palpitates as I wait for her to listen to me without having me force the rest of my cock down her throat.

Once more, she pulls her mouth from me and does exactly what I told her not to do: speak. "If you want me to take more, then make me take more."

Just like that, I'm working on autopilot, acting from a primal, desperate place within.

Perching on the edge of the couch, I pet her face, using a gentle touch to outline her features as I swipe my thumb over her wet lips and high cheekbones. Placing my thumb on her chin, I press it down to open her jaw, slipping my thumb against her bottom teeth, and enunciate gruffly, "Open that pretty mouth wide for me, G."

She does, her willing tongue peeking out. I put my hand over hers on my cock, slapping my dick there, and the corner of her lips tug in a grin as her lashes flutter. She knows damn well I loved when she did that before. Leveraging a hold in her curly ponytail, I guide her head forward and direct her.

This time, there's no teasing. There's no hesitation. In one smooth downward motion, she engulfs my entire length, choking, coughing, beautifully stuffed. At first, she keeps her mouth loose around me, simply holding me deep in her throat, braving out her gag reflex, licking down to my fucking balls. I'm holding her head there, but I can't make her suck on me.

I tug her roots, fed up by her overindulged behavior, and snap, "Swallow. Now."

Finally—*finally*—after an eternity, I'm given what I want. I've been a good boy tonight, and the culmination of my admirable behavior has come down to this moment in which Miriam deep throats me, the recess of her mouth divine, like hot, wet velvet. And if I wasn't so absorbed in the moment, I would be stunned by her near flawless execution.

She's enthusiastic and ferocious, forcing me so far down her throat that I feel like I'm dying a thousand tiny deaths. She's being rough and chaotic about it, making this lewd task all the more dirty. Her saliva coats my shaft, making it easier for her to slip me in. It's fucking messy and eager, and that enhances the sensation blazing through me. The entire time, she's moaning, that hand between her legs moving more vigorously, and I know she's loving this. She loves having me wild beneath her power, my restraint held together by a thinly wound thread. This fact alone has me ready to fucking bust.

But that's not what brings me to the brink. It's when she takes her hand away from my dick to cover the slackened hold I have threaded in her hair that I lose it.

Fuck my mouth, is what she's telling me when she pins my gaze beneath her lashes. Whether she beckons this because her arms are tired or what, I don't care.

The second she gives me the reins, I'm rutting into her throat at a force that should have anyone tapping out, but she doesn't. She accommodates me completely, maintaining the glorious suction, moving away only a moment to take a breath before welcoming my overly enthusiastic thrusts. Her eyes fixate on me, a gorgeous tear trickling from the corner, lust and pleasure storming behind them. Her tongue is everywhere, massaging my vein, wrapping around, digging into my slit.

Greta knows I'm ready when I falter and my movements become more out of control, my cock swelling in its need to let the fuck go. And still, she doesn't let up the pace, going so far as to constrict her throat when I hit the back of it, even when I pat her shoulder because I'd only been joking about coming in her skilled mouth.

She hadn't been, though.

She bobs over me nonstop, moaning, staring unblinkingly up at me with those gorgeous, hazy eyes like she's also close. I'm being worshipped by her, and it's primitive and wonderful to watch her commitment to my pleasure and—

Fuck, fuck, fuck.

She cups and tickles my balls then teases the puckered opening of my ass with a finger. One more twist of her wrist and a tight, pointed suck and flick at the tip, and I'm letting go, thick ropes of cum jetting from my cock and into her throat.

"Miriam," I shout, the name slipping from my lips like a rueful prayer, my face contorted in unadulterated desire. She says something, too, except her words are muffled, a mixture of our saliva and cum leaking from the corner of her mouth.

It's one of the most intense orgasms I've ever experienced. The volcano that is my orgasm erupts, and the lava beneath my skin saturates me in an intense heat, its flames shooting through my veins. A rush of adrenaline hits me, and my hips stutter out of beat as she sucks me dry, greedy for every last drop.

Wave after wave of euphoria swirls through me. I'm soaring high in the sky, and somehow, I'm allowed access into heaven. I luxuriate there for a minute, losing myself to the rapture that consumes my body. My entire body is not my own. My bones are liquified and rendered useless. I can't even breathe properly.

It's not possible for guys to have multiple orgasms. I know this. I acknowledge that biologically, that's not what happens to me. But fuck does it seem like that, the way ecstasy crashes into me over and over again, blurring together, seemingly endless.

How women don't have sex twenty-four-seven when they can feel like this—perhaps even better—is beyond me.

When the effects of my release dwindle and I'm tunneled back to reality, I notice that Greta is still suckling me. She has both hands on my knees as she slides along my length at a languid pace.

I shiver. "That's good, babe," I mumble, my words slurred, my brain fried. She gives me one last pointed suck and releases me, lifting herself up with a grunt and a curse. I appreciate the fact that she doesn't try to kiss me. I'm not entirely opposed to tasting my own jizz, I'm just not in the mood. She wipes her mouth and tosses herself beside me on the couch. I clutch my wrung-out dick.

Damn. She milked my balls dry. I've never felt more vulnerable in my life.

We're quiet for a couple minutes, trying to catch our breaths, not looking at each other. I'm still trying to find my sanity, what with her having slurped it out of me.

I turn to look at her, fucked out and hazy. Greta is so fucking dazzling, just sitting there pensively, unashamed of her naked form. She has a faraway look in her eyes but notices my movement from the corner of her eyes and mimics my posture. I take a mental picture of the moment, of us sitting naked on the couch, looking at each other.

"Did you get off again?" I ask, my voice cracking, throat dry.

She nods sluggishly, and when she speaks, her voice is even more hoarse, strained from her majestic oral efforts. "I really like giving blowjobs."

That's a fucking understatement.

There's another lull of silence before I speak up again. "So, are we going to talk about the fact that you screamed out Rutherford when you climaxed earlier?"

She winces. "Absolutely not."

"Cool, cool, cool." *You almost made me go soft, but that's okay. We'll move past it.*

"Are we going to talk about the fact that you started singing the Ben Ten theme song?"

"What?" I balk, horrified. "When?"

"When you were ramming your dick into my mouth like a mammoth on steroids."

I pale in horror. I don't remember doing that. The last time I did something like that was in my freshman year of college. It was one of my endurance tricks, a way for me to clear my mind and not ejaculate prematurely.

As if the humiliation I've already suffered today wasn't enough…

"We're not talking about it," I say. This time, I don't even mind the silence. At least, not until Raven lets out a hesitant meow from where he hides under his cat tree. I turn and guiltily look at the cat. "Shit."

"What?" Greta asks, her eyes droopy in exhaustion.

I point to where her black tabby sits, his contempt and judgment clear. "What do we do about Raven?"

"What about him?"

"Do we, like, split the cat therapy bill? Cause he looks like he's about to throw up."

"He'll be fine. It isn't the first time he's seen me have sex."

Lucky bastard. I lick my lips and clear my throat before asking my next question. "So, uh, who taught you how to, y'know, give head like that?"

"Some guy at my high school. He was a good teacher, and I was a very determined student."

I'm torn between jealousy and gratitude. "I'll say. You know where he lives?"

"I know where his mom lives. Why?"

"I need to send him a thank you note."

She gapes. "What the fuck. Why him? What about me? *I'm* the one that did all the fucking work. Do you know how sore my jaw is? How hard it is not to gag and choke to death on a dick like yours? What do I get for all that?"

I shrug. "Satisfaction of making me go stupid for a while?"

That doesn't appeal to her. "Get up and make me something to eat right now as a thank you before I make you go stupid for other reasons," she snaps, pointing at the kitchen.

"You're not full yet? When I fed you so well? Gluttonous girl."
I pat her adorably squishy belly. She smacks my chest, and I hiss at
the contact. "I kinda deserved that."

June 23, 2022 at 1:51 PM

GAME SCHEDULE

GAME 0	[HOME]	ASM (RANK #13)
GAME 1	[HOME]	MSB (RANK #6)
GAME 2	[HOME]	SHS (RANK #10)
GAME 3	[HOME]	CSB (RANK #3)
GAME 4	[AWAY]	FG (RANK #4)
GAME 5	[AWAY]	OMR (RANK #1)
GAME 6	[AWAY]	ACT (RANK #5)
GAME 7	[AWAY]	AT (RANK #12)
GAME 8	[HOME]	LACU (RANK #8)
GAME 9	[HOME]	AR (RANK #7)
GAME 10	[AWAY]	UMM (RANK #11)
GAME 11	[AWAY]	ASM (RANK #13)
GAME 12	[HOME]	BIL (RANK #9)

GRETA

FORDY AND THE INVISIBLE GIRL

I'M DRUNK. LIKE, off my rocker, tits flopping sideways, pissed beyond coordination. When I eject myself from James's battered sedan, I stumble out of the vehicle with the grace of a three-legged possum and plummet to the pavement.

I won the battle between myself and the door handle, but I lost the war with the gravel I'm lying on.

Regardless of how inebriated I am—which is to say completely, given how my ordinarily aloof disposition has been completely replaced by an unfamiliar peppy one—I refuse to admit I'm in such a state and behave as though I still have my full faculties.

"This is a terrible idea," my best friend says with a groan. He helps to drag me back to my feet, glancing nervously at the back seat to make sure his new situationship, Veronica, and Elise are both still asleep, undisturbed by the ruckus I'm creating. Once I'm standing, I push him away and swipe my hands over my body to ensure I'm still in one piece. I'm confident that I'm intact, though I feel like my waist is floating above me, detached from my skeleton. It's fucking freaky but kind of cool.

Teetering on my heels, I finally find my footing by spreading my legs and crouching a bit. "*Au contraire*, dear Jamesy Boo-Boo.

This is a"—I elongate the next word for flair—"splendid idea."

"There's no such thing as a splendid idea when you're drunk."

I scoff and attempt to walk toward him, only to stumble again. Luckily for me and my already scraped-up knees, he's there to catch me. But as before, I push him away to prove my vertical stability. "I'm not drunk. I'm just a little… tipsy." I sway as a cool night breeze rushes by us.

"You were tipsy four tequila shots ago. You're shit-faced right now." He might be scolding me, but there's an overtone of amusement in his disapproval. "And I know you have this invincibility complex when you're white-girl wasted—"

"I'm invisible?" I panic. Maybe that explains the funny feeling. Looking down at myself, I'm relieved to see I'm still all there. No matter how cool it might be to be invisible, now is not the time. Not when I need to talk to Rutherford and inform him of my decision.

"I'm begging you not to do this today. Sleep on it and tell him tomorrow."

I don't heed his words. Nothing can or will stop me from completing this mission. Hence how we've arrived here. The moment James finally herded us ladies into the car after some sloshed karaoke, I'd caused a ruckus until he agreed to drive me to Ender's field, where Midnight Kiss is being held this Friday night. As such, we're standing in the parking lot as we wait for the event to end. Once it's over, I'll make my move, and Rutherford and I will ride off into the sunset.

Literally. I want to ride him while he drives us toward the sunset. If you ask me, it's a better ending than anything Disney has ever conceptualized.

Of course, James understands this determination well, having dealt with my wasted antics and quirks for a while. He sighs heavily. "Fine. Whatever. Have fun embarrassing yourself, you sloppy drunkard."

I am about to react with a disproportionate level of rage at my so-called-friend's remark when I hear booming laughter.

Inhibitions stripped entirely, I react instantly. "Fordy!" I shriek, jumping up and down, frantically waving my hands. I'm not certain if he's in this group of people or not. Despite my exceptional eyesight, I'm unable to discern the individuals walking through the lot—they're too far away. Nevertheless, I continue to shout, needing to draw attention to my presence just in case. "Fordy-Mordy-Bordy!"

"Greta, maybe you shouldn't yell so loud. You're going to lose your voice again, or possibly break my ear drum." James places a cautionary hand on my elbow.

I twist out of his grasp aggressively and shoot him a glare. "I lost my voice from sucking dick too hard, Jamesy, not from shouting. Now shut up—"

"Only you would be proud of that fact."

"—and get in the car. Ya girl's got a job to finish." I shoo him away, and using every single balancing skill I garnered during my six and half years of cheerleading, I jog toward the party of people.

Satisfaction washes through me when I see him, and I slow my pace. My body reacts so powerfully as reminders of what we did on my couch bombard my mind. He swivels his head as if he's looking for something, his thick brows pinched together. My blood sizzles the second his eyes land on me, and his eyebrows shoot up.

"Rutherford-y!" I gush.

He turns to say something to the people he's with before breaking free from the congregation to head my way. "Miriam," he calls out at a normal volume once I'm within earshot. He stops a few steps from me, but the remaining distance is unbearable. I catapult myself at him, but I've definitely miscalculated.

My bones feel like Jell-O, either because of the synchronized swimming class Elise dragged me to this morning—I limped and cried my way back to the changing room—or because of the impromptu shots I knocked back half an hour ago.

Either way, I slam into him. He stumbles from the force but has enough mind to wrap his arms securely around me, saving me from another losing battle with the ground. My fuzzy head blurs even more from the contact, my senses strained from the distinct smell and feel of him. The itch that's been ailing me all fucking week soothes itself.

He's sweaty and stinky, but that doesn't matter. What I have in mind will also make us sweaty and stinky. Good thing the cabin of his truck is big.

"Uh, Greta?" he enunciates cautiously when I don't say anything for a while. His arms tighten around me when my legs falter at the sound of my name.

I'd much rather have him moaning it, but beggars can't be choosers. "Hi!" I yap. James might have been right. My throat is still a bit sore from giving him a blowjob, but every strain on my vocal cords is a wonderful, salacious reminder.

He chuckles and gently moves me back to stand on my own, wearing a fond smile.

Once again, my heart does that little flip, but it's going to have to calm down if I plan to get through this.

"Hi." A twinkle gleams in those perceptive eyes.

I wish I could pluck them out of their sockets and wear them around my neck just so I could have them with me all the time. Wait. That would actually be creepy and morbid. *Am I disturbed? Why the fuck would I think that?*

I'm about to go down a deeper rabbit hole when Rutherford speaks up again. "What are you…" He trails off into bemused silence.

He looks at me like he's seeing me for the first time, and fuck, I love it. I chose a skimpy outfit that really highlights just how fucking amazing my legs and ass are. The cold night air nips at my coochie like it's trying to give me frostbite, but at least I look fucking stellar.

They say pretty hurts. And I am the embodiment of motherfucking pain.

After a prolonged second of Rutherford scanning over my scantily-clad outfit, he frowns, his eyes linger on my scuffed-up knees.

"What's this?" he bends down to touch them, his face level with my crotch. I look down at him and blink, trying really hard not to shove his face between my legs when he's positioned so perfect for that.

"I fell," I explain, swallow a little hiss when his fingers skim over the fresh wound. The disapproval on his face deepens.

"You need to be more careful, G. I don't like seeing these cuts on you." He sighs and shakes his head. There's no time for me to react—be it swoon or defend myself—when he stands back up. "Now, Ms. I Hate Midnight Kiss, do you mind telling me what you are doing here?" What he really means is what I'm doing here now, since we'd agreed to talk tomorrow after the game.

It's been about ten days since we saw each other. The last time was at his place the morning after our fun little exception fuck. He'd committed a robbery of my bras as a means of getting revenge for my relentless mockery as he made me a snack, and I'd stormed to his place and demanded he give them back.

He agreed, but on one condition. That next, *next* Saturday, which is tomorrow—or technically today since it's well past midnight—I'd decide whether or not I'd make him a rule and not just an exception. A casual rule, he clarified, because he's not in a place to be in a relationship. His football career is too important.

As life would have it, a couple days later, I had an epiphany while I was getting mediocre head in the bathroom stall of a dingy club I frequented. It was a simple epiphany, but no less profound. I'd developed a taste for *coitus du Rutherford*, and despite my stringent guidelines around hooking up, I might actually be willing to break a few if it meant having him again.

Pride and my stubborn effort to disprove this realization incumbered me from succumbing to the reality right away, hence the sex I had with the guy in the apartment below mine this past Tuesday. I wanted to prove that I could have good sex with anyone and that letting them go was easy-peasy-lemon-squeezy. It had been nice, even fun and pleasurable, and afterward, we parted under the agreement that we would never do it again.

But the second I walked up the flight of stairs back to my place, I was hit by a feeling that it wasn't the same. The touches, the feelings, the wash of pleasure that convulsed through me at the end—all very, very nice, but not the goddamn same.

So, I came to terms with the fact that I am addicted. Not to sex, though that could be debated. Not to cigarettes, though a light would be great. Not even to alcohol—that's an indulgence, really.

No. I'm addicted to Otis Rutherford Morgan, whom I like and whose company I enjoy, and who has glasses and a charming smile, and is nice but also somehow kind of a jag, and has a funny way of thinking and marvelous hands that can wrap around my neck effortlessly and a way of reading my body without me saying anything, and fuck, I need a fix soon.

So I look at this man who I've come to crave, and I feel myself flushing with need, wonder, and happiness.

"I'm here to tell you I'm not wearing a bra." I spread my arms wide and thrust my chest out, tilting my head to the sky. "The nipples have been freed."

He looks behind him, at the group of people who still remain, before looking back at me, honing in on my chest like he's trying to confirm said statement. "That's good to know."

"It is," I affirm with excessive eyebrow wiggles. "It's splendid. My boobies are out, and I'm ready for you. No need to struggle with the bra again. We can go straight to the titty sucking and skip all that middle shit."

"Struggle," Rutherford repeats in a choked scoff. An ornate

blush makes its debut for the night, and I tilt my head, wearing a fond smile. I missed his blushes. He fumbles over his next words, clearly trying to maintain a tenor of determination as he speaks, hiding his mouth behind his fist when he hacks out an uncomfortable, dry cough. "I didn't struggle."

I giggle, the sound feminine and high-pitched. "You did, and it's okay. I found it adorable."

"I'm not adorable." But he puffs out his cheeks, looking more chipmunk than man. "I'm hunky and handsome."

That much is true. His jersey is half ripped, displaying his carved muscles. Dirt mats his neck and hair. I might actually want to get over my football-field aversion if it means seeing him tussle around on the turf.

"Hunky, handsome, *and* adorable." I reach up, my index and thumb close together as I attempt to pinch his cheeks. He bends away in a half-assed *Matrix* move.

He tuts. "You're drunk." I take a step forward, and he rights himself.

"Tipsy." Then I contemplate for a second and add with a seductive leer, "and horny." Very, *very* horny. For him.

"What a fantastic and not at all difficult combination to deal with," he says glibly.

The sarcasm goes over my head, and I reach for him, eager to demonstrate just how fantastic it truly is.

Yet again, he sidesteps my attempt to touch him.

My stomach turns, and I swallow a sudden bubble of bile that creeps up my throat. That fuzzy feeling in my head is getting thicker. My line of vision is far less clear than it should be, even in my state of inebriation. I ignore it in favor of going for what I want.

"Fordy," I whine. "Don't be like this."

"Like what?"

"A prude." I push my hair from my face and pout. "C'mon. I know you want to. Let's get jiggy with it."

"Greta, we're in public, and this"—he motions between us then glances back at his friends—"is not the time or place to '*get jiggy with it*'."

"And why not?" I cross my arms over my chest.

"Because." He clicks his cheeks and glances up at the sky, looking a little frustrated. When he speaks again, expanding on his reason, I'm hit by a wave of nausea unrelated to what he says next. "Because I'm here with someone."

I throw up all over him.

I REFUSE TO look at Otis as he drives me home. My head is thrashing in pain, my skin is clammy and chilled, and I feel like a ton of soggy balls.

This is why you hydrate while you drink, you stupid, stupid girl. I uncap the bottle of water he'd graciously offered when I got into his truck. Damn James and his piss-poor chaperoning skills. I bet all of us girls are going to have a massive headache in the morning, that useless shit stick.

"Can I say something real quick?"

I don't respond to Otis's request, given the laughter quivering in his tone. I opt to glare at my reflection in the side mirror as I chastise myself. *Tipsy, my ass. You're just a stupid drunk slut, Greta. Goddamn you.*

"Two things, actually. I wanna say two things." When I don't respond, he places a hand on my thigh, and my body reacts accordingly. I shift in my seat, my head pounding while my pussy wishes for the same treatment.

"What?" I snap a little more aggressively than I intend. But I'm utterly humiliated, and had James not been so disgusted with the stench that clung to me, I would be driving home with him and regretting my actions while he went on to gloat and sing, "I told you so."

"First, I'm very fond of drunk Miriam."

"That makes one of us." I turn my head to face the road. Snatching the bottle that's clutched between my thighs, I down the last half of it and smack my lips together to rehydrate them.

"Don't be too hard on her. She's a hoot and a half."

"I wish she were only half a hoot," I mumble, glaring at his broken windshield wipers. He chuckles and squeezes my thigh. His palm burns the skin there.

If he's doing it to drive me crazy, there's no need. Feeling like shit or not, I'm about four thigh-and-knee rubs away from turning that sunset fantasy into a midnight reality.

"Second, I want to say that I'm really happy you threw up," he adds after a long pause.

That's one way to sober up. I cringe, disgust scrunching my face. "What?"

"Not like that, not like I have a kink. I do *not* have a vomit kink." He shifts in his seat and puts his hands at ten and two on the steering wheel. "I just mean that you've seen me throw up, and now, I've seen you throw up. We're even."

"That's a weird thing to be even on, but okay. I'm... glad?" Except I'm not. I'm actually a little perturbed, but mostly, I'm fucking bothered by the claim he made and has yet to clarify from right before I threw up. I've never been one to sit on my curiosity for long. "So... That girl you brought with you to Midnight K—"

"Is no one."

I worry my bottom lip and glare conspicuously at the red traffic light above. "You seemed awfully concerned about her reaction for her to be no one."

"Call me old-fashioned, but I find it discourteous to mount other people in front of dates."

"I wasn't going to mount you," I hiss, embarrassment causing my face and ears to flush. My memory is hazy at best over what's occurred in the last hour. I can only remember overarching feelings and thoughts.

"I'm going to pretend to believe you so you can save face."

"How the hell can I save face when you're admitting to lying?"

He smirks and winks. "Exactly."

The static coming from the radio fills the cabin of his truck, and his hand remains on the steering wheel for the duration of the drive. I'm struck by déjà vu as I recall that first night we met, hauling ass to my apartment, the radio playing some folksy bluegrass song. I'd moved to change it to another station, something more modern, but he blocked my advances and claimed he didn't like to have his stereo fiddled with. Whether it was because of how ancient his truck was and fearing it would break with even the slightest tinker or some other reason, I'm not sure.

But that feeling of familiarity is overshadowed by the thoughts of how badly I want this to be a regular thing.

I want to be in the passenger side of his car, listening to the soft harmony of banjos, fiddles, mandolins, and guitars as we make our way home to fuck like uninhibited jackrabbits and follow it up with a feast that could make hippopotamuses seem anorexic.

When we arrive outside my complex, neither of us moves, and I've yet to look directly at him. Instead, I stare at the navy color of his hoodie I'm wearing. I'd gotten vomit all over my top, and he'd chivalrously offered the spare clothes he'd planned to put on after Midnight Kiss, and even patched up my knee with the Band-Aid he found in his glove compartment. He'd been all too happy to have me wear his clothes—and watch me change into them, too—and the second I donned the oversized top, he'd groaned and mumbled, "Fuck. Maybe we should get jiggy with it."

I'd ignored him in favor of keeping that rush of nausea from making a second appearance.

Still not looking at him, I collect the excess of his long sleeve into my palm and bunch up the material. I work up the nerve to fulfill my drunken objective and profess what it is I want from him, so I can be done with all this.

Grappling with the fact that I want more from Otis than just a fling or two had been difficult. James and Elise had suffered through a lot as I came to terms with the notion of inviting someone—a fucking football quarterback, no less—into my life in a more intimate and regular capacity. Had it been anyone else, I don't think I would have been as enraged.

I wanted to spend time with a man whose dreams mirrored Julien's. And that's twisted, if not a little ironic.

He cracks. "Do you mind clarifying what you meant in the parking lot earlier about the whole nipples and boob thing?"

I'm forced to face him.

The streetlight illuminates him romantically, the shadows of the waning night dancing over his stony features, softening them. He appears vulnerable in a fierce, determined way, drumming his hands softly against the wheel. I want to reassure him and just let the words rush out of me without much thought. The monologue I had prepared earlier tonight—before I got drunk and performed *Mama Knows Best* on the karaoke mic—is completely forgotten though not lost, since I still have it written in my phone. It had been Elise's idea to be mushy-gushy, and I wasn't entirely gung-ho about it.

"You don't want anything serious. I don't do serious. But you also want us to be exclusive in this… sexual situation."

He tilts his head, an adorable furrow between his brows. "True."

I continue to list more facts. "We have good chemistry. We communicate well during sex. And you actually know how to choke me."

"Why do I feel like this is going to end with me getting a gold star and a pat on the head?"

I fight the urge to roll my eyes. Squaring my shoulder, I hold his gaze. "I like the way you fuck me so… We should, like, hook up regularly."

Otis's expression is blank. He regards me with a level stare, concentrating on my face. I feel small in his clothes, and that makes me angry because no one should ever make me feel anything less than strong and tall, parents notwithstanding. North African parents can shrink their kids with just a blink.

But more than that, I'm angry that I have an expectation, that a flutter of hope courses through my nerves, making every breath I take sting.

I'm foolish—fucking stupid—for doing this drunk. Except I'm not really drunk anymore, so I'm just dumb for doing this period. I should have moved on and forgotten everything as usual.

I should forget about his stupid smile and the way he touches me and makes me see God with every orgasm he draws out of me. I should forget about the way he cooks and bakes and how he's so good at playing *Mario Kart*—an activity we partook in after he made post-coital cookies. I should forget about those pointless conversations we had that first night, the ones that made my abdomen hurt with how much laughter we'd shared, or the way it's easy to slip into discussing a controversial topic as if we already know each other's backstories.

I should forget him and just—

"What are the rules?"

"Rules?" *Was I not clear enough?*

Otis faces me more. "Yeah, like what can we do together?"

Someone is a bit slow. "Sex. No love. No dating. No relationship. Just sex. And if you don't think you can't handle that, then tell me now."

He rolls his eyes and shakes his head, letting out a chuckled breath. "Well, no shit, Sherlock. What I meant was, like, the parameters. Like… What about sleepovers? Do we stay over at each other's place if it's late?"

I make a face. "No. Too relationship-y."

"Friends sleep over all the time, but alright, whatever. What about meals?"

I consider this stipulation. I do love food. "Homemade or takeout?"

"Either."

"I'll never say no to takeout," I finally reply. But not homemade. His homemade food is one of the things that got me here in the first place.

He looks away and drums his fingers against the steering wheel again. I'm pretty sure he's taking his sweet-ass time to respond to exact some retribution against me.

I'm about to demand he gives me an answer when he stops and looks back at me. There's a smile on his lips, and my heart soars.

"Alright. Let's do it. But not tonight. I gotta get some shut eye so I'm not dead on the bus ride to Saturday's game in Louisiana."

My reaction is immediate and a little desperate. When I'm lying in bed tonight, I'm sure I'll kick myself for flinging myself at him and mashing our lips together.

It's a hard, closed-mouth kiss that lasts just a few seconds and is poignantly sweet and so satisfying, so unlike all the other kisses I've had during our time apart. And just as I'm about to deepen it, he pulls away.

Brushing a stray strand of hair away from my face, he presses a gentle peck on my nose. "I know you're happy that you're about to get some on the regular. I know. Trust me, I'm over the fucking moon, too."

I move away, my intuition telling me a *but* is about to follow.

I'm right.

"But G, you reek, like, so bad. And if we want to keep the score even, you've got to get away from me, cause I'm starting to feel a little sick."

rutherFORDY
Thu, Sep 22 5:32 AM

mornin mimi

Thu, Sep 22 8:48 AM

> dont mfken mornin me u crusty looking old man

> where did all my bra go?

idk what ure talking about :)

> my bras smartass

> where tf did they go?

how would i know

im not the bra fairy

> hmm idk

> maybe bc u told me u were gonna burn all of them after you struggled to take it off me a second time

never said that

don't know what ure talking about

maybe u should see someone since u keep making shit up in ur head

wait

hold up

hold up

hOLD uP

baby girl CHILL

FINE URE NOT BABY GIRL SO STOP THROWING ROCKS AT MY WINDOW

can u plz calm down

KNOCK ALL U WANT

IM NOT GIVING THEM UP

ULL NEVER FIND THEM

FREE THE NIPPLE!!!!!!!!!!!!!!!!!!!!

OTIS

IN WHICH LINK GETS A WOODY

IT'S THE NIGHT before Halloween and I am dressed as Link from *The Legend of Zelda*, while Herik, my counterpart, is roleplaying as Tingle. And I'm not going to lie, our getup is fresh as fuck.

"We look fuckin' good," the lineman hollers, flexing in his costume. It's pretty much a fat suit, but he's confident and working it just right. He attempts seductive faces and silly poses in the mirror, while I scroll through my camera roll and deliberate about which of the many mirror pictures I've taken I'll post to my socials tonight. I glance up and grin at his antics.

"We're definitely going to win that couples' costume contest."

He flexes again and cackles victoriously. "No shit. We look perfect together."

Rodney let me borrow his certified *Game of Thrones* Night's Watch sword, which makes my entire ensemble, though a little inauthentic in replication, look all the more legitimate and fucking baller. I'm just about to echo Herik's sentiments when there's a knock.

Quinn stands at the doorway. His gaze is critical as he assesses us. Mitchum, his boyfriend and the starring center for our school's hockey team, appears behind him a moment later, peeking his head over Quinn's. He too regards us with an impressed nod. "Lookin' good, boys," Mitch says.

Quinn salutes. "Very realistic and nostalgic, don't you think, Mickey?" he muses to his man, his head resting on his shoulder. The tall hockey player nods and wraps a reassuring arm around his boyfriend's waist. The shorter man's lips twitch in a frown. Attuned to his competitive boyfriend, the friendly giant is quick to reassure him.

"True, but don't let that worry you, babe. They don't look half as good as us." Mitch pecks Quinn's cheek, and Riverside's running back smiles confidently at the remark, reaching behind to rub the back of Mitch's neck.

The moment is cozy and cute, especially considering that Mitchum put four people in the hospital last year but is the softest guy alive and that Quinn has the temperament of a fucking bazooka but looks as intimidating as Thumper. They're dressed ironically as Toad and Wario.

I don't argue, confident in my efforts, but Herik does. "That definitely ain't true. There ain't nobody cuter than me and my boy."

There's no fighting the shit-eating grin that spreads over my face. It's me. I'm his boy.

Without warning, Herik grabs my shoulder and effortlessly spins me so that my backside is pressed to his front, then he wraps his arms around me. Herik is a fucking hottie, and my heart actually skips a beat. I'm a little frazzled by the suddenness, but I get over it quickly to play my part in this little charade. We pose before the couple like we're taking a vintage prom picture, our cheeks pressed together. Later, I'll bitch at my best friend for not shaving his stubble today, the short hairs irritating my skin.

Quinn and Mitchum scoff and mimic our stance, going as far as to kiss each other, one-upping us. I tilt my head back, looking up at Herik expectantly, lips puckered and ready for a smooch. We've kissed before—an experiment on his front, an indulgence on mine—so this wouldn't be new, but he yields, giving the actual couple their victory, and pushes me away.

"Nuh-uh. I'm not cheating on a girlfriend again," Herik huffs, shaking his head in dismay. He faces the gloating pair and wags a finger. "And you guys, you might have that whole we're-hot-and-gay shit going for you, but everyone knows me and Frosted Oats"—he wraps an arm around my shoulder and brings me toward him, patting my chest reassuringly—"are the cutest duo alive, and ain't nobody taking that away from us. Coach, Princeton, and Duger know it. The school newspaper knows it. Hell, even Otis's grandpa acknowledged it, and that old man was pretty fuckin' homophobic."

"Gotta love the conservative deep South," I say, shaking my head mournfully.

Pawpaw had always called me and Herik lover boys, but not kindly. It was more of a mock—he fervently disapproved of how attached we were to each other. Though I'm sexually attracted to men, my attachment to Andres Herik is entirely emotional, birthed from the death of my father and the hospitalization of his at the same time for lung cancer.

Ma had always encouraged me to tell Pawpaw about my sexuality before he passed away, insisting he would love me regardless, but I knew the man. I knew that he wouldn't understand bisexuality, or how I didn't mind who I was with as long as it made me feel good.

He might have still loved me as his grandson if I'd told him, but he never would have accepted me, Otis, the person, and like a coward, I kept it a secret until the very end. If I had told him, things would have changed, he would have rescinded the support I relied on him for, and I couldn't have lived with that. Hell, when he would miss my football games because of doctor's appointments, I could feel my morale crumble on the field, my performance taking a hit at times.

I loved the man with all my heart, and after he passed away at the end of my sophomore year, I could hardly bear it. There are still times when I miss him physically, my entire body hurting, but that doesn't change the fact that he was flawed. Or that I was completely relieved that I didn't have to hide it from him when I started dating Ekon during that summer between junior and senior year at the Prolific National Quarterback Camp.

A full-blown argument breaks out between Herik and Quinn over what "cutest duo" means. I pad across my room to my nightstand and aim a quick prayer to the celestials before grabbing my phone and tapping the screen, my pulse clamoring in my ears as I scroll through my notifications. When I see what I want, I swallow the victorious "fuck yes" that rises in my throat and instead casually tap on the message.

greta
Today 7:01 PM

> whats up mamacita

whats good papi chulo

> you going to the halloween bash on bueller?

isn't halloween tomorrow

> yup but your dad told us we can't go out tomorrow or he'll "whoop our asses six ways to sunday"

sucks to suck lol
loser

> wateva tipsy
> so are you going or wat

why? wanna fuck there?
never done cosplay sex but im down to get boned by link

> you gonna dress like princess zelda then?

do i look like a virgin?
besides i don't want ur princess self to feel threatened

> youre so sweet im not even gonna need a treat tonite

That had been where our messages left off, and as I read her response, the jittery hope I'd felt earlier dissipates and is replaced by quiet disappointment.

greta
Today 8:36 PM

then ill have to give you a
trick later to really show you
what halloweens about

but nah im not going

james and his roommates
are hosting a party

and im obligated to go
apparently

fyi elise is going to your
shindig

hf tho

Fuck. I stare at the gray bubbles that hold her response and attempt to rein in my compulsion to grab my pocketknife and scratch out James's name.

I debate how to reply, even going so far as to consider leaving her on read. By the time Herik and Quinn are done fighting, I've yet to come to a decision.

I reply to Greta's messages once we're on our way to the party. Rodney picked the lowest card in the deck and is our designated driver tonight. I already know I'll end up driving us back, given my distaste for drinking. All my roommates dump the responsibility on me.

For a while, I struggle to not be petty about my text, adding and removing the period at the end of my sentence at least four times. In the end, I send it sans punctuation.

greta
Today 9:29 PM

u too

ELISE IS ACTUALLY really cool.

She arrived at our party dressed like an angel, and not even a slutty one, which contributed to my preconceived notions until I spoke to her. I'd thought that because she wanted to save herself for marriage, she would be a boring, stuck-up prude, but she's not.

In fact, she's fun and flirty and even knows how to entertain when a flock of people swarm around us. So I'm not that surprised when she tells me she's the social chair of her sorority.

Five minutes with her and I kind of get how Herik fell so hard. There's something about her that's just magnetic—she's got an innocent, sweet disposition that hides a more salacious, cunning edge. The duality is beyond intriguing, and the longer I'm in her presence and learn more about her, the more fascinated I become.

If Elise is best friends with Greta, does that mean they're similar? Not in their personalities—Greta is much more straightforward and detached than Elise—but in their mannerisms. Deep inside, is Greta just as considerate and in tune with the people around her? Rather than being playfully provocative, can she appeal to others in that heartwarming manner that Elise does, if she wants to?

I want to believe that's the case. It's kind of stupid how badly I want to see Greta as more than just a sexual object. Even though that's what we've agreed on—that's all I have time for—I just have a feeling that beneath the surface, she's amazing in her own, individual way, and I just... I want to see it. Even if I don't get to experience it, I want at the very least to witness it from afar.

The party is in full force when Elise has the terrible idea of dancing in one of the overpacked rooms. The drink she has in her hand is like an accessory I've yet to see her without. Despite being wasted, she really knows how to boogie without spilling any liquid, the movement of her body replicating the fluidity of her drink.

"Were you also a cheerleader?" I holler over the music. Herik is in one of the upstairs bedrooms, playing *Smash*. I was knocked out of the impromptu tournament during the second round, and Elise during the fourth, but our counterpart is going strong and currently sitting in on the semifinals. We would have stayed and cheered for him if it wasn't so crowded.

"Also?" she replies, her lip curled in confusion. Before I clarify, she giggles, shaking her head. "Oh! Like Tata. No, I wasn't. I was a Merry Miss dancer. She and I couldn't stand each other in high school. We only became friends when I started seeing her brother."

My eyebrows shoot up. "Greta has a brother?"

Her movements slow as she takes a sip of her drink. The way she speaks is candid, and had I not known she were so drunk, I'd have deemed it hostile. "Yeah. Julien. But don't mention him to her. He's..." She swipes her thumb over her neck and rolls her head to the side, her tongue poking out.

It's hard for me not to react, to behave casually about what she's just said, and continue to dance and laugh and smile along with her, forcing a perception of joy as the drunkard in front of me has the time of her life. Despite the overwhelming urge to interrogate Elise even further, to inquire about why or how he died, I swallow my inquiries out of fear that if Greta ever found out I knew this personal fact, she would end our arrangement. And next week, I'm supposed to fuck her tits, so there's no way I'm going to mess up what we have now.

I force myself into a state of distraction. It's a special skill I've acquired, a tactic I learned at one of my football camps to clear my mind and focus on one specific thing.

With my body damp and my ears ringing, I concentrate on how badly I don't want to be here. I'd much rather be at home, re-watching *The Witcher*. I wish the costume contest would just happen already so I could use up the last of my savings to take an Uber home and crash, trusting Mitchum, a fellow alcohol hater, to drive the crew home.

After dancing for what seems like an hour, though it was only ten minutes, Elise suggests we take a break and head back up to Herik. I tell her I need some fresh air and that I'll see them in a bit. It's still loud outside, and there're a lot of people, some of whom try to talk to me about my thoughts on our upcoming game, but I keep my replies curt, pushing through the throng with a callousness that would put our football team's marketing manager on edge. I'm sure Linda is sick of calling me into her office for a "chat."

When I'm alone, I get an urge to do something stupid. I haven't even drank, yet my brain operates at a weird frequency, as though its inhibitions have been lowered. I call her, because even if I was able to distract myself before, about her brother, I could never entirely get Greta out of my head.

Maybe I'm just an addict who needs a fix. I refuse to attribute any more value than that. I'm hooked on sex with Greta. That's all. Her unusual takes on toes and fingers and stupidly off-key laughs aren't at all what comes to mind when I think of her. At least, not entirely.

"Hello?" Greta yells when she answers. The background is loud, filled with roars of laughter and incoherent hollers.

"Sounds like someone is having fun," I drawl.

"I can't—hold up. I can't hear you. Give me—" The noises become muffled and die out entirely after a few seconds. She speaks breathlessly, her voice clearer. "Sorry. What did you say?"

"Sure sounds like someone is having fun." I lift my knee and rub it subconsciously, doing my best to not scowl. "Clearly this party wasn't just an obligation."

"Who's to say obligations can't be fun?"

If I close my eyes, I can just imagine the way her lips curl into a smile. Better yet, I can see her lips wrapped around my dick, peering at me with wide, watery eyes as she sucks me off in the library bathroom while I try to stay quiet. That was last week, and the last time we hooked up, since both of our schedules are busy.

There's a delay in my response as I revisit this moment, my mouth watering as it remembers the flavor of her on my mouth, too. A chill runs down my spine and straight to my dick. *Shit. This is not the outfit to get a woody in.* "Everyone. Everyone says that. An obligation is literally defined as a duty or commitment."

Greta clicks her tongue. "It just so happens that as of two minutes ago, I was deeply committing myself to having a good time by dancing my ass off. I'm sore all over."

My next words come out without much thought. They slip out like a passing comment, one that's meant to simply be heard but not dissected. "Not with too many guys, I hope."

"Define 'too many,' Merriam Webster."

"More than or equal to one."

She regards my words with a disapproving tut. "That sounds a little possessive, don't ya think, fuck buddy? You jealous or what?"

The use of our label irks me for some reason. "I was just dicking around." I kick the mound of dirt beneath me a little more aggressively than I should. "I don't care who you dance with."

"I think you do," she coos. "I think you wish you were the only one that could dance with me."

"You sure you're not sore from jumping to all those conclusions? Cause you sure have an active imagination." My mind runs with the image she's put in my head. A hand around her waist, her body grinding against mine. That would be splendid right now.

"You should know how active my imagination is. Didn't you get my pictures yesterday?" she asks in a low whisper.

The noisiness of my surroundings prevents me from hearing her clearly, but I catch enough to draw a reasonable conclusion. My heart stammers out of beat. *Are we about to have phone sex?* I mean, I'll do it, right here and now. But I gotta admit, I'm not too fond of doing it in this costume. It seems a little blasphemous.

"I got a picture. Singular, not plural," I mumble, mimicking the sultry timbre of her tone. I walk farther away from the house. A random person tries to catch my attention, but I ignore and bulldoze past them.

"The rest must not have sent. What a shame." She snorts a little at the end, giving way to the bullshit in her explanation. "Do you want to know what they were?" She takes my silence as a yes. Smart girl. "Remember that video you recorded of me at your place? The doggie one."

It's my favorite. With one hand, I had locked her wrists behind her back, the other preoccupied with filming. The sounds, the angles, the imagery… My mouth goes dry, and I respond with a cracked, "Yes."

"I was watching it and playing with myself," she confesses, just as breathy.

My face is scorching to the touch. "And where was I?"

"Busy chilling with the boys and watching films with the D-line."

I know exactly what day she's talking about, and I curse myself for putting my football career before her. "And how did you take care of yourself while I was busy?" My breathing has become uneven.

"With my favorite dildo." I know the one. We've used it on me. "And the entire time, I was wishing it was your big, gorgeous cock inside me instead, fucking me the way you did in that video." She moans softly, her breaths wet and heavy. "You know how much I love it when you're rough with me, and especially when you come inside me." There's a pause and a whimper.

I'm just about ready to die, my ears on fire, my nose runny.

"You've seen the video I'm talking about, right? Seen how much of a whore you turn me into when you fuck me."

I run my hand through my hair and tug at the ends, fearing I might go insane. Since recording it, I've only had the opportunity to luxuriate in our porno skills once, and I can recall the amateur footage hazily at best. I hate myself for not putting it on repeat. "Jesus, G. You're such a fucking tease."

"And what are you going to do about it? Punish me?" Her breath hitches, and I freeze in my step as my mind sifts through different scenarios that might have caused her to let out such a familiar, whiny moan. She speaks again, and I swear she's pressing her lips into the receiver, gifting me with the sound of her every gasp. "I'd love if you did that again. But this time, make sure you spank me harder, okay? That way, I can feel how good it hurts weeks later."

God, you really were looking out for me when you put her in my life, weren't you? But then I look around, and that gratitude disappears. I actually have to bite my tongue to stop from screaming in frustration. Moving the phone away from my face, I swear silently into the air as I double over to try and calm down my growing erection. I'll have to fucking hike half a mile to get even a modicum of privacy, and that's just not possible, which means this—whatever filthy phone sex she wants to engage in—isn't possible.

When I finally regain control of myself, I clear my throat. "Sorry about that, I had to—"

"Touch yourself too?"

Too? Too? I'm about to fucking lose it. I'm pretty sure this is what insanity feels like.

"You're killing me, babe." Placing a shaky hand on my forehead, I attempt to stay composed. "But I can't do anything right now. There are too many people around."

Immediately, her tone and volume shift. She makes a noise of disapproval. "Damn. That sucks, huh? No sex in person or over the phone. What'd'ya think the universe is trying to tell us?"

"To persevere, because waiting makes everything better." At least, that's what I've been telling myself every time our plans fall through. Since the start of our arrangement, we've fucked nearly every day, except for part of last week and this week, my busy schedule all the more hectic, and hers less accommodating than usual.

"I've told you already. I don't care for patience."

I shake my head and don't respond. And as I try to recall what she looks like, to conjure up an image that isn't her naked and convulsing in ecstasy, a pang of longing hits me. I sigh, disheartened, and mumble, "Is it too sappy to say I miss you?"

"Me, or the kitty?"

"I definitely miss Raven, too."

She busts out laughing.

The sound is so nice that I can't help but smile in return. The urge to hear it again fills me. "That's not—God, sometimes I just want to boink you on the head."

"Why boink me on the head when you can just boink me?"

"I'm trying, dude. But apparently, I have to play *Tetris* with your calendar to get some."

Relief washes through me. It's nice to know we're equally addicted to each other—that I'm not the only one going crazy here. "Right back atchya, *dude*."

"I'm much more flexible than you." There's a pause followed by a light chuckle. "Remember?"

One time, she'd actually done the splits on top of me, my hands constrained to the headboard, bouncing her ass to ride me all the while, one hand around my neck, the other circling her clit. Another time, she'd placed her legs behind her head in a harmless demonstration of her skills, but that had inevitably turned sexual. "I do. I remember very well, and I have to say, I'm quite fond of that skill."

Greta says something, and I'm trying to pay attention when the sound of my name resonates in the air. It's being called over and over again, booming, urgent, angry. It's Herik.

I tune in midway through to catch the tail end of her exclamation, "—and next time, I can bend down and touch my toes while you—"

I'll kill Andres. "Shit, I gotta get off the phone."

"Oh." There's a hitch of disappointment in the exhale. Or maybe I'm hoping there is. "Okay? Well before you do, I just want to say thanks."

I hasten my strides. "For what? For calling?"

"No. For that game. You were the one who sent me the *Settlers of Catan* game thingy, right? The package was dropped off right before I left my apartment."

"Oh, yeah. It's no big deal. You've never played it, and I really think you should. It's great."

"Great as it might be, it can't be better than sex."

I'm panting hard as my pace turns into a light sprint. Herik is waving at me like a madman, which tells me the costume contest has already started. If I'm the reason we miss it, he'll kill me. "Debatable. Just wait 'til you play. You'll see." Then, I'm in front of my best friend, and he looks like he's going to sucker-punch me in the face if I don't get off the phone. In a panicked rush, I slur, "Okay, gotta go. Bye."

"Bye," she hums. It's a wonderful sound. I stare at my phone after hanging up and smile slowly. It's a little sappy, my reaction, but definitely warranted. Then, Herik grabs me by my prosthetic elf-ear and drags me into the house.

What a fucking ass.

AUTUMN IS HERE, and I can't breathe. One moment, I'm shouting along as Jenner whoops Benjamin Crown's ass at beer pong—the basketball player might know how to shoot threes, but he couldn't ping a pong to save his life—and in the next, my head turns slightly and I see her, and it's like the entire room is stripped of oxygen.

I'm fucking stunned, not understanding why she would be here. But the shock wears off quickly, replaced by rumbling irritation.

I try to evade her, but it doesn't work. Right as I'm about to escape out the door, she finds me. She places a gentle hand on my forearm, and I jump out of my skin. The beat of the music is loud, and still, I hear her whisper my name. Not *my* name but the name she uses for me. She looks at me with those eyes—those big, perceptive eyes that always flashed pity and sadness rather than outrage or indignation any time I lashed out at her—and I swallow the bile that rises up my throat.

I hated those eyes, and how understanding and sympathetic she'd been. I'd felt caged in because of that compassion. I feel caged in right now.

Herik ends up saving me. He happens to see us, notices the way I've frozen, and beelines our way. He barely even acknowledges Autumn before making an excuse for me to leave; something about Quinn crying in the car because he got into a fight with Mitchum. I don't ask questions. I just bolt.

When I get into the car, I locate Quinn, except he's not crying. He's actually moaning very loudly as he gets head from Mitchum in the back seat of Rodney's car. They jerk apart when I aggressively slam the car door behind me.

"You good, dude?" Mitch coughs. He wipes his lips and leans over the center console as Quinn frantically shoves himself back into his pants.

I grunt and turn on the ignition. When Quinn makes a noise of protest, I snap, my temples throbbing and muscles tense. "Shut the fuck up. I'm not leaving. I'm just going to the gas station to get some cigarettes." I turn to glare at my teammate, who appears both worried and defiant. "Snitch on me, and I'll make your life fucking hell during practice, Francis."

That night, I smoke half a pack and hate myself the entire time.

greta

wanna catan?

now?
give me a bit to find more players

lemme rephrase
wanna fuck?
so much for using code

when did we decide to use catan as
a code word for fucking???
i would NEVER defile the game like
that

well u did after i pegged u the other
night

oh
tbh i dont remember shit after i
came
was probably fucked out
anywayyyyyy ill be at ur place in 30
instead of settling in catan ill settle
in u

youre so lucky youre hot

bring lube

Wed, Nov 8 12:19 PM

tonight?
cant
boo :(

Wed, Nov 8 4:37 PM

im sorry
its fine
is it really tho?
cuz i feel like ure saying its fine
when really its not fine and ure
actually super mad

what do u want me to say?
do u want me to stroke ur ego?

yes
or u could stroke something else ;)

hard pass one minute man

that was just hurtful
:(

:(all u want
idc
just make sure you beat your meat
before you come over tonight
i need you lasting for what i have
planned

damn ure so romantic

you just wait til i hand cuff you
ill be romancing the shit out of you
then

dont make promises you cant keep

GRETA

THINGS WE SHOULDN'T SAY

OTIS WON'T STOP staring at me. We're standing in an elementary school playground, surrounded by children, and this giant, yoked-up man refuses to lower his gaze, his eyes obviously carving out my naked form from memory.

And for a while, I indulge him, reciprocating the look as I recall the dirty things we did to each other yesterday—dirty, pleasurable things that rendered both of us still in exhaustion and awe.

It's a week after Halloween, and it's been a while since Otis and I have gotten together, what with the football team working extra hard to prepare for Game Nine against the Pit Bulls, one of the few teams in Riverside's conference that has comparable star power. Last night, Otis texted me a little before midnight, stating he couldn't sleep because he was stressed, and needed a nice rendezvous to get his mind off the upcoming game.

Lucky for him, I was awake, re-watching Disney movies with Elise since she'd been sad her very important father had canceled their plans to see each other this weekend for the umpteenth time this year. It boggles her mind that she sees her mother, who resides in Australia, more than her father. It hurts her too. She'd been nice about me abandoning her, opting to stay at my place while I left to get railed by the quarterback.

As I stand here in the present and stare into his eyes, all I can see are all the things we did at his place.

The touches and kisses. The fucking and moaning. The name calling and praises.

I'm thinking of all this, my ears growing hot and my heart stuttering out of rhythm, until I'm snapped back to reality by Clementine, who rushes over to remind me it's time for her after-lunch snack. She throws a fit when I don't comply right away, and I require her to ask me in full rather than just hold her hand out and say "gimme." She's not having a good talking day, the pitch of her voice is so low that I have to bend down to hear her, but she gets through it. I offer her a compliment when she's successful, which would usually make her smile, but she scowls and snatches the bag of animal crackers with a haughty huff before scampering over to where the rest of the students stand.

That girl has got some attitude, and though I find it cute when she directs it to Mr. Marbury, I'm starting to see why she gets put into timeout a lot.

After she leaves, I make it a point to ignore Otis. There's a storm brewing in those ocean eyes, and I would be lying if I said I didn't want to be shipwrecked and laid to waste in the carnage it would reap.

However, there's a concept I'm quite fond of, one I put into practice with my day-to-day life. It's called "time and place." It is a novel notion which dictates that for a specific situation to unfold in perfect totality, there has to exist an intersection in the universe's continuum where time and place intertwine at just the right moment.

An elementary school with about thirty or so second graders separating us is not the right place. Now, with my father standing not two feet away from Otis, facing my direction as he enthusiastically puts on an upbeat show for the kids about the wonders of football, is not the right time.

Despite this, scandalous passion remains in his eyes, and it's too obvious.

"He looks like he wants to eat you," Elise observes softly. She's standing directly to my left, Mr. Marbury to my right. She doesn't normally assist at our school, doing most of her education preparation at second chance schools, but we'd needed extra help today with the makeshift career fair, and Elise had been nice enough to offer.

I glance over at my supervising teacher and clear my throat dramatically, turning to my best friend in order to breathe inconspicuously. "He can do that later. Not now."

"Later might just turn into now," Elise snickers.

I make a noise of reproach.

The sound alerts Mr. Marbury, and he snaps at us. "Ms. Sahnoun, Ms. Pillar, you're being rude. Be quiet while Coach Sahnoun presents."

I mumble a feeble apology, embarrassed by the brusque reprimand. I grant all my attention to my dad, doing my best to appear engaged. He stands just twenty yards ahead of me, all the children in awe of his animated personality and hilariously relatable quips as he explains his job as a football coach.

He's always been charming and funny, exceptionally good with kids that weren't his responsibility. But that's how most parents are, I guess.

My dad is the last presenter for my class before school is out of session. He's a great public speaker, retaining most of the students' focus effortlessly. Dad's presence today was last-minute. Isla Xiao's surgeon mother had called to inform Mr. Marbury and me that she couldn't make it to the time slot she'd signed up for due to a work emergency.

Lucky for my teacher, my mother had my father wrapped around her perfectly manicured finger. I made one call to her, and the all-powerful matriarch had dispatched my dad within the hour. I'm sure that had I asked him personally, he only would have agreed to come if I bribed him with my efforts to do better academically.

Ever over the top with his finesse, he brought goodies for the little rugrats—footballs, sweatbands, jerseys, whistles, and other assorted hullabaloos—and was accompanied by two players for a demonstration, just so it could be more fun. I hadn't known they would be making an appearance until they sauntered into the classroom during lunch, asking where they should set their boxes of supplies. Good thing I'd taken theater classes in high school, because had I not, I would have appeared shocked to see Otis standing in front of me, wearing a confident, easy grin.

That sniveling little shit didn't even tell me he was coming, and we'd been texting five minutes before he showed up. Granted, they were dirty messages, with the last one I sent being IF YOU BRING SOME DUCT TAPE, I PROMISE TO USE IT ON YOU, and him replying with WHAT COLOR?. But still, sending a quick BTW, I'LL BE SEEING YOU SOON wouldn't have killed him.

By the time my dad is done talking about the different types of positions on a team and the role he plays in shaping—I call it breaking—his players, ensuring they perform their roles successfully, he requests some volunteers to assist Otis Morgan and Jefferson Rodney in demonstrating a few of the most common plays in the sport.

Carter Rodriguez, one of the four students I'm responsible for, breaks away from the crowd of kids and approaches me, doing his pee-pee dance.

Oh no. This isn't going to be good. Carter's incontinence is infamous, not just at Hillcroft but at his previous elementary school, too. The second I realize what's to come, I'm making my way toward him.

There are firm rules set in place regarding the children I assist. Given their speech impediments, we have to allow them as many opportunities to talk throughout the day as possible. They aren't the type to seek out conversation and speak voluntarily, so putting them in a situation where they're required to is really important for practice and building their confidence. Of course, this can be difficult, since there's always a line to toe between pushing them positively and causing them severe discomfort. Even if I'm aware of what one of them wants, I have to wait for them to ask and can't offer any assistance unless they're really struggling to get the words out.

But given the potty emergency, I disregard the rule, concentrating more on keeping Carter dry and happy. "Do you think you can make it to the bathroom?"

He looks at me with doubt. Shit. Whether or not he thinks he can, this kid better try, because I'm not trying to handle anyone's piss. We make a quick break for it.

Thankfully, the cafeteria workers failed to lock the doors after lunch. We take a shortcut through there and make it to the bathroom just in time.

I wait outside while he does his business. Three minutes later, there's still no Carter. Concerned, I enter apprehensively to find him posing in front of the mirror. He pretends to hurl an imaginary football in the air, loosely mimicking the Hail Mary Otis demonstrated earlier. Carter even pats his pretend helmet twice after the invisible ball leaves his hands, something the Heisman-winning quarterback does after every successful play.

It's beyond adorable. Heartwarming, actually. His antics melt away some of the hatred I naturally harbor for kids. I mean, what twentysomething who's not Elise loves children?

I smile fondly at the kid. "Carter?"

He freezes at the unexpected calling of his name.

I keep my tone light and kind. "What are you doing?"

He looks at me nervously. "Sorry, Ms. Sahnoun," he replies. Sorry is easy for him to say. He's quite familiar with it and frequently apologizes for taking too long to say something, for not saying something, for various reasons I don't fully understand but that make it obvious that too many people have treated him like an inconvenience and forced the word out of him to the point that his elocution is always perfect.

My last name, however, has always been a struggle for him. It usually takes him an elongated attempt or two to wrench the surname out. When I started in late August, he'd avoid saying it altogether, opting to refer to me as plain ol' "Miss."

Time and patience I do not possess but have managed to extend is all it took to get him to this point, and I'm proud. "Don't apologize," I reply with an airy chuckle. "I was just asking cause it looked like you were launching that football straight into space. Were you trying to see if you could be like one of those football players?"

Carter blinks at me, his stance becoming smaller as he nods shyly, staring at the floor instead of me. I bring his attention back to my face and maintain eye contact as I murmur encouragingly, "You know, I think you're even better than that Mr. Morgan. But *shhh*"—I place a finger to my lip and dramatically look side to side—"don't tell him I said that, okay?"

"Really?" he squeaks, doubt bleeding in his tone. Carter has always been a dreamer, but he doubts himself. It's easy to do, given how most people around him speak for or over him.

I nod fervently, and when he beams at me, he's the epitome of joy. My heart soars. I almost stumble back from the force of his expression. It's been a while since I've seen such bright, uncorrupted happiness. It steals my breath.

"Of course. I'm the daughter of a coach, so I know these things. I saw the way your hand extended back so perfectly. If you had a real football in your hand, you would have sent that ball straight up to heaven. I swear."

Carter gets on the tip of his toes and does a little dance,

demonstrating my words by extending his arm far back like before then letting the imaginary football fly. I do the dance with him again before ushering him to wash his hands one more time for good measure.

Before we head back to the others, I turn to face him completely. "Since you had to go to the bathroom really bad, you weren't able to ask me for permission, but you need to ask me now, okay?" When he makes a face, I continue with authoritative resolve. "And we're not going back out to watch the fun football demonstration until you do."

He pouts before taking a deep breath. As per our guidelines, he meets my gaze, and I hold eye contact, showing him I'm alert and attentive. In a volume above a whisper but below a shout, he asserts, "Ms. Sahnoun, may I go to the restroom?"

"Yes, Carter, you may go to the restroom. Thank you for asking." With a nod from me, he's released from his obligation and strides out with a skip in his step.

I don't follow immediately. I let myself linger for a moment, my composure compromised. In my head, I'm replaying all the fake games my brother and I would play in our backyard when we were younger and listening back on all the conversations we had about our dreams—his was to play in the NFL, like our dad, and mine was to be a ballerina, like Mom. Those dreams never became a reality.

Swallowing the burn rising in the back of my throat, I close my eyes. I miss Julien right now, but the pain I feel from his absence is the good kind, the type of hurt that's accompanied by an affectionate smile.

I'M HAVING MY way with my pet for the night—no, not Raven. He's asleep, given his crazy day of eating through my TV and humidifier cords—when I hear a series of sharp knocks and bangs.

Otis is seated on the floor of my bedroom, his back against

my mattress, gagged and restrained, when this startling sound interrupts us. Alarmed, I tear my mouth off him and stare down the hall, disoriented.

I've been edging Otis, and after a tearful plea in which he threatened to use his safe word—"pineapples"—if I didn't give him permission to come soon, I'd promised that his release was imminent. His fulfillment is again interrupted by the aggressive knocks on my front door that grow louder and louder.

Still in a daze, I alternate between looking out my open room door and at Otis. By the seventh time I turn back and forth, I get whiplash.

"Who's that?" I whisper to him suspiciously, a sinister feeling stirring in my gut.

Otis looks at me with desperate, wide eyes and shrugs. The gag makes his every word unintelligible. I remove it quickly, but the insistent banging cuts through the air again, muting him.

Following the aggressive raps, a sickeningly familiar voice calls out, "Greta, open the door." Any and all lingering arousal that coursed through Otis and me is effectively sliced, diced, and sacrificed.

"Oh my God. *Oh my God*!" I shriek, hysterical but quiet. I bolt up and look for my robe, dread turning me dizzy. I think I'm about to faint. I rush out of the bedroom only to have Otis hiss my name in terror.

"What?" I snap, turning back to look at him. He looks scared and nauseous and in pain.

He holds out his tied wrists and jiggles his bound legs. "Hello? Aren't you forgetting something?"

Fuck, fuck, fuck. Why is my dad here? Since when has he ever visited me without obligation? Did Mom send him? Damn that woman.

And the timing! Mr. Paternal Blue Balls has to appear out of fucking nowhere and ruin the big finish I've been building up to.

The plans tonight had been to edge Otis, but that didn't mean the process hadn't been torturously fun for me, too.

"Greta," my dad calls again. "I know you're in there. Open up. It's *Baba*."

Exasperated, I stop trying to divest Otis of his restraints. That's when I hear a knob twist, followed by a metallic rattle. My soul actually leaves my body and levitates to look down on me. I can see the door from where I'm crouched, and I wait for it open—wait for doom to descend on me—only to find that it's been delayed.

That's when I remember that the ever safety-conscious Otis had twisted my deadbolt in place when he came in after lecturing me about keeping my door unlocked once again.

When this is over, I'm going to thank this guy so fucking hard, we'll both lose function in our legs.

"Hurry and get these off," Otis hisses, his voice ragged.

"There's no time." I look around my room, frantic for some sort of escape plan. Today is not the day to reveal the nature of my relationship with one of my dad's football players. Under normal circumstances, my dad probably wouldn't be pissed. Irritated and disgusted, yes, but not pissed. I'd disseminated every vestige of conservative proprieties he harbored in high school with my overtly promiscuous behavior. But given our current predicament—Otis with a cock ring, a tube of lube, and an array of toys scattered on the floor—blood will spill.

Still looking around my room, I catch a glimpse of the light that's on in my bathroom. The closet.

"Get up." I go to his side, wrap my arms under his armpits, and haul his heavy-as-fuck quarterback ass onto his feet. We move with a lot of struggle, my father's presence and persistent knocking only adding to the mania.

"What are we—"

I don't let Otis finish his sentence before I'm dragging him into my closet.

Realizing what I'm about to do, he gapes at me. "No way am I gonna—"

"Shhh." I take the gag that I'd tossed on the floor and stuff it into his mouth. The betrayal and horror in his eyes make me feel bad.

But only a little, because honestly, what's the alternative? Out him as the reason for my limps? I've already been lying to my parents about the cause, citing the gym as reason for my injuries, and the upside has been fewer comments about my weight.

Fewer, but not zero.

Otis makes a sound, his eyebrows knit together in resentment, but I push him farther in.

"Stay calm, okay? Just give me, like, five minutes to get rid of him." I shove him, and he falls flat on his ass. "Please. I won't be long, I promise. And then once I'm done, you can do whatever you want to me. Okay?"

He's hesitant at first but acquiesces after a few more pleas.

I occupy the next thirty seconds by frantically getting myself and the apartment ready, aggressively wiping at my mascara-smeared face and collecting the discarded clothes to toss them into the coat closet. When I finally go to unlock the front door, I'm sweating.

"Greta, what the hell were you doing?" My dad bristles, toeing off his shoes then pushing me aside to storm into my apartment like he owns the place. Which, to be fair, he technically does. His name is on the lease. He stops to stand in the middle of the living room and looks around suspiciously, sniffing the air. Hints of Otis's cologne linger—a scent I've grown accustomed to—and I think I might just die. "Do you have a boy in here?"

Play it off. I thank fuck for Otis being half-white and keeping his shoes on in the house. If he'd taken them off in the living room rather than my bedroom, we'd have been outed about now.

"On a school night?" I shake my head and do my best to behave normally, keeping my expression light rather than frenzied.

"Nuh-uh. I was just in"—*what takes over a minute to do?*—"the bathroom."

"Oh." He relaxes his face and shoulders. "Good. I mean, I know you're sexually active, but I don't want to *know* know, *tu vois ce que je veux dire?*"

I do know what he means, and that's why I'm tempted to ask him to leave, but that would be too suspicious.

"Of course not," I dismiss with a breezy and not at all forced laugh.

He nods.

"Where's Mom? She with you?"

"At a fancy function with her girlfriends, using up all my money with some charity. It's just you and me tonight. And Raven. Where is he? He usually comes to say hi to me at the door. I even brought him some food, too."

Too? That's when I register the bag of takeout in his hand. Fuck, this won't be quick at all.

My dad locates my actual pet on the window behind the couch. He leans over and makes kissy noises. The feline eats up the attention, tired ears flicking in joy.

"Let me change into something more comfortable real quick. You can set the table," I say before rushing to my room and slamming the door.

When I open the closet, Otis looks up at me expectantly, and I'm awash with overwhelming pity.

"I'm sorry, baby. My dad wants to have dinner with me." I reach over and grab a pair of pajamas. Changing as quickly as I can, I take out his gag, remove his cock ring, and remind him to be quiet, but he's so pissed by how this situation has unfolded that I don't think he'd talk even if he could.

Back in the living room, my dad has a plate of food ready for me. He criticizes me for my lack of clean dishes, inspecting the dishwasher to ensure that it works, since I've been blaming my frequent home visits on appliance issues. He should know better, though.

Dinner proceeds with little to no friction, a rarity for us. We mostly discuss movies and football, his reason for such a random visit remaining unexplained. I indulge him, entertaining his questions about my life—thank God he avoids the topic of grades and classwork. The verbal reaming I received last week was enough to last me a month.

Oddly enough, it's nice. So nice that at some point, I stop checking the clock and forget how much time has passed since he arrived.

Until he brings up Julien.

"You were so determined to kill him, I honestly thought you were a psychopath." Dad chuckles in mock horror. "I told your mom that I wanted to have you committed, especially after I saw the collection of severed teddy bear heads in the backyard."

"They were ugly bears. Besides, the only reason I hated Julien so much was that you guys gave him all the attention," I huff defiantly, finishing off the last of the gala apple he'd brought me before crossing my arms as I lean back in my seat.

"But now, all the attention is on you."

He doesn't mean it in the way it comes off. I know that. I know he means that he's here with me and only me—Otis being stowed away in my closet notwithstanding.

But his poor word choice has an unintended consequence. It serves to remind us that I am the *only* one who will ever receive my father's attention. There's no other child to share it with, and it makes all the jealousy I ever harbored against Julien, no matter how juvenile and innocent it had been, sickening.

"I actually wanted to talk to you about him," Dad says quietly. He picks up his crumbled napkin and wipes his mouth, staring at anything but me.

My heart pitter-patters violently in my chest. "What's up?" I chirp, doing my best to sound upbeat and not at all hostile and incredulous.

Still, he broaches the topic with excessive discretion. "I didn't realize you were working with children who have speech impediments," he says warily, as if testing the flavor of each word before pronouncing it.

My unease grows. "Really? I thought I told you." This is a bald-faced lie. I told Mom and assumed Mrs. Snitchy-Snitch would inform my father of my career decision. I'd only confided in her out of necessity, requiring her permission as a former CEO to put her down as a "professional" reference. She'd been encouraging and nice about it at the time, and has tried to bring up the topic on more than one occasion since then. I always shut it down, not wanting to speak on the matter or delve into my motivations.

"No, you didn't."

I wonder why. But I remain visibly unaffected, my response nonchalant. "It's not that big a deal. You already knew I wanted to be a teacher."

"Yes, but it's more than just that." He takes a sip of his drink before placing it down and continues breathily, as if in awe, "This means you're moving on."

What a funny concept: moving on. How does someone move on from an event that's so integral to their existence? "Uh, I guess." In so many words, I'm trying to make it clear just how much I don't want to have this conversation.

He doesn't get the memo. Or maybe he does, and he tosses it into the trash just because he can. Because he's Farid Sahnoun. "Can you *guess*, then, if you're willing to come to the game next weekend?" Dad beseeches more mockingly than gently. "It's important, and your mother would love to have you there." He purses his lips and sighs. "I would love to have you there."

Since he began his job as head coach of Riverside's football department, my father has never once requested I come to one of his games. The burden of demanding my presence is always shouldered by my mother and always done via text.

But here he is, asking me, as if it's his right and this is the momentous day I'll definitely say yes.

Joke's on him.

"I don't think so." I feel my face twist in obvious disdain. I'm on high alert, that sinking feeling in my gut pulling even tighter.

Keeping calm, Dad responds. Each word he speaks is obviously chosen with precision, the delivery deliberate. "So you're telling me you can work with children that remind you of Julien, but you can't come to one game? You can't watch your dad from the stands and cheer him on?" I remain unblinking, and his brown cheeks turn red. "I raised you. I took care of you when you were younger. I tolerate your immature behavior and consistent failures. Still, I love you, and I ask you for one thing. To come to a game. And you can't even do that? *C'est bizarre, non?*"

Had he yelled at me, I don't think I would have gotten so enraged.

It's funny, the way family can get under your skin. They do it better than any stranger or friend ever could. They latch on to one's nerves, their words making the blood boil.

He's always had this skill. Sadly, I've yet to develop a healthy coping mechanism to fight off my irritation. That's why, when I speak, it comes from a place of pure loathing. I want to share my hurt and anger with him for all the times he's been so cavalier about sharing his unsolicited thoughts and advice.

"It's not weird. Being around children who remind me of his life is different than being on a field, around a man who reminds me why he died."

There it is.

It isn't fair to place all the blame on my father, not when I share in it. It isn't fair, but it's how I feel, sadness and contempt weaving an entirely different tale for me now.

In this story fabricated by my pain, Julien is alive because he doesn't play football. He doesn't try to follow in my father's footsteps. He doesn't work himself to the bone to be good enough. He doesn't agonize over his "mediocrity," doesn't take the harsh words and constant barrage of criticism to heart, doesn't drown himself in narcotics to relieve himself of the internal agony and chase a moment of relief from the stress.

In this story, Julien is alive because my dad isn't my dad. My dad is just Farid Sahnoun, a Kabylia-American that didn't fall in love with football but instead worked hard in a different, less competitive career to provide for his family, loving them with compassion rather than toughness.

But that isn't real.

It's sudden, the way our fragile relationship crumbles. The strain of this moment disseminates before it truly begins. What I'd asserted barely scratches the surface of how I feel—years of bottled-up emotions released in one pointed accusation—but it must have been enough, because my dad already got up and left the apartment without another word, anger etched on his face, devastation watering his eyes.

Regret doesn't hit me right away. In fact, I preserve my indignant outrage while clearing the plates and stowing away the dishes, ignoring Raven, whose concern manifests in leg rubs and broken meows. All the while, I think of every bad thing my father has ever done to me, to Julien, and allow it to fuel the flames, to justify my cruelty.

It's not until I go to the bathroom that I remember Otis, and just like that, the topic is dropped from my mind.

Oh, fuck. Otis.

Flinging open the closet door, I look down at the man in question. *Shit.*

"Hey." I kneel in front of him.

There's malice in his eyes, and even when he's capable of

forming coherent phrases, he opts for silence.

I clear my throat and flash a guilty, lopsided smile. "How you doin'?"

He remains silent, using a death stare to communicate his feelings.

"So that took longer than I expected."

More silence.

"He came over for some father-daughter bonding." Which will probably never happen again, given how this attempt turned out.

Even more silence. But this time, the lines of his face soften.

"If it's possible, can you just forget about all of it?" I mean this in more than one way. The likelihood of him hearing what my dad and I said is low, but if there's a chance…

A look flashes in his eyes, and his lips twitch like he wants to say something.

"If you do, I'll give you whatever you want." It's a reward for the both of us.

It's this suggestion that breaks him. What a simple man.

"Grab the pink duct tape and start practicing the phrase, *"Spank me harder."* You're going to scream it a lot tonight."

REMINDERS
shit to do

- ○ make lesson plan for marbury
- ○ schedule meeting with academic advisor
- ○ finish degree plan for academic advisor
- ○ gift ideas for dad's bday
- ○ RSVP for lisey's sorority banquet
- ○ raven's grooming appointment
- ○ more econ homework :(

OTIS

AS FALL COMES TO A CLOSE

IT'S A SATURDAY morning, and rather than spend it in bed, perusing social media and selectively engaging with the pictures that cross my timeline, I'm on campus with Jenner, Brody, and Quinn.

We're going ham, studying last minute for our final round of midterms. We've already downed two energy drinks each and are jittery as fuck.

Ever the gracious teammate, Brody had offered us some of his prescription Adderall as we settled in, knowing damn well we'd be here for a while. Jenner accepted, but Quinn and I refused, afraid of being picked for one of Coach's random drug tests.

Normally, we wouldn't spend more time than needed on campus. We would study at our place, gathering in the kitchen or living room, our respective tutors coming in and out of the house to help last-minute.

That isn't an option today.

Rodney, a nutrition major, is using our place for a project, where he's the only guy in a ten-person group. I wouldn't be surprised if we walk in on an orgy when we get home tonight. There's also Mitchum's place, but he's out of town, which has made Quinn a sad boy over the last two days. Then there's Herik's, but when I texted him this morning, he denied me.

dr. dre-ik
Today 6:25 AM

stay the fuck away from my house

else is coming over

im serious otis

i kicked the boys out so you better not fucking show up or on god i'll ruin you

well shiiiiiit my guy

is she also gonna be coming over u

or just coming over to your place?

Today 7:56 AM

u mad?

don't be daddy

prayin u get the nut

He never gratified me with a response. I'll have to have a discussion with him later about leaving me on read. No one puts baby in a corner—or leaves baby on read.

Alas, with all other options inaccessible and most study-functioning cafés at capacity during this time of year, we ventured to Ginnik Library in search of silence and seclusion.

It's on the STEM side of campus. It's the quietest library, with a lot of traffic from students who care more about their grades than getting a picture of their favorite collegiate athlete. I come here every now and again for an extra layer of privacy.

But today, the study rooms are taken. Not at all surprising, considering how close we are to finals.

What is surprising is being on the seventh floor—the least populated level, due to its sub-freezing temperature and the fourteen flights of stairs required to get there—and finding it practically empty, only to have it flood with students not one hour later. They all stare at us, some even stopping by to drop sticky notes on our tables. I crumble most of mine and make a point to toss them in the trash. They stop appearing after the fifth alley-oop.

Dismissive of this attention we're receiving, our little quartet ignores everything and everyone in favor of absorbing as much knowledge as we possibly can to scour a C for the semester. Because C's, they get degrees, and anyone who says otherwise is lying.

While I'm staring diligently at my janky laptop screen, cross-referencing the formula I see there with the application of it on my paper and wondering where the fuck I went wrong and why my answer is incorrect, I feel a tap on my shoulder.

My face twists in annoyance. *Jesus fuck, I'm trying to study. Leave me the hell alone, you annoying shits.* Unadulterated spite rattles my bones, and I yank off my headphones, tugging painfully at my tragus in the process, and just before I turn my head, I hear an old nickname.

"Otty," she whispers.

Surprise overcomes me. Instincts kick in, and I scramble to stand. Everyone else simply gawks in bemused astonishment, knowing damn well I didn't call Autumn over here and that whatever is about to happen is going to be juicy. It's been a while since our team has had gossip.

"Autumn. What are you—"

"Someone took a picture of you guys and posted it with the location captioned." She glances over her shoulder at the people doing their best to appear busy despite the frequency with which their eyes lift to observe my group. For all the perks that come with going to a football-obsessed university, sometimes it really fucking sucks.

I make a face and narrow my eyes, looking past her to shoot a formidable scowl at the nosey creepers.

"Must be nice to have time to stalk even with finals around the corner," I reply dryly. My volume is well above what's appropriate for a quiet study floor, but that's intentional.

Autumn shakes her head with a rueful, slightly amused grimace on her face. "Would you like me to hand you a megaphone? I don't think you were loud enough," she chides sheepishly, playfully elbowing my ribs.

The air between us turns stuffy and charged. My back is turned to my teammates, but I can feel them staring.

I know what they're thinking: *Holy shit, isn't that the bitch who broke Otis's heart while he was recovering from a career-defining injury?*

But they don't know the truth. No one but Autumn and I knows the exact truth, and I am too ashamed of how I behaved to elaborate. They knew that we hadn't been good for each other, but they had excused the behavior due to my injury.

"I texted you," I croak when she doesn't fill the thick silence.

She stares at me, and I'm held captive by her gaze, imprisoned by the emotions brewing in them. Even if I want to look away, I can't.

Those eyes haunt me. They remind me of the way she used to look at me when I had an outburst, and my blood runs cold. The emptiness, the exhaustion, the hurt—they were always there, always directed at me, begging for an iota of affection after it all went to shit.

No matter how terrible she must have felt, Autumn never said anything. She only stared. At that point in my life, I used her silence to assuage my guilt.

Our relationship wasn't great, sure, but it wasn't *that* bad, right? She would have said something if it was unbearable, right? She would have left *me* instead, right?

In the end, she stayed put, and she remained silent. To the very end, it was all me.

"I know. I replied," comes her delayed response.

"Yeah, I saw. I was going to respond after midterms since

I'm"—I tilt my head toward the table that has all my shit scattered on it—"busy."

Coward. Coward. Coward.

"Oh. You're busy." Autumn looks somewhere between annoyed and disappointed. "Well, I was going to ask you if you wanted to get a cup of coffee, but if you're busy, then..." Her gaze darts awkwardly to the side.

I'm about to confirm her speculation with a hearty, "Fuck yeah, I am," when Quinn, the nosy, stupid son of a bitch, interjects, "Actually, we were all just about to take a break."

You fucking liar. Oh, I'm going to kill you. Murder you during practice. I'm going to work you until you pass out, you smarmy fuck.

"Why don't you guys just grab coffee for us instead? I know Otis was complaining about a headache earlier."

"I bet you're all about due for a caffeine fix." She points at the empty cans cluttering the table.

"Definitely. Here." He raises himself off his seat to grab his wallet and hands me three twenties. I only need one for the purchase. The other two are meant as a bribe. Those forty bucks wadded in my hand ask me not to kick his ass later.

It only infuriates me even more. I'm no cheap bitch. I'm worth at least fifty.

Watch your back, I mouth to him after writing down the guys' orders then grabbing my keys and phone. I fall into step with Autumn as we make our way to the coffee shop next door. Their coffee is absolute shit. They brew it at the same temperature hell boils, making it burnt, sour, and devoid of flavor. At least their teas aren't too bad.

I consider their menu, pondering intently what type of tea I'm going to order and whether I'm in the mood for a tasty pastry. Duger has me on a strict diet since my muscle mass has dropped according to my last weigh-in. Usually, it isn't a big deal what my weight and muscle density is since I'm not a lineman, but Duger takes being offensive coordinator seriously and micromanages every aspect of my life to ensure we both don't get reamed by Coach.

"You're quiet," Autumn comments when we've reached the third-floor landing.

My head snaps in the direction of her voice, aware of her again. All my efforts to remain quiet and unbothered vanish, and my heart lurches nervously. I'm sure my expression gives way to the looming trouble that hangs over me.

"Trying to conserve oxygen," I mumble. It's not entirely a lie. My abs are starting to burn a little, my hamstrings and glutes stinging from the strain.

"Good point." Autumn has never been the athletic type, always preferring a sedentary lifestyle with a book or a remote in her hand. She's slender and small, her frame fragile, but that's mostly from her poor eating habits.

Before my injury, I made it a point to text her to eat and drink water, concerned for her well-being. She used to reply with adorable pictures of her and the food or drink. I used to stare at those photos constantly, using them as a pick me up on the days Coach would ride us really hard. But not anymore. According to my phone, we never even existed.

As we continue to make our way down, she's huffing and puffing like the big bad wolf, and when she turns to make a comment or two, her breath wafts over me in vigorous pants, making me feel like that piggie in the straw house, about to be devoured by her whole.

Except, in our relationship, Autumn wasn't the wolf. I was.

When we're finally on flat ground, no longer tortured by the stairway, we both take a second to catch our breath. She doubles over with a hand on her thigh and the other clutching her stomach as if its contents are about to spill.

I can't help but regard her fondly before tapping her.

"Yeah?" She heaves.

I motion for her to straighten up, which she does. "Stand up when you need to breathe. It's better for oxygen consumption and helps circulation."

Rubbing the ridges of my belly, I suppress a groan. One might think that with my body looking the way it does, cut at every angle, strenuous activity wouldn't have me feeling like a freshly fucked grapefruit. But damn, do I hate stairs.

She nods, placing a hand on my shoulder to steady herself. The gesture causes me to react subconsciously. Immediately, I'm bending so she doesn't have to stand on her tiptoes.

And I look at her. Like, really look at her—who she is now, and not who I remember her to be. And just like that, I'm thrown back to the first time we met. Back to the first time my eyes fell on her as she ran after a departing bus headed to South Campus.

The moment is crisp in my mind. I see, hear, and smell everything in high definition as if I'm witnessing our first meeting all over again.

Vibrant, silky, red hair flies into her face, licking like flames around her head. Cherries spotted on her cheeks, the bloom of color gorgeous on her ivory skin. The gloom in her eyes darkens as she watches the bus accelerate down Loading Market Street before turning the corner and disappearing.

She bites her bottom lip and looks around in defeat. The smell of the warm, butter croissant in my hand has my mouth watering, eager for the first bite, but the sight of her makes it go dry. Mopeds and cars honk, exhaust pipes rattle, and the faint hint of carbon monoxide permeates the air around me.

I walk toward her subconsciously, my eyes transfixed on her. I have no idea what I'll do once I reach her, I just know I have to be in her presence.

Just before I reach her, though, she spins and bumps into me. I

*juggle my coffee and pastry but tingle with awareness, a giddy rush
of joy fluttering through me at the contact. It's a chance meeting
that would put Katia's favorite rom-coms to shame.*

*"Oh, shoot," she hisses, an apology shining in those expressive
green eyes of hers. "You almost dropped your croissant!"*

*Just like that, I want her in my life. I got out of my last
relationship only three weeks ago, but that doesn't matter. The best
way to get over someone is to get under someone else, and I swear
by that motto. Since the eighth grade, I've never remained single
for longer than two months.*

*Herik and Katia say it's unhealthy. I say it's nice to fall in love
a lot.*

When I'm pulled from my reminiscing, Autumn's brows flicker
in that tell-tale sign of mild annoyance. I guess I have been standing
here and thinking for too long. I wonder whether she knows I'm
ruminating on this particular memory. I told her the story a hundred
times at the start of our relationship, my narration causing her to
beam each time. Her happiness always made me happy, until the
end. But that hadn't been because of her. Nothing had made me
happy at the end.

The lines on her face round out and soften as her gaze pierces
my soul. I'm held captive again.

"You know what?" she whispers, a secret grin on her face.

"What?" I'm so mesmerized by the delicate incantation of her
voice that it's as though I've been transported back in time and am
no longer Otis, but Otty.

"I'm craving a croissant."

Just like that, I'm aching. Stowed in the dark recess of my heart
are memories of what it was like to love her—at least what I had
thought was love. The sliver of light in my chest that used to shine
so brightly in her presence flickers dimly, reminding me of what
it was like when things were good. I might not have truly been in
love with her, but before my injury, I genuinely believed I was. And

nothing—not even Doctor Time—could ever erase the memories and feelings I once harbored for her.

"We should go," she finally murmurs, tugging me from my thoughts. I agree, and her hand slips from my shoulder. Habitually, I reach for her but stop myself at the last second, shoving my fists into my pockets. She crosses her arms over her chest and digs her fingers into the skin of her biceps.

It's a short walk to the café and an even shorter one to the register.

Once we get our drinks, we beeline for an isolated table positioned in the corner near a window. I pull out a seat for her, the one that faces but isn't against the window. It's November, and the weather hints at winter's approach.

Because I'm a petty bitch, I place Quinn's drink near said window. He can drink shit—or in this case, a black block of bitter ice—and die.

A moment of silence falls over us as we prepare our drinks the way we like them. My phone keeps vibrating, my group chat with the guys popping off. I flip my phone screen down, a habit that used to irk Autumn to no end—"It's like you're trying to hide something," she would comment, suspicious—and glance at her to see if she's wearing that same expression of irritation. She isn't.

"So," she says, pausing in case I hint interest in initiating the conversation she wants to have. I don't, and she frowns. "Should we start with small talk or just get right into it?"

"Small talk would be nice," I murmur, warming my hand with the cup. It's scalding, but I welcome the burn.

At first, I don't pay attention to what she says, drawn instead to the slight differences in her appearance. She's still very much the Autumn I once knew, but there are little tweaks that make her a stranger. She's gained weight from when we were last together, and her angular face is fuller. The exhausted hollows under her eyes are gone. Even her hair is gleaming, radiant, having improved during our time apart.

She's still prattling on by the time I'm done with my observations, offering excessive details about her life. It's cute at first, but after a while, it's annoying. She used to do this when we were together—offer me every detail, every tangent to a story. I'd told her it was endearing, but that was when everything she did had that effect on me.

When it's my turn, I keep it short, simple, and impersonal. I tell her I'm okay, that I'm better now. My knee isn't giving me too much trouble, and when it does, I manage. My mom is fine, thanks for asking, and so is Katty and Icka—I'm purposeful in calling them Katia and Monica, correcting the intimate nicknames she freely uses. And that's it. That's all I say.

Autumn makes a face, and I'm sure it's due to my brevity, but she doesn't press.

She sighs. "Now that that's out of the way, let's get straight to it, shall we?"

"What is it you wanted to talk about?"

"Closure."

I swallow the snippy refusal that crawls up my throat. "We broke up, like, six months ago, Autumn."

"I know." She fiddles with the charm bracelet on her wrist, a gift from her stepdad. It feels wrong that I know the backstory behind each charm that dangles from her wrist.

"And you want closure now?"

She stares over my shoulder, refusing to meet my eyes. "Yeah."

"Why?" I'd given her the chance to say what she wanted when I told her it was over. It had been her decision to simply walk out of my place without a word. A week later, she left for a summer abroad in Spain. The study abroad reminds me of our last fight, the one that broke us up.

"Go, Autumn. Just fucking go if you want to go. Stop bringing me into it. Jesus. You think I need you that bad? Are you fucking

kidding me? Leave. Live your life. Stop acting like I'm keeping you here. In fact, what do you think about breaking up? That way, you don't have to be 'sick with worry,' and I can finally have a moment of fucking peace without you nagging me all the fucking time."

"Because I'm ready now." She speaks with conviction. If we were still Otty and Autty, I would tell her how proud I am of her for taking the initiative. "And because I'm not scared anymore of what mean thing you might say to me."

I suck. I get it. Even if I've worked to erase that part of my life, remnants of who I am—was—will forever exist in me and in her, no matter how hard I try to prove otherwise.

And that's why I kind of hate her. I know I don't have a right to. She'd been there for me at my worst, when the pain I felt in my knee was minor compared to the agony of the unknown. There was no saying whether or not I'd be able to play football again at that point, and I was barely holding onto my sanity. Football was my world—it was meant to be my ticket to the good life so I could take care of Mom and Katia and Monica. And trying to come to terms with the fact that this might no longer be an option killed me on the inside. All the hard work I had put in, all the hours of sleep I had lost, all the aches in my muscles I withstood, would have been for nothing.

In those dark moments, she had been there, always speaking so kindly, so encouragingly, trying to undo the damage my torrent, pessimistic thoughts had delivered.

But that wasn't what I wanted—what I *needed*—at the time. I hated that when I would snap and throw away the dinner she made me because I didn't like the way she cooked the steak tips, she calmly cleaned the dishes like I'd polished off the plate and complimented her efforts. Or that when I came home from physical therapy and needed help into the shower, she was there, offering to shampoo my hair and wash my body like I hadn't bitched about how she should have already had the bath ready when I texted her

I was on my way home.

Nothing she did was right, nor was it enough. Reminiscing on everything she did for me, her patience, her kindness, her willingness to simply be there, I can recognize that it wasn't her flaws serving to upset me. It was my pain manifesting in a way that I couldn't control, in a way I hadn't wanted to control.

Looking back, I cringe at how she got caught in the crossfire of my hurt and saw all the ugly in me. She was the person I cherished the most at that moment in my life, and yet, I'd treated her like she was my servant, a nobody.

And I hate that. I hate not being able to go back in time and change the way our relationship unraveled. I'm subconsciously aware that this isn't what I should hate about the situation, as if my treatment of her doesn't warrant every bad thing she thinks she knows about me. It's just that I hate that she walks around every day so aware of how terrible I can be. I'd much rather have the entire world have unsubstantiated opinions on what a jackass I am than this.

"So, why?" she says. The question is vague but specific at the same time. Despite how timid and quiet Autumn might appear, she's strong. I used to tell her that when I apologized after getting particularly nasty, the ache in my knee so tremendous that I couldn't help but pass the pain onto someone else. I would tell her she's strong, beautiful, and kind. I used to tell her she was as close as it got to being an angel on Earth.

I didn't deserve her. I told her that, too. Not that I believed it in the moment, more so saying it because I wanted her to forgive me, but in hindsight, it ended up being the truth.

She waits for me to say something, refusing to shoulder the burden of my turn this time.

I clear my throat, clench my jaw, and sigh in defeat. I look at her, and there before me is a tsunami of anger she'd never unleashed but had lain dormant out of pity for my condition. I deliberate on my response, juggling my options. I can either be stubborn and remain silent until she explodes, or I can tell her what she deserves to hear, what she came here to hear, what I should have said long ago.

"I'm sorry, Autumn."

She doesn't respond, and I'm tempted to get up and call it a day. But I don't.

Because even if I hate that she's bringing this up now, I owe her—maybe not entirely, because it was her choice to stay with me, but stay with me she did. She was there in February, right after it happened, for three months of wheelchairs and crutches. She stayed when I was doing physical therapy, standing by my side, encouraging me despite the sardonic cynicism and passive aggressive retorts I hurled her way, simply because she was around and would take it. It's unfathomable now that she withstood more than a day of my terrible moods.

I know she had held onto hope that after I recovered, I would revert back to the person she fell in love with—the one who thought he loved her. There had been glimpses on days when things weren't as bad for me. But holding onto that hope was her fault, right? I never said or did anything to indicate I could be better, especially when I was still existing in my own personal hell. And it's not like I made her stay or anything. And yet...

"I'm sorry for being the worst boyfriend imaginable after... I'm sorry about taking all my anger out on you. I had no right to let my feelings out in that way. I know I didn't hit you or do anything physically, but..." Fuck. This is hard. "I never meant to say such ugly..." I don't finish the sentence, the words caught in my throat. Her eyes are glossy, and my heart burns. No matter how badly I want to crawl out of my own skin and drop dead on the floor, I push on. "You didn't deserve to be treated that way, and I'm sorry for making you feel like complete shit when all you did was support and love me."

But why didn't you leave? The words slice my tongue in a plea to be released. *If I was so bad, if you couldn't stand it, if it hurt you so much, why the fuck didn't you just leave?*

Better yet, when I was getting mad at nothing, why hadn't she ever asked me to calm down, to stop? Why did she let me go through the motions with her there?

As if reading my mind, she robs me of my silent question, alters it, and throws it back in my face. "So why did you? If you knew that I shouldn't have been treated that way, why did you make me go through that?" she whispers. A tear falls from her eye.

"I-I…" Words elude me. What am I supposed to say? I'm a selfish asshole? I was hurting physically and mentally, so I wanted to hurt everyone else around me, too? Except everyone but Autumn was smart enough to avoid me.

"That's all I want to know, Otis," she whispers, speaking my Christian name for the first time since our first date last fall. More tears spill down her face. If I didn't know Autumn, I'd think they were tears of sadness for the loss of what we had.

But I do know her, and I know that more than anything, they're from frustration of what I'd put her through. I cough and sniff, uncomfortable and empathetic to the display.

"If you knew you were hurting me, why didn't you stop?"

I can't look at her anymore. Every fiber of my being wants to get out of here and wallow in bed, because even if it had been nearly a year since I tore my ACL, it feels like it was just yesterday.

"I know you've changed," she says, her voice broken and soft. "Milton told me."

I knew it. Tuckerson knows what happened between us. Stupid fucker. "I have."

"I'm glad." She wipes her tears away, leaving her eyes puffy and red. She squints in rugged determination. "I'm happy that you're not in that bad place anymore. That wasn't you in February. I know what a good person you were—could be." She hesitates,

273

her breath catching for a second. "But if I'm being honest, I kind of wish you didn't get better."

When the fuck did I order a ton of bricks? I blink at her, my lungs dry, not even bothering to conceal my astonishment. "Huh?"

She grabs a napkin, dabs her face, and expels a sour laugh. "That didn't come out right. What I meant to say is that I just... I don't think it's fair that for you to have become a better person, I had to suffer. I never signed up to be a life lesson for you. I only wanted to be your girlfriend."

I sag in my seat.

She takes a deep breath, fanning her hand over her face to cool down. Honesty is her manifestation of anger.

"I'm sorry," I repeat, hollow.

"About what? Making me feel bad or for what you did?"

Like there's a fucking difference.

I'm a broken record, unable to divine better words. "I'm sorry." *I was shitty. I get it. But I was in a really bad place, and the way I acted then wasn't the real me. That version of myself is the antithesis of everything I'm working to become.* Injured Otis had been awful, no doubt, and she happened to be there when he appeared. And that's not fair to her, but it's not fair to me for her to continue to put me in that box. It seems like she gets that, but she still won't let it go.

She lets out a sardonic chuckle and shakes her head, biting her bottom lip, like she's saying *how typical.* She wears an expression of fierce resolve. "Fine. You're sorry. Just sorry."

It bothers me that she doesn't believe me, but not enough that I'm going to argue with her until she does.

It takes a heartbeat, but Autumn collects herself. She grabs her coffee and takes a sip.

Now for the goodbyes. It hurts to be forced to rehash old memories, good and bad. But at least it's done. I've apologized. Granted, it was a little pitiful, and maybe it won't make the Apology

Hall of Fame, but it's the best I can do, given how overwhelmed and bombarded I feel. "Autumn, I—"

"Is there someone else in your life? Is there someone who gets this better version of you?"

A version that I helped create is what she means. I don't get the chance to respond when a notification dings on my phone, as if summoned by Mother Fate herself. I haven't checked my phone since we sat down, but for some reason, this time, I do.

Had the message been anything other than WANNA FUCK TONIGHT, I probably would have responded differently to my ex. But this very text reminds me just how unattached I am to the girl who I've been having exclusive, casual sex with on the regular.

"Everyone gets a better version of me now, but if you're asking if I'm with someone romantically..." I let the term linger in the air, willing myself not to be as stupid as I am. After that text, I'm spiraling into my own thoughts, wrapped up in the nuances of my relationship with Greta and the many rules we've already broken. I take a sip of my green tea. Too bad I'm a fucking idiot. "No. I'm not seeing anyone like that."

I'm not sure if this is the closure Autumn wanted or expected. I'm not sure if her feelings have been resolved. Hell, I'm not sure how *I* feel about any of this.

But what I do know is that when we get up to leave, the Autumn I once knew and the Autumn walking away from me are not the same. And maybe, just maybe, she's walked away thinking the same about me.

REMINDERS
task list

- O films for game 10
- O meeting with o-line abt annual prank
- O meal prep (pay herik $30 for groceries)
- O flash cards for SRA midterm 3
- O remind mom to pay car insurance & electric
- O send icka allowance
- O cake for rodney's bday

GRETA

FOLDED IN THE BACKSEAT

I'VE NEVER BEEN fond of car sex. Due to a specific incident involving the reverse cowgirl, a 1998 Corolla, and a basketball player who jumps when he climaxes, I'm traumatized. The humiliation of having my whole family come to the ER, where the doctors regaled them with how Reggie sprained his neck, still has me a little scarred.

But it's Otis's turn to choose what we do for our fuckdevous, and since he didn't put up a fuss when I requested he dress as Indiana Jones last time, the least I can do is comply with his fantasy. So, I'm cramped in the backseat of his truck in my high school cheer uniform.

The safety shorts barely cover my ass, the skirt revealing the meaty underside. The hair bow is too scratchy and big. And don't even get me started on the top... It fits like a glorified Band-Aid.

Not that Otis minds. "C'mon cheerleader," boob dude grunts, grinding his hips into me, "spread those gorgeous legs wider for your quarterback."

"How much wider?" It's not like me to complain, especially where sex is involved, but I'm exasperated by the small confines of his truck.

We started off in the front, where I gave him some road head, determined to have him come at least once before we actually fucked. The sight of me in the small uniform had excited him beyond belief, a prominent bulge appearing at the front of his football pants the second I slid next to him in the passenger seat. Before I even fished him out of his *Hunter X Hunter* briefs, he'd been leaking, eager. With just a few tight, twirly strokes, a half-dozen head bobs, and a quick suckle-and-tongue combo at his tip, his balls tightened, and he busted. I didn't want a repeat of what happened last Wednesday in *195 Extraction's* bathroom, when he'd come too quickly, leaving me high, dry, and too agitated to finish myself off.

Rather than respond, Otis takes matters into his own hands. I'm beneath him, sitting in a curl up. My back is pressed against the door jam, my head smashed against the cool glass window. One leg settles straight out atop the seat under us, while he pushes the one hooked over his shoulder away from his person until the heel of my foot is flat against the window, forcing me to do the splits midair.

My spine arches as he forces my leg back, and I let out a pinched whimper when he slides in deeper, his large hand pressed between my stomach and my mound. A sweet fire spirals through me from having his full length buried in me so completely. We're pressed pelvic bone to pelvic bone, and when he twists his hips, it angles him better and stimulates me further. I actually see stars, my breath stolen from me by a sudden flow of longing.

"Fuck," Otis says, feeling it too and closing his eyes to hang his head in mindless bliss. My walls welcome him with repetitive squeezes. As good as it feels for him to luxuriate inside me, the fat helmet of his cock bumping against places that hardly ever get stimulated, I'm concerned for when he starts thrusting.

I thoroughly enjoy being wrecked, but I also have to drive home and would rather not do that with my lower half bent out of shape.

Just as I'm about to ask and maybe even add an offhanded

comment about being gentle, he wedges his hand under the tight confines of my top and with a firm yank, bunches it up, exposing my breasts. He grabs the thigh not being folded back like it's origami and wraps it high around his waist.

"We're going to have to be quick," he murmurs, pulling out for a moment. He licks his hand then grazes it against me, slipping his middle and index finger inside flawlessly, parting them repeatedly to stretch me. I lean up into him, aching for more. He gloats and pushes the pad of his wrist against the tip of my vulva, placing an exquisite force on my clit, and winks. "I have a game soon, and I can't be late."

Channeling my cheerleader persona, I squirm and bat my lashes prettily. Bending forward some more, abs protesting, I too lick my hand and grab hold of him, tugging to slot him against me. Immediately, his hands are replaced by the tip of his cock. His eyes flutter wide open. He's always impressed by how flexible I am.

"Just make sure you finish inside me, stud," I murmur, speaking against his lips, my tongue flicking out with every word. "I want to feel you drip down my leg while I cheer for you."

He bites my bottom lip then soothes my mouth with licks and sucks. When he releases me, my lip sufficiently swollen and red, he smirks. He inches back inside, and I suck a deep breath through my nose, my core tensed.

"Only if you promise to keep some inside. It'll be my good luck charm. If I see even a drop spill"—with a slow push forward, more than the tip is inside me, and he bites my ear as he finishes breathing out a blissful promise disguised as a threat—"I'm going to ruin you."

I purse my lips and close my eyes as he slowly, decadently, sinks inside me, taking his time, just as I like it. With every inch he reintroduces, his hard length rubs wonderfully against the hot, slick surface of my pussy. I'm tossing my head side to side and letting out high pitched whimpers to play my part in the fantasy, but my hips bucking is entirely involuntarily. The dull strain that comes from my contorted leg is overshadowed by the ripples of pleasure that seize me as my body molds and accommodates to the shape of him.

Once he's bottomed out, all bets are off. We've already been at this for a good ten minutes, and my body is strung tight, vibrating with desperation. He skims his hand against my waist and lowers his head to tend to my breasts. I bow my back to grind against him, enjoying the friction.

"I'm going to need you to relax that messy little cheer pussy of yours," he commands, words muffled as he continues to mouth my nipple. I don't listen at first, still drawn stiff. But he's zealous in his effort to divert my attention from the soreness in my legs to the tingles around my chest, alternating from one breast to the other, circling his hips to impart more pressure. Once I've turned sufficiently pliant in his arms, he gets to work.

And boy, does my big, naughty quarterback *work*.

With a sharp inhale, wedged deep within me, stretching my snug cunt just right, he begins to move, our hot, perspiring bodies slapping together rhythmically, each sharp thrust deep and precise. The pace is steady. A little slow, but that's okay since he's hitting a spot inside me that makes me aware of everything, even the trickle of sweat beading down his jaw. I stare up at him, mouth open in an attempt to breathe better, soft moans and breathy whines of joy escaping as our sex turns into full-blown fucking. It's authentic. There's no extravagant persona to channel.

I'm panting, he's growling. I'm clenching, he's twitching. I'm bucking, he's thrusting. Over and over again, he plows into me. It hurts, the pounding I'm receiving, but because it's so continual, so persistent, and because he's rocking into me, my hips canted in the air to receive him better, all the pain is eclipsed by perpetual, sweet pleasure.

He's been doing so well, holding out for so long, but I can feel the pulsing at the base of his cock. He no longer leans forward, instead standing tall in his full glory, his jersey tucked into his shoulder pads to offer me a splendid view of his carved abs. If I had the capacity to move, if my muscles had even a speck of energy left in them or if my bones weren't molten, I would glide my hands over his sculpted frame just to feel the way those muscles contract from his efforts.

"I'm close," he warns, his gaze fixated on our joined bodies as he tries to keep the rhythm steady. The plunge of his cock is less jackhammer and more frantic ruts, the depth shallow, the pace quick. I clasp my pussy as tightly as I can around his cock, trying to pull him in deeper, but to no avail.

Penetration won't be enough. It's definitely good, but not enough. Immediately, my fingers make quick work of my clit, knowing full well that while he's definitely going to get his, I've got to put myself first to ensure I also get mine.

The knot of tension that collects in my gut swells just in time. Eyes fluttering shut, I focus and drown myself in the stimulations— the taste, the touch, the smell, the sounds.

It's just as I'm about to topple over, his hand moving over mine to help reinforce this finish, that he grabs my chin aggressively. "Look at me," Otis snarls, looming over me, gasping over my face. My eyes snap open, and I admire how beautifully ruined he is above me, *because* of me. "Watch your quarterback while he fucks and fills his cheer slut up."

I think the day that Otis learned of my degradation kink was the best day of our sex lives.

I oblige. And though I don't actually watch the way his cock pulses its release in me, I watch him. I watch the way his eyes glaze, his face alight in enigmatic satisfaction, and the way his lips part as a primal sound of ecstasy rips out of his throat as he rears in and out and comes.

As he spills inside me, he continues to move in short, messy strokes, attempting to extend the release. The sound of his orgasm and my arousal blends in a dulcet melody. My hand touches where we're joined to feel his release, and he shudders over me. "That's my cheerleader. You love taking my cum, don't you?"

It's these words, compounded with the scalding, sticky sensation of him pouring into me, that catapults me over the edge. Concentrating on everything I feel, him inside me, beating, my body tingling, alive, I pinch my nipples and firmly tap my clit before finally letting go.

The base of my spine goes molten, liquefying from the heat it radiates. The tension coiling in my body breaks, exploding as it dismantles me into tiny particles. I'm soaring, letting out an elongated shriek of pleasure that he has to muffle with a clasp of his hand over my mouth. "We don't want anyone to hear, do we?" he says, still partaking in the façade. "Only I get to know what a whore you can be."

Fuck if I care. I'm absorbed in the afterglow. I'm not sure how I remain immersed, but I do know that by the time I snap out of it, I'm hypersensitive and in a daze.

"You're dangerous, Greta Sahnoun," Otis slurs when we've regained most of our faculty. He's panting, marveling down at me. The look in his eyes is one I'm familiar with, and though I would never admit it to anyone aloud, it's growing to be my favorite part of our moments together.

I hum in affirmation and try not to wince as I grow aware of what I've just put my body through, a dull, sore ache blistering throughout me. At this point, I'm convinced Otis thinks I'm Elasti-Girl, the way he contorts me as if I'm malleable beyond human limits. But the sting isn't just from the position we've taken on, it's from the sheer force of our release.

As much as Otis would have enjoyed remaining in this position, having a fondness for growing hard while still buried inside me, I bring my leg back in front of me, away from the foggy window, and shove him off me.

Our aftercare is pretty minimal, given our locale. He grabs the wipes I keep in my backpack and cleans us up. He does his best to be gentle with the sensitive skin of my pussy, apologizing when I suck in a sharp hiss of pain. Then he helps me change into a baggy hoodie and a pair of shorts, knowing full well I've yet to receive full faculty of my limbs, before changing himself. When I mention that my legs hurt, he kisses along them and apologizes before pressing a peck on my lips.

I actively ignore how intimate the gesture is—pretending like my heart skipping a beat is due to some health-related reason—and instead remind myself that that's what aftercare is like, I'm supposed to feel cherished and appreciated. Last time, when he spanked me so hard that I actually had to use my safe word for the second time, he'd practically groveled in guilt, massaging my ass for an hour as an apology.

Otis is more civilized than I am, and exits the car to get to the driver's side, while I climb over the foldable console to the front seat. I immediately twist the keys he's left in the ignition and turn the heat up, warming myself against the icy night air. The rigor of our strenuous coupling made me forget the weather. It's the week of Thanksgiving, and our exams ended about two hours ago, signifying the departure of fall and the beginning of winter.

"I'm freezing," I chatter, rubbing my palms together.

He'd refused to keep his glasses on during sex, much to my chagrin, and he puts them back on before he shifts into drive. He pauses at my complaint, reaches behind us to grab his discarded jacket from the floor, and tosses it at me.

Eager, I drape it over my shivering legs and pat his shoulder in appreciation. I'm about to ask if he has a mint or hard candy when one miraculously appears in front of my face. When I try to thank him, he holds a hand up and shakes his head in mock humility. I'd roll my eyes and sneer at him if I wasn't so used to this.

With that, he peels out of the vacant parking lot and we make our way to his place.

"So how was the performance today?" my fuck buddy asks.

"Good."

"*Good?*" I could have stepped on his neck and spat in his face, and he would have appeared less offended. "You better elaborate on what you mean by 'good' before I get insecure and run us both off a cliff."

He asks this nearly every time we get together. I've never given him such a bland response before, always taking care to stroke his ego. But the crick in my neck, my aching thighs, and the swollen beat that reverberates between my legs have me behaving otherwise. "If I were to put you on a letter-grade scale... a B? Maybe a B-plus."

"B? B-plus? Egg-squeeze me?"

"Was that a sneeze? *Gesundheit.*"

"Don't change the subject. We're talking about this," he demands. "What the fuck do mean you're giving me a B-plus? You can't just kick me off the honor roll without explanation."

"You're the one who wanted me to tell you how it was."

"That's true. I did ask." His voice fades as doubt crinkles his eyes adorably. "But how? You came so hard, I actually thought you were squeezing the circulation out of my dick."

If his career as a football player ever fails, I'm sure Otis would thrive as a thespian. "Well, for one, I feel like my neck was sawed in half."

"That's an issue with logistics, not my performance. We can remedy this easily by bringing pillows next time." With two successive snaps of his fingers, he urges me to continue. "*Andale.* What are your other grievances? And remember, you're grading me solely on my performance. If your guts were rearranged, then give me an A-plus in exchange."

I let out a tepid chuckle. To be honest, there's one thing I've really wanted to talk to him about but have always ignored since there was nothing much he could do about it. But if he's really asking, then I should tell him. "You know, I wouldn't mind if your dick was an inch or two smaller."

"An inch *what*? Smaller?" He peels his eyes from the empty road to gawk at me.

"Yeah, I mean, I just think it's a little too big."

"Too big?"

Does Polly want a cracker? "Look, I'm just saying that a solid five—maybe even six—inches is just as good as that python you pack. Sometimes it can... hurt."

"You like that, though. Wait." His voice hitches. He glances at me from the corner of his eye, anxiety and doubt glimmering there. His grip on the steering wheel tightens. "Do you?"

"Of course, I like it," I reassure. "But—"

"Why is there always a but? Are you trying to hurt me?"

I repeat myself, stressing him to understand and listen. "I like it. But, when you get a little too excited, you don't really, uh, take care to get it in right. Y'know? I feel like I'm being pummeled instead of fucked."

Genuine concern overcomes his features, and he rapidly divvies his attention between me and the road. "Maybe we should stop doing it so rough. I know you like it hard, but you shouldn't be hurting that bad after."

"Pish-posh. By the time we're done, I want my pussy to be beat. If I'm not wondering how fast I can call PETA, I don't want it." I rub his thigh in reassurance. "Besides, if I really can't handle it, I'll 'papaya.'"

He purses his lip to keep from laughing at my safe word. His is pineapple, so he has no leg to stand on if he wants to make fun of me.

"I was just informing you of what lowered your score."

"But if my big dick is a contributing factor, then why have you been giving me A-pluses the last couple of times? I mean, you weren't riding me, and I was…" A lengthy, awkward pause lingers between us, and he gasps in horror. "Oh my God! You've been giving me pity scores."

"They were not pity scores," I say quickly. Too quickly. He glowers at me. "They're just inflated for ego accommodations. Besides, I do like it when you fuck me, and I like your dick. Really. Your girth is fantastic."

But he's shaking his head. I sidle up to him. With one hand on the wheel, he uses his other to push me away, light in the force he exerts. "Yeah, right. Don't try and talk me up, you traitor. I—No, stop it, woman! Get away. I don't need you trying to schmooze me after betraying my trust."

"Aw, c'mon. Don't be such a ninny." He huffs resentfully at this accusation.

I'm not sure if I actually offended Otis. If I did, he gets over it fast and changes the conversation to what we'll be doing for Thanksgiving break.

By the time we're parking in the driveway of his place, we've moved from the topic of our plans for Thanksgiving and the party my dad is hosting the following week, to which cartoon is better: *Kim Possible* or *Dexter's Laboratory*.

"You can't just use Shego as your only argument!" I shriek, frustrated by how stubborn he's being.

"I can if it's the only argument to be had," he responds just as loudly, just as impassioned. "Shego is not only the finest woman to ever grace the fabric of this universe, but she's also one of the most versatile, well-thought-out villainesses to be created."

"You could also argue that about Dee-Dee." I scoff. "She's just as beautiful—"

He makes an error sound. It's loud and obnoxious, and my fists ball up the second it rings in my ear. "Wrong! Dee-Dee is cute, sure, but definitely not beautiful."

"Same difference."

"No, not 'same difference.' You're not cute. You're beautiful. Hence why I want to fuck you and not Dee-Dee."

Heat rises in my cheeks from his admission. He's called me hot, gorgeous, sexy, ravishing, fuckable, slut, and pretty little whore—all of which were uttered during sex—but never beautiful. It's new, and surprisingly pleasant. My heart beats in my ears but I ignore the clambering to maintain the momentum of our argument. "Well, I would hope so. She's a cartoon and a minor."

"Don't—" He's interrupted by a sharp rap of knuckles against the driver's side window.

It's Elias Jenner, the tight end, coming to inform Otis that Coach and Duger had stopped by their house to go over some tapes. My fuck buddy tenses while my mind considers possible ramifications in the event that we're found out. My deduction concludes that they'll be limited, but I'm still on edge.

There's not a lot of time to dwell too long on any of these concerns. A sigh of relief lurches Otis forward when his friend informs him that his teammates had his back and simply told Coach that he was out.

Otis flops back in his seat and covers his face, shouting "thank you" to the ceiling of his truck. "All right, crisis averted." He turns to look at me, peppy as ever. "Want some dinner? I heard your stomach growling earlier, and Quinny Boy made fajitas."

"Actually, Mitchum made fajitas. Quinn threw a tantrum since Mitchum watched ahead on *Attack on Titans* and spoiled episode six for him on accident," Elias corrects. With a brisk wave, he takes his leave.

I shift in my seat and stare at Otis's lap rather than his face. "Alright, well, this was fun, but I'm going to head home now."

"You sure? Mitchum is an even better cook than Quinn. We can eat some free dinner and watch some tapes." He nudges his knee against mine and wiggles his brows. "What do you say? Will you allow me the pleasure of hearing you roast a team that isn't ours?"

"Sounds like an ideal date," I mumble. For some reason, I'm hesitant to refuse outright, and I hate that fact. I hate that a part of me really wants to say yes.

"Maybe for you, but not for me. My ideal date is you topless in my kitchen, me eating sushi off your naked body."

"Where are your roommates? Watching?"

He looks both disgusted and jealous. It's playful in the same way it's serious, and his words come out more threatening than he likely intended. "Nowhere in sight. I might be kinky, but I ain't no exhibitionist."

Though I don't laugh, I do smile. I bite my bottom lip as my mind kicks onto overdrive, desperate to come up with a good enough reason not to go inside with him and chill. The only excuse I come up with is boundaries. Otis and I have been doing very well at keeping our relationship purely physical.

Well, not purely. We do talk a lot after sex, between rounds, or while we're in the bathroom, cleaning up, him on the toilet and me in the shower, or vice-versa. And there was also that one time we had a sleepover when we'd both been too exhausted to move after a four-hour playtime, but he'd left before I even woke up, leaving a note on my pillow that read, HOTEL MIRIAM GETS 4 STARS FROM RUTHERFORD. GET FLUFFIER PILLOWS IF YOU WANT 5.

And sure, there was another instance when I really needed someone to help paint my nails since I'm the least ambidextrous person alive and thought it convenient to use him, given how good he is with his hands and how accessible he was since we had just finished fucking. I'd done his nails, too, painting them a pretty green. There was also that day last week when he'd brought me takeout from Ricky's Burger, my favorite fast-food joint. We didn't have sex since I was on my period, but in order to add some sexual energy, I did watch three episodes of *Narcos* with him while I was topless, so it isn't that big a deal. Granted, he ruined it by being sweet and making me cinnamon-honey tea to help with my ailing cramps, a home remedy his mom trained him to make.

There was also this other time—

"You know you want to," he taunts. "You enjoy shitting on people."

"And beef fajitas," I mumble. I'd marry a cow in a heartbeat if it wasn't frowned upon. "I really love beef."

He puts on an obvious, valiant effort not to make a penis joke, and I'm proud of him for succeeding. "Exactly. Beef and talking smack. Nothing beats that. What d'ya say?"

A current passes between us, one filled with possibility that I know we shouldn't explore. Despite how tempting his proposition is, I shake my head. "I think I'll just head home."

Even if I don't want to. Even if the vision of sitting on his couch and shouting insults at the TV with a homemade meal is most appealing, I just know it's a bad idea. I can't explain it—can't properly put to words the unease that rumbles low in my belly. I want this relationship we've worked out to last as long as possible, and if I can avoid pushing our boundaries, I should. Even if I hadn't before, I should now. I already feel myself growing attached to him.

"You sure?"

I nod and scoot away, and just as I open the passenger side door to go grab my stuff from the back, he adds, "Let me at least bring you something to take home to eat by yourself."

He's being pointed with his remark, but I ignore it and agree.

It's when he rushes inside and I go to grab my shit from the backseat of his car, kindly looking around for his phone, that I see the note.

Normally, I would never have picked up a discarded piece of paper, half crumbled with tracks of dirt on it. But in the soft glow of the porch light, I see five letters: MIRIA, and I have a feeling the last one is an M.

I straighten it out and read what it has to say, my heart falling to my feet.

TO MIRIAM
CIRCLE ONE
BREAKFAST AT MY PLACE NEXT TIME?
YES   NO

VOICEMAIL

mamounette
Columbus, Mississippi
November 16, 2022 at 10:15 AM

Transcription

"I'll be late to the mall please call your father I don't care if you're in a fight with him it is not okay to ignore him we did not raise you like this you're being so disrespectful I honestly cannot believe you're my daughter right now"

papa sahnoun
Columbus, Mississippi
November 15, 2022 at 2:16 PM

Transcription

"I hired some men to fix your washing machine while your mother was gone and put dinner in the fridge don't go out and eat and waste money or I will cancel your cards study hard"

22

OTIS

CRYING OVER SPILLED WINE

MOM IS GOING to kill the next person who calls me Otis.

"I'll never forgive *su papa* for naming you after his father." She seethes when Rodney's parents finally walk away from us. *"Te ves gringo. No sacaste herencia mía. Qué vergüenza."*

I snort, rolling my eyes at her assertion that I look like my gringo father instead of taking after her. "So much for loving and honoring Dad's memory." Though I understand Spanish, I'm incapable of responding in kind, embarrassed by my poor grammar and limited vocabulary. Still, it's better than Katia and Monica, who both barely understand our mother's native language at all.

"Don't get me started. I loved your father, *pero su nombre es— Me revienta! Me vuelve loca! Ai!* Don't remind me."

"I didn't remind you! You brought it up yourself, and now you're getting pissy."

Mom doesn't have a chance to snap back at me when Katia and Monica come huffing and puffing toward us, their eyes bright. The looks on their faces make it clear they have a mission: to spill the tea.

"You know how I don't like to get messy?" Katia asks as she stands in front of us.

I choke on my wine and place a hand over my lips to capture any drop that might shoot out as I cough. "That's a joke, right? You're making a joke because you're bored."

My sister scowls and whacks my arm. I'm not sure if she intended to put her whole fucking chest into the strike, but it doesn't matter, because the second the back of her ring-covered hand makes contact, I go cross-eyed, delirious from the agony. Mom doesn't bat an eyelash, only ever intervening in our sibling fights if hair is pulled or blood is drawn.

To save face, I swallow the rumble of pain that crawls up my throat. If I concede to the fact that she's capable of inflicting tangible, poignant damage to my person, my sister—the personification of Bowser himself—will definitely do it more often.

Besides, I'll take a physical reprimand over a verbal one. Whoever created the saying 'sticks and stones may break my bones, but words will never hurt me' has clearly never been verbally assaulted by a Morgan woman.

What Coach does to us is nothing in comparison, which is why I've yet to snap back at him, my tolerance high.

"I don't," she rebukes in a low hiss. "I'm a very clean, very holy girl."

"The day you're holy is the day I start lactating."

Monica snickers. Mom rolls her eyes. Annoyed by my attitude, Katia reaches for me. I don't have time to evade her impending torture before she's pinching and twisting my nipples. This time, the whimper that escapes me comes from deep within my soul. It's a reaction I can't suppress, try as I might.

Ma's reaction is delayed, but she slaps my sister's hand off me. "*Comportate*, Katia! We're in public."

"Sweet baby Jesu—" I exhale, the words coming out in a soft vibrato. I stop from saying the Lord's name in vain. The vein on her forehead is frightening enough.

Katia glances innocently at Mom then turns to smirk at me,

snorting quietly. She then moos mockingly. "Give it a minute, Bessy." Combing her bangs behind her ears, she clears her throat and speaks more clearly. "As I was saying, you know how I don't like to get messy?"

"Yes," I bite out between clenched teeth. I close my eyes and I swear a tear nearly spills out the corner. Being away from Katia for so long had me forgetting our dynamic and how aggressive she is. I'm always at her mercy. My dad beat the shit out of me the one time I ever retaliated when I was six, and I've never touched her since, nor will I ever touch her again, a fact she takes advantage of.

Thankfully, Monica doesn't share the aggressive attitude. Rather than her fists, the broody teen's weapon of choice is her words, or lack thereof.

"Guess who I saw walking in?" She pauses for effect before whispering, low and daunting, "Autumn."

I turn to stone, my pain forgotten. "What?"

Fuck. Had Tuckerson invited her as his guest? Why? Were they that close? I've seen them on campus before, but this is a dinner for close family of the chosen players. That must make her close family to him, right? They probably talk shit about me. Did they tell other people, too?

An ugly feeling reverberates in my chest, my stomach flipping as I scan the room for her, my breathing a little labored. She's nowhere in sight, and I'd like to believe in out of sight, out of mind, but Coach's house is so big, she could honestly be anywhere.

"She looks good, too," Monica adds.

"Should we say hi?" Mom muses quietly over the rim of her glass. When I flash her a look of betrayal, she winces. "*Lo siento, mijo*. I just really liked her."

"I liked Harrison more. He was so freaking hot," Katia chimes.

"And so freaking gay," I reply. Harrison had been my first very-super-duper-serious boyfriend during freshman year.

"That's not a problem for her. Katia looks like a man," Monica mocks.

Mom sucks in a deep breath between her teeth, giving a threatening look. Even I chastise Monica with a severe scowl. We all have our insecurities, and Katia's is her looks, a fact Monica knows but feels like exploiting. Still, the teen refuses to appear apologetic and holds her head high, her arms crossed in defiance.

Never one to appear phased, Katia waves off her little sister with a snort. "Talk to me when your chest fills out, Cutting Board."

Monica glowers and gapes at Mom expectantly, but Mom just gives her a *you-deserve-it* look before mumbling a half-hearted reprimand at her older daughter. This causes Monica to whine about how mistreated she is in the family, always the one to dish it but never take it.

Mom grumbles, "*Mal agradecida*," sauntering away to mingle with the other parents, having had enough of her kids.

"Now that Mom is out of the way, is it true that you're dating a girl?" Monica asks. "I thought you liked dick."

I'm unfazed by her crass remark. She's in a phase of her life where all she wants is a shocking reaction. "I'm into people, not dick, Icka. But yeah, I'm, like, with—" Then I stop and scowl. "Why are you asking?"

Pushing her little sister out of the way, Katia makes herself the center of attention, effectively bringing back the conversation about my ex. "Are you sure you don't have feelings for Autumn? I mean, you look pretty fucking spooked."

"I don't," I bite out. But Katia won't stop looking at me like that, and I'm just about ready to stamp my feet and pull a Monica. "Seriously, Katty, I don't have any feelings for her."

Her eye twitches, and she shoves the drink back into my hand. "Don't call me Katty."

"Whatever you say, *Katty*." I'm able to dodge the Hulk smash she's about to deliver, but my drink sloshes on me, and I groan, my victory short-lived.

"You fucking idiot!" Katia hisses. "You almost spilled wine on the carpet."

I cut her a leveled look. "No thanks to you."

She rolls her eyes and steers me to the bathroom to clean up the stain that's marinating on the crisp white dress shirt Mom made me iron three times before we left. And it's while we make our way through the maze of a house that we bump into Greta.

"Greta!" I scream, the suddenness and volume of my exclamation causing both girls to jump.

"Otis." She looks me up and down, thoroughly inspecting my outfit. If I were a peacock, I'd be cocking the fuck up right now, my feathers bright and wide.

I inspect her, too, starting at her face and end at her boobs, which are pushed so high up her chest, they could substitute for the loose lace scarf she's hung around her neck, covering her mouth-watering collarbone.

"Greta," I repeat because my brain has short-circuited. The necklace she has on is draped low, stopping just above where the mounds of her breasts press together, and all I can think about is whether or not it would stay in place if I were to fuck her, her sweat working as an adhesive.

"Oats," Katia says. "Aren't you going to introduce us?" My sister looks between Greta and me, appearing scrupulous then triumphant as the gears in her head click into place. Whatever notion she might have had of me being hung up on Autumn are eradicated, the drool dribbling out the corner of my mouth from all the tit-ogling a clear indication.

Damn Greta and her sexy dress. "Oh, Katia. This is Greta, Coach Sahnoun's daughter." I awkwardly motion at Greta with a hand before directing it to Katia. Katia barely conceals her shock as I continue, "Greta, this is Katia." I pause before emphasizing, "*My sister*. Katia, my sister."

Greta arches an interested eyebrow at me before facing Katia and smiling kindly. "Hi, Otis's sister Katia."

"Hey, Coach Sahnoun's daughter. Sorry for roaming around. We're looking for a bathroom," Katia says following a lingering awkward silence between the three of us. "He's not potty trained, so I'm on dooty-duty."

"Why am I not surprised?" Greta snorts.

I simper and glance between them. There's just something terrible about having my bully and the woman I love to have bully me in the same room. "We're actually going to try and clean this stain off my shirt. Mind pointing us in the right direction?"

Greta jerks her thumb over her shoulder but before she can speak, a voice comes that isn't sultry or feminine. At first, it's in that unfamiliar language before suavely transitioning to English.

"Greta, you can't just abandon your mother in the kitchen. You know how hard today is for her. Get back in there and help —" Coach's stern words cut off abruptly when he stomps toward his daughter and realizes Katia and I are in company. "Morgan, what're you doing in this part of the house?"

"Uh," I reply dumbly. My stomach twists in knots and sweat drips down my back at the thought that I might get caught by Coach. There's no reason for him to know about Greta and me, but I'm ready to piss myself.

"We were actually looking for a bathroom to clean up a stain on his shirt," Katia rushes to supplement when I falter. Then she holds her hand out and flashes him a charming smile. "I'm Katia, Otis's sister."

Coach grabs her hand and gives it a firm shake. "Ah, so you're the infamous Katia. Otis talks a lot about you and your younger sister—" He looks at me for help.

"Monica," I quickly interject.

"Yes! Monica."

Katia tosses an arm around my neck in a false gesture of friendliness. "Aw, I didn't know Otis was such a family man."

She digs her nails into my bicep. *You better not be talking shit*, the clawing signifies. I try to shrug it off because technically, I didn't talk shit about Katia. Too many of my teammates know her personally and have her socials.

It's Monica that I trash talk. Despite being hundreds of miles away, the kid still manages to give me severe anxiety and stress, given how often Mom calls me to vent about my kid sister's terrible behavior.

"That appears to be so, though I don't see the resemblance between you two." He points between the two of us. Katia has bright-brown locks, which she got from my dad and that shine golden red in the sun. I have my mom's dark hair. "I actually thought you were Autumn for a second. I heard she was here and assumed you got back together with her."

The sound of her name causes me to react involuntarily, my body going rigid, goose bumps rising on my arms. I glance at Greta, waiting for her to react, for that foul green monster to rear its head. I'm prepared to reassure her with honeyed words and artful expressions of seduction and faithfulness.

But all that preparation is for naught. Rather than jealousy making its appearance, I get nada. Literally. Her expression is completely blank.

"Nope," I reply, squaring my shoulders and ignoring my now bruised ego, putting in a concerted effort to ignore Greta's presence as I focus on Coach's face. "Autumn and I are no longer involved."

Coach blinks at me, the corners of his eyes wrinkling. But just as quickly as the doubt appears, it vanishes, a charming smile in its place. "The locker-room talk must be wrong, then."

I give a nod and look at Katia. "Let's go find the bathroom on the other side of the house."

"There's no need," Greta interrupts before we can even make a move. "It's right down the hall. Make a left, and it's the first door on the right."

I look at Coach to see if this is okay, and he gives me a curt nod. Still ignoring Greta, I make my way past the two, the father-daughter duo standing flat on opposite sides of the wall to give us room. But I'm stopped as I try to walk past Coach.

He claps a steady hand on my shoulder and leans forward. "You did good today, Morgan. I've heard from higher-ups that if we win this next game, the committee will put us in the Peach Bowl. Keep it up."

There's a skip in my step as I continue down the hall because what he's just said outshines all the cruel, demeaning jabs he's thrown at me since I've come back to the field. The insults I've withstood all mean something. They've led to more than just frustrated locker punches and discarded cigarette butts. It affirms one very important fact to me: My career isn't over.

Even if I'm hard pressed to admit it, I know he's one of the reasons that's the case. Even when he was scouting me, Coach made promises, and to my surprise, he's fulfilled them all. He made me one of the best quarterbacks in college history, my stats pre-injury are proof enough. And yeah, he's a piece of shit most of the time, pushing my limit, all our limits, with stern admonition rather than encouragement, but when it matters, he softens.

Those moments are few and far between, but for me, it counts. Especially when he'd come to my hospital after my surgery, genuine tears of worry in his eyes. "You'll get through it," he said. He never offered much else, but I held onto that sentiment with each visit he made.

No matter how much of a shithead he is, no matter how many times I daydream of stabbing him through the heart, I'm grateful for him and that he chose to move on from high school football two years before he announced he would. Without Coach Sahnoun, I wouldn't be the player—the man—I am today.

I bet he'll honor me at dinner as the most valued player. I'm so fucking pumped.

"Did Daddy Sahnoun pay you a compliment? Is that why you're wearing a psycho smile?" Katia asks when we get to the bathroom.

Well, that'll kill anyone's mood. My face contorts in disgust. "Did you just say '*Daddy Sahnoun*'?"

Katia hums, grabbing the hand towel from the hook to wet it and squirt some soap on it. "Absolutely. The man is yummy."

"That's your rebound brain talking. Being single has fucked up your eyesight."

My sister glares and tightly grabs the collar of my shirt, yanking me forward with a strong jerk. "His attractiveness has nothing to do with me being single. Being a DILF has nothing to do with a person's position. He might be your coach, but he's a daddy coach."

"As a person who's attracted to men, I'm going to have to strongly disagree with you."

"You're just saying that because you're boning his daughter," she says too loudly. "It would be totally wrong of you to find both daughter and father attractive."

I inhale sharply and glance out the door, panic surging through my veins. When I stare back at my sister, my blasé attitude disappears and I snatch the rag from her hand.

I'm so fucking done playing docile like I've done with her all week. Right now, I could give two flying fucks about how depressed she still feels over her breakup. I'm done taking the brunt of her sardonic attitude. "You need to learn when to shut the fuck up, Katia," I snap, heat licking up my neck.

She looks taken aback, my sudden shift in behavior unpredictable, even to her, a person attuned to me.

"Not every fucking thing has to be announced or made into a joke. Some shit you can keep to yourself. It wouldn't be the end of the world if you learned to shut the fuck up every once in a while. Jesus Christ."

When Katia is truly upset, she shuts down. Her frustration manifests itself in flustered, darkened silence, which is maybe where Monica learned to be so broody.

When I say what I say, angry by how flippant she's being about all this, how she's making light of my love life like hers isn't just as convoluted, she goes quiet, a scowl on her face, the skin of her lips creased.

Still, she snatches the rag back from me to help rub as much of the stain off my shirt as she can. The other thing about Katia and our family in general is that anger doesn't deter us from being there for each other.

But right now, I wish it did. That's why I brush her hand away with a reckless nudge, refusing to meet her eyes. "I got this," I whisper, still fuming. "Just… go find Mom and see if she has a Tide stick or something."

With a mute shove as she turns away from me, she leaves.

In an effort not to think about how much of a dick I just was, I work harder on trying to remove this petulant stain. I rub vigorously for a solid two minutes, sure that if I go at it for another, I will burn a hole straight through.

I'm interrupted by someone entering and closing the door, and I assume it's Katia. Without looking up, I grumble, "Please tell me she had a Tide stick, cause this shit is not coming off and I'm drenched."

"Who has a Tide stick? Autumn?"

Snapping my head up, my foul mood dissolves at the sight of Greta, the playful glint in her eyes, and her seductive smile.

"Autumn? Why would I want anything from her?" I'm grateful I don't stammer.

Greta gives me a suspicious look, eyebrows raised to her hairline, her trademark aloofness in place. Without a word, she reaches for me, and my hands drop on their own accord, ready to offer her unencumbered access to my body.

The first few buttons of my shirt are already undone, and she continues to open the rest of them, her touch lingering at the belt of my slacks. I forget myself, where we are, and what I'm doing here as I zero in on the gorgeous girl breathing heavily over my chest.

"Isn't she an ex-girlfriend?" Greta asks, resuming our conversation.

It takes me a second to realize which ex she's talking about. My hands go to her waist, and as I draw her closer, her fingers dip beneath the tight fit of my undershirt, lifting it to expose the smooth expanse of my abs. I flex at her cool touch, the ridges of my muscles appearing from the exertion. She enjoys this and she skims the soft pads of her fingers over them several times before tracing the line of my sternum to my shoulders, her palm rubbing circles around the defined muscles there.

I lift my hand to touch the dainty necklace she has on, trailing the tip of my nail up and under her scarf to feel her collarbone. The outfit she has on should be illegal, and the fact that when she walks out, other people will be able to see her in it, makes me a little upset.

"An ex," I respond slowly. Wanting to lighten the atmosphere, I add, "Which means I'm ready for the next."

"Otis is a *play-uh*, is that it?" She whistles, her lips hovering over my chest. "Does this make me a pit stop for who's to come?"

It takes me a second to respond with her lips pressed against my Adam's apple. My hold on her body tightens, trying to bring her closer. "Who's to say you're not that person?"

I'm so immersed in this moment with her and what she's doing that I don't realize I've crossed a line until she withholds her touch from me and I'm left chilled, the reality of my actions dousing me in regret.

"That's a mood killer if I've ever heard one," she grumbles. She tosses something at my face, and that's when I realize she came in with another crisp, white dress shirt and undershirt for me. Taking a step back, she leans against the sink and crosses her arms over her chest, staring at me with disapproval.

"It was a joke." I pull off the rest of my clothes and get dressed. I try to be quick, ruffled by what's just transpired, but that only makes me fumble more. Greta remains, watching me patiently, impassively.

Once I'm dressed and move to leave the bathroom, she stops me. "We've got to talk," she begins carefully.

I blink stupidly at her, my blood running cold. "Talk?"

"Don't look so scared. It's not anything big." She snorts, quick to pick up on my thoughts. "It's just about that note I found in your truck before you left for break."

"Note?"

She reaches into her chest and produces a rumbled scrap of paper. Immediately, my heart drops. Before she even reads it aloud, dread seeps through me.

"Remember this? 'Breakfast at my place next time?'"

"Oh." How I react to this discovery will determine the trajectory of us.

Greta bites her bottom lip and nods, crumpling the piece of paper back up into her fist. "I'm assuming this is old."

I nod.

"Before we had our agreement, right?"

Another nod.

"Okay. Well… You said that you don't have time for a relationship."

"I did say that, and I don't want a relationship." *But I wouldn't mind making time for you.* My pulse patters nervously.

"Then what's this?" She carefully sets the wadded paper on the sink and stares at it like it'll give her all the answers she needs.

"It was… It was me having a good time with you."

"And wanting to do it again."

"Yeah. Sex."

"Just sex, and no relationship, right?"

I don't answer.

"You *don't* want to have a relationship with me, right?" She's begging me. Even if her tone is detached, her eyes cold, she's begging me. It's obvious in the way she breathes and sucks her kiss-swollen bottom lip.

"I—No. When I told you I didn't want a relationship then, I meant it. I, y'know, was too busy. I *am* too busy." I make the mistake of looking at her. Like, really looking at her. Not just at how hot she is or how confident she appears. I look at her the way you'd look at your favorite meal. I'm hypnotized, enthralled by her everything, my mind torpedoing through all our moments together to slam me with this feeling.

Then I make another mistake of not concealing that look when she raises her eyes to mine. I could deny it night and day, claiming that I don't want anything with her and that the sex we have is all I want and nothing more. That I'm happy—not satisfied, but completely happy—with our dynamic.

I could do that, but I would be lying, and there's no point in lying when her crestfallen expression tells me that she knows.

"Oh, Morgan."

VOICEMAIL

GM Preston
Buffalo, New York
October 12, 2022 at 7:44 AM

Transcription
"Otis it was a pleasure having dinner with you and Coach Duger I am really looking forward to seeing you at the combine next year you have proven to be a formidable force on the collegiate league despite your injury and I have full confidence you'll be just as unstoppable with us in Buffalo call me if you have any questions and let me know your thoughts on coming down here for a visit during our off-season"

GM Wilson
San Antonio, Texas
October 29, 2022 at 8:08 PM

Transcription
"Morgan I was really happy you could make it to dinner with our managing team today and I wanted to let you know that we're very keen on seeing you wear yellow, blue, and green come this next season call or text me at any time if you have questions and just know we'll have our eyes out for you at the combine next year"

GM Bernard
Saint Paul, Minnesota
November 6, 2022 at 6:53 PM

Transcription
"Otis Morgan what a great Tim I'm on the phone what the fuck can you need that's so"

GRETA

KISS ME TWICE UNDER THE MISTLETOE

TODAY IS A fucking terrible day. Like, cry-buckets-of-shit-while-throwing-up type of terrible. So when James has the asinine audacity to hit on my mom, I feel better. Especially when my dad walks in to witness it.

"I welcome you to my home, invite you to my party, let you eat my food, celebrate with my family and my team, and this is how you treat me?" my father booms, hands on his hips, a vicious scowl on his face. "This is how you thank me? By offering to service my wife when I'm not around?"

"Don't yell, Farid. We have guests over," Mom whispers as she puts another tray of food in the oven. She's not actually paying attention to what's going on, focused instead on ensuring dinner is perfect. Despite the kitchen looking spotless, she grabs a disinfecting wipe and rubs the counters again. She looks at me for the umpteenth time, and I meet her gaze for a second before turning away, the faded longing in her eyes making the hollow inside me pinch and ache.

She's distracting herself from today by cleaning, cooking, and driving me fucking insane.

"*Don't yell? Don't* yell? I'm going to—" Dad's rampage fractures into disbelief, his face red. If looks could kill, James would be the one stuffed and set on a platter for us to feast on, instead of the turkey Mom spent all day preparing.

"It was a joke, sir," James squeaks. He glances at me for help, but Elise and I are too busy eating the chocolate strawberries she brought me to do anything.

Besides, this is quality entertainment. Who are we to disrupt it?

"Do you hear or see anyone around laughing? Jokes are meant to be funny. Do you think objectifying my wife is funny?"

"Greta is smiling and—"

My dad takes two strides toward him, grabs his sweater sleeve, and drags him to take a seat next to Elise, twirling the stool so that it faces the wall instead of my mom.

"*Tu es chiant.* Sit down, shut up, and wait for dinner. Look at my wife, and I'll rip out your eyeballs and have them sautced into the *tajin zitoun.*"

I bet it would still be delicious. It's a recipe from my *setti*, dad's mother, who's very old and still lives in Algeria and can make dirt taste gourmet.

"I don't know what that is," he mumbles meekly.

"What did I just say?"

James whines and shuts his mouth. All three of us remain silent as my dad rages to my mother in French, frequently throwing in his mother tongue—his command on Kabyle is feeble at best, his years in America withering away his fluency—and she responds with manufactured serenity. James appears terrified at the volatile manner in which Dad enunciates.

I'm the only one who doesn't react to their conversation. That's because I understand what they're saying and the only one that knows this angry outburst isn't specific to James. It's toward the day and how ineffective the dinner party is in diverting his attention from the bleak significance of it.

At its inception, the idea wasn't bad. Having a gathering of football players and their parents seemed like a clever way for my parents to vicariously compensate for their loss. They could relish in the blessings these parents have, though they wouldn't ever be able to experience it again themselves.

But they underestimated how affected they still are by Julien's death. They thought that just because my mom doesn't go to bed crying every night and Dad doesn't drink himself stupid after work, that things are okay. They thought they had weathered the worst and it was now past them.

As if three years was enough time. How stupid of them.

Consequently, their party is causing them pain rather than solace. It's especially brought Dad an unequivocal sadness rather than gaining a sense of comfort in seeing happy families joined together, mothers fussing over their children's attire, fathers waxing on and on about how proud they are. It's no wonder my father has been frequenting the kitchen and neglecting his duties as host.

As for me, if someone were to wonder what I'm doing, hiding out in the kitchen, I would say it's for one reason and one reason only.

Otis motherfucking Rutherford Morgan and his stupidly handsome face and that perfectly snug suit. Can one spell "delicious" without Otis? Yes. But it would be such a shame to do so, especially with how absolutely edible he looks in formal wear.

Otis and his stupid note that makes me want to melt and scream at the same time. Otis and his stupid feelings that are complicating what should be a perfectly straightforward fucklationship.

"Greta," my mom calls suddenly. I snap my head in her direction. Dad is already stomping out of the kitchen to tend to his neglected host duties.

"*Oui?*"

She doesn't respond right away. Three seconds pass and her shoulders sag, the tension released with a gentle exhale. With a smile, she shakes her head and whispers, "*Laisse tomber.*"

If only I could let it go, Mom.

Elise nudges me with a knee. I turn my attention to her. "How ya feeling now? Still cranky?" she asks.

"Like I need a good lay," I grumble faintly, leaning back in my seat. I twine my fingers together and press my joined palms against my forehead, closing my eyes for a second. Damn Otis for ruining my bathroom-quickie plan.

"Isn't *he*"—she wiggles her eyebrows in a very conspicuous way— "here tonight?"

I jerk my head in a short nod.

"Then grab him and head upstairs for a quick hanky-panky."

Opening one eye, my mouth twists in disgust. "You did not just call it 'hanky-panky.'"

Elise pretends to brush her hair behind her ear and innocently bats her lashes. "You guys don't make love, so what else am I supposed to call it?"

"Sex. Just sex." Or fucking, but I'd be hard-pressed to convince Elise to say that.

It's Elise's turn to make a face. She polishes off the last strawberry.

So much for being a gift.

"That sounds so technical."

"It is technical." I sit up straight, scowling. "What's wrong with making sex technical? Not everything has to involve feelings."

"But feelings make everything feel... better."

"I agree with that," James interjects, turning to look at us, his chair still facing the wall. "You're just emotionally crippled, which was cute in our freshman year, but as juniors, it's getting a little old."

I roll my eyes and point a finger at him. "You, lover boy, are in timeout. Keep running your mouth, and I'll inform my dad about all the other shit you said to my mom *before* he walked in."

"Evil, petty woman." He goes silent.

Elise shakes her head and frowns. She places a hand on my knee, the touch gentle, understanding. The way she's looking at me makes everything inside me feel heavy and frosted, and a crack appears in my defenses. I bite the insides of my cheeks to maintain my outward expression of apathy, my slightly labored breaths the only indication of what I'm actually feeling.

"I know I've already offered this, but if you want to talk, I'm here," my best friend whispers.

Rather than sneer at her concern, I nod and give a tight-lipped smile. "Thanks, Lisey. I'm good for now."

It's a lie, and both Elise and James know it.

But there's nothing that can be done. The inconsolable sadness that gnaws at me is an insatiable fiend, surviving on my trepidation. And so I give way to it, allowing it to feed on me, feeling barren. That's all I am for tonight. That's how I'll survive this.

JEFFERSON RODNEY MAKES a speech during dinner, towering over the rest of us as we remain seated. He looks handsome and clean, his suit tailored wonderfully for his stocky body, the blue tie complimenting his clear, cool-brown skin and perfectly wavy black hair.

The fullback is being honored as the most valued player on the team. The coaches made the right decision. On the field, the man is an absolute menace, with the speed and agility of a fucking hyena and the stamina of a bulldozer. He's always been a good player, but this season, his skills have developed tremendously. Last week, I overheard Dad talking to NFL recruiters about him.

At the end of his speech, Francis Quinn, Jefferson's counterpart and fellow running back, the person Jefferson is tasked with protecting and paving the field for, stood to give his teammate an enthusiastic standing ovation, causing the rest of the packed tables to follow suit.

And the only reason I remembered this moment is because of

the way Otis hesitated to react in kind. His indiscernible façade transforms into complete disdain and outrage.

But like a blink, the look disappears, and in its place is a tight-lipped smile. Otis lazily stands tall and claps appropriately, bowing his head and partially concealing his face.

But I know what I saw.

MY MOM IS driving me up a fucking wall and I've only just scurried away from her after she captured me while I was relaxing on the couch and talking to Elise, Katia, and Autumn. The fun conversation about adopting strays was cut short in favor of me standing by Mom's side so she could feel soothed by my presence while I'm left irritated by hers.

"If that woman grabs me by the elbow one more time, it's on sight," I snap at James, who's playing a game of Jenga with the shortbread cookies on the table.

"She's just sad. It's her son's death anniversary. Give her a break."

I glare at him then at his plate. I want to knock it out of his hand and force him to clean up the mess. But alas, I'm a pacifist. And my mom will literally make me suck the crumbs out of the carpet if any fall. "He was my brother, too, jackass. I'm also sad, but you don't see me nagging her all the time."

"That's because you have the emotional range of an elephant. You're either grazing the fields, all relaxed and shit, or terrorizing villagers and stampeding their homes."

I blink, trying to process what he just said. "Are you saying I look like an elephant?"

He stops building the world's first dessert-scraper and looks at me, baffled. "What? No. How the hell did you get that from what I said?"

"You said I was an elephant." I take a bite of a cookie, willing the sweetness to bring forth a rush of endorphins so that my internal frown might turn upside down. Sadly, no happy hormones flood me.

He shakes his head ruefully, adds two more cookies, then snatches his drink from my hand, ignoring my question as we leave the kitchen.

Right as we cross the short distance into the living room, there's a loud cheer and the room bursts into laughter.

"We finally got one!" an indistinct male voice shouts from some corner of the room.

"Kiss! You're under the mistletoe, so you have to kiss!" a girl that looks like a mini-Otis says. Monica, I'm assuming.

James and I look up to confirm this exclamation. I let out an internal sigh—seriously, who the fuck puts Christmas decorations up this early?—but make no qualms. James is already leaning down to kiss me when I turn to face him. It's short and friendly.

It's funny how this kiss inspires no feeings in me, only serving to remind me of how my kisses with Otis feel. It's not that kissing James is unpleasant, but kissing Otis is passionate.

When we break apart, we pause to smile at each other, and the reassurance in his eyes, the one that tells me *I'm glad you're still in my life*, makes my chest fizzle in relief. I reciprocate the look before turning to look at the room. Most all are jeering, whooping, and winking.

But not Otis. I barely get a glimpse of his profile before he walks out of the room.

RODNEY IS BOLD—extremely bold, and a smidge sleazy, even by my skewed standards.

"All I'm saying is that as the guest of honor, I should be rewarded with a lil' sum-in' sum-in', y'know?"

"I hear you." I toy with my necklace subconsciously but stop when I notice the way his eyes follow the strumming of my fingers against the thin gold cord.

He's been flirting with me for at least five minutes, smart to do so now while my dad is lounging in the backyard with the rest of the parents. We're standing in the living room with the rest of the guests our age, everyone paired and absorbed in their own discussions.

"You hear me, but are you willing to do anything about it?" he purrs, leaning forward. He's only an inch or two taller than me, but his confidence and mannerisms add to his stature.

"What would you like me to do?"

He places a hand on my waist. At first, it feels nice. He has a firm grip, and his hands are hot but not too sweaty. Our bodies are close but not too close.

A protest sits on the tip of my tongue, a knot twisting in my stomach. But nothing comes out. There's no tangible reason for me to want to distance myself from his gesture. And yet...

"I'm sure we can think of something," he whispers, his lips dangerously close to my ear. I place a hand on his chest to keep from having our torsos flush. The knot grows tighter as my eyes nervously dart around the room. One word and he would back off, but I'm stubborn, wanting to prove a point, one that I don't even know.

"Chill, my guy. Shouldn't you be worried about my dad?" My response is breezy, but my pulse stammers out of beat. And it's not because of Coach Sahnoun.

"Aw, c'mon. I know you and Frosted Oats are messin' around. If he ain't afraid, then why the fuck should I be? I'm the golden boy tonight."

This time, I don't disguise my surprise. His flagrant disloyalty prompts me to push him away slightly, disgusted. "If you know I'm with Otis, why are you still acting like a clown?"

It's his turn to appear disconcerted. "Oh. So, you *with*-with him? I thought y'all were just fucking around for fun, not like in a relationship and shit."

"We aren't in a relationship," I sputter.

He's backed away from me as well, though his touch remains on my hip. Doubt wrinkles his face. That knot in my gut tightens. "Really. We're just having fun."

"All right, then," Rodney responds slowly. The back of his hand skims up my side, stopping just before my breasts. "If that's the case, then how 'bout 'just having fun' with a real man?"

I don't get a chance to respond before Otis appears out of nowhere, wearing an expression of disinterest, the lines of his face soft and placid. But there's a threat in the way his imposing body looms over us.

Without warning, he wraps what seems to be a friendly arm around Rodney's shoulder, but I observe the way Otis effortlessly grips his friend's massive bicep to tear Rodney's hand off me. "Jefferson," he begins softly. "I thought we talked about this?"

"Talked about what?"

"Talked about you"—he strengthens his grip while the running back appears confused—"staying away from Coach's daughter."

"We were just talking."

"And touching." The lilt of his tone is relaxed, but the malice in his eyes belies his true feelings. He pats Jefferson Rodney's chest, and it's a harsh gesture. The running back leans back from the force. Otis has yet to look at me. "And unless you want me to rip your hand off your body and use it as my new Reacher Grabber, I would advise not doing that."

"Bro, I was just—"

Otis's eyes twinkle in an eerie way, his smile somehow turning more serene. He speaks carefully, pausing between every word. "Get the fuck away from her right now before I lose it."

Rather than appearing afraid, Rodney looks annoyed. He gives me a final once-over while I remain motionless, an uncomfortable feeling simmering beneath the surface of my skin.

Both Otis and Rodney leave me, neither of them acknowledging me on their way out. It enrages me, and I look around the room, self-conscious about Otis's display, struggling to contain an outburst.

I'm torn between shoving Otis into the closest room and fucking him until this tension wracking my body disperses or yelling at him for making me feel… anything but hollow.

I CAN'T LEAVE my parents' house quickly enough. Right as the last batch of guests say their goodbyes and walk out the door, I follow, despite my mother's insistence that I stay over. I swear, if I have to look into those sad eyes for another second, I'll combust. The harrowing dullness in them could turn Medusa herself into stone.

Elise and James already left a while ago but sent me a text asking if I wanted company tonight, probably afraid that alone, I'll do something stupid like buy a pack of cigarettes and smoke the whole thing. Feeling a little anxious, I check their location to confirm they haven't preemptively arrived at my place.

Nope, just at a Dairy Queen.

The drive to my apartment is quiet. I should have put on some music or a self-righteous podcast about healing and finding oneself—hell, even an erotic audiobook would do—to drown the melancholy thoughts fighting to reach the surface. But I don't. I'm an emotional masochist, an elephant ready to terrorize the villagers.

Ironically, the memories that come to the forefront, the ones I conjure in the saddest of moments, are happy ones. Even more ironic is that unlike the sad ones, happy reminiscing leaves a more poignant nip of sorrow in their wake, making it hurt a little too much to smile without pain.

The memories are random, but the pattern is simple: They're all instances when Julien laughed. Like the time we went to that summer lake and Julien taught me how to do a flip off the tire swing. Or how, when he was first learning to drive, we stole Dad's vintage Mustang convertible and took it on a joy ride at two in the morning. Or when, at his homecoming dance, he was crowned freshman homecoming king and was asked to choose a girl to dance with, and he chose me instead of his actual date since mine had gotten sick and couldn't make it.

I beam so hard my cheeks ache, but the happy memories also give way to hurt. When I close my eyes, I see a faded apparition of him, the goofy grin he wore when he scored a touchdown or made a good pass, or the stupid dance he would do when his teammate caught an interception. In my memories, Julien exists only in a state of utter happiness. Even if I know that's not the case, I preserve him like this, incapable of processing him in any other form.

It hurts even more when I open my eyes because he's not there and never will be. I miss him, and I hate it. No amount of yearning or wishful thinking will ever bring him back.

The worst part is expending myself on these emotions only to have them yield nothing in return. At least the pain keeps him alive, even if just in my memories.

WHEN I ARRIVE at my apartment, I don't get out of my car immediately. In fact, I don't even shift into park. Temptation looms. The gas station isn't too far from my place. What's so wrong with grabbing a pack and lighting it up for two hours, just until the day ends? It doesn't count as caving if I really, *really* need it, right? It's not my addiction speaking, I rationalize. It's my need for self-preservation. And when I'm well-preserved, I won't do it again.

I argue with myself for a while, sitting there, one hand on the steering wheel, the other on the gear shift. However, right as I'm about to surrender and put my car into reverse, there's a knock on my window. I shriek in surprise, a hand on my chest as I turn to look at the perpetrator.

"Otis, what the fuck?" I snap, feeling my face contort with rage. I'm still shut in my car, and he motions for me to lower the window. "You scared the absolute shit out of me," I exclaim. "What're you doing here? Are you trying to apologize for being such a jealous ass? I get that you might want something more out of this, Morgan, but I've made myself perfectly clear and if you can't—"

Otis dangles something green and red just above the window frame, cutting off my monologue. I don't get a proper glimpse of it before he leans his head into my car and grabs my face, silencing me.

This kiss is unlike any of the ones we've shared before. It's hard to describe why that's the case. The technique is the same. There's nothing different about how our mouths move. It's a familiar dance with our tongues, our lips opening and closing, sucking, drawing patterns. Even the way he licks his way inside, oscillating between passionate and teasing, is the same, the wet sounds the same, too.

But it's different, the intensity of it all. His breath comes out heavier, hotter, through his nostrils, or on a sudden exhale when we break apart for the briefest of seconds to readjust. He sucks my bottom lip, holding it for a moment too long, almost like he never wants to let it go. I don't even think I want him to, not when he cradles my face like this, making me feel like everything is alright.

He toys with my necklace then trails beneath my translucent scarf to touch my collarbone. The slippery material falls off one shoulder. Otis traces the skin there with the callous pads of his fingers, and I arch into his touch, wishing away the barriers between us.

Even I'm behaving a little out of character. My hands itch to feel him. They move to lace into his hair and caress the thick cords of his muscular neck. My palm flattens against his pulse. It beats wildly, but he's perfectly fine, his soft grunting indicating as much.

He's an inferno, blazing with fire so pure and molten that it's white.

He's a midway point on my journey to *Somewhere*, and I'm basking in the wonders and horrors he's willing to show me—to give me—before I'm burned by his existence and walk away. I'm frightened, this uncomfortable feeling of déjà vu overwhelming.

Suddenly, I'm left cold by his retreat. Shivers wrack me from both the absence of his touch and the frosty air billowing into my car.

Otis tosses something into my lap, and I glance down to hear him say, "There's your real mistletoe kiss."

When I look back at him, he's rubbing a thumb over his lip and staring at me like he wants to say something dangerous but just doesn't know how.

In the end, however, his eyes cool as he grows quiet and amenable again. "I don't need a relationship."

"Okay."

"I just need... I want you, Greta. However you'll have me, I'll be that man for you. Whenever you want me, I'll make the time. And if that means we're just fucking, then so be it. But whatever it is we're doing right now..." He looks into the distance.

I hold my breath, and when he gazes back at me, I actually feel robbed of something. My breath? No. Something deeper.

"I think it's worth something."

There are so many things to say, so many counterarguments to make, so many points I want him to clarify after dropping this fucking bomb on me. Part of me recoils entirely from his admissions and the subtext. But there's another part, quieter but more influential, that is soothed. More than that, the thought of this ending terrifies me more than the prospect of him wanting me in a capacity I'm not willing to give him.

Already feeling emotionally overwhelmed, I simply swallow, nod, and chuckle insincerely. The window slowly raises before he walks away.

I GO TO the gas station. I don't get a pack of cigarettes, but I do buy a bottle of Everclear.

I thought it would help me cry, but I only get angry. I storm around my apartment, yelling wildly at the ceiling fan as if I'm talking to Julien. I say a lot of mean things I would never say sober.

I tell him that I hate him for being so weak. That he was so stupid for overdosing when he should have known better. That I truly wish it was me instead of him who died—at least, that's how our parents feel, I'm sure. And that he should have talked to me if he was so stressed, because I hadn't thought it was that bad. Sure, Dad was riding him harder to make varsity and get invited to football scouting camps, but he was doing well, wasn't he?

But most of all, I yell at him for leaving me and for making me an emotionally decrepit elephant with two extremes and no in-between.

Raven approaches me in the middle of my tirade and boops his soft nose on my foot, and I break. The tears that had been caged in my body, compressed and suppressed by the dinner party   who wants to deal with a sobbing, grieving chick?—spill out of me. I hug Raven and cry into his fur. He's nice enough to absorb my tears without scratching me much.

I end up falling asleep on the floor of the living room with the bottle half-empty, my eyes swollen, my makeup running, and my heart hurting.

When I wake up in the morning, I go about my day like last night didn't happen.

Inbox - hanselngreta@rsu.org

✉ Marbury & Greta (46)

Ms. Sahnoun, Have you finished grading the student's homework? They're completion grades. Please finish them as soon as...

✉ Republic Bank

Hi, GRETA, your available account balance is low Account: COLLEGE CHECKING - 4269 Available balance: below $5 Please remedy this...

✉ Dr. Myron

Extra credit assignment has been posted. Please complete it before midnight tomorrow for an extra 5 points to your exam average. If you have...

OTIS

NEW TO LOVE

"ARE YOU READY to be thanked?" Greta purrs. She sets her pen down, pushes away from the kitchen table, and swivels in her seat to face me. I mimic her, our knees brushing, and electric delight rushes through me.

Wedging her legs between mine, she places her hands on my thighs, dragging them over the coarse material of my jeans until she reaches my crotch. I jolt, thoughts of price determinations and inflation rates eluding me.

I had high hopes when she asked me to help her with economics. Despite having my own schoolwork to do and being exhausted from practice and watching game tapes, I'd rushed over here when she'd texted Tutor me tonight?.

I can't really afford to waste time this week, but pussy is pussy, and no matter how dedicated I am to getting into the NFL, finally receiving a message from her after radio silence since my mistletoe confession had me rearranging my priorities for the day.

Had I known tutoring meant actual tutoring, I would have taken my time getting to her place. I'd have eaten dinner with my roommates, washed my hair a little longer in the shower, and maybe even outlined my term paper that's due Monday.

The text had left much to the imagination, and given our pattern, I'd assumed a dirtier subtext, thinking that maybe she would finally indulge my schoolgirl fantasy. But no. She'd requested my assistance in earnest.

Being summoned for a non-sexual reason had been a pleasant surprise. Granted, I couldn't help but feel slighted when she successfully comprehended a new set of theories and applied them to her own problems, wondering how much work I could be getting done at home with my textbook instead of hers, but all this goes away the second her hand rubs my dick.

Greta nibbles on my jaw, traveling lower until she reaches the nook between my neck and shoulder. Keen fingers undo the buttons of my pants. I tilt my head back to provide more space, my lips parted to pant in uneven breaths. The suction of her mouth on the sensitive area, the way she tries to puncture my skin with her teeth in bruising intent only to apologize for her aggression with sweet, soothing licks, all have me as high as the cow jumping over the motherfucking moon.

I make a noise somewhere between a whine and a growl, trying hard to guide her mouth onto mine. Greta resists for a bit but then obliges me, those decadent, luscious lips slotting against mine, stealing my coherence.

She pushes the mint she's been sucking on into my mouth, and I moan at the cool taste mixed with her flavor. We make out passionately. Our lips collide in heavy, open-mouthed kisses, the smooth surfaces of our tongues sliding along each other sensually, sharing her candy until it dissolves. We're invested in this drawn-out exchange. The longer it goes on, the sloppier and more intense it gets.

I love all of it. I love the way her tongue curls and rubs against mine. I love the way her hand strokes me, the strength of her grip fluctuating, her other hand finding purchase at the nape of my neck as she settles over my legs. I love the way she attempts to dominate me and the way I readily concede to her prowess.

She tickles her thoughts onto the roof of my mouth and the inside of my cheeks, knowing I'll understand and chase her back into her mouth to inscribe my own reflections.

I want to remain like this, in her embrace, for the rest of forever, her dainty hand jerking me into a state of readiness, mapping the hard, smooth ridges of my length in tight, precise pumps. The pads of her nimble fingers massage my scalp and lips as our tongues and teeth mingle, making the soles of my feet tingle as my chest constricts in painful wonder.

But as all our sweet moment do, the mood turns volatile. My hands, once rubbing soothing trails beneath her shirt to trace her perfect profile, skim the underside of her bare breasts and clasp her ribcage to draw her closer until she's on my lap.

Her pussy replaces her hand. I emit a hoarse groan when she grinds her mound against me in concentric circles, and my cock jolts, ready to slide into her. Through the material of her shorts, she beats against me, hot and ready. I can't help but let out a light chuckle.

She nips my bottom lip and pulls back a little, arms twined around my neck, curbing the movement of her hips. "What's so funny, Princess? Share some of the giggles."

"You're burning up for me, sweetheart. I just know you're dripping," I whisper, repeating what I'd said to her that first night we met when she'd asked me for a cigarette and let me kiss that addictive mouth of hers. I press a kiss on the hollow of her collarbone, going lower, my chin dragging down the collar of her shirt as I peck along her sternum. It can't have been more than three months ago, yet I feel like I've been with her for the better part of my life.

Her eyes light up immediately as she's recalling the moment with perfect clarity. My heart flips, and she smiles, wiggling her eyebrows suggestively at me. "And if I was? What would you do about it?"

Just like that, it happens.

I never understood what my dad meant when he told me that finding that one true love was terrifying. Every time I've fallen in love, it's felt great. Freeing. Wonderful. And every single time, at the beginning, I always thought they were *it*.

I blink just for the tiniest of moments, but my world reforms once I open my eyes. Before me is a woman, so ethereal and exquisite that I can't believe she's real. She has flushed cheeks and bright eyes and thick, kiss-swollen red lips that are curved into a familiar, mischievous grin. She looks at me with equal parts arousal and glee, a divine dimple indenting her cheek, and I'm done for.

Without so much as a warning, I topple over the edge to an abyss I've experienced before. Except this time, the altitude is higher, the fall harder. There's a rush in the plunge—a heart-wrenching exhilaration that rivals even the best of releases. As I plummet, I do nothing to hold myself back, to slow the descent, or even to brace myself for the catastrophic landing. Because for as breathtaking as it was, the touchdown wreaks havoc on me. My reality shifts as it's casted in ominous shades of navy, violet, and gray.

I'm in love with Greta Miriam Sahnoun, and I think I have been for a while. I just hadn't realized it, my incessant need to have sex with her obscuring my desire to be around her, to be *with* her.

"Rutherford?" she probes when I go lifeless beneath her. Concern emanates from her.

The sound of my middle name snaps me out of my daze, and with all my might, I gather my wits and force myself to appear normal and not at all devastatingly lovestruck. "What's up, Miriam?" I choke out.

Her eyes narrow, and she purses her lips, inspecting me carefully. It's clear from the way she moves her mouth from side to side that she wants to say something. But I kiss her first, afraid of the prospect that she might accidentally crush my soul with a harmless tease.

I lose myself in the kiss, allowing the gesture to serve as a confession. My chest explodes with burning desire, and I know I have to tell her I love her. Even if it's without words. I have to. So I get creative.

The tip of my tongue traces the letter "I" against the surface of hers. My hands move to cup her bare breasts, squeezing only her left one, the one protecting her heart, to communicate "love." Finally, I speak the "you" by holding her tighter against me, never wanting to let go.

I'm forced to, though, when she pushes away from me. "Move your chair and take your boxers off," she commands, leaning over the kitchen table we'd been studying on to grab her discarded hair tie.

Immediately, I know exactly how Greta is going to thank me. She collects her hair into a tight ponytail, shoving off her shorts and panties but keeping her oversized shirt on. My hand instinctively goes underneath to grope the curve of her ass, only to test the dampness between her slick legs. I moan. She's fucking dripping, just from rubbing that pretty cunt against me.

Right as I try to slip a finger inside, she steps away, turning to scold me with a glare.

"What?"

She scoffs. "You must be a nightmare at museums. All touching and very little looking."

"I mean, if we're talking about looking... How about you take those titties out? I wanna see 'em."

She ignores me and rolls her eyes, one corner of her mouth tugging into a smile. Her eyes remain stern even as I wiggle my eyebrows and cup my hands over my chest, pretending to juggle the jugs.

"Quit playing," she chides, clicking her tongue.

I pout and *harumph*. "Yes ma'am."

As domineering as Greta can be, I've observed that she likes to be in control while beneath someone else's control. It's hard to explain how she establishes that dynamic in our sexual trysts. One second, I think I'm the one doing the fucking, and in the next, she proves me wrong, unexpectedly taking charge.

That's what she does now. She pushes me down onto the chair and then turns around. With her back flush to my torso and me still seated, she squats over me. She swats me away when I offer any assistance to spread her pussy or align my dick into her. She's going to do it by herself.

One hand grips the edge of the table, the other on my shaft to keep it upright and steady while she drops onto me. Greta lets out a throaty whimper as she lowers herself past my bulbous tip, her sopping entrance blossoming. She glides lower, taking me in about halfway before needing to adjust.

My face overheats and a knot forms in my spine, my body wrought with tension as she clutches me, her warm, slick walls simultaneously sucking me in and pushing me out with every clench. I keep my hands to myself but they itch to grab hold of her, to shove her down and relish in the sensation of being encompassed by lush, wet walls.

"You feel so good," she babbles, her limp head falling back onto my shoulder, legs bouncing in short strokes, taking more of my cock at every pass. "So fucking good. So big and thick. Fuck, I love your cock."

Pull yourself together and do not *nut right now, Otis.*

"I thought you didn't like how big I am." I clutch the seat of my chair to keep from plunging upward in brutal need. She's almost there. Almost settled on my lap completely, clasping all of me. It would take just a small—

"I lied. I love it. Love your big cock. Love how it wrecks me. Fills me."

My self-control snaps, and without pretense, I wrap my arm

fully around her waist and thrust violently, eliminating that last inch of unoccupied space. "And I love"—*you*—"filling you up and hearing you scream because of me." I grunt, dropping my ass back onto the chair only to push back up again. My balls churn when she bucks, her pussy fluttering around me.

I pull her closer to bury her against my chest, holding her there, fully seated, my cock sheathed deep inside her, squeezed and soaked.

She twists to awkwardly face me, curiosity flitting over her face when I inhibit her movements, my biceps rippling to anchor her in place. "Otis," she whines, trying to bounce and create delicious friction. "C'mon, move. Fuck me."

I shake my head, gasping like I'm asphyxiated. "Just—a minute. Give me a minute."

She keeps resisting, and the desperate movements cause me to slacken my embrace immediately, giving in to her request. But then, just as she's about to lift off to slam back down, she surprises me and stops. Greta looks me in the eye and bends her arm to cradle the back of my skull.

I bask in the undisturbed sensation of our joined bodies, in the vibrancy that strengthens my heart. There's no movement, no dirty talk, no kissing. Just us, breathing together, our eyes locked, a cloud of ambiguity festering in hers. She gives me this moment, and for that, my heart expands and loves her infinitely more.

But like all good things, this sweet moment comes to an end when she seductively commands me to fuck her.

Without another word, I perform the role she wants. It's time to satisfy this insatiable woman pressed against me.

At first, it's just a simple reverse cowgirl. She slides up with gradual, deep strokes, grinding against me when the helmet of my dick bumps her g-spot, my hands working languid circles onto her clit. I assist her movement with a hold on her knee.

But then she stands, and I slip out. There's no time for me to protest and ask what's going on before she's bent over the table, her torso flat on the surface, ass wriggling desperately from side to side, indicating what she wants to happen next. She doesn't have to say a single thing before I'm scrambling to my feet. Settling behind her, I kick her legs farther apart, bend down and sink back inside her tight cunt in one frictionless thrust.

I fuck her as innocently as backshots can be, each whiny exhale an indication of the pleasure escalating within her. But then she starts to roll her hips and shove back against me, redirecting my focus from her pussy swallowing my dick to her unmarred ass, the skin rippling each time our skin meets, her backside smacking into my hip.

And the compulsion to smack that thick, meaty flesh is one I cannot control. It takes hold of me before I can ask if she's cool with getting rough today.

"Yes," she squeals. My rhythm stutters out of beat at her exclamation, her moans drowned by the scraping of the table's legs against the tiled floor. Balling the back of her shirt into my grip, I ram into her violently. Her upper body bows perfectly, her head tossed back. I slant and position my torso over her even more to nuzzle my nose against her neck, fighting away a grin. I feel her every whimper, her hips grinding.

This time, when I leave a sharp sting on her ass, I do it in a desperate need to possess her, to leave my mark on her.

We go at it like this for a while. I only slap her ass one more time before she says her safe word, our night together from two weeks ago still affecting her.

But that doesn't mean she wants me to go soft on her. She's quick to make clear just how badly she needs to be wrecked by me. I angle her and thrust downward, our sticky flesh beating together to create a concerto with the moving furniture and our moans.

"Yes," she shrills, spasming around me, holding me hostage in her luxurious depths. A sob escapes her when I circle my hips to bump against her favorite spot as she works her sensitive clit with her hand.

I'm high on her pleasure, each sound she makes tabbed as a new favorite of mine. "You're a dirty girl, aren't you?" I taunt. "A dirty, slutty girl that likes how hard I fuck this tight, gorgeous pussy."

She presses her cheek into the table, but I know the cool surface offers no respite from the fire building in her body. "I love when you fuck what's yours, Otis."

My name slips from her lips like it was meant for her, and immediately, sanity eludes me. At first, it's brutal but slow. I have her blubbering, plowing so deep that her knees buckle and she clutches the ends of the table. When I slide back out, I do so completely, making her whimper from the loss while I stroke my length, delighting in how slick it is from her, before slamming ferociously into her again. I'm mindless from the euphoria that shoots through me, the sight of my cock entering her serving to heighten the sensation.

Soon, the torturous tempo I've established isn't enough. "More. Faster," she bites out.

I obey, plowing into her warm, wet heat, reaching the hilt with each stroke. The muscles of my thighs quiver in protest, but the effort is worth it. Every moan she lets out, every bow of her back, every buck against my body, makes anything worth it.

It becomes even more worth it just a moment later. Her ponytail is swaying from the intoxicated movement of her head, hypnotizing me. Under its spell, I grab and yank, tugging her head back forcefully because I just love the way her body curves under me. This produces a scream of agonizing approval, the sound shooting straight to my balls and making them clench. I'm close.

"Harder," she chokes out. "Pull harder."

I ruthlessly oblige, compounding the sensation with a sharp, harsh drive of my hip that has me wrapping an arm around her to keep her from collapsing. Her torso arches into the forceful pull while I spoon her from above, following the concavity of her form, and I love it. Love the lewd sounds of our flesh meeting. Love the sobs that escape her and the breathless pants that leave me. I fucking love it.

Love this.

Love her.

The buildup to our climaxes is quick. The punishing pace I've established overwhelms me, and soon, I'm shaking in the effort to maintain my thrusts because she's bucking into me wildly, chanting how close she is, how much she loves the way I'm pulling her hair, how good it feels to have her needy pussy fucked by my thick, gorgeous cock. My legs start to shake as streaks of iridescent white glimmer in my line of vision. It feels so good.

She feels so good.

We are so good.

"I need you to come around me right now, okay, G?" I plead, tugging at her hair to leverage myself deeper inside her.

She jerks her head, denying my appeal.

I grab her cheeks and pinch them to tilt her face up. I still can't see her to make out how beautifully ruined she is, but I can feel it in the way she trembles around me and hear it in her staccato breaths. Normally, I'd take a more aggressive stance, but I'm so desperate for release that it's not even funny, and all I can do is whimper, "Please. Please come for me."

"Fuck. More. Beg me more. You do it so well," she moans. And I do. I plead with her, praising her, telling her how I won't be able to take another second without feeling her cum spilling over me. And with that, she grabs the hand I have on her breast and yanks it down between her legs. "Fuck," she shrieks when her body seizes with pleasure and comes all around my cock, her pussy spasming to trigger my release. I'm pulled into the depths of a hot, silky heaven, cocooned in the pure bliss of her body.

I make a plea, something about wanting her—needing her—and

follow a second later, biting her shoulder to keep from making an undue confession. I pray the venom of my bite somehow seeps into her bloodstream and infects her with the unrequited infatuation I feel.

For a solid ten seconds, I'm immortal, basking in the light of her aura, feeling nothing but rapture as I soar to new heights. My toes curl, my mind numbed by the electricity that fizzles through me.

As I let go, I continue to fuck her, filling her with my cum. She absolutely adores it and reach around to grab my ass to help me pour every drop of it inside her.

My body gives out a few seconds later, and by the grace of God, I topple onto the chair rather than the floor, bringing Greta along with me.

I go blank after that, catatonic, limp, the urge to take a nap weighing heavily on my tired eyelids.

The only thing that breaks me out of my dreamy state is a loud, clear meow. When I turn my head, Raven is looking up at me, his judgmental face filled with reproach. My eyes flicker to Greta, who's resting against my chest, equally exhausted.

She stares at Raven then looks at me with a frown. "Yeah. I definitely have to take him to a therapist."

YOU KNOW WHICH bitch just killed my vibe? Greta's friend.

"What did he want?" I inquire, trying to maintain a semblance of casualness. I stand in front of the bathroom sink, a towel wrapped loosely around my waist, watching keenly as she makes her way into the bathroom and lifts her shirt while she approaches the toilet.

I'm lathering her face wash in my palms just as she taught me, but I'm distracted, staring at her sitting on the toilet, phone in hand.

Just two minutes ago, our harmonious post-sex routine was disrupted by a ring of the doorbell. Rather than take a second to get dressed, Greta decided to saunter out of the bathroom, clad only in an oversized shirt with no bra or panties, to answer the door, my cum still tacky on her inner thigh. "It's only James," she'd said when I suggested she put more clothes on.

"Something," she replies vaguely, concentrating on her phone. My face ticks in irritation.

"Something?" I repeat for emphasis. When she doesn't get the hint, I try again. "What something?"

"This thing he left at my place on Monday. I dunno what it is."

Two days ago, Monday? The Monday after the Sunday where you kissed him under the mistletoe and I pretty much told you that I liked you and that you could play me like a marionette? That Monday?

"Oh?" *Don't ask. Don't do it, Otis. You are not her boyfriend. She's made that clear. All you're going to do is hurt your own feelings. Don't ask. Don't ask. Don't—* "What were you guys doing Monday?"

"Playing that Catan game. It was fun."

Had she told me that she fucked him, I would have been less offended. "The game I bought you?" I try so hard to rein in the anger that rattles through me. I'm a poor, poor boy who spent my hard-earned money on her, and this is what she does. "You played it with him?"

"Yeah." She's still paying close attention to the screen in front of her, not having looked up at me once. She taps her foot as she types, speaking to me absentmindedly, as if I'm not even worth her undivided attention. "We had a game night."

"Who's 'we'? Just you and James?" I turn away from her, my face twisted in an ugly scowl. I'm being grumpy, but I genuinely can't help it. I can't keep my mouth shut when this cardinal board-game sin has been made apparent to me. "Cause you can't play with two players. You should be playing with four. Three at the very least."

"We made it work since everyone else flaked."

Was it Elise? Was she a part of 'everyone else'? Did she flake? Is she the reason why Greta played my game alone with that fucker? I'm going to have to have a conversation with Herik about his girlfriend's lack of commitment. If she can't commit to a fucking game of Catan, then how the fuck can he trust her to commit to him? I'll text him once I finish moisturizing.

I don't say anything else. I'm abusive to my face as I wash it, rubbing forcefully, murder on my mind. I pause every now and then to glance at Greta to see if she's looking in my direction. When she isn't, I'm launched further into a state of despair.

I'm the color sage, green with hints of furious red and mopey brown.

"You've been washing your face for a while," Greta comments after a minute. She turns on the bidet then wipes herself with toilet paper before standing beside me at the sink. She scrutinizes me for a second then hip bumps me aside and washes her hands.

"So?" I grumble. I glare at her in the mirror, hating how oblivious she's being. I would bet a lot of money that it's intentional. How rude.

"So?" She snorts and shakes her head, staring back at me, still unbothered. "Your face is totally irritated. That's not good."

"I don't care." If I had a bib and a binky, I'd be the world's tallest baby.

She waves dismissively. "Fine. Keep acting up. See if I care."

"You don't," I snap. That's the problem. She doesn't care that another guy saw her practically half-naked or that the guy got to kiss her and play *Catan* with her.

I mean, seriously. How could she? How could she take my heart and smash it to bits like that? Catan? *My* game? With that bozo? If the world swallowed me whole right now, I would thank it for the sweet relief.

Greta turns to look at me, holding her hands up as the water drips down her arms. She regards me with a level gaze before snatching the towel I was using to dry my face. "Otis," she says calmly. "You can't act like this."

"Like what?"

"Like *this*. It's confusing." She stops, an unnamed emotion creasing her beautiful face.

My heart leaps to my throat, ready to suffocate her with my newfound feelings.

But she doesn't give me the opportunity. "Seriously, stop. You can't be feeling jealous like this."

"What's 'like this'?" I prod stubbornly.

She smacks her hand on the counter and cocks her hip, her expression severe. "Like a boyfriend."

As if I needed another reminder that I'm not.

In about ten minutes—maybe less—I'm going to walk out that front door, just like James had. The only difference between the two of us is that he got to fuck her back then and I get to fuck her now. Except, I'm a prideful shit—a Morgan through and through.

"Like James was?" Admittedly, that is not the best thing to have said.

"Better him than you," she snaps.

Now I've done it. I've made her angry.

"Contrary to what rom-coms might have you think, jealousy is fucking ugly. And you're looking a lot like Frankenstein right now."

Okay, I did not deserve that. "What you mean is Frankenstein's monster. Frankenstein was the scientist that made him, genius. And if that's the case, then I'm the hottest monster alive!"

"Still a monster, you brainless fuck."

I don't take the insult too kindly, and that's when we go at it.

Greta calls me a shithead, I call her a pretty, empty-headed, piece of ass. She says I'm being a Neanderthal, and I ask her how she knows such a big word when she can hardly multiply.

Right when she calls me a hacked-up sycamore tree with hairy areolas, I sort of just lose it, and rather than respond, I kiss her. I'm so beyond turned on by her insults, it's not even funny. Even the most tolerant therapist would raise an eyebrow at how much of a masochist I am.

It's barbaric, the way I launch myself at her while we're in the middle of a fight, but it's effective. Our anger turns into passion, and soon, her shirt is off and my towel is dropped and we're going for round two against the bathroom wall. It's messier than the sex we had at the kitchen table, and I'm actually proud of how fast my dick stands at attention and even more proud of how long I last. She's already come once by the time she's begging me to fill her up a second time, her cunt so willing and wet.

I respond with a circle on her clit. "You haven't earned it yet, slut," I say, which feeds her second orgasm.

She whines for me to stop. She's sensitive. At first, I slow down, taking her at her word, but she's quick to correct my line of thinking by kicking her heels into my back. That's when I remember that "stop" between us doesn't mean stop. It's just her way of expressing how she feels. "Papayas" is what means to stop, and until she says that word, I'm going to keep fucking her.

By the time I finish, all my anger is gone, replaced by desperation. Greta is mewing, tame, and amiable to everything I want to give her. When I nuzzle her neck, she responds with a gentle nudge of her head, fitting me in better. When I kiss her collarbone, she wiggles her hips, settling me in deeper. And when I silently mouth the words "I love you" into her cheek, I swear I feel her heart skip a beat.

I'm left weathering the brunt of my climax with an actual tear escaping the corner of my eye, her fourth and final one having crashed into her as I let go. My body trembles and tingles, and I go dumb for a minute, holding us both against the wall like that.

"Four orgasms because of jealousy?" She pants, running her hand through my hair. "Shit. I should invite James over for a threesome and tap into your real potential."

"Do it and see what happens," I croak, doing my best to sound menacing but sounding instead like a dehydrated toad.

"Oh, trust me. I will." She smiles and tilts her head to press a kiss on my nose.

THAT NIGHT, GRETA lets me make her dinner, and right before I leave, she offers to let me sleep over. Not because we're both tired. Not because she owes me. Greta lets me sleep over for a reason I'm going to keep locked in my heart, just for the time being, afraid that speaking it might jinx what we could be.

✉ **Emerson Loyn**

Otis, Dinner last time was great. Sorry for the late follow up. Attached to this e-mail, you will find our rubric for ranking prospective players at the 2023 Combine. Please do not forward or share this document. Your recovery has been amazing, and given our confidence in your ability to outperform...

GRETA
PILLOW TALK: TAKE TWO

I CAN'T SLEEP. My body is wrung out from our strenuous sex, but my mind is awake, hyperactive, and vividly alert. I lazily gaze at the satiated man resting peacefully beside me.

How did this happen? How did my brain short-circuit and allow me to invite him to stay? We'd been on our way out, ready to grab some takeout from Ricky's when the first lapse in my judgment occurred.

"You could save so much money if you'd let me make you a homemade meal." He'd tutted, shoving on his shoes.

I'd shrugged. "Go for it, then, Princess."

And despite claiming he needed to go home to finish something or the other, he accepted the proposition under one condition: We use paper plates.

It was nice, watching him maneuver seamlessly around the kitchen. Raven and I sat on the kitchen island and feigned interest as Otis narrated all that he was doing in a poor British accent, clearly hoping he was teaching me something. All it did was make me chuckle.

We had dinner and talked about a variety of different topics, like whether bowling should be considered a part of the official

Olympic sporting roster and how blueberries are the worst of the berries. And we were still talking even after we'd finished the pasta he'd made, bickering, fake scowls, and boisterous laughs bubbling out of our lips until we both naturally hushed because it had already been half an hour since we'd last taken a bite. Technically, it was time for him to leave.

"Am I likely to be kicked out like some common street whore if I offer to throw away the disposable plates and spoons?"

"Don't offer." As before, it came out without thought, the invitation emerging from a dormant, hidden place inside me. There were no excuses for the invitation, no logical explanation for why I would so blatantly and explicitly break the rule for him—why I had been breaking the rules for him from the start.

But here he is, lying beside me, blissfully unaware of my inner turmoil.

With nerve-jittering caution, my body angled far enough that my irregular breathing won't disturb him, I focus on the way his body rises and falls with slumber. I watch the way his nostrils flare adorably in random intervals. I notice how his fingers furl and unfurl atop the pillow. Every new sleeping habit I take note of makes my heart lurch ferociously and echo loudly in my ears.

My mind reels, split between two polarizing thoughts: one laced with bitterness, the other with a giddy thrill. I'm bitter because of how this stupid boy with blue eyes and a breathtaking smile is inserting himself into my life and upending my plans to remain happily single. But I'm giddy and thrilled because of how this gorgeous boy with soulful eyes and a deep, dimpled smile is squeezing himself into my life and offering me a type of comfort and company I didn't realize I wanted. The latter sentiment has me fabricating imaginary scenarios and ruminating on how they would make me feel.

Waking up to Otis and his stinky morning breath, his eyes alight with adoration and amusement. Reading a book on the couch while

Otis watches some stupid documentary. Arguing over whether or not mashed potatoes should have cheese in them or not. Playing rock-paper-scissors to determine who gets to use the shower first.

Every scene that flits in my mind brings a smile to my face, intensifying until I'm full-on cheesing, my cheeks sore, butterflies breaking free from their cocoons to infiltrate my insides with ticklish wonder.

The gimmick with these made-up moments is that they're not fake. They've actually occurred. The fiction is the way I react in my mind, versus how I have reacted in real life.

In the morning, I should have kissed his mouth and chided him to brush his teeth with the toothbrush he bought that first night, the one I have stowed in my bathroom drawer. He doesn't know I have it. The one other time he slept over, he left early and brushed his teeth at home.

While we're on the couch doing our own things, I should have dug my feet beneath his thighs, which he would grab and set them on his lap to massage absentmindedly, his focus entirely on the documentary. His hands would be firm and soft, kneading all the knots that've collected on the soles.

When he served me the mashed potatoes with cheese, I should've told him that they're actually really good, rather than stubbornly denying it. Seeing him grin in victory would have been worth it, I bet.

And when we played rock-paper-scissors and I lost, I should've joined him in the shower rather than behaving like a sore loser, pushing him aside and rushing in before he even had a chance to get to his feet. Either way, he would always let me go first.

Fuck, I think, willing myself to stop beaming. It doesn't work. My mind is no longer in control of my muscles. *Fuck. Fuck. Fuck.*

There's no denying it. I like Otis. I *like*-like him.

It makes me want to giggle and squeal as I smother my face into a pillow, arms and legs flailing about in uncontained excitement while I think of his rumpled hair and his sultry voice. I want to reach over right now and brush my fingers over his face, tracing the outline of his rugged features in marveled disbelief that someone like him exists, so beautiful and so wonderful.

When did this happen? When did I start wanting him? At what point did he become more than just a good fuck?

Was it after the party, when he drove to my place to give me that unforgettable mistletoe kiss? Or was it when he invited me to his place to formally meet his roommates and analyze football films while we ate dinner together? Perhaps it was two hours ago, when he was making dinner and proving to me that he's better than I am at twerking, wearing a pink apron and holding a spatula.

Or was it when we were fucking, my back to him, and he asked me to give him a minute? He'd held me against him, and I'd been foolish enough to look into his eyes and let him kiss me, forcing me to taste all the tender feelings he had for me—feelings I'd first seen that night of my dad's Thanksgiving dinner. Had there been some sort of transfer of emotions that way? Did his erratic heartbeat against my back, his cock throbbing inside me, change the fabric of my emotions?

No, that can't be it. Emotions can't just get fucked into someone. I would be in a relationship and in love by now if that were the case.

It has to have happened over time, small things chipping away at my resolve, conversations and moments we shared that I thought were fleeting and meaningless but had actually permeated me, altering him into someone I genuinely care for and wish to be around.

But that's how it always is, isn't it? Someone becoming important doesn't happen all at once. They seep in. It's nature. It always takes a small seed to grow something profound.

Otis's smile was the seed. His laughter was water, his touch my sunlight. And just like that, I've blossomed into someone I wasn't before, my composition restructured.

"Fuck you, Rutherford." I sigh, clenching my fists into tight balls to keep from reaching over to touch him. "This is not what I wanted."

Except, I do want it. There's no other way to explain the satisfaction that settles over me as I simply watch him. I've been defeated, and honestly, I'm okay with that. Of course, I'm scared. Terrified. But I trust Otis.

"Why are you staring at me?" he rasps lazily.

I flinch, surprised by the sound of his voice. I'd been so lost in my own thoughts. I lick my lips and wince, doing my best to behave as I normally do. "Because you're so handsome when you sleep."

"More than when I'm awake?"

"Yup. You look so gorgeous with your mouth closed."

He lets out a feeble scoff. He closes his eyes, and I assume he's about to fall back asleep when he suddenly reaches for me. One arm wedges itself beneath me, the other looping around to grab a handful of my ass. He draws me toward him, and when we're flush against one another, face to face, he positions his chin above my head.

I burrow into him, listening to the rhythm of his heart, exhilarated by the fact that it matches mine. My toes tingle.

"Is that so? How about I keep my mouth closed the next time I eat you out." He shimmies his hips against me, not hard but not entirely soft.

I'm not given a chance to take back my words. He moves his hand from its perch on my butt to delve under my shirt, pressing the flat of his palm against the bare skin of my spine. His thumb strokes a nearby vertebrae soothingly. Pressing a kiss on top of my head, he says in a throaty mumble, "Let's go back to sleep, baby."

I don't relax. For a few minutes, we remain like that, pressed against one another, his eyes closed, mine wide open. I'm still woefully awake, but now, there's only one thought in my mind.

How do I get him to confess? I mean, it's obvious, right? He likes me. He wants me however I'll have him. That's what he said.

Part of me wants to rouse him awake and tell him what I'm feeling, about the rays of liquid gold beaming within me. Tell him about the way he makes me fight to keep a straight face, my natural reaction to the sight of him a gleaming smile.

But another part of me is hesitant and wary. I should get to know him more, right? Because I don't know a lot. The time we've spent together hasn't afforded me the opportunity to delve into his psyche. This is mostly my fault, of course, given the transactional way I've treated our hookups and how quickly I change the subject from anything serious.

Will I be able to tolerate his imperfections and accept his past mistakes? Will he accept mine? I'm not perfect. I'm so aware of that. But I hope he'll want me all the same.

And what do I do about the questions I have about what I've already observed? I wonder about his past relationships, especially the one he had with Autumn, whom I've determined to be the person he mentioned that first night when we talked about love. And I have questions about that barely-concealed rage he revealed first at the coffee shop and again at the dinner, during Jefferson Rodney's speech. He's notorious for starting arguments and fights with others on the field, especially during those first few games when he came back from his injury. Ejections weren't unknown to him.

I've never been a patient person or pretended to be, so I'm not going to apologize for stirring Otis back into a state of consciousness. I won't ask him the questions I have lingering in my mind, but I'll talk to him about something substantial. I'll force a conversation that, for the time being, will reassure me and lay a proper foundation for my feelings.

"Are you awake?" I whisper.

He groans and slackens his hold on me. I take that opportunity to reach over and turn on my bedside lamp, quickly burrowing back into his hold. "What gave it away? The closed eyes or the even breaths?"

I wiggle my hand between us and palm him over his boxers. He can't help but react, no matter how sleepy he is. "It was your twitching dick."

"You try to stay soft with a hottie pressed against you," he says with a simper.

"Let me find a hottie to press up against, and I'll let you know how it goes."

He lets out an indignant puff of air over my scalp. "That's just plain rude, Miriam."

"Should I take backsies?"

"I wouldn't believe you even if you did."

"Aw, don't be like that. I'm sorry."

"What a lame apology." He sounds more awake, leans back, and takes a long look at me. There's a dark, hazy cloud swarming in his eyes. My stomach lurches in excitement. "Say it like you mean it."

"How about you make me mean it?"

He does. He places his mouth over mine. It's soft and chaste, but the effect it has on me is that of a searing kiss. Electricity collects at my fingertips and travels through my body, and I'm ignited. I suppress a shiver of delight when his tongue peeks out to lick the seams of my lips, rubbing gently against my own when I meet his wet licks.

I open my mouth to deepen the kiss, but he retreats, our lips breaking apart with a sucking sound as he pecks me repeatedly, enthusiastically, sweetly. I'm ready to wrap myself around him and devour him whole, but then he pulls away completely.

Silence hangs. When he finally speaks, his words come out in a gruff gasp. "Are you going to mean it this time?"

"Mean what?" I'm in a daze, desire fogging my judgment. I

can't even remember why I woke him up in the first place. Was it to have sex? I'm sore, but apparently, I'm ready for another trip to pound town if my slippery thighs are any indication.

"Your apology."

I can't suppress a smile. "I sincerely apologize for not calling you a hottie."

"And?"

I make a face and try to think on the spot for what more I should be guilty of. "And for not waking you up with a blow job?"

"Yes, well, that would have been nice. It's a travesty that we've missed this opportunity, but that's not quite what I was looking for."

I can't keep playing this guessing game, so I resign with a sigh. "Help me out here, Princess. I'm blanking."

"You should also apologize for…" He waits, eyes wide, nodding like I'm going to follow along, but I don't. "For waking me up." He huffs. "I was tired today."

"Oh shoot, I forgot. Go back to sleep."

"Too late. I can't sleep when I know you're wide awake." He groans, wiggling in place as if nesting deeper into the mattress.

Fuck me. I actually feel pricks of joy jolt through my body, the sensation more vigorous than when we kissed. I swallow to keep from letting out a whine of adoration. "Aren't you such a gentleman?" I try to tease, the intonation of my voice wavering.

"Pawpaw raised me well."

We're both wide-awake now. Deep exhaustion is still present, but our awareness of each other and of the moment we're sharing supersedes the need to rest. "I have a question."

He stops drawing a pattern on my shoulder and tilts his head farther into the pillow. "I might have an answer."

"Why do you have tattoos?" He's wearing a T-shirt. I'd objected to the article of clothing when he padded to bed with it on. But apparently my apartment is too cold, even though I turned up the heat. I reach behind him, digging under his shirt to skim the edges of my fingernails lightly against the patterns on his back.

Otis shivers, his muscles rippling delightfully beneath me. "What'd'ya mean? Am I, like, not supposed to have any?"

I shake my head. "No, I just mean that you don't seem like the type."

"My type being?"

"Squishy."

"Feel free to ask my teammates… I am not squishy." He brings his palm against my left breast and presses down. "What about you? You have a tattoo, and you don't seem like the type."

"Are you saying I don't look like a grungy, dangerous girl?" I put on a mean mug in demonstration.

"No, you're very much a good girl. A good girl who loves to please." He smirks then kisses me before I have time to protest, and the butterflies in my stomach transform into rowdy mutant bats. "The tattoos," he rasps when he breaks away from me, his wet lips glimmering in the faint moonlight, "are a thing between Herik and me. We started getting 'em when were, like, fourteen, I think?"

"Show me." I've noticed the tattoos before, but I've never actually gotten a proper look at each individual one.

Otis untangles himself from me, tears off his shirt, then flops back onto the bed facedown. I turn on the nightstand light and settle myself atop of him, resting on his voluptuous ass.

Tentatively, I trace the collage of ink, unsure of where one tattoo starts and ends, each stroke blending together. "Is it, like, one big piece of art or a bunch of small ones?"

"Bunch of small ones. We got one after every game we won in high school, from freshman year until we both signed with your dad."

"And you said you started at fourteen?"

"Yeah. Herik is younger than me, though, so he technically got his first one at thirteen."

"Fuck, that's young. Who the hell would tattoo a kid?"

"Herik's brother. Duh."

"*Duh*. How didn't I know that?" I scratch him lightly, and he hisses in mock-pain before laughing when I dig my nails in for real, the sound shaking the mattress. "So does each one have a meaning?"

"Not really. They're pretty much random. We picked whatever designs we thought looked cool."

I press a kiss at the base of his spine then map a scatter of pecks, mesmerized by the intricacy of the designs. "Andres's brother is a damn artist."

"Jordan might've tatted us, but the designs are actually my dad's. I found a box with his old templates when I was cleaning the garage before high school. That's how I got the idea."

And there it is. The substance. I've never heard him speak about his dad. "What does your dad do now? Is he still designing tattoos?"

His body goes tense. "Nothing, I imagine." His excessive nonchalance immediately alerts me that something is off. "My mom thinks he plays poker with Bon Scott in heaven, but the guy really liked to sleep, so I feel like he's just having a good, long nap up there."

He's saying his dad is dead.

People reply in a lot of ways when they learn a loved one has died. "I'm sorry for your loss" is the most prevalent, followed by, "You must miss them."

But the truth is that they're not sorry. And the hurt doesn't lessen just because they apologize or even acknowledge the pain. And when they try to give advice—like the fact that time heals all, and you'll feel better, just give it a while—they're wrong. It will always hurt so fucking much, it just won't hurt as often.

I don't say anything, because I understand. When I roll back onto my side, I place a hand on his cheek, and he closes those sad eyes to burrow into the touch.

I get it.

"What about you? That tattoo that you have here." He presses a kiss just above my heart. "Why'd you get it?"

I, too, try to play it off. "If I said it was commemorating my past relationship with James, what would you do?"

His lips fight a grin as he lightly swats my thigh "Don't test me, woman."

My laughter continues until it dwindles into short, uneven chuckles. When it dies out, I settle deeper into his hold and press my cheek against his chest, the corner of my mouth tugging down. "It doesn't say James."

"Then who?" And the way he asks, the way his body goes stiff, the corners of his eyes crinkling, makes me suspect he knows already.

Which doesn't ease the knot that turns in my gut. *Do it. There's no point in keeping it a secret. It's not even a secret. I bet Elise blabbed. Someone has got to superglue her mouth shut.*

"Julien."

Recognition flares in his eyes.

"He's my younger brother." *Was.* "He passed away the semester before my high school graduation."

"Oh." Otis is being polite, feigning surprise. It's kind that he would try to play dumb, but I'm still upset, unable to contain my annoyance.

"You know already, though," I accuse. He opens his mouth, but I speak over him. "Don't even try denying it. It's all over your face. I'm just wondering who told you."

"Elise. But in her defense, she was super wasted."

Of course. Just as I suspected.

"There was also the conversation you had with your dad while I was in the closet. I, uh…" He looks away and sucks on his bottom lip. "I kind of heard that, too."

Every carefully regulated function in my body stops. I go lifeless, frozen in horror. He'd heard me blame my father for my brother's death. I think I'm going to be sick. "You never said anything," I squeak. I sound weak and pathetic. I feel weak and pathetic. The proximity to him no longer brings comfort.

"That's because you told me to forget about everything." He says it so simply that it's like we're talking about the weather instead of the murder accusation I'd laid against my dad.

My clambering heart twists painfully, and the back of my throat burns. Suddenly, excuses start to form, the shame and regret of my spiteful censure manifesting itself in a rapid-fire expulsion of words, an honor-bound need to defend my father overwhelming me even if I don't believe the words entirely.

"I didn't mean what I said to him that night. My brother overdosed on accident, and it's not like my dad gave him the drugs or even encouraged it. He used to smoke, but he stopped when Julien was born. I know my dad has this total ban on you guys even smoking cigarettes, and that's because of Julien.

"It's just—you know my dad. You know how he can be. He can put a lot of pressure on people, and Julien was young, and I never helped him field the expectations, and it really was an accident. He's never—Julien had never done anything that reckless before, he always knew his limits, but that night was bad, and he just…

"But it's not my dad's fault. I was just angry that time he visited and didn't want to go to the game, so I said what I said out of anger and not because it was true. I don't want you to think of my dad as this evil guy when he's not. He loved my brother. *Loves* my brother. And me… too. He's not, like, an evil Satan or whatever. At least not entirely."

Otis doesn't try to stop me from explaining, or interrupt me to soothe my panic. He lets me speak in long breaths until I've exhausted all the oxygen in my lungs. The anxiety settling deep inside me fizzles the moment he places a warm hand on my face and whispers, "Okay. I believe you. Your dad is not an evil Satan.

At least not entirely."

And just like that, I know. He doesn't pry for more information. He doesn't counteract my claim and regale me all the times my father has been terrible to him. He doesn't even ask how or what my brother overdosed on. He just gazes at me with overwhelming understanding, his palm neutralizing the dread climbing my cheeks.

I look in his eyes and I *know*.

In the comfortable silence that follows, I wait for the regret to settle in. I wait for my body to recoil like it did when I first told James about Julien, when I felt nauseated, then promptly hurled. He'd been nice about it, holding my hair back and soothing me as best he could, but that hadn't helped. I hated his words of comfort—he didn't really understand. Since that day, I haven't brought it up again with him.

But with Otis, none of that happens. My body, once wrought with unease, settles into a quiet peace. Nestling my face in his chest, I feel safe and close to him, and it's weird how much closer I want to get. Not physically—Otis and I have pretty much done everything under the sun to be close to one another physically, reaching limits that shouldn't be possible—but emotionally.

"Can I... Can I tell you something?" I'm emboldened to venture into deeper waters, even if my mind tells me to slow down. I crave intimacy that cannot be satiated by sex, and I've never been good at depriving myself.

"What's up, buttercup?"

Deep breath. You want to be closer, so be closer. Take a step so he'll run the mile. "It's something I've never actually told anyone."

He swallows. "And you want to tell me?" I nod, and he holds his breath before he lets out a breathless, "Okay."

I close my eyes and muster enough courage to broach the subject again. "I miss Julien."

"You've never told anyone that?" His tone isn't judgmental. Just curious.

I shake my head.

"Why not?"

"Because saying things like that out loud makes them hurt a bit more, y'know?" It's true, at least for me. That's how it's always felt. Speaking it aloud has me feeling like pieces of myself are going up in flames. The situation feels too real. If I keep Julien to myself, at least there are times where I can pretend I've gone crazy and that I've imagined it all. Even if it's just for a moment, I can doubt myself just enough to make it all go away.

"Yeah. I get that," he whispers. "I don't talk much about my dad, either. I can talk about the good times. But I never—I don't—I ignore all the bad things and erase them from my mind."

I don't ask him to expand, because I get it. Julien had his flaws, but aside from his addiction to drugs and the solace it brought him, I can't recall a single fault, nor can I conjure the disgusted outrage I felt about his addiction. The relatability makes me feel for Otis.

"Now I feel like I should tell you something," he says with a nervous exhalation. But I don't need him to. In fact, I don't want him to. What we're doing is not an exchange of information, it's a glimpse of affection.

"You don't have to. I just..." I wanted to give him something. Something only he could have from me. Something to hold on to and know that there's a piece of me that wants him in the same way I think he wants me.

"I want to." He bends down, pecks my lip, and swipes a thumb against the high rise of my cheek.

I feel so precious like this. Hugging him is like hugging moonlight, his iridescence bleeding warmly into me, filling me with a calm intensity until I'm shining just as brightly as he is.

"Sometimes, I feel like what I do is never enough. No one... No one really tells me it's enough."

My moonlight dims at the confession, his eyes losing its luster, casting us both in the dark weight of his insecurity. I wish I could dive into his heart and dust away his worries. But I don't know him well enough. I want to—and God, I can't wait to—but right now, I don't. So I say what I wish I could have told Julien. "If it's your best, then it's enough. It's everything, and no matter what others might think, it matters. It's everything."

He doesn't respond. But it's okay because he looks at me like I'm a dream, and I hug him like he's the best version of my reality.

It doesn't take long for us to fall asleep, our heartbeats synchronized and our breaths even. He asks to turn over because it's more comfortable for him that way, and I acquiesce, spooning him. He holds my hands against his abdomen. As I slip into that space between being asleep and awake, I run toward my waking thoughts instead of going the other way. Once I'm unconscious, Julien and I bask in the blissful memories of what it was like to be together in the former.

In my dream, I get to apologize to him before he leaves. He doesn't say anything in response, but at least he knows how badly I wish I could have been there for him. For a moment, so finite it could be mistaken for nothing, my guilt is absolved. For the rest of my dream, I chase the feeling.

Seeing him in my subconscious is amazing. I'd like to believe it's why I wake up happy.

But disappointment hits me a moment later when I open my eyes to see that Otis is gone. His side of the bed is empty and cold, but the molded indent of where he'd been remains, reaffirming everything that happened. There's also a small note on the bed.

TO THE HUMAN LAWN MOWER
CIRCLE ONE
WAS LAST NIGHT A DREAM?
YES   NO

A smile brightens my face. A pang of need reverberates through me, and I ache because I miss him. So, just like that, I make up my mind.

It's time to fuck up this friendship.

so this is like ♡

greteleatsbread · 16 songs, 55 min 35 sec

👤+ ⏮ ❚❚ ⏭ ⤬

Moonlight Ariana Grande	♥	3:22
Sparks Fly Taylor Swift	♥	4:20
24/7 Celina Sharma, Harris J.	♥	3:04
Adore You Harry Styles	♥	3:27
Right Back Khalid	♥	3:35
Like I Want You Giveon	♥	4:20
Skyline To Frank Ocean	♥	3:04
Lucky Russ	♥	3:20
Foldin Clothes J. Cole	♥	5:16
About You Now Sugababes	♥	3:32
I Think I Like You The Band CAMINO	♥	3:03
Feel A Way. Kiana Ledé	♥	2:47
I'm Yours Alessia Cara	♥	3:49
Come Thru (with Usher) Summer Walker, Usher	♥	3:01
Thinkin Bout You Anthony Russo	♥	2:57
I Like That Bazzi	♥	2:38

OTIS

DISHWASHERS SAVE LIVES

"WHERE YOU AT, Baby Girl?"

Said Baby Girl lets out a disgruntled scoff. "I just threw up in my mouth. Disgusting. Don't ever call me Baby Girl."

I release a heavy, sad sigh. "Didn't answer my question. I asked where you're at."

"Why?"

"Cause I wanna see you." Gnawing on my bottom lip, I hold my breath and wait for her response, tethered by her silence.

"Again? You saw me last night." She chuckles. If I didn't know better, I would think she's playing coy. But Greta—gorgeous, tenacious, spirited Greta—is not coy, and if she were, I'd need a pacemaker.

"And?"

"No dice. I gotta study. Bye now," she sings off-key but stays on the line just long enough for me to plead.

"No! Wait. Don't hang up. I have to see you. Please."

The hesitation gives me hope.

"I'll bring you dinner," I bait. I cringe and pretend that how pathetic I'm being bothers me. In my twenty-plus years of existence, I don't think I've ever begged someone to keep me company, not even when I was a scrawny loser.

"From where?"

"Ricky's."

"Say less." She moans. "Imma say this once, so open those big ears and listen closely, okay? I want a number one with no cheese, extra pickles, no mustard, add mayo. Get me root beer with light ice, and if they don't have root beer, then Sprite, and if they don't have Sprite, run your car into the establishment because I'm sick of their soda machine being out." She doesn't even wait for me to confirm her order before she hangs up.

I remain frozen, dazed, amazed, a smile plastered on my face. I stare at my phone and swear there are birds singing and angels humming in my ears.

I'm lost in thought when I get into the truck, the lull of the radio soothing me into a reflective state as it always does. Since Pawpaw passed away, I haven't touched it, allowing whatever station the radio was set at to play anywhere I go, even if all that comes out is crinkling static. Back home in Dayton, 96.1 played the top country music, a genre I could take or leave beyond the comforting nostalgia it brings me. Here, it plays broken, crinkly bluegrass music.

When I get to the drive-thru, I'm a little relieved by the fact that one of the employees recognizes me and offers to give me my order on the house—one of the few times being locally popular is good. Herik calls as I wait for them to prepare the meal, and we have a quick discussion about the strategy sheets he's just caught up on.

Once I secure the bag, I'm eager, driving a little faster than the speed limit, pushing my ancient truck a little harder than I should, and right before I turn into the parking lot near her campus study spot, I get another phone call. At first, I fear it's Herik, ready to continue our discussion, since I'd hung up after saying, "You're a fucking idiot and I'm tired of repeating myself. Read the plans one more time and then watch the films again. Rotter's center barely nose tackles," but when I see a G and a yellow heart on the screen, I beam.

"Hello, this is your delivery dri—"

"Where are you?" she snaps.

"Ma'am, I'm going to need you to stay calm."

"You're late," she snaps, cranky by my tardiness.

But how the hell am I tardy if we didn't even set a time? "Look, if this is how you treat all your delivery men, I'm gonna need to talk to UberEats and DoorDash to have them terminate your account."

"Don't get smart with me. I'm hungry."

I wish I could see the adorable pout that's set on her lips, the one that complements her whining perfectly. "And I'm at Suleiman's parking lot. Come down and meet me."

"Meet you? Me thinks you don't understand the concept of a delivery," she replies, but I hear her breath quickening, the sound of air pushing against the receiver as though she's walking fast.

I grin like an idiot.

There's a shuffle and huff on her end of the line. My nerves become hyperactive. I squint out the window, watching for a form to approach me. We're both quiet, phones pressed to our ears. I make a mental melody out of her gasps, drumming a backdrop beat against the steering wheel. I'm gripped by anticipation, practically bouncing in my seat, when I see her silhouette, her figure becoming more clear as she gets closer.

We don't hang up even when she stops in front of the driver's side window. She knocks, but I'm already rolling it down. Placing a hand on the door sill, she glares at me. "Where's the food, quarterback?"

I lean back in my seat and give a suggestive look. "Hop in, cheerleader."

Greta scrunches her nose and shakes her head. "I don't want a repeat of last Wednesday. I still haven't gained full mobility in my legs." She kicks them back and groans dramatically.

"You were bouncing on 'em just fine last night." I wiggle my brows while she raises hers dangerously. I heave a sigh. "No repeats." Putting the phone down, I lean forward, my nose millimeters from hers. "I want to take you somewhere."

A thoughtful look crosses her face. "Neverland?" She flings her arms out dramatically and tosses her head back. "Take me away, Peter."

I chuckle, basking in her perky mood. This is good. Hopefully my plans won't turn her completely sour. "Let's fly, Wendy."

A smile tugs her lips. Inching forward, her mouth ghosts over mine, hovering close enough to make it tingle but not close enough to touch. "Fine, but there better be food in your car."

I just stare at her. Fuck, she's so beautiful. Fucking divine. Glamorous. Exquisite. In all honesty, language cannot capture how magnificent Greta is.

Under the faint glow of the streetlight, she glows, illustrious in her own right, shining brighter than the closest star. I melt, hardly able to believe that there was a point where I merely found her physically attractive. But she's beyond that. She's perfection in its most vivid, natural form.

Shit, she's got me all sappy. I'm down so fucking bad that I could win even the most difficult limbo contests.

I'm about to bridge the small distance she's established between us when she pushes away and begins to skip out of sight. "Let me grab my things real quick."

Something happened last night. Somewhere between falling asleep and waking up to her heavy breaths and soulful eyes, a shift between us occurred, and I can't begin to understand what or how or why. All I can do is enthusiastically accept it. When Greta looks at me, instead of casual amusement, it's with attentive curiosity, and I can't just blurt out how I feel simply because I'm overwhelmed by love. I can almost swear she feels the same, but past experiences have taught me that the intensity of my feelings is usually not matched by their feelings. I can get ahead of myself sometimes.

So I'll let her control the pace. I'll let her be the one to change the fabric of our relationship. If she wants us to be labeled as fuck buddies still, then so be it. I can wait for her. I'm eager—desperate, even—but I'll wait.

Greta hops into the truck. "Alright, Fordy, where we headed?" I've already lifted the center console to give her room to sidle up to me, which she does. She stops just an inch from touching me.

"Don't call me Fordy," I grumble, shifting the gear into drive. "And it's a secret."

She snorts, and suddenly, there is a fry in front of my face. I accept it wordlessly, lurching toward her to bite it, intentionally nipping at her finger. She makes a sound in the back of her throat and retracts her hand, whacking my shoulder lightly.

"You're not supposed to bite the hand that feeds you," she scolds. "Didn't anyone ever teach you that?"

"Sure, they did, but I happen to know how much you like biting and thought I'd ignore the rule for a second."

Greta titters. We then engage in a serious discussion over which is best: kettle corn, caramel popcorn, or traditional buttered popcorn. The closer we get, the more nervous I am, so I get quieter and let her take over the conversation.

During practice, my plan had seemed so thoughtful and clever. Coach had cut it short today and instead assigned us tapes to study since we've been slacking on strategy. The stadium should be empty at this point, the staff gone for the day since it's a little past eight and there's nothing going on there.

I'm starting to sweat by the time I turn into the back of the lot, where all the players, coaches, and employees park. There's a direct entryway to the turf through here. I park really close to the building, in one of the rare spots not reserved for accessible parking. I don't make a motion to exit the truck right away.

She's going to recognize where we are and lose her shit. You need to get ahead of this, Morgan.

"—like, my lips shouldn't feel numb after I eat a couple handfuls, y'know? And don't even get me started on the salt—"

I'm quick to interrupt her tirade. "First, I need you to stay calm." All right, so that wasn't the best opening line.

Greta sipes her root beer straw and blinks at me grimly. "Oh, no. Have I been Ted Bundy-ed?"

I gape, appalled by the joke. "Greta, that's not something to kid around about."

"The fuck you mean, 'kid around'? I'm being serious." She drops the bag of food between us, using it as a barrier. Shaking her head in dismay, she folds her arms over her chest and grumbles, "Damn it, I knew you were too good to be true."

My breath catches in my throat. In a daze, I marvel, "You think I'm too good to be true?"

Greta rolls her eyes and reaches for her door handle. Immediately, I wrap my arms around her waist to keep her with me. She pauses and turns to look at me, her lips set in a thin line. She speaks with a calm chill. "Otis, either let me out of the car, or so help me God, I'll make like Mike Tyson and kith your dick with both my fists."

Genuinely frightened of her follow-through, I slacken my hold and clear my throat again. Immediately, she pushes the door open and steps out. Shit, shit, shit.

I stumble out of the truck and rush to stand in front of her, not knowing what to do. "Ta-da," I sing. Extending my arms in a diagonal line, I widen my stance and give her jazz hands. No one can be mad when they're being jazzed.

Her eyes flicker between the stadium and me, and I watch her anger turn into shock before returning to that familiar aloofness. "Rutherford, I'm about to fucking ta your da."

I'm concerned I might be fucking a psychopath.

"Here?" I pretend to play stupid and rock innocently on my heels. "I mean, I'm a little tired from practice, so we might have to work to get me goin'. But there's no one around, and I'm always down for new experiences, so I guess—"

"Morgan."

I wince at the sound of my last name. Players refer to one another only by our last names unless we're pissed, but the opposite is true for Greta and me. Sniffing, I blink rapidly and flash a sheepish grin, rubbing the back of my neck. "Can I at least explain myself before I'm murdered?"

"Why? That's how the villain always gets away in the movies."

"Am I the villain in this situation?" I sulk.

"I'm being so serious right now when I tell you that you have ten seconds before it's"—she creates a makeshift gun with her fingers and pretends to aim at me, closing an eye for precision shooting—"*pew, pew, pew* time."

"How do you make everything sound so wonderful?" Her nose wrinkles in warning, and I start talking very quickly out of fear of destroying the progress we made last night. "Okay, so you don't like football fields—which I totally get and respect, contrary to what my actions right now might show—but when you told your dad that you don't like them because of him and the game and all that hoopla, I got this idea." Fuck, did I just say 'hoopla'? I sound more and more like Pawpaw every day. "And I know it's none of my business—"

"It's not."

Is this what it feels like to die inside? "But I thought some moderated exposure therapy would help you to overcome your dislike because I know you love football, and I'm sure you know that it's so much better to be in the stands and watching with the rest of the fans, and I thought maybe you'd want to have that. And yes, I know, I rhymed but that was totally an accident. But look, we're here at the field, and there's no one around—no staff is ever here on the Thursday night of an away game week since it's a half-day for them—so I thought it would be a good idea to just sit and bask in the grassy glory of it all and eat some Ricky's."

"Exposure therapy," Greta repeats.

"Not the nude type, but yeah." She doesn't react to my frisky quibble, and I want to kick myself. Sadly, I'm not flexible enough to do that. "And if you don't want to do it, that's totally fine. We'll go somewhere else to eat. My place, even. I bought a new body pillow, and I swear you'll love it. It's like hugging a cloud that knows how to hug back."

When she remains frozen for five seconds too long, I brace myself for outrage, setting my face in a preemptive grimace. I'm sure her anger would manifest itself in a silent way, where she shuts me out and maybe even calls someone to come pick her up rather than have me drop her off. And if James appears, I'll have to fight him out of principle, which will only infuriate her more.

Greta bites her bottom lip, regarding me with a vacant look. I open my mouth to rescind the idea completely, but then she raises a shoulder in a meek shrug. When she speaks this time, she does so with a certainty that doesn't reflect in her frightened eyes. "No. I don't want to go to the field with you. The fact that you thought this was a good idea to even suggest is a little... baffling. I mean, exposure therapy is something you do with a therapist, not some guy you're fucking."

I feel bludgeoned. Her words, though honest, are also cruel, and I'm humiliated. My gesture, meant to be sweet and thoughtful, now registers as rude and thoughtless, and the progress we made last night crumbles before my eyes. The rejection is—

"But I really appreciate the effort, I think it's sweet. And since we're here, let's eat in the bed of your truck and face the field. I'll at least try it that way." She doesn't wait for me to respond but opens the trunk door.

Try. She's trying for me. Does this mean I can confess now?

When I break out of my daze, I help her, and soon, we're seated side by side, our backpacks serving as cushions. We've toed off our shoes and are facing the stadium. I'm about to apologize and grovel when she speaks up.

"God, I love Ricky's," she says with a moan. She takes a juicy bite of her burger.

My appetite isn't as voracious as hers since the supplements Duger gave me suppress it. "If I'm being honest, I like Barton's more."

Her jaws lock mid-chew, and she stares at me. "What did you just say?"

I make a face. "Say it, don't spray it, lady."

"Don't make me—"

I can't make her do anything, though I pinch her lips together to keep her from talking with her mouth full. No matter how attractive I might find her, there's something about food spraying out of someone's mouth that makes them... unattractive.

She bites me. I apologize. We proceed to eat and chat about our day. The conversation is mundane and familiar—dare I say even couple-y. Just like the good-morning text I sent her today, it's natural, like this is something we do all the time and not a new routine we're picking up.

She laughs when I tell her about practice and the ball I threw at Tuckerson's head on "accident," and I scowl when she tells me that James owes her a foot massage because they had a bet about which one of them would leave the library first, and they'd bet against themselves.

"I see you still haven't gotten over your jealousy." She shakes her head in dismay when I make a face. She finished most of her fries on the drive here then polished off her burger almost as quickly. Now, she's eating my fries as we lie back and stare at the sky.

Normally, I'd be annoyed. But this is Greta, and she could eat my heart as a late-night snack and I would thank her.

"Didn't we have a talk about that?"

"We yelled about it and had sex about it, but I don't remember there really being a talk about it."

"Fucking, talking... They're both effective means of communication."

I sip her drink. "Look, everyone gets jealous. It's natural."

"I don't get jealous." When I flash her an incredulous look, she raises an eyebrow, eyes wide, and insists. "Seriously, I don't."

"I don't believe you for one second." A hothead like Greta most certainly gets jealous. I might be overt about manifesting my little green monster, but I'm certain she has one, too, even if it's dormant.

She clicks her tongue in frustration. "I'm being serious, Otis. Cross my heart, hope to die, I don't ever get jealous." Then her expression brightens, and she wags her index finger at me. "Wait. Actually, you might be right. I have been jealous *once*."

I give her an arrogant look. "Yeah? When?"

Out of nowhere, Greta pushes up and kneels in front of me. I look up at her. My heart stops, the tension created by the movement is palpable when she places her hands on either side of my face. I turn my head to burrow into her touch.

Then, without warning, she's squishing my cheeks. I make an unintelligible sound, and she snorts. Bending forward, she presses a kiss on the bridge of my nose, right where my glasses sit, and then another on my forehead, the gesture lighting my entire body on fire. Her thumb brushes over my cheekbones to lift the frames for a second. "Right now. I'm jealous of these things." She lets the glasses drop back on my face. "How come they always get to sit on your face, but I've only had the privilege a couple of times?"

The silliness in her comment catches me off guard, and laughter rumbles out of me. It comes out distorted since she's still sandwiching my face between her palms. A blush crawls up my neck. I'm starting to hate my glasses a lot less.

"Can you blame me?" I wheeze, doing my best to remember to breath.

She lets go of me so I can talk properly. My hands go to the back of her thighs, pulling her toward me. She holds onto my shoulders, arching her body into me.

"They're lighter than you are," I tease, trying and failing to be playful.

She shoves me back then pushes away from me. I watch as she settles beside me again.

I collect our trash before following her example and lay myself by her side. Our shoulders brush against each other. My body tingles with the urge to wrap my arms around her, to hold her the way I held her last night. But she's looking up at the sky, and I don't want to disturb the serenity that's fallen over her.

For a while, I just stare at her, her eyes glazed over, her face relaxed. I memorize the outline of her profile, each curve and sharp line. At first, she appears stoic, but then a perceptive smile tugs at the corner of her mouth. She knows I'm staring at her, and I swear, she makes herself appear more brilliant, robbing me of even the most basic instincts. When I feel like my lungs are about to collapse, she sucks in her bottom lip—those stunning, plump lips—and tilts her head in my direction.

My stomach jolts, and words of adoration burn in the back of my throat, echoing in my head. To keep from scaring her with my feelings, I tear my eyes off her and gaze up at the sky, finally capable of taking in a much-needed gulp of air to soothe the fire radiating in my chest.

"How are you feeling?" I ask after a stretch of comfortable stillness, the type that allows the heart to reach out to another, traversing the *anima mundi* to find each other.

"Okay." She doesn't sound as self-assured as usual.

Tinges of concern drip into my voice as I parrot her. "Okay?"

"Yeah. I just—I don't actually feel anything." There's a rustle, and I turn to see her looking at me, a hand placed over her stomach. The expression she wears is thoughtful. "I thought I would, like, feel something, y'know, magnanimous while we're here, but I don't."

"Is that a good thing or a bad thing?"

She sucks in her cheeks for a moment, then shrugs. "I dunno. It's an okay thing, I guess."

My pulse spikes, and my palms get clammy. "And that's good... right?"

She moves her mouth to the side and nods.

I let out a relieved sigh. "Okay, good."

We go back to staring at the sky, the front of our bodies inclined toward each other, and lie there in silence. It's a beautiful night, the glittering stars illuminated brilliantly behind a canvas of navies, blacks, and violets. The colors gloss together in a gradient, homogenous and still distinct. There are no clouds, just a clear view of this masterpiece. The moon, a slim crescent, is bright.

I want to take a picture of the sky. I haven't seen it look like this in a while.

Greta feels okay, I think, focusing on a particular star that fades and dims and glows and glitters. *She's okay.*

And that's what matters. Sure, she's not just magically over her brother dying or even feeling much at all, but that comes with time. Maybe not imminent or soon, but in the future, she will be okay and that's what I want. I want there to be a future with Greta, one where she's finally able to walk into a full stadium and watch a game—watch me—on the field.

"You know what I've always been curious about?" I say absentmindedly.

"I imagine there's a lot of things, but what's on your mind right now, Princess?"

It's funny how she always manages to get an upper hand with me. It's also funny how much I adore that about her. "I've always wondered why you kicked me out that first night."

"That first night?"

"Day, really. I made you breakfast, and then I was banished."

"You're wondering why I kicked you out? All this time, you've been clueless as to why I would ask you to leave after you changed my sheets, fed my cat, spent the night, cooked me breakfast, and then offered to wash my dishes. This, mind you, was within fourteen hours of meeting each other outside a dirty house party—"

"Our house is usually clean, thank you very much."

"—and sharing cigarettes and nothing else—not even our first names." Greta finally takes a deep breath. "All this to consider, and you're seriously wondering why I wanted you out of my apartment?"

I blink at her and remain stupidly stubborn despite it being glaringly obvious. "Yeah."

Greta scoffs and shakes her head, nudging me with her elbow. "Don't be dumb. You were playing boyfriend when we'd barely exchanged middle names."

"I wasn't playing boyfriend. I was just trying to show how much I appreciated the time we spent together."

"Oh, please." She inches closer to me.

"Besides, we did more than just fuck and sleep. We talked for, like, hours that night."

"About nothing." Another inch. Her chest brushes mine.

A jolt of excitement swells in me. "And yet, I remember everything you said."

"That's creepy." A hand slithers beneath my arm to wrap around my waist. Her knee digs between mine. "Someone's a bit obsessive."

"Attentive," I rasp.

She considers my words in silence. A finger grazes my forehead, pushing away the curly strand of hair that's fallen there. My eyes flutter shut for a moment, opening only when she speaks again.

"Next time, don't do that."

"With you? Or with another person?"

She doesn't respond but pinches me. Her breathing is shallow, aimed at my collarbone.

My throat flexes with hard swallows. I'm sure she can feel the erratic beats of my heart. "Miriam?"

She presses herself almost entirely against me. I'm unable to resist any longer and wrap my arms around her. She sits up slightly to help me snake my arm beneath her. My chin rests just above her head. "Yes, Rutherford?"

I'm still afraid of the ferocity of my feelings and the slow burn of hers. I'm terrified that if I say something, it'll shatter the fragile porcelain that holds our undefined relationship together. I've always been quick to fall headfirst, and if I want this to work, I need to be patient.

And for her, I'll try.

"Would it have been better if I offered to load the dishwasher?"

she's the ♡ne

frosted0ats · 13 songs, 33 min 21 sec

👤 ⏮ ⏸ ⏭ 🔀

I.F.L.Y Bazzi	♥	2:45
She Looks So Perfect 5 Seconds of Summer	♥	3:22
this is how you fall in love Jeremy Zucker, Chelsea Cutler	♥	2:54
Phases PRETTYMUCH	♥	3:35
More of You JP Saxe	♥	2:34
Yellow Hearts (feat. Audrey Mika) Ant Saunders	♥	3:00
Love Songs - Bonus Kaash Paige	♥	2:28
Damn Baby Alt Bloom	♥	2:54
My Girl The Temptations	♥	2:45
Lover Taylor Swift	♥	3:41
Tattoos Together Lauv	♥	3:07
Pick Me Wafia	♥	2:58
Sweet & Sour Nic D	♥	2:21

GRETA

A KISS AT MIDNIGHT

ELISE AND I are at an upscale club that opened two weeks ago, and only one of us is having the time of our lives.

News flash: It's not me. It's Elise. She's dancing it up with an expensive bottle of Prosecco in hand, while I sit here, bitter and cranky in sobriety. And yet, no matter my mood, I can't help but shimmy my shoulders to the beat of the Latin music blaring boisterously.

Fuck, I hate being the designated driver. How I lost a coin toss three times in a row, I'll never understand. I might fucking suck at statistics—my borderline C in the class proves it—but even I know I should have won at least once.

Maybe I've angered the gods of probability. And so, here I am, prohibited by the rules of Designated Driver from indulging in a favorite vice of mine.

Normally, I'd scream, "Fuck all," and get sloshed anyway, relying on the fact that good ol' Jamesy-Poo would come to my rescue and assume my role. But my Mongolian counterpart decided to turn our inseparable trio into a duo, meeting with his project group for his signals and circuits class instead.

Alas, tonight is not my night to blow off steam. Normally, I would fight Elise, but she's understandably upset since her father canceled plans on her for the millionth time and with little warning. It's worse this time, though, since he'd missed Thanksgiving, too. A time for family.

"I'm parched," she croaks, waddling toward me in her nine-inch Dolce & Gabbana pumps—the glossy white ones that I'd tried to steal from her overnight duffel since they match my skimpy ensemble better than hers. With no regard for hygiene, she grabs the first drink she sets her eyes on and makes a face, sticking her tongue out repeatedly to draw out the flavor. "What is that?"

I shrug and pout.

She notices this and joins me. "C'mon, Tata," she coos, getting to her knees in the booth. She stumble-crawls toward me, faltering when the sharp heel of her shoe catches on the tablecloth. "Stop being a pooping party pooper and dance with me." When she reaches me, she drapes her body across mine, locking her hands around my waist.

I cringe and try to push her off, not wanting her foundation to rub onto my clothes. "I can't." I wrestle with her, not taking kindly to her invasion of my personal space. *When the fuck did she get so strong?* "My legs hurt."

Lisey gasps and moves back. "Do you want me to massage your legs? I'm really good at massaging. You can ask Herik." She bites her bottom lip and lets out a small giggle.

I'm about to inquire about that when a popular club mix comes on and she suddenly abandons me. Apparently, she can't help but dance.

Left on my own once more and wanting to distract myself from how bored I am, I grab my phone, and slide my thumb straight across my screen to open my unattended notifications for the umpteenth time today.

And for the umpteenth time today, I read the texts I've yet to respond to but have memorized entirely.

princess
Today 6:42 PM

miss u

i wish i didn't have midnight
kiss tonite

i just wanna snuggle w u

I can't stop thinking about these messages. When my mind ventures into the darkness nurtured by the verbal reprimand I received from my supervising teacher this morning and kindled further by the ugly fight I got into with my parents at lunch today—a fight over grades and football game attendances—Otis's texts stop me from free-falling into the somber abyss.

In fact, at random times as I brood in my seat, using my straw to play with my lemon or draw with the mildew on the table or the perspiration on my glass, an unexpected smile blossoms at the thought of him, my heart beating harder and faster.

Since yesterday, when Otis took me to the football stadium in that grand, well-meaning gesture, I've struggled to decide what I should do about *us*. I know there should be, and that we both want there to be, an us, but it's all unspoken. All those times we bent the rules for each other were in quiet understanding. All those lingering looks and touches were reciprocated in covert agreement.

Soon, however, that's all going to change. Because I have a wonderful plan, the type of plan that won't fail since it follows Occam's razor to the tee. Because after Otis's game tomorrow, when he comes home, win or lose, I'll be there in a darling little teddy. I'll have his jersey number painted on my face, and in my hand will be my own little note for him:

TO RUTHERFORD
CIRCLE ONE
HOW ABOUT YOU BE MY BOYFRIEND?
YES   NO

"Whatcha drinkin'?"

Immediately, the overwhelming scent of desperation and cheap cologne permeates the air around me. Turning slowly, I give the strange guy who's brazenly taken a seat beside me a blank look. When he doesn't get the hint and remains in place, shoulders squared like he thinks he's something, I purse my lips.

"Acid. Want some?" I remark in monotone. I raise the glass to him.

He regards the offer in amused confusion and shrugs, sidling closer to me.

I don't move away, unwilling to appear uncomfortable.

"You're hot."

Famous last words, I think, a little offended by the low effort he's putting into hitting on me. Honestly, if I were a sleazy guy, I could woo a woman better. Closing my eyes, I swallow a rumble of revulsion that rises up my throat and instead mumble a quick, "*Va te faire foutre.*"

With as much self-control as I can muster, I face him again and smile. Leaning forward, I beckon him with a curl of my finger, projecting a false allure of desire with every fluttering bat of my eyes. His head moves closer. I stop him when my cheek hovers over his and whisper, "I know I'm hot, but you smell bad. Shoo." I pull back and usher him off with a reckless wave of my hand.

"What the fuck?" The prick gives me a sinister look, his chest puffed out in a bid to seem macho. "Who the fuck do you think you're talking to, bitch?"

"A degenerate chimpanzee, clearly." I hold my hand out in front of me, not quite touching but hovering close enough to bother him. "*Au revoir, blaireau.*"

The French throws him off a little, but he's quick to recover. "You're too fucking fat to be talking like that, bitch," he fumes, slipping out of arm's reach. The first time he said "bitch," I was willing to let it go on account of it being an ego-punching moment for him. But this second time…

"You should feel lucky I even came to talk to you."

Lucky? First, this guy calls me fat like that'll have me on my knees, crying and sucking his dick for approval, and now this. To say I'm royally pissed is an understatement.

However, I have no time to react and throw my own targeted insults in his face before he topples onto the table, scattering the drinks and making a mess. Initially, I'm thrown for a loop as to what's just happened, partially convinced the Invisible Woman does exist. Then I see.

Elise must have heard what he said, and she'd been the one to punch him. Her arm is still raised, hand balled in a fist, fingers curled over her thumb in terrible form, her chest heaving. She looks so fucking hot right now, and it's not just because she's punched a guy for me but because she's done so without mussing a single hair.

"Who's the fat bitch now, you crusty-looking motherfucker!" she shrieks.

I place a hand over my mouth, touched by the number of curse words she's used to defend my honor.

Over her shoulder, I see a crowd forming, and given that I've partaken in my fair share of public disputes, I know that in about thirty seconds, security is going to show up. To avoid Elise being charged with assault and to maintain the advantage of anonymity, I scramble out of the booth, grabbing our purses and jackets, before taking hold of Lisey's wrist and pushing through the swarms of individuals that have gathered. She stumbles behind me, protesting against my grip, oblivious to my frenzy. I don't stop until we're out of the club and clambering toward where we parked.

Overwrought from the exertion, Elise groans and plops down on the curb, rubbing her ankles. Looking up at me with a scowl, she snaps, "What was that for?"

"You just assaulted a guy. I was trying to save you from prison."

I double over for a second to regain my breath before taking a seat beside her. My skirt is too short, and my bare ass scrapes against the concrete. I have my legs close together to keep from getting charged with public indecency.

"Prison?" she repeats in panic, blinking rapidly as her mind toys with the thought. "I can't go to prison. This is a new lace wig." It had taken Elise over an hour to do her hair, and all that effort going to waste would be a shame.

"You're welcome."

A burst of wind brushes by, and I toss our jackets over our legs.

She cuddles into her faux-fur coat, burrowing her face in it. "Wait," she says with a gasp, turning to look at me, panicked. She fumbles to open her small clutch. "I didn't close my tab."

I place my hand over hers. "That's fine. They'll close it for us at the end of the night."

We should probably head back inside somewhere. It's a cold night, and the initial warmth of our getaway is starting to wane.

But when I turn my head to say something to Elise, I notice that she's looking at me. And not just looking, but staring, her eyes barreling through me as if she's peering at my very essence. Her cheek rests on her knees, her arms wrapped around her legs, her hands rubbing the smooth expanse of her model-esque legs.

I mirror her posture and scoot closer to her, wanting to share our warmth. "What're you looking at, lady?" I say in a playfully aggressive tone.

The corners of her eyes wrinkle. "Someone pretty."

Her comment disarms me, and my breathing falters. Still, I try to maintain a lighthearted pretense. "Why Lisey, if I didn't know any better, I'd think you were hitting on me."

"I'm serious." She cups my cheek.

I go still beneath her touch, her eyes captivating.

"You're so beautiful, and I just want you to know that."

I don't know what prompted her to say it. Maybe it's what the guy said. Or maybe she remembers the way the bouncer looked at her and barely glanced at me. Either way, the sincerity in her words warms me to the core. I place my hand on top of hers, an appreciative smile on my face.

Being overlooked for my looks because of Elise has never bothered me. Not really, at least. I know I'm attractive in my own right, and I also recognize that someone more physically captivating than me will always exist. Sure, I get insecure at times, comparing myself to her or other girls, but that's natural. Plus, I've always been good at being indifferent when something starts to really affect me. "I know. Thank you."

The way she beams lets me know that she understands all that I mean. "You're feeling better, right?" Elise drops her hand from my face and shivers. "I know you were upset before we left."

Despite how oblivious and ditzy Elise can act at times, she's actually pretty perceptive. Somehow, I forget that a lot, doing nothing to disguise my feelings around her. A part of me wants to be honest and open up about all that happened today with my parents and Mr. Marbury, but another part really wants to end the conversation so we can get somewhere warm and not have our nipples fall off.

The latter wins. "Yeah, I'm feeling a lot better." I'm careful to shuffle onto my feet then extend a hand to her. "Let's go inside before we both die of hypothermia."

She grabs it, and I yank her up. It's only when we get into the car that she makes an absurd suggestion, one I'll oblige since she's my knight in shining armor tonight.

"Before we go back to your place, let's get sundaes. It's a little hot in this car."

SINCE I CAN'T sleep and Elise's dog, Hanson, snores like a pig for slaughter, I've voluntarily evicted myself to the couch. It's late. We weren't tired right away when we got back to my place and decided to stay up to watch YouTube tutorials on re-twisting hair. She wants to surprise Andres tomorrow by doing it for him, finding the activity intimate. I hope he takes an anesthetic beforehand if the residual pain throbbing my scalp from her practice round on me is any indication of her skills.

At first, I tried to watch TV to numb my mind into a state of slumber, but then a particular book, haphazardly stacked atop my messy pile next to the entertainment center, catches my eye, and I decide to indulge in a guilty pleasure of mine: Alien porn.

Lying on the couch book in hand, I immerse myself into an aptly cold, other world featuring rugged horn-and-tail men with ridges on their tongues and monster dicks. I'm completely comfortable on the couch, a throw around my legs, which are firmly pressed together, my face flushed in equal parts intrigue and arousal, and my cat resting above my head, reading with me.

Right when the cold alien man is going down on the heroine, the door to my apartment swings open.

"Why is your door unlocked?" a man booms in greeting, standing imposingly in the doorway. I can't help but squeak in surprise.

Initially, I don't register that it's Otis. He's dressed shadily, donning a dark black hoodie and gray sweatpants. Even his expression is menacing, emanating an I'm-going-to-rob-you aura.

Placing a hand over my violently beating heart, I scurry to my feet. "What the fuck is wrong with you? Who fucking barges into someone's house like that?"

"Who the fuck leaves their door unlocked in the middle of the night? Scratch that—who the fuck leaves their door unlocked at all?" He's equally outraged. Unlike me, he doesn't modulate his volume. I glance down the hall, anxious that our commotion will wake Hanson. That would be bad on all accounts—his barking will wake everyone up, and then I'll have Elise's peppy, romantic ass down my throat about why Otis is here so late.

When no noise or motion comes from the direction of my bedroom, I whip back to face my intruder, glowering at him. I'm still shaken from the rude and unexpected way he barged in, even if part of me is a little relieved to see him after twenty-six Otis-free hours. "You cannot just—"

"Nuh-uh." He takes a step forward. I've never thought of him as threatening before, his burly build attractive rather than intimidating. But right now, as he looks down at me with his eyes narrowed and his lips twisted into a dark scowl, I'm a little on edge, almost frightened. "Don't even try to make an excuse. I've told you so many times: Lock your fucking door. You live alone. You have to lock your fucking door."

I clench my jaws. I don't like how many times he's cursed at me. I push at his chest to create distance between us. Even if I can rationalize where his angry concern is coming from, I don't appreciate his reaction. "All right, tough guy, stop shouting and back off," I snap in my best effort to appear menacing. A part of me is definitely afraid now. The rage in his eyes is volatile. I recognize that he wouldn't ever hurt me, but that doesn't mollify my intuitions.

It takes him a second to register just how uncomfortable I am, and once he realizes it, Otis steps back, the dark edges on his face softening, and brushes his hand over his hair, frustration still marring his features. "Greta—" he falters.

I don't bother to speak, weaponizing my silence by folding my arms over my chest, expression blank.

It's effective, and he grows visibly anxious, tapping his foot. He takes a deep breath, closes his eyes, and shakes his head before trying again. "I'm sorry. I shouldn't have talked to you like that. I just got worried."

Gone is Otis's anger, replaced with genuine worry and misery. "You didn't text me all day, and then your door was unlocked, and for a split second I thought..." He licks his lips and shuffles toward me cautiously. When I don't back away, he takes another step and reaches out to brush his hand over my bare shoulder. The touch elicits an invisible shiver to roll down my spine. I stare at his neck, watching the way his Adam's apple bobs when he swallows repeatedly before continuing, "I'm sorry. I didn't mean to scare you. And I know—I swear, I know I shouldn't have spoken to you like that."

"No, you shouldn't have." My body relaxes from his acknowledgment of wrongdoing. I hear the jingle of Raven's new matching Tiffany collar, a gift from Elise, and the feline comes down from his perch on the armrest. He stretches and purrs as he makes his way to our new house guest.

He's quick to greet Otis with a face-to-shin rub but doesn't bother to linger for a pet before making his way to his feeding bowls.

Otis takes two more steps toward me, his arms extended. When there's barely any space left between us, the fronts of our bodies flush against each other, he bends to press his forehead against mine, his hot breath fanning over me. He wraps his arms around me while I grip my T-shirt to stop from grabbing hold of him.

"You still mad?" he whispers, his mouth brushing over me. I bite my tongue. My lack of response causes him to hold me tighter, my face nuzzled in his chest. He lets out a heavy sigh that I feel more than hear. "I really am sorry I yelled. I didn't mean to. The door was unlocked, and I freaked out. I don't want anything to ever happen to you, I don't know what I would do. And the fact that we didn't talk all day…" He inhales rapidly. "I'm sorry. I'm really sorry. I just… I couldn't stop thinking about you and I wanted to be around you."

This is cheating. His tone. His sentimental admission. It makes it hard to be angry, and my attitude melts.

"You better not do it again, or I'll just—" I don't bother to finish my threat and instead wrap my arm around him and lean back, straining onto my tiptoes to press a kiss to his lips.

Otis responds enthusiastically, his hands grabbing the curve of my ass, hauling me against him. A sound of approval escapes me when he wrenches his lips from my mouth to my neck and—*oh, yeah, right there*—kisses it in a way that turns me into putty.

My peck of forgiveness is evolving into more, not that I mind. Releasing a placid sigh, I strain into him, my head lolling back to give him better access. On their own accord, my palms slide under his shirt to feel the cold, corded muscles of his back.

I enjoy myself thoroughly, absorbed by his doting affection until he starts to peck back up the column of my neck and presses his cold nose into the crevice beneath my ear. My nervous system jolts. I flinch and dig my nails between his shoulder blade in reprimand.

"Ew, get off me. You're cold," I protest. I wriggle in his grasp, using his defined hipbones to try to push away, but he holds on tighter, burrowing his face deeper in the crook.

"No, don't make me let go. You're so warm." He groans. Frosty the Snowman—or is the Abominable Snowman more accurate, given his stature?—nibbles at my shoulder and rocks his hips against mine. I roll my eyes but keep him there, doing my best to warm him up since he's always done the same for me, even if I didn't realize it at the time.

Our embrace loosens, and we veer toward the couch. Rather than falling gracefully onto it, we lose balance and crumble, leaving me with two-hundred-something pounds atop me. I'm suffocating under his ginormous ass and have to tap his arm incessantly to get him to lift off, which he does once I start to see the light on the other side.

"Sorry." He grunts, hovering over me.

"It's okay," I whisper when he settles more of his weight onto me again, just enough so that I can feel him but not enough to smother me. "Why aren't you at Midnight Kiss?"

"Cause you're here and not there." He kisses my nose. I move away and give him a flat look.

"Wanna try another line? Cause Lisey already showed me the pictures Herik sent her from the night. You and your date looked super chummy."

He clears his throat. "Did we? I thought it was more respectful than chummy."

"Uh-huh. Sure."

"Not jealous, my ass," he mumbles unintelligibly. Victory brightens his face, and he's speaking again. "Look, you have nothing to worry about. Malik and I are just friends. And despite being tired as hell, I'm here now, and I want snuggles. And you can't be mad at a guy who wants snuggles," he mumbles into my chest.

I purse my lips to keep from snickering. He's right, and so I reward his adorableness by scratching his scalp.

And just like that, we're talking about stupid shit. We talk about his day and how badly he wants to create a punching bag out of my dad's and Duger's faces. Then we talk about my night, for which I give an embellished and entirely false narration about all the guys I took to the bathroom for a quickie. When I do admit to dancing with a guy at the start of the night, he smacks my ass but calmly asks to be my only dance partner. I agree, obsessing over how we can say so much about what we want from each other without actually saying *it*.

"Do you plan on sleeping over again?" I ask when the conversation dies down and all we're doing is holding each other, still wide awake.

Otis looks up at me expectantly, as if that wasn't his plan the whole time. It's already three in the morning—he's lucky my dad doesn't have them wake up early on afternoon-game days. "Can I?"

"If you like being relegated to the couch."

"Am I in timeout? Was it the ass smacking? Did I hit you too hard?" He cups my butt cheeks then starts rubbing them. "Sorry, babe."

"You know I don't mind the ass smacking," I murmur, brushing his hair out of his face. I grimace and suck in a breath dramatically. "But actually, you've been replaced."

His eyes narrow, and he growls in warning. "Greta—"

"What?" I'm quick to challenge. "You think you're the only person warming my bed?"

"Are you trying to be funny?" He starts lifting up on his elbow, still keeping an arm wrapped around me.

"My dad did call me a comedian earlier today." I don't mention that it was because I said I would get a job next semester should he decide to cut me off because of my grades.

"Really? He called me a dilapidated seal."

"That's basically a compliment."

"Sure, if you're hearing impaired." He lets out a deep breath, his lips flapping together, then juts out his bottom lip. "Are you going to explain why I'm being banished from your bed?"

I jerk my head to the bedroom. "Elise and Hanson are sleeping in my room."

Visible relief washes over him. "And I'm guessing she's not into threesomes."

"Not really. But I can always call—"

Otis slaps his hand on my mouth to stop me.

I bite down to remove his touch.

"Let's not continue to play this make-Otis-jealous game."

"Would you rather play *Catan*?"

He's quick to untangle himself from me and sit up. A grin splits his face, and his eyes gleam with excitement. "Really?"

We play for two hours, making up our own rules. He whips us up some hot chocolate when I make a passing comment about craving one. And as I watch him seamlessly navigate around my kitchen, I'm even more convinced of how I feel.

Sipping the warm drink while we play is the most fun I've had in a long time. The setup gets ruined three times—twice by Raven, who gets angry and lashes out when we don't shower him with attention, and once by Otis, since he's such a sore loser.

When it's time for him to leave, he gives me a kiss at the doorway, deep and slow and sweet, swallowing my face between his palms. It lasts forever—if forever were short enough to be bittersweet—his hands on my cheeks, mine balling the material of his shirt. My senses are consumed by him, and it's still not enough.

I reach for him again when he pulls away, wanting another touch, my entire body thrumming with need I haven't felt in a while.

But he's already slipped away, and by the time I step back into my place, he's texted me.

princess
Today 5:21 AM

lock your door or i'll rob u

and thx for being my real midnight kiss

goodnight G

predictions for game?

I'm really nervous about this next game cause we've been doing so-so. Last year there was no doubt in my mind that RSU would be going to the conference cause we dominated the whole season but this year we only picked up after game six. What do you guys think about this next game? And do you think the collegiate football committee will let us advance to the nectar bowl?

1 comment   92% ⬆ ⬇

jillianmillerhal · 33 min. ago
it's all on morgan. coach S is playing him more so he better not fuck up this next game or we probably won't qualify for the plum bowl

OTIS
HOW I SLEEP AT NIGHT

COACH SAHNOUN HOLDS me captive in his office, staring at me in an attempt to intimidate me into confessing my side of what's just happened, to give him a reason to not kick me off the team. But if he thinks he's going to win the quiet game, he's Cuckoo for Cocoa Puffs.

That makes two of us, given what's just transpired. But I've reached my limit. Acting crazy was actually the most sane of the options I had at my disposal.

It feels like we've been sitting here for at least an hour, though the clock on the wall says it hasn't even been fifteen minutes. I swear to God, time slows in this fucking room.

"So," he says, breaking the silence with a clap. *Ha! I win.* "D'you wanna explain what happened on the field?"

I shrug. Mimicking his posture, I maintain a nonchalant expression, running my tongue over my teeth repeatedly.

Coach's jaws clench in response, his eye twitching in barely tethered rage. He should have already blown a gasket at this point, as my uncooperative behavior is intolerable for a formidable man like him. I'm genuinely impressed by the fact that he's remained so calm throughout all this.

"Why're you so quiet now, hm? You had so much to say earlier. Speak up. Let's hear what you have to say, big man."

I tilt my head and arch an eyebrow, blinking slowly, refusing to be goaded.

"Is it because you're scared of me?" he taunts, letting out a lighthearted chuckle then spreading his arms out in mock invitation. "Don't be. I'm a lot smaller than Rodney and a bit nicer than the referee." Placing his hands behind his head, he ushers me with a firm nod. "So, c'mon. Talk. Let it out. I won't bite. Or are you too much of a pussy?"

I roll my eyes but tuck my arms closer to my chest in irritation. *Scared? Pussy?* Far from it. A pussy wouldn't have gotten into the referee's face and yelled like a fucking barbarian until they were ejected from the game, nor would they have tried to beat up the biggest guy on the field. Then again, a sensible person wouldn't have done that, either, but that's not the point.

"Listen," I drawl lazily, my voice cracking and dry from the exertion I put on my vocal cords earlier. I motion between us. "Can't you just get on with whatever this really is and punish me already?"

It's his turn to appear skeptical. "Punish you how?"

My arms drop, and my hands slap loudly against my thighs. Releasing a heavy breath, I roll my neck in vacant disinterest. "I don't know, but I need you to"—I clap my hands twice—"chop-chop and get on with it. I have plans."

Any other day, I wouldn't have dared to speak to Coach like this, but today wasn't any other day. Today is The Worst Day Ever™. Plus, I'm already in hot water, so what's the harm in burning a little more, especially when it feels so good to let out the vapors?

"What plans?" Coach snorts. "I know your family couldn't make it, and the parties don't start until ten or eleven. So where…" His voice trails off, and a knowing look crosses his face.

Suddenly, the world around me slows even further, and my guts float. The hairs on my arm raise. It's a feeling I'm too familiar with—call it an intuition of sorts—omniscient in its predictive powers but helpless to what follows.

I felt it before my mom told me my dad died and the morning I opened the door to Pawpaw's bedroom to bring him breakfast and medicine, only to see that he'd passed away in his sleep. It curdled through me when I was informed of the severity of my knee injury earlier this year and on that late-summer afternoon when Autumn and I called it quits. And now, here it is again, announcing itself just seconds before he speaks.

My blood runs cold when Coach's mouth twists into a sour smirk, his eyes narrowed, gleaming with resentment.

He knows.

"Do you have something going on in your love life, then?" He places his elbows on the desk to rest his chin on clasped fists. The dreamy smile he wears could put the Cheshire Cat out of business.

I struggle to swallow, my chest flooded with unbridled anxiety.

"Hm? Is that why you want to leave so badly? To meet up with my daughter?"

Every organ in my body takes pause. My face pricks with frosty chills, drained of life. I sit completely still, my bones coated in rigid marble, terrified that even the slightest movement might set him off.

"You look surprised," he says. Shaking his head, he sucks his tongue and squares his shoulders, his eyes shining like a famished predator ready to strike. "Don't be. I told you before: I listen when you boys talk. So naturally, I would find out about you and Greta." His smile darkens and fills with malice as he leans forward. "I know everything, Morgan. Every. Fucking. Thing."

I exhale out of necessity, my lungs ablaze, my heart struggling to find a rhythm. Surprise causes me to choke on a bubble of air and I cough to dislodge it. I expected to get my ass handed to me by Coach today after what I pulled, but now, I'm pretty sure I'm going to be murdered. Clearing my throat obnoxiously to bide my time, I grapple with the fact that I'm done for and stare at him in utter disbelief and horror. Admittedly, I'm afraid now.

"I'm not fucking your daughter," I blurt automatically. Lack of forethought has me choosing my words poorly. What's worse is that I don't even sound remotely believable.

The dangerous smile curling on Coach's lip deepens, and he shakes his head. "Lying will make this worse."

I don't believe that. After this, there's absolutely nothing on Earth that could make today, or even this situation, worse.

Slight after slight had compounded since this morning, forming a harrowing amalgamation of dread that was delivered to me in one fell swoop so the universe could have a final giggle before the end of the semester.

First, I awoke to texts informing me that no one in my family would be at my game today, regardless of their promises. I wish I could say I was surprised, but I wasn't. Disappointed, yes, but that's not unusual. After Pawpaw left, it became rare to see Katia, Mom, or Monica in the bleachers, watching me. It only ever happened when I dragged them there. Just because I was used to it didn't mean it sucked any less.

Next came the locker-room talk. Surprisingly, it had been going well during the first half. Instead of being a fuckwad, Coach was actually kind, offering words of genuine encouragement with no subliminal or targeted remarks thrown into the mix. It was a stark contrast from yesterday, and whatever foul mood I was in had dissipated the closer we got to the end of his pep talk. Because after his speech comes the captain's, and that's me.

Except, it wasn't me. Rather than gesturing for me to stand at the center, he grabbed Rodney. Mister Mother Fucking MVP, Jefferson Rodney.

To say I felt decimated was an understatement, but I was determined to persevere, to get that *"You're the real MVP"* from

Coach and Duger by the end of the game. My performance would show up Rodney—and this would be post knee surgery, which would make it all the more impressive—and it would be glorious.

The third "fuck you" from the universe arrived soon after the start of the second quarter, when Herik stumbled forward right as I initiated our third down. The opposing team's defensive nose tackle rammed me into the ground, and my bad knee took the brunt of his weight. Before I even stood up, I knew something was wrong. The ligament pinched and throbbed in a way it hadn't for a while. No amount of acting on my part could conceal the instability in my leg.

Tuckerson took my place during our next offensive turnover, and from that moment forward, we sucked. I'm not saying it's his fault, but we were up when I was playing.

I knew for certain we were going to lose after the third quarter, and if that agonizing realization wasn't bad enough, what happened two minutes before the game ended was.

That was when I got ejected.

Quinn fell to the ground in a terrifying tackle that had everyone in the stadium gasping in shock. When Rodney neglected to follow the route for that play—failing at doing his fucking job, which is to protect Quinn, who'd caught the ball—I lost it. I was strung too tightly already, bludgeoned half to death by the day, and it was the last straw.

It was like an explosion. The agony and rage compressed inside me burst and lit my whole world in shades of unrestrained torment. The strings that kept me rational were severed, and I went ballistic.

Adrenaline allowed me to ignore my injury and storm onto the field, tossing Herik aside when he frantically rushed to stop my rampage. My sights were on Rodney, who was jogging to his toppled teammate. I tackled him to the ground. And just like that, I let my body take over, manifesting my anger physically because I was sure that would make me feel better. It didn't matter that my

Kinesio tape was coming undone or that my knee was swollen and screaming for me to be kind to my body. I only saw red, and until that color waned, I wouldn't stop.

Too bad it didn't get to that point. I was yanked off of Rodney and ejected from the game, my standing at the university immediately called into question.

So yeah, you could say I've had a fucking terrible day, and evidently, I haven't taken it well. But this right here, this revelation from Coach, has got to be one of the worst things to have happened.

"How did you find out?" I choke out, my face hot from the shame of getting caught.

"You ask as if you were trying to hide it."

And that's when he tells me all that he knows, like a man revealing his cards during the showdown of a poker game. He regales me with all the telltale signs, the clues that Greta and I had recklessly left. My bruised knuckles turn white from how hard I clutch the armrest of my seat, willing it to ground me. I'm seconds away from leaving an Otis-shaped hole in the wall.

"I know all this," Coach says with a grunt, the lines of his face etched in disappointment, "and yet, I'm not upset about the fact that you two are together. All I want to know is why you would fool around with my daughter and not have the decency to tell me about it. I've known for a while. I've just been waiting for you to say something, since I knew she wouldn't."

Shocker. Your own daughter doesn't trust or want to confide in you.

I'm on the defensive. Unlike before, when I felt justified and entirely blameless in my reaction, I know I'm in the wrong here. Still, I can't back down when I've done my damndest already to appear strong and unphased. "Am I supposed to run all the people I'm with through you?"

"Don't be intentionally dense, Morgan. There's a difference between you fooling around with somebody you met at a bar and fooling around with my child."

I know Greta's parents are chill about her sex life, but he's being too calm, and I don't know how to process this. I'd feel so much more in my element if he were yelling.

Seriously, why isn't he yelling?

"I didn't realize you cared." I snort sarcastically. A part of me is aware that every word coming out of my mouth is leading to my destruction, but the angry and irrational side is louder, calling for carnage.

"I'm warning you this last time, Otis. Respect yourself," Coach warns, his appearance pleasant, his tone deadly. "If you have a problem, be a real man and say it. Quit with this tough-guy act."

Whatever faint plans I had before of giving in and apologizing go out the window. I've never thought of myself as a hypersensitive person who cared about concepts revolving around masculinity, but hearing 'be a real man' from Coach—from the same guy who puts on a mask of cruelty in a bid to appear tough—it's too much, too hypocritical.

But just like him, I'd put on an uncaring front to conceal the fact that inside, I'm hurt. I'm hurt beyond belief, and in truth, I want him to hurt as much as I do. So for the second time that day, I break. Despite my better judgment, I lose my grasp on myself. Misery loves company, and I hope Coach enjoys mine.

"You really want me to tell you what my problem is? You."

"How theatrical and riveting." He sits up and smiles, and God, I can't wait to fucking wipe that look off his face, smear its gloating remnants on the walls, and dance around in victory.

My scorn tugs my mouth into a scowl. "Very riveting. Just as riveting as your attitude."

"*My* attitude? Perhaps you're speaking into your reflection, no?"

I stare, projecting all of my pent-up frustration and feelings of inadequacy onto him. "I'm looking right at you, aren't I? I'm not the one who tears down his players and calls it encouragement."

"I tear you guys down? How?" I don't get a chance to speak before he's raising his voice. "Was it when I told all of you that win or lose today, you're all amazing players?"

I throw my head back and let out a chilling laugh. That's his only defense? That he sprinkles a little sugar on top of shit and calls it a dessert? Miss me with that fucking bullshit. Sporadic guffaws escape me as I stare at him in humored disbelief. "Don't be intentionally dense, Sahnoun," I mock. "Do you have selective memory? Did you happen to forget what you said to us yesterday during strategy review? Or all the insults you throw our way every day during practice?"

Coach blinks at me. "What? The constructive criticism I give you all? That's what's got you throwing this temper tantrum?" He shakes his head. "Wow. Wow, I'm in shock right now. I was really wrong about you, wasn't I? You'll never succeed in the league. *Never.* And you want me to tell you why?"

No. "Go for it. It's not like you've been shoving candy canes and rainbows up my ass these last three years."

The corners of his eyes wrinkle, and I wish I could take back time so I wouldn't have to hear what he has to say next. But more than that, I want to take it back, heed my wounded pride, and not speak so cruelly like the old Otis.

"You, Morgan, are insecure." He maintains that calm, chilling tone. "Even before your injury, I saw it. I could see the way you checked out the crowd when you made a good pass but especially when you messed up. I would see the way you lashed out at your teammates when they criticized you. I noticed how you would react when I paid you a compliment. I watched you, and I kept thinking: *Maybe he just wants to be better. That's why he's so unsure. He doesn't want to get complacent. He tells himself he's not good so that he'll continue to strive for more.*"

Coach Sahnoun looks down and pauses for a moment. It's for dramatic effect, to wring my anxiety tighter. He raps his fist against the table twice before looking back at me, unbidden sadness on his face. When he speaks, he does so caustically, every word burning me to the core. "But then you messed up your knee, and they say you don't know a man until they're at their worst. And you were at your worst—are still at your worst—and that's not a man I want to coach anymore."

He doesn't mean it. It's not true. He's just saying all this to hurt you. But that doesn't change the impact of his words or how heavily they weigh in my mind, heaving me further down the dark hole of sadness and rage. I have to bite my bottom lip to keep from letting out a pained whimper, my heart pinching and thumping and burning. My throat itches.

It takes me a moment to compose myself. Swallowing a rush of bile, I clutch at the frail metal armrests of my seat, wanting to pull them from their anchors to toss at him. "I am not at my worst. This was one bad game in a streak of good ones."

Coach holds his hand up the whole time I refute him, shaking his head, obviously disillusioned and weary.

He means it. I want to crumble to the ground right then, but I don't. Like I said, misery loves company, and I'm the embodiment of unadulterated suffering.

Before he even has the chance to say anything, I speak softly, the words escaping me so effortlessly, with no regard for reality and repercussions. "Y'know what, Coach? I don't care what you say."

He smirks with mirth and doubt. "Oh?"

"Yeah. I don't. Cause no matter what you say, at the end of the day, I know I'm better than you, even at my worst."

"And how do you figure that?"

Shut up, a voice in my head shrieks, fighting for salvation. But it's too late.

"Cause at the very least, I get to go to sleep at night knowing I don't have a daughter who hates me for murdering her brother, when all it would have taken was a little compassion to keep him alive."

And there it is. It doesn't matter that my words were motivated by a need to hurt Coach as much as he's been hurting me for three years—and especially in the last two minutes. It doesn't matter that I don't truly believe my words, that I speak them simply because I know the pain they'll cause. I've crossed a line that I can never take back, but at least I've achieved something no one else on the team—probably even the universe—has ever done: I've made Coach speechless.

The taste of victory is sweet and potent, and for a few heartbeats, I get to see agony marring his face and wetting his eyes. I'm invincible. I'm a king in a land that's not my own, indestructible.

And I know that my fall from grace will be terrible, even soul-crushing, but that's the problem with wanting to exact retribution: It marginalizes consequences and makes everything seem worth it.

Coach physically tosses me out of his office. I can't even slip out a word of half-hearted apology, one I won't truly mean but realize is necessary for my salvation. I fall to the ground outside the door, and everyone in the locker room stares at me, no one offering a hand of help.

He'd said my injury was my lowest, hadn't he? Well, he'd been wrong. This, right here, is it. And sprawled helplessly on the rough carpeted floor of our locker room, staring intently at the nameplate plastered on the door before me, I can't help but wish I was man enough to get up and apologize and mean it. I wish I could muster an ounce of regret.

It's not until I get to my empty house and walk up the creaky stairs that I remember Greta, that I feel regret. Not because she comes to my mind naturally, obsessively, but because when I open my bedroom door, there she stands. Devastated, beautiful, and ready to knock my world asunder as payback for tearing her heart to shreds.

I might have ripped the ground from beneath her feet, but she's about to bury me beneath the wreckage.

that game was a joke right?!

WTF happened today? I'm actually in shock.

5 comments   100%

jillianmillerha1 • 5 hr. ago
I said it was all on Morgan in that last post... and yeah... I was right

laserthosetags • 5 hr. ago
not only did he beat up J. Rod but he also punched the shit out of Andres Herick and that's his "best friend" what a dick

killjive • 3 hr. ago
Did you guys see coach s's reaction? He looked like he was about to have an aneurysm. Never laughed so hard in my life

manntis1for1 • 4 hr. ago
The referee is GOATED for getting in there and pulling Motherfucker Morgan off J. Rod. Thought we were about to be out of a running back LOL

harp33r • 4 hr. ago
Anyone else remember that post on here a few months ago talking about what an asshole Morgan is...

GRETA

HATE HOW MUCH I DON'T HATE YOU

"LIE TO ME."

Otis shifts his weight from one foot to the other, his eyes downcast and shoulders sagging, still holding his duffel bag. His clothes are rumpled, and the bedroom door is wide open behind him. I didn't give him a chance to greet me before speaking, confronting him head-on with what he'd done.

Initially, I'd planned to play it cool, to lull him into a state of security and comfort before launching my attacks. But that gave way the moment I heard his heavy footsteps barrel up the stairs.

I stand a few feet from him, my posture rigid, my demeanor stern. I'm sure my expression is harsh. A random bystander might assume I'm ready for battle, but even if I appear formidable, I'm bleeding on the inside. Heart, lungs, soul… Everything is weeping from his treachery.

My throat burns with the urge to shriek in frustration at him and at myself. Fuck. I wish I could fast-forward through this painful conversation and arrive at its conclusion, wherein I decide to leave or stay.

Better yet, I wish I hadn't been so adamant about coming over to comfort him. Earlier, we'd gathered at James's place to watch the game, and after seeing the fight on TV, I'd become more insistent despite my friends insisting otherwise—I wanted to be there for Otis.

I thought I knew him. The last couple of nights had been amazing. We'd been completely connected. I told myself that his actions, though deplorable, came from a place of pain. He wouldn't have lashed out at my father like that for no reason, and though I couldn't condone it, I would be there. I had to be there.

The number-one thing to do in a relationship is to be there for a partner, through the good, the bad, and the ugly. Granted, I'm assuming my role preemptively, but I want to. We'll be official soon enough, and we already treat each other like we're *together* together.

"Lie to me," I repeat. He talked all that shit to his teammates, to my fucking father, and now, here he stands, mute like a coward, obviously not caring about the harm his words had on those beyond his intended audience. The repercussions ricocheted, and they'd hurt me. "Lie to me and tell me you didn't."

For the first time since he walked in, Otis raises his chin and looks at me, jaws clenched. I'm held hostage by his gaze, and even if I want to look away, I can't.

Looking at the man I'd once imagined as my moonlight, in the wake of everything he said and did, makes me feel like I've been struck by lightning, his gaze the bolt that's marred me.

This very look makes it all come together. It hadn't before. I'd thought of Otis just as Otis, my Rutherford. The guy on the TV, the one Elias and Jefferson had talked about downstairs, not knowing I was upstairs listening to every word, was someone else. I was aware that they're the same person—they share the same body—but they were different to me. Maybe detaching quarterback Otis from the man I kept company with all the time was how I was able to get over my initial qualms about being with a footballer.

But I can't do that anymore. Now, when he looks at me with

eyes that belong to both of them, I'm forced to confront the truth, and it makes me want to crumble.

I'd been dead fucking wrong about him.

Disillusionment is a funny feeling, and that's only because it's not a feeling. Or if it is, it mostly feels like nothing.

Initially, there's a physical reaction as actualization dawns. The ground beneath will feel as though it's been stolen, followed by a spiral down an endless abyss, every internal organ churning with the descent. There's no landing, but the feeling will stop, and when the mind clears, there's nothing there. Self-loathing persists, for being stupid and naïve, but it doesn't feel like anything.

And that's because disillusionment is all mental. There's a mirror in the mind, reflecting a manufactured reality, but when the die is cast—once the stone is thrown and the mirror shatters—it's all over. The picturesque fantasy of that person is dismantled at the hinges, and one is left wondering what to do.

What's fucking up this situation nine ways to hell is the fact that, at this very moment, I truly wish I'd never discovered the truth. That way, I could remain in my fantastical world, where the blissful notion I'd fabricated of Otis and me exists.

Sometimes, it's better to live in a lie than face the devastating truth.

I need for Otis to let me live in the world I've created where the both of us are happy, we're together, everything is great, and none of this happened, because the Otis in my mind would never do something like that.

I'm weak, and as much as I hate myself for it, I hate myself more for how much I don't hate him.

"Lie to me. Do it," I taunt, but he doesn't take the bait and my chest swells, tingling. "Fucking do it. Tell me you didn't!" I'm shouting. I don't think I've ever raised my voice like this to someone who isn't my family, but I'm crushed and find solace in the screaming release.

After all that, he had to do *this*? Ruin *this* for me? Does he not know how hard it was for me to accept the idea of us? How could he?

As much as I want to fault him entirely, I can't. I know I bear some of the blame. Because the truth is that I know Otis, but I don't *know*-know him. I'd allowed myself to fill in the blanks, to manufacture a version of him without cross-referencing it with what existed before me.

Just because he'd been inside me, made me laugh and smile, and had taken care of me in a capacity that was beyond his obligation doesn't mean I know him, and today's events have made that more than clear.

The volume of my voice had been too high, and he turns his torso to shut the door. Turning back to face me, he sighs, his tone mild. "Can we sit down and talk? My knee is fucking killing me right now."

A part of me wants to rush forward and coddle him. I've been fighting that urge since he got here. He must be having a shit day, the exhaustion etched on his crestfallen face evidence of this.

But no matter how shit his day was, he had no right to do any of the things he did and I'm not about to let go of my convictions because I'm pussy-whipped for a guy named after a cow on Nickelodeon.

Letting out a sarcastic snort, I roll my eyes at him, needing to appear tough. "What the fuck does this looks like? A therapy session?"

He flinches and stares my feet. The fatigue disfiguring Otis's face turns to sadness. He heaves a labored sigh and shakes his head a little, closing his eyes to hide the emotions storming in them.

I don't know what I'm still doing here or what I want to achieve with a conversation like this. I know what he did, and he knows I know, so I should probably leave.

Except I don't. I stay. I tell myself it's to hear him out, so I can swiftly and unequivocally end things. Deep down, however, I know that's not the extent of it. I harbor an ember of hope that whatever he has to say—whatever excuse he offers—will be good enough for me to forgive him. That way, we can move on, and he can be mine. It's been so long since I've felt like this about another person, and I deserve to be happy just like everyone else, right?

Except my guilt and protectiveness of my family forces me to pretend like that part of me doesn't exist.

"If you're not going to sit, then I am." He walks past me, pausing when his arm brushes against mine. He tosses his duffel on the floor and lets out a grunt as he plops down on the bed, extending his bad leg.

I keep my back to him for a while, wrestling away that feeling of devastation wrangling through me, grappling for more strength before turning to face him. "Are you going to lie to me now?" I ask. "Are you going to tell me that what I heard isn't true?"

"What did you hear?" he asks cautiously.

"Lots of things. The sounds in your house travel really well and your roommates are pretty fucking loud."

"Everything?" I nod, and he lets out a sound between a chuckle and a groan. Swallowing thickly, his Adam's apple bobbing, he mumbles, "I bet you don't know everything."

What the fuck is he playing at? Why is he being so passive? "Yeah? How about you surprise me."

"Your dad knows about us."

Questions multiply in my head, and I'm starting to doubt the narrative I'd overheard his teammates tell when they got home from the game. Otis's arrival had been delayed significantly for some reason or the other... Maybe this was it. "Did he get upset?" *Is that why you said what you said?*

I can't imagine my dad being super pissed. He's never been the type to be overprotective of me in that way. He might be displeased at first, but only because he doesn't like the idea of his players doing sexual things with his daughter.

Otis purses his lips before shaking his head slowly. "Not really. Just annoyed I didn't respect him enough to say anything about it."

I'm back to square one, frustrated as all hell. "If not that, then… What? How could you?" I take a step toward him, giving up on my previous attitude. Shuffling to stand in front of him, I tower above his tired, slumped frame. He's staring at the wall behind me, the defined muscles of his jaw ticking as he clenches and unclenches his jaws. "How could you say *that* to my dad?"

"I didn't mean to." It's almost like he's not here with me, his mind in another place. "I didn't mean to do—say—any of it. It sort of just came out. I never meant to…"

I don't respond.

The crushing silence that settles over us snaps Otis out of his trance, and he looks at me. I don't know what induces him to reach for me, but the movement makes me lean just out of reach. When the calloused pads of his fingers graze against the soft skin of my arm, I flinch and jerk back as if burned. His eyes reflect the slight he feels from my rejection.

It's time to leave. I got my reason, pitiful as it is. I've done my part by trying to reason the motive behind his behavior, and now, it's time for me to let him go, to sever ties, to move on. And yet, that stupid, pathetic part of me that's in like-plus—not love but a little deeper than like because this doesn't feel like a simple crush anymore—won't let me.

I become one of those people I despise, and I stay, allowing myself to hurt even more with every passing second I stand in his company, confronting the truth of him. "So why did you do it?" My eyes are dry, but sadness drips into every word I utter. "You didn't mean to, and you probably knew you shouldn't have, but you did. Why?"

He waves a hand, opening and closing his mouth like a pufferfish. "I was angry."

I expected some magnanimous response. "You were angry," I repeat, testing out the logic in his response. I pinch my brows together. "You were angry, so you decided to... What? How could you... How could you even..." I can't conjure the words. They're stuck in my throat, disbelief hindering its passage.

"I wasn't thinking." Otis expels a deep breath, then pushes his messy hair back, places his elbows on his thighs, and plops his head onto the heels of his palms. "Look, G, I'm fucking exhausted. And I'm so glad you're here, but can we talk about this—"

"You don't want to talk about this now because you're tired? Then maybe you shouldn't have tried to beat the shit out of one of your teammates. Maybe then you wouldn't be tired."

"No," Otis enunciates slowly, almost like the words are being hauled out of him. "I shouldn't have."

"And what you said to my dad?" A gasp catches in my throat. "When you used me and my brother's death against him and called him a m-murderer? Should you have done that?" Fire licks up my neck. Had I really called my own father that a month ago? It's unfathomable to me now.

This time, Otis isn't too quick to concede his wrongdoings, and fuck if that doesn't hurt. I bite my bottom lip to keep from keening over in misery. I'm starting to realize that I'm not going to get what I want from him, no matter how badly I wish to.

"I'm sorry I hurt you," he whispers.

"That's not what I asked." It's not what I want to hear. It's not the apology he should be delivering.

"I am sorry."

I'm close to screaming again. "That's not what I asked, Morgan. I asked if you should have said what you said to my father."

His eyes are dull, unrecognizable. "What do you want me to say, G?" He weaponizes the affectionate abbreviation of my name, a nickname he'd previously used during intimate and playful moments, tainting it. "Do you want me to lie and tell you he didn't deserve to be hurt? Because he did. He really fucking did. And you might not think that's the case, but you also don't know the context."

"Context isn't necessary. Wrong is wrong." My hands curl into fists.

"But you didn't hear what he said to me," Otis whispers, sounding lost and out of focus, as if he's reliving it. "You didn't hear the way he was talking about me. How he always talks to me."

"That doesn't mean you can—"

"You don't get it." His voice is no longer meek and gentle. He's stern, defensive. "I'm always small to him. I'm nothing. I could be the best of the best, and he'd still talk to me—he'd still *treat* me like I'm less than scum."

Dad called me useless today. At least that's better than a piece of shit, amirite?

Dad said he'll get me a car for my sixteenth birthday if we win the championship. I have to be the best out there. Make sure you cheer extra hard, okay, Gretel?

Sometimes, I feel like nothing. But sometimes, I feel great. I don't get it.

I feel sick, like I might puke.

Otis lets out a quiet groan before speaking again. "Look, I know it was wrong, and I'm sorry. I'm sorry I hurt you. But I just... Fuck, I only intended to hurt him, not you. Never you. You have to believe I would never ever have said it if I knew it would hurt *you*." He lets out an exhausted grunt, struggles to stand, then takes a step, reaching for me again. Everything he's saying is making it worse.

My body aches to stay still, to let him bridge this gap, because even if I don't *know* exactly how Otis feels, I do understand.

"I wanted to hurt him as badly as he hurts us. I mean, c'mon. You know how he can get. You know how—"

"It doesn't matter." I sound severe despite the hum of my wavering conviction. "It doesn't matter if he's the biggest jackass alive." *It does matter. That's why you hate your own dad sometimes, Greta.* "You had no right to say that to him. No right to try and hurt him like that. There are other ways to go about it, but to use my brother? How could you think that was okay?"

"It's—"

"No!" I shout loudly enough to make him jump. "No. No, you don't get to excuse yourself. You don't get to justify your actions. You don't get to—" I take a deep breath and let out a strangled screech of irritation, looking at him with all the grief I've kept inside over Julien. I'm drowning in sad, terrible memories I've fought so hard to suppress, to never recollect, and no matter how hard I try to break the surface, I can't. "It wasn't your pain." I flare my nostrils and will the tears that burn in the back of my eyes to stop before they crumble my composure. "I know my dad isn't a great guy, and I know you wanted to hurt him as much as he hurt you, but it wasn't your pain. You didn't see how broken he became after Julien died. You didn't see how it crippled our family. And yet you felt justified enough to use it against him as if...

"It wasn't your pain, Otis. It didn't belong to you. You had no right to use it in that way. You could have done anything else to—" My lips tremble, and my outrage softens to a whisper. "It wasn't yours."

"But you said—"

"I'm his daughter!" I howl. I don't care if I appear hysterical or crazy. I don't care if I'm coming off as an emotional, neurotic mess, something I've never been accused of before. "I'm Julien's sister. We're his family, and we know what happened and we feel his loss every day. I can say it, but you can't. I don't care who you think you are—what you went through—you didn't have the right to say that.

"For three fucking years, I held that feeling inside me, despite how angry I was with him. Three fucking years before I exploded and said one of the worst things I could ever say to a father who's lost a child—who lost a part of himself afterward—and I regret it. You heard me say it *once*, heard me talk about it *once*, and even *after* I told you I didn't mea—even after that, you go and say that shit to my dad's face?" My voice cracks and I let out a mangled sob. "Seriously, Otis? *Seriously?*"

Maybe he knew it before but just didn't want to face it, like how I didn't want to face who he really is. But now, with my fortitude decaying, my eyes wet with the need to sob, he seems to recognize that he's wrong, and rather than persist in justifying his actions, he relents, remorse cutting into his handsome face. "Greta, I didn't mean to—I didn't realize it would hurt you like that. I wasn't thinking. I—" His breath catches and this time, when he apologizes, he means it. I know he means it because he talks like it's the last time we'll ever speak again. "I'm sorry. I'm so fucking sorry."

The hope inside me is extinguished, leaving only a dull pang. I want to double over and scream and cry because this incident is opening old wounds that I'm not drunk or high enough to handle. I'm hurting everywhere, and I want it to stop. I want to go back to a time when I didn't have any feelings.

It's fucking twisted that what pains me the most right now isn't even the thought of Julien. It's not even what Otis said to my dad or how badly he's hurt him.

What coils my guts is that even if I know I should hate him, to toss him out of my life and out of my sight the same way he tossed our trust out, I can't. I don't want to. The hope might be gone, but the motherfucking feelings are as sturdy as ever.

For the sake of not giving in to my emotions, I let out a noise of choked outrage and turn to leave. My departure is long overdue. I've already given him more than he deserves, and if I stay, I'm only punishing myself.

Otis rushes to obstruct my escape by standing in front of the door.

"Get out of my way," I snarl between clenched teeth.

"No." His face is tense. "No, you can't leave. Not like this."

"Oh yes, I can. And if you don't let me, I swear to God, I'll punch you so hard, you'll be wearing dentures."

Instead of the calm, sad boy I'd been speaking to earlier, Otis transforms into a frantic, desperate version of himself that I've never seen before.

Truth be told, there are many sides of him I haven't seen before today, and I detest most of them. But not this one. I pity this one.

"Don't leave." It's a request, not a command. When I open my mouth to deny him, he continues, "Please. Please, I'm begging you."

I hold my hand up and wave it in front of his face, shaking my head, signaling him to stop because I can't take this. I don't have enough time to evade his touch when he grabs and looks at me, his blue eyes misty.

"I know what I did was wrong. I know it was and that you don't want to be around me or see me."

I try to wriggle from his grasp, but he grips me tighter, and I stop trying.

"I swear, I'll do anything to fix this. But right now, I need you to stay." His voice cracks and those stormy eyes finally give way to a hurricane. Tears drip from the corners of his eyes and down the sharp terrain of his handsome, angular face. "Today has been terrible, and I have no one right now, and I need you, G."

There he goes with that pet name. I shake my head again. "No."

Though he doesn't let me go, he slackens his hold. "Please." He inhales a shuddering breath.

Even more pitiful is the way I want to hug him and forgive him if it means this will stop. I close my eyes to keep from looking at him, to keep my willpower in check. I know what I have to do, and I just need to fight against my longing until I can escape. Then I can break down.

"Fuck, Greta." He drops to his knees, his arms around my waist, and presses his face against my stomach. I feel his tears against my skin, soaking into my shirt. "Please. Don't leave. Please. Please stay. I was wrong. I'm sorry. I'm so fucking sorry. I lo—"

My eyes snap open, my body arrested in terror. This time, when I shove him, I put all my might into it and detach myself. The protest that leaves me is urgent, filled with disgust, anger, and quiet yearning. He can't say it. He can't. This isn't how it's supposed to happen. He can't. "No. No, don't you dare. Don't you dare say—"

He ignores me. "I love you."

7:48

Saturday, December 3

NOTIFICATIONS

james
the sluts + a virgin
i get that youre sad and all that but you have to text us back. or answer the door. we're really worried dude

lisey
the sluts + a virgin
you're scaring us babe :(

lisey
the sluts + a virgin
can you open the door? please. your neighbors are tired of us knocking

lisey
the sluts + a virgin
tata please

lisey
the sluts + a virgin
james im outside come out

james
the sluts + a virgin
k lets get cfa on the way to tata i already ordered the oreo shake on the app

mamounette
Je vais tuer ton père...

mamounette
Comment peut-il continuer à me briser le coeur comme ça?

papa sahnoun
Is your mother with you?

papa sahnoun
Answer the phone

ORBITING HER SPACE

SHE STAYS FOR a moment. Greta hesitates long enough for my heart to contract and then expand in a single stroke. It's finite, her hesitation fleeting, but I've ventured into a secret realm in time's dimension where blinks draw out and the stroke of a hummingbird's wing stretches infinitely. Here, the sand drips down the hourglass as though it never wants to leave its narrow stem, suspending me in limitless hope that ultimately won't end well.

For the rest of my life, I'll replay the moment, feel the pinch of tethered helplessness jerking within me as I gaze upon her. The flush that rests on her cheeks, the moisture saturating her thick, dark lashes. The tremor in her jaw, her gorgeous, swollen lips parted, my honest, desperate confession robbing her of words.

She's in an obvious state of disbelief, her dull, sad eyes gleaming, and it's not until she twists her body to turn away that I see the longing, the desire, the shattered affection, all sentiments I reciprocate. I reach for her from my place on the ground, but it's too late. She's left, and my injury has rendered me immobile, the pain reaching a crescendo, so intense that I can no longer tolerate or ignore it.

Fuck.

Herik doesn't answer when I call, and neither does Quinn nor Jenner. I hear someone downstairs, and I'm certain it's Rodney, his footsteps distinct, the hum of his loud, deep voice unique. I have enough remorse not to bother him.

Duger ends up answering and taking me to our team's doctor. We don't say a single thing about what's transpired today. He just lets me stare out the window to hide the trickle of tears that sporadically fall from my eyes.

THE ONLY REASON I'm still sane is because she didn't block me.

G 🖤
Yesterday 1:13 PM

can we talk?

i know i fucked up

i promise ill do better this time

Yesterday 4:09 AM

i wasnt in the right headspace before but i am now

i just wanna talk

thats all i want

i swear

Today 8:29 AM

please

Today 11:46 PM

Give me space.

If only I were an astronaut.

THE UNIVERSITY CLEARS me. They call the outburst an anomaly and say it was due to stress. They recommend a therapist, and I pretend to be up for it until we're out of the disciplinary hearing, when I toss their referral in the trash. I'm not about to waste time with a therapist for a one-time lapse in judgement when

I could be focusing on my career.

But I no longer feel certain about that, either. Two implied offers from the NFL are suddenly reconsidered. It's insinuated that I shouldn't go for the draft, and that my invitation to the Scouting Combine, though standing, might be rescinded. I would bet all of my money that Coach has something to do with all this. If not him, the media coverage surely did me in.

I ace my finals, but it doesn't matter. I've more or less been kicked off the team, so my academic standing no longer has a bearing on sports. When I go to talk to Coach the following Monday before practice, Duger intercepts me with disappointment etched on his face and implies that my status as a player is uncertain. By now, I'm sure everyone knows about the exchange between Coach and me.

Over the course of the next week, I make more attempts to approach Coach as winter break inches closer and closer, my return to Texas imminent. During my last try, I leave him a note.

I find the note under my door the next morning with the words GO FUCK YOURSELF, BITCH scrawled across it. It's from Rodney.

I'm pissed, but I don't do anything. I deserve it.

THE SECOND I roll into the driveway of my childhood home, I transform into a shell of a person. I'd barely been keeping it together, but once I crossed the state line and merged onto Route 90, my demeanor shifted. Here, there's nothing to distract me. No football. No classes. Nothing. Just my family, and given how many times Ma has called me since the outburst, I know I'm in for some hovering.

"*Bendición, Ma,*" I call out as I crack the door open. Chairwoman Meow attempts to bypass me, but I'm quick to bend down and capture her.

"*Bendición, mijo,*" Ma sings back.

When I open the front door completely, I see Monica sitting on the couch with her legs propped onto the coffee table while Mom cleans, her music loud, shaking the picture frames on the wall. Monica barely glances up at me and grunts a greeting before turning to Mom and shouting, "Can I go to the diner now? I'm late, and Mary already ordered for me."

The music stops, and Mom clicks her tongue loudly. "*Ay, como si te importara tu familia, niña malcriada. Vete, ya!*" She's clearly fed up with something that happened prior to my arrival. She shoos her youngest daughter away with a scowl and a reckless wave of her hand.

Monica is clever enough not to back talk, and she swerves around me and my suitcase to slither out the door. I drop our cat then, confident he won't escape again.

Mom barrels toward me in glee. She hugs me extra tightly, cooing and awing at how big I've grown and how handsome I look. It's an overreaction, since it hasn't even been a month since we last saw each other. At first, I don't return the gesture. I'm a little stunned by the affection, having sorely lacked it recently. But she smells like orange blossoms and yeast, and she holds onto me like she's freezing and I'm her only source of warmth.

We stand like that for a while. I rest my cheek atop my mom's head. She tries to pull away from me, but my hold on her tightens. She rubs concentric circles on my back, patting me every now and again. That's what she used to do when I was younger and fighting off sleep, the rhythmic motions soothing, lulling me into a state of rest.

"*Pasa algo? Te duele la rodilla?* You said you were feeling better," she murmurs.

I shake my head and don't say anything, holding her tighter still.

Mom pushes away from me and takes a step back, her eyebrows knit together in concern, her lips turned down in a deep frown. She reaches up on her tiptoes to place a tentative hand on my face, swiping at invisible tears. I don't think she realizes how emotional those maternal caresses make me feel. *"Por qué estás triste?"*

The urge to confess bubbles up inside me, simmering intensely. It would be so easy to blubber all that had transpired and have my good ol' ma comfort me. She was always on my side when I was younger, even when I was in the wrong.

But that was when she had Dad. When there was someone to shoulder the burden of being a parent. Now, it's just her, and Monica is being difficult, and Katia has been spending a lot of money, and I...

Well, I wasn't supposed to be such a disappointment, such a fuck up. I was supposed to be her perfect first child, the easy-to-manage one. And even if she won't say it to my face, the tone she took when she called me after the game made it clear that even if she would stand in my corner no matter what, this was an instance where she didn't want to be there.

"Mi amor, háblame. Quiero—"

"Ma, I'm really tired. I think I'm going to go sleep." I offer a pursed smile and walk away. I hear her sigh heavily, muttering unintelligibly to herself. She would have put up a fight, but she has a shift coming up.

When I get to my room, I plop facedown onto the bed and sleep.

I dream of something terrible and awake to a wet pillowcase stained by my tears and sweat. Though I can't recall exactly what my subconscious conjured to terrify me, the distraught festering inside me tells me all that I need to know.

For the rest of the night, I reread all the texts between Greta and me, hurting as I recall just how close I'd been to happiness with her by my side, only to have opened my palm, parted my fingers, and let it slip from my grasp.

WHEN I WAKE up the next morning, I busy myself. I stretch, patch up my knee, feed Chairwoman Meow, and make breakfast. Monica acts like a brat and only takes two bites, complaining that the eggs are too runny and that I put too much ham and not enough hotdogs in them. Mom grabs a banana and a cup of coffee, leaving forty dollars for groceries and a list of things that need to be fixed around the house before heading to the hospital. I'm left to scarf down nine whole eggs and twelve strips of bacon. I struggle to get through it, my restrictive diet from the semester still diminishing my appetite. I feel like a boulder afterward, but at least I get to skip lunch.

Then I unpack my shit and rearrange my room, though there's not much to do since it's pristine, untouched since I moved out my freshman year. The house is already clean, too, so I just get on with the list. I get through most of the items on my own, but when I need Monica's help, it takes about an arm and a leg to get her to comply.

By the time I'm done with that, it's eleven in the morning, and I feel like I'm going crazy. I'm tempted to do something I haven't done since Pawpaw passed away and open our garage. It used to be Dad's workstation, where he fixed cars and drew tattoo designs, but when he passed away, it became Pawpaw's room.

I can't muster the strength to do it, though, so I mow the lawn and stare at the door, thinking of all the ways Pawpaw would cheer me up if he saw how sad I was. We'd smoke together, and he'd let me sip on his beer, watchful of Mom. It makes me smile a little.

A trip to the grocery store, a lukewarm can of beer for nostalgia's sake, and three stress cigarettes later, I'm back in my room. I shower and change, burying my tobacco-scented clothes under my bed. I stand there for a while, doing nothing but gazing into empty space, my mind retroactively repressing that one thought.

By two in the afternoon, I give up. Putting forth pretenses means nothing when I can't distract myself, so I go to sleep.

When I wake up, it's midnight, and there's a covered plate of *picadillo* on my nightstand, along with a glass of mango juice. As I eat, I stare out the window and reminisce about sneaking out during my high school days.

And then I sneak out the very same way, wedging my big frame through the small opening. Instead of making my way across the lawn to jump into a friend's car and smoke some weed in an abandoned parking lot or secretly hook up with William at the back of the abandoned Arby's, I lie on the freshly mowed ground and stare at the vast, glimmering night sky. It's a clear view, the streetlights dim. I can't make out any constellations, but that doesn't detract from my admiration.

Space is vast and endless, and as I gaze at it, I feel closer to her.

The day had been deceptively warm for winter, but the night air is cold. I'm not layered enough to be out here for long, my teeth and bones rattling with each gust of wind, but I can't go back inside. I won't sever this connection I've created.

As I marvel at the night sky, the persistent pain in my chest eases and the pressure in my lungs dissipates. In my semi-lucid state, I allow myself to imagine another life. I'm another person, unencumbered by the stains of my character. In this world I create, I'm perfect and the life I lead is, too. No one hates me, no one is hurt by me. And my affections, intense and true, are desired rather than rejected.

Words fall from my lips, floating in the air. "I miss you. I love you."

When I go back inside, I'm once again subjected to the harrowing pain of my reality. The day has already gleamed over the horizon. I'll have to wait for the cover of darkness to come once more in order to be at peace again.

MY LIFE IS a daydream I desperately wish to wake up from. By the fourth night home, I've turned into a corpse. I've entirely given up on trying to behave normally. It's too much effort, and I can't. I wake up and wonder what the hell I'm doing all this for, and I'm left devastated when no answer comes to mind.

At first, Mom lets me dwell in that liminal state without interfering. She's too busy, picking up shifts because she got into a fender bender last week and insurance isn't covering all of the damages. So she leaves me alone for the most part but comes into my room to see if I'm alive, chides me for not eating or drinking, and sprays some Febreze because "*Ay, hueles horrible.*"

But by the fifth day, she's refused to let me wallow alone. I've been living a nocturnal life—though calling it that is too generous since I'm barely existing—lying in bed, doing absolutely fuck all or sleeping. Only in the cover of darkness do I take action. I get up, climb out my window, and lie in the grass.

It's Ma's day off. She wakes me up at nine in the morning and forces me to go on a walk with her. She tries to get me to talk, but I'm so afraid of what I'll say or how I'll behave that I keep quiet, my responses bland and short.

But that's okay, because she talks. She tells me about how her life has been. Her favorite surgeon moved hospitals, so now, she's mostly assisting a young, up-and-coming cardiothoracic surgeon. She doesn't like him. She says it's because he's too new and he's unaccustomed to the workflow, but I know there's more to it. I wonder if she's getting mistreated, and a flare of rage burns through me. I suppress it, though, cowering from its appearance.

"I can't wait for you to be a famous football player," she says wistfully, linking her arm through mine as we turn the corner. "I'll drive into work in one of your fancy cars and make everyone jealous. They'll all be nice to me and try to be my friend."

I barely muster a smile, my heart plummeting. My self-loathing intensifies. This is the perfect moment to tell her about Coach and what I said to him and how that has put me in a precarious position where I'm not only unsure about my status on the team but my future career as a football player. She doesn't know about *that* part of the day. She only knows about what happened on TV.

But I don't. Mom looks up at me, her lips stretched out in good humor. I want to give her this, even if it's a joke. I want to give her the world and all that's within its orbit. And if I can't do that, then at least I can let her live in hope for just a little while longer.

"When I'm a famous football player, you won't have to go to work at all. I'll take care of you, Ma."

MONICA SCARES ME. Not because she's a particularly scary person, but because she's weird and unpredictable.

Like right now, she's standing beside my bed, quiet as a mouse, petting Chairwoman Meow in her arms. I'm napping, dreaming of blue melancholy, when I get the sense that someone is watching me. I open my eyes and squeal.

"What the fuck, Monica?" I holler in surprise, rolling over to stuff my face into my pillow. My heart beats at a mile a minute. If anyone in my family were to become a psycho serial killer, it would be her.

My younger sister doesn't reply right away, and when she does, she sounds apprehensive. "Katia is coming home tonight."

I grunt into my pillow.

"And Mom says you have to have dinner with us."

Another grunt.

"If you don't, she's going to get mad."

"Not as mad as she'll be when she finds out you have a boyfriend." The walls between our rooms are paper thin.

Monica inhales sharply, and there's a meow. Her cat topples to my bed and makes a disgruntled sound before climbing over me to settle on the other side of the mattress.

"Have you been eavesdropping? You friggin' pervert!" she shrills, slapping me.

I yelp in surprise as I roll away from her reach, catching myself before falling off the bed. "Monica, hit me one more time. I dare you," I growl, putting on that scowl that used to always scare her straight when she was younger.

It doesn't serve its intended purpose, though. Steadfast defiance is etched on her face, but at least she lowers her smack-happy hand. "If you tell, I'm going to—"

"What?" I sit up to bunch the comforter over my lap. "What are you going to do?"

She worries her bottom lip, eyes narrowed, but says nothing.

I smirk. "That's right. Nothing." Turning away from her, I wave my hand in the air to shoo her out.

She doesn't get the cue, and the springs of my mattress creak as she sinks down. "Actually…" Her breath hitches, and she audibly swallows. "Can I… Can I ask you something?"

Oh please, God, please don't make it about sex. Anything but sex. I am begging you. She's my baby sister. I'll have to murder whichever fucker touched her, and I'm trying to be less violent here, dude.

"Uh…" I tentatively lift my head to look at her. "Sure?"

Monica purses her lips, and I can see her mouth moving like she's trying to find the right words. That only increases my anxiety, and to keep myself from blowing up, I interject.

Don't be a dick and call him a shithead. Don't do it. "Is it about your boyfriend?"

She nods, a light blush staining her cheek. Maybe she remembers the lecture I gave her over Thanksgiving break about how men are the root of all evil and how she's not allowed to date anyone until she's fifteen, a ruling Ma backed me up on without hesitation. The debacle that was Katia's young dating life left us both scarred.

"Is he not treating you well?" I supplement when she hesitates.

The tone of my voice is calm, but I've already come up with several ways to lure this guy into a back alley and beat him to a pulp.

"No!" Monica all but shouts. She places a hand on the taut muscle of my bicep. "No. God, no. He's not—he's so sweet."

"Is he really? Or is he just trying to get in your pants?"

Monica blanches in horror at my remark.

I stand, jostling Chairwoman Meow. "Don't look at me like that. I've told you a hundred times: All men are dogs who are not to be trusted."

"Then that makes you a dog," she snaps. "And you're not to be trusted."

An image of Greta's crushed face flashes in my mind, and my throat burns. *You have no idea, Icka.* "This isn't about me. This is about you and that twerp you're dating."

"You're not being helpful," she grinds out between clenched teeth.

I rub my face and sink back against the creaky metal bed frame, but she's already getting up to leave.

"Aw, c'mon, Icka," I urge. "Tell me what's wrong."

She snorts and shakes her head. "Forget it. It's obvious you're going to be a dick about it, so I'm just going to talk to Katia when she gets here."

Two responses sit at the tip of my tongue. The first is her use of the word *dick* and the verbal lashing I'm desperate to serve her for speaking disrespectfully to me. The second is her obvious attempt at making me feel useless by bringing up Katia.

But alas, I'm above that, and more than anything, I'm genuinely concerned about her. Ever since she started middle school, Monica has been confiding in us less and less, and even if puberty had a similar effect on both Katia and me, too, it's upsetting to see, given how young she is.

Swallowing, I soften my expression and speak to her softly, kindly. "Okay, but do you swear he's treating you well?"

She doesn't say anything.

I resign myself. "Fine. Whatever. But if you want to talk about it again, I'm here, and I promise to listen." I lick my lips and dart my eyes to the wall, wishing Greta could hear me. "Just know that I care about you."

Her nose scrunches in disgust. "*I care about you*," she mocks, deepening her voice. She pretends to belch and storms out of my room, shouting, "You're literally so gross. Don't ever say something like that to me again."

I wonder if she understands how sincere I'm being.

HERIK CALLS AFTER Mom drags me out of bed to prepare Katia's favorite lasagna. It's an awkward, stilted conversation. We haven't spoken since he stopped by the house before I left for break. Normally, we would drive home together since we live four streets away from each other, but he's meeting Elise's family. And he's also mad about what happened on the field.

"You back in Dayton?" I ask when a lingering silence collects between us after we grunt out unusual, formal greetings.

"Not yet. I'm heading back Wednesday."

"Isn't your ma upset you're barely spending any time with her?"

"Perks of being a Jehovah's Witness. Christmas isn't that important."

"Yeah, but your mom is clingy." Overprotective is more like it. Like clockwork, Herik gets a call from the woman at 8 p.m. and if he doesn't answer, she'll raise a special type of hell from hundreds of miles away.

"Yeah, but she knows things between Elise and me are for real. And I'm not abandoning her completely, y'know. I'll at least spend a few days with her before we head back to school." There's a pause. "Actually, about that... Do you mind giving me a ride back? Elise drove us here, and her dad's flying me home, so I have no ride, and plane tickets are fucking bugging."

Is that the only reason you called? To ask for a ride? "Yeah, sure. When did you want to head back? I was going to drive down the Saturday before the semester starts."

Herik clears his throat. Then coughs. Then sniffs before clearing his throat again. "Well, uh, Coach sent us a text saying that we needed to be back by that Thursday."

I stop laying out strips of pasta. My heart falls to the ground. I place a hand on the counter and hang my head, my blood curdling in dread. Swallowing thickly, I maintain a steady voice despite the sob licking up my throat like fire. "Oh, th-that's okay. We can... Yeah, we can leave Wednesday morning. That's fine."

"Are you—"

"I'll text you about it later. Katia is almost here. Gotta go." I hang up and leave the kitchen, beelining to my room. Mom yells, trying to stop me, but I swerve from her grasp. When I close the door, I lean back against it, frantically checking my phone for a notification I know isn't there. Nothing. I log into my university's financial aid portal to see if my athletic scholarship is still there. It is.

I clutch at my chest then crumble to the ground, my body still barricading the door. I'm confused and lost, stuck in limbo.

Mom bangs and roars behind the door, her rage evident in the aggressive way she speaks exclusively in Spanish, detailing how disrespectful and childish I'm being, but I don't budge. I'd rather deal with her wrath than face her and realize I'll never be able to actually care for my family.

I just sit there, pressing my forehead against my knee, the cotton of my sweats absorbing the silent tears that spill out of my eyes. In that moment, I hate Coach for being so cruel. And what's more, I hate myself.

What do I do? What the fuck am I going to do?

MA HITS HER breaking point on New Year's Eve. I'm surprised she made it past Christmas.

I'm in bed, doing nothing, per usual, scrolling through my social media to torture myself. I stalk pages I shouldn't and see my friends—former friends, I guess—hanging out and playing video games together. Some even go to each other's places during the holiday, posting fun gift exchanges or bad sweater contests.

"That's it. *No puedo más!* I'm done!" She slams the door behind her. I jolt in surprise at the ruckus then lift myself up to bear witness to my intruder. Chairwoman Meow, who has decided to take her nap times with me since our sleep schedules are in sync, gets up from her perch near my head to stare Mom down. She ignores the feline, stomps to the edge of my bed, and yanks at my blankets.

Letting out a garbled protest, I try to grab them, but she's in Kraken mode, which means she has the strength of a thousand suns, and a second later, my body is exposed to the chilly winter air.

"Get up."

"I—"

"*No me contestes,*" she hisses, and immediately, my lips seal together. Balling my shirt in her hand, she forces me to my feet.

I stand in front of her, a little frightened she might beat me. I haven't been disciplined by her since I was twelve and she found Pawpaw and me smoking and drinking on the porch when she came home from work early.

Heaving deep breaths, Mom stands a foot away from me. She lets go of my shirt and crosses her arms over her chest. I really want to ask her what she's about to do so I can brace myself, but I know better than to talk first.

"I have tried to be patient," she begins calmly. "I have tried to be understanding. I have tried to give you time to… I have tried. Really, I have. But I can't take it anymore. *Esto.*" She gestures at me and my room. "This is not okay! *Sé que no quieres hablar conmigo, pero no me importa*! Katia has been home for a week, and you've barely even said hi to her. *Llego a casa y te encuentro durmiendo, o si no, estás mirando las estrellas.* You're smoking and hiding your clothes under your bed instead of doing laundry *y a veces te escucho llorar*! And I can't take it. *Me estás lastimando. Yo—No puedo más, Otis. Soy tu mamá y* you will talk to me."

I stare at her, feeling neither resistant nor affable to the notion. At this point, I'm broken, and Ma knows that and can't stand seeing it.

"*Hablame*," she commands, authoritative in her compassion when I don't speak up immediately.

Bile rises up my throat. I close my eyes for a moment, and all the things I'd wished I'd said—all the things I'd thought to say only after it all happened—come rushing out of me. I tell her all that happened from the moment I woke up that horrible day to the pathetic love confession I made just before Greta left because the worst she could say was no. And I tell her that the worst very much happened.

Mom doesn't interrupt, which is really uncharacteristic of her, but maybe she senses that this situation is different. Before today, the most intense discussion we'd ever engaged in had been about my sexual orientation, and even then, it had barely been a conversation. It had been more of an awkward acknowledgment, one I was surprised by given her intense religious beliefs, and an agreement never to tell Pawpaw.

"And all this happened because we couldn't make it to your game?" she finally says when my words die out. I've been talking for so long that she took a seat on the bed while I paced in front of her.

"Not just because of that," I counter mildly. "But I guess I was a little sad you guys weren't there. It was an important game and… I know you were working. I just… I really wish you guys were there."

Mom frowns and wrings her fingers. "*Mi amor*, I didn't realize—"

I cut her off. "Don't feel bad for me. I—it shouldn't have mattered if you were there or not. I shouldn't have done what I did."

That's what I should have said to Greta. 'I shouldn't have done what I did.' *That's it. Maybe then I wouldn't be miserable like this.*

"But still. I should have…" Mom runs her hand through her hair and lets out a loud exhalation. "I should have come. I should have taken off work. But I guess I thought you never needed me, *mijo*. You always did things by yourself, and I didn't think…" She stands and looks at me remorsefully. "If I knew how important it was to you, I would have come. You believe me, right? You know I would be there for you."

"I do." I'm not sure if I do, but a part of me yearns for it to be true.

"Good because I was watching at work. I had them turn on the game on every floor." She cradles my face in both hands. "And I know things are bad with Coach right now, but it'll be better once you get back."

"I don't think it will." In fact, the more I think about what I said—how I'd hurt him—the more I'm certain there's nothing I can do to make it better.

"I do. Look, I've lived a long life." Then she pauses, a little disgruntled. "Not *that* long since I *am* young, but long enough to know that you can get far in life if you apologize and own up to your mistake."

I squeeze the bridge of my nose, pinching my brows together. "I tried."

"Try more."

"But—"

"*Papi*, it's not supposed to be easy. Life isn't easy. You know that." She lets go of my face and heaves a heavy sigh. "You know that more than anyone. I wish you didn't, but you do."

I don't say anything, taking a minute to mull over her advice.

"And I also think"—her face twists in uncertainty—"you should go to therapy."

"Are you calling me crazy?"

Mom rolls her eyes and gives me a look, shaking her head. She doesn't like the joke. "*No me malinterprete.* It's just... With everything you just told me... I didn't realize you had these types of ugly feelings in you. It's not good. It's not healthy. You're usually so kind. So nice."

"Only when it's easy," I whisper. That's what I've learned during my nights staring up at space. Coach had been somewhat correct. When things get hard for me, when I'm uncomfortable or don't feel too good, I'm not a good person. And that makes me not a good person, period.

"*Ay, pobrecito.* I didn't even realize." A tear falls from the corner of Mom's right eye. I don't know if it's from the disappointment of realizing her son isn't the person she thought she raised him to be, or because she actually does feel bad. Nor do I ask, afraid of the answer. "We'll take you to a therapist, okay? To work out these problems. You should have gone when you were younger, but we couldn't afford it."

"And now we can? C'mon, Ma, you just told me you couldn't even come watch my game because we're tight on money."

"I'll make it work." She's resolved, undeterred. "*Soy seria.* You're going to therapy, and that's final."

"Lucky bastard. I want to go to therapy. I'm just as fucked up," Katia's muffled voice complains from the other side of the wall, effectively cutting through our very serious moment.

"Shut up! They'll hear you, idiot," Monica says. A slap resonates, then a yelp, and like that, my two sisters are going at it. Mom leaves to handle the situation. I sit alone in mine to contemplate my own.

MOM FINDS A therapist back in Mississippi. My first appointment is set for the Thursday Herik and I get back. The shrink is expensive and out of network, but every time I try to mention the costs, Mom starts singing "Bidi Bidi Bom Bom." She's afraid I'll bail and goes so far as to call Herik to make sure I attend the first session.

I go back to a somewhat normal life for the duration of winter break. I don't apologize for my behavior to my family, but the feet massages I offer to give them say as much. Just as I'd promised Monica months ago, Katia and I take her out and let her have fun to her heart's content. It's a good time because we're all dancing and laughing at the dumbest things and we're not arguing the way we usually do when we're around each other for too long. Mom yells at me when we get home half past four in the morning—Katia, the rat, scurried out of sight to have me bear the brunt of Ma's rage. But the reprimand proves to be worth it because the next morning, Monica lets me watch a documentary on the industrial revolution without putting up too much of a fight, and she even clears her makeup and skin care off the bathroom sink later that night.

When I get back to Mississippi, I go to my therapy session with Dr. Toner. Herik waits in the lobby until the hour is done, even though that makes him late for practice.

Things are not totally okay yet, but I'm working on it.

2:22

Tuesday, January 10

NO NEW NOTIFICATIONS

GRETA
GALA APPLES

"**GRETA, TELL YOUR** father that I'll be staying at Jacqueline's house tonight and that he needs to make dinner for himself."

I look up from my phone and blink at the woman whose voice could break the sound barrier. "He heard you." At first, I'd been completely on board with how angry Mom was with Dad, but now, it's getting asinine, especially when I had to moderate interactions during our trip to France over winter break. Lord have mercy, I almost committed murder.

"I don't care. Tell him."

I stare between them, wondering how I, of all people, have become the peacemaker in this household.

In the end, no matter how much I protest playing Mom's lackey and getting roped into my parents' fight, I do as she says. She and I are on the same side, even if our motives differ a bit.

Heaving an exhausted sigh, I swivel in my chair and stare down the Sahnoun family leper. "You hear that? Mom is staying at Jacqueline's house tonight, so fend for yourself."

"Oh, I heard her. Even wheat farmers in India heard her." He grunts, glancing up at us.

Mom mumbles French curses under her breath, and even if he

doesn't hear her, his eyes narrow—he knows whatever she has to say to him isn't pleasant. It hasn't been since she learned about what went down in his office after the championship game.

I'd had my heart broken by a guy I'd foolishly caught feelings for, but Mom had hers broken by the man she'd given her past and present to. She'd become aware of what Otis had said, blaming Dad for my brother's death, and though she didn't fault me for feeling how I felt or behaving and reacting how I did, she'd instantly forgiven Otis.

For her, learning about her husband's treatment of his players and discovering he hadn't changed in spite of what happened with Julien had been a betrayal of the highest order.

"He promised," she'd said, sobbing to me over the phone after Dad came home and narrated what happened, thinking he would receive support.

I'd been doing my own crying, still parked in Otis's driveway when she rang.

"He promised he wouldn't say things like that again. After Julien, he promised. He promised."

I didn't know how to comfort her or what words would soothe the gut-wrenching anguish that plagued her, since I, too, felt something akin to that and was in need of comfort.

So, I simply let her cry about how much she misses Julien and how Dad had dishonored him by continuing to be just as cruel to his players as he had been to his son, even after everything. I let her cry about how she wishes she had divorced him already, because a man like that can't have a heart. "There's no way," she kept saying. I let her cry about how she still loves Dad because he's *her* Farid, the same Farid that sang to her belly when she was pregnant.

Farid, who always went above and beyond for her birthday and their anniversaries. He woke up in the middle of the night when Julien was suffering from colic as a baby, insisting that his son needed his father, not his mother, to care for him. Farid, who had carried her out of that hospital bed as she clung to the lifeless body of her son, reminding her that though she lost one child, there was another who needed her, so asking God to take her away to be with her youngest son wasn't fair, not when he and I were both hurting, too. He'd worked hard to coax her out of her despair, despite being wrapped in his own. He'd reminded her that she couldn't just leave him—leave me—even if she really wanted to in that moment.

He was her Farid, not Coach Sahnoun. Unlike me, she couldn't see Dad as a dichotomy. To her, he was one person.

And I got it—I get it. I understand. Not to the same degree, but enough to make more tears fall from my eyes at the relatability of it all, my wounds still fresh that night. By the time I got back to my place—with Elise and James banging violently at my door in panic—I'd wrecked the collar of my shirt, using it to dab my tears and snot, telling myself I'd been crying so hard because of my mom. That had been a lie.

"All done," Mom sings when she finishes tying a sky-blue bow on the basket. "Make sure you put the leftovers in the fridge when you get home."

"*Tinquilète je gère.* This is the third time you've told me that. I'm not a child. I know how to take care of leftovers."

"Please. I've seen unfinished takeout containers left on the kitchen table when I come over to clean. *Fille irresponsable et sale.*" She balks, shaking her head, then extends her long arm to smack me. "Wasting all that food. Think of all the starving kids in Africa."

"Starving children aren't exclusive to Africa, Lina. There are plenty of starving children here in the United States, too," Dad says with a grunt.

Mom's left eye twitches, and she lowers her voice to speak rapidly in French to me. "Tell that man to not address me unless I address him."

"Mom, I'm not—"

"Do it!"

I do as I'm told, behaving as a messenger parrot.

Dad scoffs and rolls his eyes, which causes her to relay more stuff through me about his attitude, and soon, they're actually yelling at each other directly since it's much easier that way.

"I'm leaving," I shout over them. They don't acknowledge me. I grab the basket and make my escape, giddy that my car requires maintenance, which means I get to take my dad's vintage Cadillac.

The drive to the cemetery isn't long, but I take my time, enjoying myself in the car. I wish I could put the windows down like we used to, but it's almost the end of January, so I settle on letting the stereo play some of Julien's favorite songs. The lyrics are depressing, but the music is good enough.

When Dad took the job at Mississippi, he'd had Julien's cremains and grave marker moved from where we first buried him in Kansas, wanting to keep him close. I'll never know why, since neither of my parents visits him much. Mom has only gone once since moving here, and Dad only goes on Julien's birthday to lay down some flowers, too auspicious to stay long. The only person who makes a regular effort to see and hang out with him is me.

Contrary to how horror movies might convey gravesites, Julien's appears more like a garden than a cemetery. The grounds are well maintained, the grass vibrant and green year-round, an array of flowers mazing around the site. A variety of trees is planted about—my favorite is the orange tree beside Julien's spot, shading him from the sun. It's a prime location, and Dad had to beg the old couple who owned it to sell the lot to him.

"What it do, Juju-Bee?" I holler when I get close. I huff and puff as I make my way up the torturous incline. "You're looking as lovely as ever. Stone-gray really suits you."

Being dead and all, Julien is unable to respond. But I can imagine what his frozen-in-time, fifteen-year-old self would retort, something along the lines of, *You look good, too, Gretel. Love the hair. Were you going for Einstein today, or was that an accident?*

I glare at him, wearing a rueful smile. "A happy accident, thank you very much."

Thank God no one is around right now, or they'd look at me and think I'm insane.

When I finally stand in front of him, red-faced and out of breath, I offer a silent prayer and then get right to the good stuff. "All right, so I brought three different types of cigarettes. I know, I know. You're dead, so you've kicked the habit, but I've just picked it back up, and let me tell you, it's wonderful." I go to reach into the pocket of my jacket, only to curse, realizing I've left it on the banister at my parents' place. It's a little chilly, but given the physical exertion I underwent to get up here, I'd hardly noticed.

"Psych. No smokey-smokes for you." I take the blanket under my arm and place it nicely on the ground. Plopping front and center, I grab the edge of it and wrap myself in the soft material. "But on the bright side, Mom did make *makroud el louse*. Don't worry, it's *setti*'s recipe." Peeking my hands out of the blanket like a T-Rex, I reach into the basket and present the dessert to him. "Ta-da. There are six in here. I'll take five, since that's only fair."

Why do you get five? Are you planning on leaving crumbs on the ground on your way back home?

I roll my eyes. If he were beside me, I would nudge him. "Oh, shut up. You should be grateful I'm even sharing." Leaning forward, I place a cookie in front of him. "Besides, I like these more than you do."

Just because I don't wake up in the middle of the night to eat a whole tray doesn't mean I don't like them just as much.

Ignoring the jibe, I fill him in on my life. I haven't spoken to Julien since finals week. I'm animated, feeling light as I speak to him.

I tell him about how I passed all my classes this semester, which means I don't have to move in with Mom and Dad, thank God. If

Mom does follow through with her divorce threat, I do not want to be there. I'd rather just witness the highlights—my mom can be entertaining when she's upset. I recognize I should be a bit more upset about my parents' divorce, but I'm too absorbed in my own issues to care.

I tell him all about our trip to France to visit Mom's family in Lyon, and how our parents had fought most of the trip, acting lovey-dovey only in front of my grandparents. He asks about our *mère* and *père* and the rest of the extended family, and I give him a rundown on how they're doing. Our frequent trips to France and rare visits to Algeria had been the highlights of our childhood, our living grandparents doting and our cousins abundant and fun.

I tell him about all the shopping Mom and I did in Paris—the Goyard luggage mom bought came in handy—on top of the tens of thousands of dollars she blew on paying for renovations at our grandparents' place.

What about Otis? Any updates on him?

I'm not sure if the question comes from the imaginary Julien or the part of me that doesn't want to forget about him in spite of what happened. "Since I texted him to give me space?"

Yeah.

"Nothing." I cling to the blanket. "Which is fine. Great, actually. I asked him not to text me, and he respected my wishes and stopped. And it's not like we were…" But I don't say "together," because saying that would mean I would have to explain what happened in Paris. Where I'd kicked What's His Face out of my hotel room before things could go anywhere because it felt disgusting to have someone who wasn't Otis kissing me. And frankly, I don't want to admit that, much less explain it.

You can't ask for one thing but actually want something different. That's not fair, Julien scolds. He always was perceptive and wise for his age. He might have been younger than me, but he behaved more responsibly and maturely than I did. Everyone who met us would make comments about how he was really the eldest. Sometimes, I wonder if it's because of how much he had to bear at the hands of our dad. I used to get annoyed by those comments, but now, I yearn to hear it just one more time.

"Elise has been telling me about him. Unsolicited, might I add." I worry my bottom lip. Anytime she mentions him, repeating what Herik said or pretending to talk to James about it, I feign disinterest or force myself to react with tepid annoyance. Yet, my pulse kicks up a notch, a mixture of relief and excitement twisting through me from any speck of information about him. "They're pretty sure he was kicked off the team. Dad wasn't too happy with him after what he said, and y'know how much of a dick he can be when he's unhappy."

"You shouldn't talk badly about people behind their backs. And I didn't kick him off the team. He's just on probation."

Immediately, my head whips around to locate the voice, and there is Dad, effortlessly trekking the incline to where I sit.

My heart drops. *Fuck, he heard that. Am I going to get in trouble? Is he going to take the Caddy away from me? Fuck.*

"What are you doing here?" I ask a little rudely, a little surprised but mostly ashamed. I'm sure my dad knows I don't have the highest opinion of him, but it's not as if he needs confirmation.

"You forgot your jacket."

"You drove all this way for a jacket?"

"It's cold out, *ya tafla*. Besides, I've driven a lot further for a lot less." He huffs. He's referring to the time when he made the three-hour trip to my cheer camp the same week I got my driver's license. I was supposed to text him when I arrived, and when I didn't, my phone forgotten in the console of my car as I caught up with my friends, he panicked and made his way to me. He'd looked absolutely wrecked, and I'd chided him for being overdramatic, embarrassed by my parent showing up. It wasn't until I hugged him goodbye and he held me tighter than usual that I realized just how worried he was. I've never forgotten to text him since.

I let the blanket fall from my shoulder as I reach for the coat and slide my arms into it.

"You were trying to get away from Mom, weren't you?" I ask accusingly when he doesn't leave right away. Why'd he have to come after me? It's not as if I've been any nicer to him than she has. I just can't curse him the way she does.

Dad doesn't admit it right away, but I continue to stare until he breaks, sulky in his admission. "You caught me. She keeps pretending to put a curse on me every time we're in the same room."

"I don't think she's pretending."

"I don't think she is, either."

There's a lingering silence, and right as I'm about to ask him to leave, to give me privacy with my brother, Dad holds out a pack of Vogue cigarettes. I close my eyes, muscles tensed as I brace myself.

"Before we veer off-topic, would you like to explain these?"

"They're James's," I lie automatically. It's worth a shot.

"He has asthma. Try again."

Doesn't stop him from smoking weed. Rather than unwittingly incriminate myself, I bite my tongue and hold back all my excuses, glancing at Dad from the corner of my eye.

The disappointment etched on his face is worse than anger. He berates me in a gentle tone. "C'mon Greta, you know better than this. You were doing so well. What happened? What's going on? Why would you lapse?"

Otis. Except it seems a little pathetic to admit a measly guy drove me to do something so self-destructive. Of course, the situation is a little more complicated than that, my feelings layered and perspicuous, but I'm not about to wax on about my almost-love-life and elephant-ness to my dad. I shrug. "I don't know."

"I won't accept that. Tell me. Tell me why you started smoking again."

I feel both cornered and aggravated by his intrusion on what should be a pleasant day with my brother. "Why don't you tell me why you did it?"

"Why I did what?"

"Why did you break your promise to Mom?"

It takes a second, but he registers what I mean. His eyebrows relax as he frowns.

"The promise," he muses to himself. He takes a seat and leans back, pressing his bare hands against the ground then squinting intently at the sky, as if he's searching for the words there. "It wasn't a promise I made to Mom. It was to Julien."

Sullenly, he drops his head and gazes at the tombstone before us. THE MOST BELOVED BROTHER AND SON. The inscription is generic and cliché, but that doesn't make it any less true.

"That makes it better." I snort. "The dead love it when you break promises."

"At least I haven't been haunted." It's easier to joke than to face the somber truth.

"*Yet.* Julien's favorite holiday was Halloween. You never know what could happen this year. He could be biding time."

"He did get into the spirit of it a little much, didn't he? I always had to pick him up from abandoned houses."

I scoff. "And you thought I was difficult."

Dad grunts in disdain, curling his lip. "I would take picking up my son at a haunted warehouse over a pregnancy scare any day."

"Still, you didn't answer my question. Why?"

"Why, why, why?" He closes his eyes and hangs his head. When he finally speaks, his voice reaches just above a whisper, and I strain to make out his confession. There's transcendent sadness etched on his face, a sadness only true love can deliver. "I wanted to prove I wasn't wrong." He pauses and purses his lips, clearly struggling to articulate himself properly. "I wanted to prove that it wasn't me, that I wasn't the reason he… That it wasn't my fault. It's easier, staying the same. It's easier to be the way I always was than to admit—than to *face* the truth of who I am."

I can't stand staring at him any longer, so I turn to face Julien. No matter how hard I try to imagine what my younger brother might say in this moment, nothing comes to mind. Even I struggle to figure out what to say, only conjuring accusations. "So you treated all your players the same way you treated him to… What? See if someone would accidentally kill themselves, too? Then you would have stopped? That's fucked up, don't you think?"

Dad adamantly shakes his head before I've finished speaking. He swallows over and over again, and still, his words come out raspy, gruff with emotion. A tear escapes the corner of his eye. "It's not that simple. I—" He clears his throat. When he speaks again, he sounds small and not at all like the terrifying man who threatened to end the life of a doctor if he didn't resuscitate my brother again. "I treated my own son that way, and then what? I have to treat everyone else better when he's the one who actually deserved it?" He shakes his head again. "No. I couldn't do that. No."

"Two wrongs don't make a right." Our roles have reversed. Now, I'm the one teaching him a lesson.

"I know that. I know. But how am I supposed to live with myself, hm? How do I exist, knowing that I'm the source of so much pain?" He turns to look at me. His eyes are red. I haven't seen him this devastated since… Well, since Julien.

It hurts, seeing someone so strong be reduced to *this*, to realize he'd been faking his strength. That deep down, he sees himself as nothing, causing him to behave as if he deserves nothing. It makes it difficult to pity him.

Difficult, but not impossible.

His logic doesn't make sense to me. I can't traverse the path he's created from point A to point B. If I knew the imminent consequences of my actions—if I knew the repercussions would hurt not just myself but another person—I wouldn't do it. I would abstain, or at least try to.

"You could have been kinder," I mumble. It's not just about Julien or his players. It's about me, too.

"I could have. Should have. And when I was younger, I would tell myself over and over again that I wouldn't be like my dad, that I would be different. Over and over again, I said this, and then I grew up, and without thinking—maybe it happened *because* I wasn't thinking—I became just like him."

It's hard to imagine *jedi* as cruel. But then again, it's hard to imagine my father as a son, in Julien's shoes. "I'm not going to be like you," I whisper vehemently, the declaration acting as a plea to the fates to make it true.

Dad looks at me with the same fierce determination I wear. "I hope you aren't." There's a stretch of silence before he speaks again. "Greta," he begins softly, turning to look at me.

I stubbornly face forward.

"I can't change the past. I regret it, but I can't... I can't make what I've done go away, and I can't change myself overnight. But I want you to know that I will try to be better. I should have changed with Julien, and I didn't, but now, I can. I will try."

I close my eyes to keep from visibly rolling them.

"I want to be the father that you can praise behind his back when he's not around, not the dickhead you describe anytime I'm away."

Whether or not he says this last part to guilt me or to accuse me for revealing my feelings to Otis, the very feelings that were thrown back in his face, I don't know. All I know is that he's said it, put it out there in the world, acknowledging his wrongs in a way I've never witnessed before. And for the rest of my life, if I see him act to the contrary, I will remember this moment and hate him a little more for it. "Okay."

"I promise you, *mon chat*." He seems unsatisfied by my response.

I make a face. "I'd rather you didn't promise. I don't need to be disappointed anymore."

Dad flinches at my bluntness but remains undeterred. "I promise."

I nod mutely. I don't trust myself to talk. The moment feels fragile. It's not every day my dad is vulnerable with me. In fact, the last time he spoke so emotionally was during family grief counseling, and even then, Mom had to beat the feelings out of him, inspiring the therapist to suggest couple's therapy.

We're alike that way, Dad and me.

"So, how—how do I do this?" he asks, waving his hand at the tombstone.

"Do what?"

"What you do here. With Julien."

My posture relaxes, and I drop my legs to sit crisscross. "What do you mean? You just talk to him." I don't mention that Julien responds back to me.

"Like, a conversation?"

I nod in the affirmative, and Dad appears more puzzled.

"Do you not pay your respects?"

"I mean, yeah, you do that first. And then you just"—I gesture between myself and the grave—"converse about anything."

"Anything?"

Another nod.

He regards this notion thoughtfully. "Anything." After a moment, he begins. First, he speaks of missing him, envying Julien's perch up in the heavens. Dad wishes he could gaze upon his son, too. He'll settle for the photos and happy memories, though.

Next, he talks about soccer, which he affectionately refers to as the "other football," and gripes about how much money he lost on bad bets during this year's Premier League. He informs Julien that his favorite team, Arsenal, is doing well this year, much to Dad's chagrin. On and on he goes, hopping from one topic to the next, having so much to say after never having done this before.

I'm amused. I've never heard Dad be so chatty. He doesn't take any pauses and rattles on and on like a man starved of conversation.

It's a little cute, even endearing, to witness him in such an excited state. I've seen him be sensitive before, especially during movie nights. Between the three of us, it's Dad who's the bawler— Mom and I are usually unaffected.

But this is different. This isn't just sensitive Farid Sahnoun. Or father Farid Sahnoun. This is playful and lighthearted, with Dad beaming from ear to ear like he's having the time of his life. Hell, he didn't even smile this much when Mom took him to the World Cup for his birthday.

The one-sided conversation dies down, and he lets out a satisfied sigh. Lifting the lid of the basket with his index finger, he reaches in to grab a bite and pauses. "You didn't eat anything," he observes disapprovingly.

"I'm not hungry."

"You sure?" There's a shuffle, the sound of nylon rubbing together, and just like that, he wrestles a plastic baggie from his big puffy jacket. In it are gala apples.

Sliced gala apples.

And I don't know why my eyes water at the sight, why my nostrils flare, why my throat burns no matter how many times I swallow to quench the flames. I don't know why, but that doesn't stop me from holding out my hand to receive his offering.

He sighs in relief, almost like he was afraid I would reject his affectionate gesture.

While I eat, I look at my dad in all his imperfect glory. And as he watches me munch on slice after slice, the smile on his face grows, as if he's the one being fed.

For all the mistakes he's made, all the pain he's caused our family in the past, and all of his inevitable future fuck-ups, I love him. Even if life with him hasn't been perfect, even if he makes me miserable sometimes, rattling deep in my soul and settling heavy in my bones is the actualization that, at the end of the day, no matter what happens between us, there's always a connection: Love. Moments and gestures like these make the bad disappear. It's clear that no matter what, he'll always be my dad. I'll always be loved by this flawed man.

I haven't forgiven him, and nothing is made better or fixed by this moment, but I, too, want him to feel somewhat at ease and to know how I feel, so I offer him a piece of my apple.

"Only half?" Dad teases, but he pops it into his mouth without hesitation.

"You have to earn the whole."

He nods solemnly and makes a face like he's in deep thought. "Fine. But you have to quit smoking, or there will be consequences." He uses that tone—the one that reminds me he is *the* Coach Sahnoun—and I agree. We shake on it, but we don't let go of each other's hands immediately. Instead, I lean against him and rest my head on his shoulder while he rests his atop mine. I can't ever recall being so close to my dad, but it's nice. I guess I never realized I wanted a moment like this with him until now.

And if I could have something like this with Dad, then maybe… My heart pinches in my chest. For a short, lingering second, I allow myself to daydream about how a reconciliation with Otis might pan out.

"Now, to get your mom to forgive me." Dad lets out a heavy sigh, tugging me from my thoughts. "Any ideas?"

Mom and I are two peas in a pod in a lot of ways, but nothing bonds us more than our materialism. "Besides actions, there's one thing I can think of." I raise my head to stare at him. "Ever heard of Harry Winston?"

He turns to precariously look at me. "Rings a bell, but tell me more. Who is this Mr. Winston, and what does he have to offer my wife?"

I drone on about Mom's favorite jeweler, and the entire time, I feel like someone's watching me. I know it's Julien, and he's smiling at us. I don't see this smile, but I feel it when the clouds above part and the sun shines a little brighter, the branches on the tree overhead swaying and dancing, seeming a little happier.

For the first time in years, the congestion in my heart clears, the locks and chains barricading it fall away, allowing more space for all those emotions I'd desperately fought after Julien died. I feel...

Content.

🔒 January 11, 2020 at 4:24 AM

Julien's Eulogy

I miss you. Not every day or all the time. Only sometimes. It's usually on a random Tuesday, when I'm driving and a song we used to listen to comes on. I'll go through life as if you never existed, but in that moment, you take over me. You're all I can feel. You weigh me down with your absence, crushing me in your nothingness. I'll have a smoke and pretend like you're beside me, sharing a drag like we used to, and it'll be better, until only the butt is left and I'm crying, wishing you were here.

How can you no longer exist and still consume me so entirely? Why can't you just leave me alone? Are you punishing me? Trying to show me just how hurt you were when you were alive?

They tell you in grief counseling there's something to be learned from tragedies. And after a lot of introspection, I think I found my life lesson.

I've learned that I don't want to feel. I knew I always loved you because you were my baby brother, our little Juju-Bee, but I didn't realize just how much. I didn't even know I had the capacity to care for someone the way I care for you. Did it magnify after you left me? Is it because you were a part of my life for so long and now you're not?

I don't know what it is, but what I do know is that I never want to feel like this again. I never want to love anyone else again only to feel their loss later. I never want to find happiness in another person's smile or feel at home in their laugh if there's a chance I'll experience this again.

I don't believe in the afterlife simply because I'm existing in pure hell every time I'm reminded you're not here anymore. But if there is one, I know you're in heaven, and I hope there are angels telling you how amazing you are every second of every day. I wish I had told you that every second of every day.

I'm sorry I'm writing this a year late. I'm sorry I left your funeral early. I'm sorry I didn't do more to keep you here. I'm sorry I didn't help take away your pain.

I love you so much, Julien, and even if it hurts, I can't wait to miss you again.

With every last bit of love I have,
Gretel

OTIS
I.F.M.Y

"**YOU LOOK SO** handsome in a suit," Mrs. Sahnoun gushes. Head tilted, she makes a V with her hand and clasps her cheek, smiling in adoration. She turns to face her husband and lightly thumps him with the back of her other hand. "Doesn't he look handsome, Farid? Tell him he looks handsome."

Coach stops glowering at me long enough to give his wife a what-the-fuck side-eye. She responds with a scathing glare, and immediately, he's subdued. Begrudgingly, he mumbles, "Meh. He's looked better. But the suit does compliment that black eye well."

The apple doesn't fall far from the tree.

Mrs. Sahnoun reproaches him with a hiss and kicks him.

I'm unfazed and stare at his feet, mumbling, "Thanks, Coach."

A lull of silence falls over us, and I rub my wet palms over my thighs. Sweat collects at the collar of my dress shirt, and my formal wear feels too tight.

Why had Quinn suggested I wear a fucking suit? I want to choke him, or better yet, steal all his do-rags so his waves will look fucked up. God, I'm hot and clammy and am feeling really fucking stupid, what with how dressed down the Sahnouns are.

"Would you like some cold lemonade instead of tea?" Mrs. Sahnoun asks. Maternal concern crinkles her eyes, and without pausing, she gets up to fetch me a glass, patting my thigh sympathetically when she stands.

After two seconds alone with Coach, I'm ready to follow her. Neither of us speaks. I look around the room, staring at the array of family photos set on the fireplace mantel. The ones with Greta and Julien make my stomach drop in remorse. My courage, bolstered by my boys just before I got here, wanes.

Thankfully, Mrs. Sahnoun comes back with my glass before I have a chance to back down. She doesn't take a seat until she's satisfied with how much I drink. I suck on an ice cube, praying that its coolness will somehow give me the strength to do the right thing.

"Otis," Mrs. Sahnoun begins, hesitant.

My attention, previously focused on the pattern of the rug, snaps up to her. Her wariness puts me on edge, and I'm starting to doubt her kindness. Did she mean to put my guard down before she launched an attack?

"I came here today to apologize to you and Coach," I rush to clarify.

Her small smile assuages my fears. "That's nice, but before you do that, I would like to apologize on my husband's behalf for how he—"

"Lina!" Coach barks.

Mrs. Sahnoun holds a hand in front of his face, commanding obedience. "—for how he treated you and the other players over the years. He has difficulty in leading with love, given his own experiences, but from here on out, he will do better to correct this behavior." *Or else.* She doesn't say it, but it hangs at the end of the statement. Leaning forward, she captures my hands in hers, beseeching me with her eyes. I'm jarred by how much they look like Greta's. "I'm so sorry for all the pain he caused you. He should have known better."

"That's enough. I can speak for myself," Coach spits between gritted teeth.

She lets go of me and settles back against her chair, remaining quiet, her defiant gaze lasered on him expectantly.

Coach clears his throat a few times. He starts to say something, a broken syllable escaping before he goes quiet again. He shifts in his seat and clears his throat once more.

His display of nervousness, compounded with what Mrs. Sahnoun just said, gives me the confidence to speak, to swallow the crippling fear and shame that's infected me since Jenner dropped me off in front of Coach's place. "Before you say anything, Coach, I had something I wanted to say." It doesn't feel right to be seated, so I stand, hands behind my back. Only the coffee table is between us, yet I feel detached from him and this moment.

He presses his lips into a stubborn line, his eyes downcast.

It's not an encouraging reaction, but I power through. I knew it would be hard. Mom told me as much. My therapist told me, too. It's supposed to be hard, and I need to do it anyway.

You're not doing this for him. You're doing this for you, I remind myself, repeating Dr. Toner's words. My hands curl into tight fists behind my back, and when I speak again, I make myself clear. I enunciate slowly and deliberately, taking the time to process every letter of every word that spills from me, determined not to let my emotions get the better of me.

Even if it isn't anger, Dr. Toner told me, it's better to communicate with a level head.

"First, I wanted to thank you for not kicking me off the team and for the training you've given me these last three years. I came out of high school thinking I was the best I could be, and you showed me that improvement is constant, and perfection isn't a fixed state. It's a metric that can always be redefined and reimagined, and that alone always helped the team push to do and be better."

Coach raises his head, but his gaze remains averted.

"Second, I wanted to let you know that I have decided to stay another year under you and Duger's leadership. I know you might've heard that through the grapevine, but I wanted to inform you of my decision personally. You were right before, and I don't think I can enter the professional league without working out my problems. And if you're willing to keep me on your team next year, I'll show you I can be better and that I've changed, just like you have showed our team you're doing."

Mrs. Sahnoun's shoulders visibly relax. Coach focuses on my tie. It's old, and the pattern is wacky, but it's a favorite of mine—it belonged to my dad, and Pawpaw before him.

"Finally, I wanted to..." I hesitate for the first time since I began my monologue. I've more or less been following the script I drafted with my mom, but I deviate, wanting so badly for my sincerity to shine through. I knew what I said was wrong even before Coach lifted me from the seat across from his desk and tossed me out of his office, and I truly regretted it when I spoke to Greta. But only recently have I come to terms with just how much Coach hadn't deserved it.

I straighten my spine and jut my chin to force myself to stare him in the eyes. Shame commands me to hang my head low, but I fight it. "You're a wonderful dad, Coach."

He rolls his eyes, and panic settles in as I frantically try and salvage the genuine sincerity I feel. It's not that I want to be exonerated from what I did. It's that I want him to know how serious I am.

"Really, you are. A really good dad. And I know this because Greta has told me you are, and she always defends you. I didn't treat you with the respect you deserve as a dad, but also as a person. When I s-said..." I struggle to find the right words. Rather than fumble through, I take a deep breath and give myself a moment to collect my thoughts before continuing, "*What* I said came from a place of hatred and disgust. I had no right to speak about your son in that way. I never should have even thought it. I was tainted by a need to hurt you so badly that I—"

My breath hitches, and humiliation thaws the coolness in my veins. Now, I can't help but hunch forward, the weight of my behavior heavy. Remorse collects in my throat and makes my eyes sting. I'm at a loss for words again, so with one last exhalation, I rasp, "I really mean it when I say I'm sorry. I'm so sorry, Coach. And to you, too, Mrs. Sahnoun. I know you both loved your son very much, and I'm sorry I ever doubted that."

Mrs. Sahnoun's eyes gleam. Coach remains stoic, but I feel his eyes on me. I wince prematurely, preparing myself for a well-deserved verbal lashing about all that I've done wrong. It wouldn't be anything new.

Except it doesn't come. When he speaks, his tone is casual, not severe, and his disposition is loose, not poised to attack. I raise my head in astonishment, feeling like I've been transported to another dimension.

"If you're starting next year, we're going to need to work on your reflexes. Duger and the other offensive coaches were telling me you're evasive maneuvers are off by two-quarters of a second from your average last year, and if you really want to impress the general managers at next year's Combine, you're going to have to decrease your response time."

And there it is. I take a seat, and the conversation keeps going, Coach babbling about my future on the team, behaving as though nothing happened. It's as if I stopped by for a routine performance review over tea. There's no touchy monologue from him, no endearing exchanges of forgiveness and gratitude. We just do what we do best: Talk football.

And though he says nothing to me directly, even after telling his wife he would, he offers to fill my glass of lemonade, and that speaks volumes.

A little later, I text Jenner to come pick me up, giving a thumbs-up emoji in our O-line chat to indicate that all is well.

The front door opens, and a familiar, beautiful voice begins to speak a mile a minute. The hairs on the back of my arms stand immediately, and my heart flutters out of rhythm, my body more alive than ever.

"Hey-yo, where's the mayo? I'm home. Not for long, though. I'm here to borrow some things and be fed before I gotta skedaddle. Dad, I need your leaf blower. Don't ask. It's for a stupid art project Elise has in mind. She goes to Wine'n'Paint once and thinks she's freaking Monet. I already checked the garage and didn't see it there, so can you grab it for me? I feel like it's in the shed, and I don't wanna go in there. There are spider webs everywhere.

"Mom, I'm going into your room to grab that Van Cleef set Dad got you for your birthday last year and that cute Burberry bag we bought in France this Christmas. I've got a Valentine's Day party to go to tomorrow, and I'm tryin' to look shnazzy. And before you say anything, just know that I'm a responsible adult and I'm not gonna lose anything, so spare me the lecture."

Finally, there's a pause and the sound of bare feet padding against tile. We all freeze in the living room at her unexpected arrival. "Where are you guys? We've gotta hurry. I'm starving, and I told James I would meet him for pedicures in, like, thirty minutes, and if I'm late again, he's going to make me pay. I know you guys don't want me to charge the credit card. Mom? Dad? This is not the time to play hide-and-seek. Wait—did you two kiss and make up? Or did Mom finally commit murder? I hope she wore gloves. C'mon, where are you guys?" She lets out an adorable, annoyed *harrumph.*

I panic and look at Greta's parents for guidance. Coach and his wife turn to look at each other, whispering quickly in their native language as if trying to figure out what to do. Their planning is cut short when the woman of the hour suddenly appears at the entryway of the living room.

"Are you guys in the fancy living room? Wow, I see how it is. You guys throw a freaking fit if I even sniff around it, but if you go in, it's okay. What are you guys doing in"—her voice tapers into a whisper when her eyes fall on me—"here?"

"Greta, what a surprise! Look who stopped by!" Her mom oversells the excitement.

I'm as still as a statue, my muscles turned to stone in terror and glee. My pulse thrums in my ears, rattling my skeleton with every beat. I'm suspended in utter disbelief, and had I the capacity to say anything at the moment, it would probably be "fuck me."

"I'm looking." Greta folds her arms over her chest, appearing more cautious than shocked.

"Otis came to apologize to Papa and me."

Not how I wanted her to find out, but beggars can't be choosers. My responses are delayed, but I scramble up from my seat and turn to face her. A wave of elation crashes over me at the sight of her—*holy fuck, she's so close!*—and I nearly stagger back from the force of it.

Despite her disheveled appearance, she looks beautiful, almost ethereal. Her hair is tied up in a sloppy ponytail, and dried mascara is smudged beneath her eyes. Even the mustard stain on her shirt adds flair to the rumpled ensemble.

"I didn't know you were coming," I admit, because saying nothing for this long is actually the worst. Mrs. Sahnoun and Coach observe the two of us like zoologists in the wild, noting every micro-reaction.

"Obviously."

The way I ogle her, absorbing every second I can while in her presence, is shameful.

She regards me nonchalantly in return. If not for the way her chest rises and falls in quick, succinct movements, I might think she truly doesn't care for me. But it does—she does, and fuck, that gives me hope I shouldn't be feeling.

"If I'd known you'd be here, I would have planned my visit differently."

"That's courteous of you."

My desire to hear her speak more—albeit in choppy, pointed one-liners—propels me to continue this stilted exchange. "I was just talking to your parents."

"They're brilliant conversationalists."

"And I didn't know you were coming."

"You already said that."

I'm perspiring so much, I'm the personification of Niagara Falls.

"Give the poor guy a break," Mrs. Sahnoun finally snaps, unable to watch us any longer. I flinch at the severity of her tone and nearly whimper in relief when she gets up to stand in front of me, her arms crossed. "He likes you, and you're being mean."

Love. I love her.

"I didn't say anything!" Greta says defensively, staring at her mother as if utterly betrayed.

"Watch your tone," Coach Sahnoun warns his daughter.

She gapes at both of them.

"What the—how are you guys—I mean… This is ridiculous! You guys realize I'm your child, right? Me! Not him! You're supposed to be on my side."

An argument ensues in a language I don't understand.

Coach apologizes to me for the display his wife and daughter are putting on. "Women, right?"

I don't think this is the time to tell him that's sexist. Not when I just got on his good side.

As the bickering continues, I catch Greta's gaze darting toward me, her countenance impassioned, her face flushed. It reminds me of the arguments she and I had. Not the serious kind, but the ones where we were knee deep in our opinions about what the proper shape for a door handle should be.

I've missed her so much—so fucking much—that I've somehow fallen deeper in love with her.

The sound of a car horn blaring interrupts my adoring thoughts. It's Jenner. I swallow a groan and force myself to leave. I awkwardly interject in the family squabble, "That's my ride."

The Sahnouns turn to look at me, but I'm fixated on Greta and the way her mouth tugs down, almost in a frown, before resuming its neutral position. Her knitted eyebrows soften, her forehead free from any worry creases. For the few heartbeats that it takes me to turn around—to turn away from her—she locks eyes with me.

I tell myself she does that because she misses me the way I miss her.

PARTIES AREN'T MY thing, like, at all. And this sentiment is further reinforced the longer I stand here and watch another man touch the woman I desperately wish was mine. Before we got here, I'd been determined to enjoy myself like any collegiate athlete would. I'd put on a happy face, smile, and laugh with people I don't know instead of behaving like a reclusive ass who only knows how to scowl and snap.

I've been trying to distract myself by chatting with other people, making flirty conversation with two guys and a girl. They're nice. Cute. Friendly. But it always ends with me wearing a scowl when I catch sight of Greta with that guy.

And now, here I stand, alone, my temple pressed against the wall after the third person caught on to where all my attention was going. Closing my eyes, I welcome the darkness veiling my line of vision. That way, I won't have to witness the very definition of Hell.

Greta with her hair framing her face in luscious, bouncy curls, her lips thick and kissable with that red lipstick she has on. Her jewelry is delicate, and that necklace—fuck, that necklace makes me salivate. It draws attention to the dainty wing of her collarbone, and all I can think of is all the ways I've kissed, licked, and bit it while we fucked.

Greta in a gorgeous, near-transparent, sequined corset paired with a tight black-leather miniskirt that clings to her like a second skin and falls just below her ass. She compliments it with sheer, lacey, black pantyhose and a garter. Had she tried to appear any sexier, I genuinely think I would spontaneously combust.

Greta walking into the same room I stand in, near yet far, her gaze flitting over to me, her breath catching then accelerating as she doubles back and lets her stare linger.

She's devastatingly gorgeous tonight, the shape of her voluptuous body perfectly outlined. Her tits look so fucking good. On God, I got a semi watching her walk in, her hips swaying naturally to the music, her eyes glimmering with excitement as she peered around.

Some person hands her a drink—it's not a person I know—and two Solo cups later, she's dancing, swaying her body to the beat of the music. I'm trying my best not to stare so blatantly, trying to give the girl beside me at least some of my attention, but of course, that gets shot straight to hell the moment a guy approaches her.

At first, Greta doesn't seem interested. The guy leans forward and says a few words in her ear. She says something back but keeps her distance. My relief, however, is short-lived when not a minute later, their bodies are pressed together. Her hands twine around his neck, his leg slotted between hers as he crouches to sway and grind against her properly.

My heart drops repeatedly, constantly, and my legs shake. I brace a hand on the wall to keep from doubling over. A knot collects in my stomach, tightening impossibly, and my palms tingle.

A deep, inconsolable ache clambers inside me. The hollowness from her lack of presence in my life is suddenly filled by an unscrupulous demon. The sight of her in another man's arms enrages me, and I stiffen, fixated on every way their bodies touch.

Then that demon swells and threatens to consume me, igniting

454

every cell in my body until I'm burning like an inferno whose flames can't be extinguished. Yet my blood is ice, cooled to the point where it burns. Hatred, resentment, and irrational anger curdle inside me. It's painful to carry and conceal, and I want it to stop. I don't want to feel like this, like my body is about to give out any second.

Fuck. I need a drink or a smoke, and since the first one is more accessible, I go with that. I open my eyes and glance at her, unable to control myself. Our eyes meet. She holds my gaze for a lingering moment before whispering something into the guy's ear. He leans down and presses a kiss on her cheek before walking away. And I could just die right then.

Flames lick up my chest to my throat. I swallow once, twice, and tell myself all the things Dr. Toner told me to chant when I'm feeling emotionally overwhelmed, hoping that will calm me down. When it doesn't work, I stalk toward Jenner and snatch up his drink, hating the way it tastes but loving the immediate buzz it gives me.

Before I have a chance to consider my next course of action, the Jell-O shot I just threw back decides for me, the liquor absolving me from taking full responsibility. I stalk toward the guy Greta has been paying attention to tonight. I won't approach him, I tell myself. I'll just see who it is.

But then I realize it's Nelson Himmer, the enforcer on our hockey team. I've never liked him and always found him excessively aggressive on the ice, and the fact that Mitchum also doesn't like him—

"Sup, man." I do my best to appear friendly and blasé.

Mitchum's teammate barely acknowledges me as he continues to rummage around the table for a clean cup. "Yo."

"You're Nelson, right?"

This catches the guy's attention. He stands up straight and regards me skeptically. "Yeah. And you are?"

I extend a hand. "Otis Morgan."

Nelson stares at my outstretched arm. He's slow to reciprocate, and his grip is a little too firm. "Right. The quarterback that beat up his teammate."

That day will live in infamy. "The one and only." I plaster on the fakest smile of my life.

"You come to punch me, too?"

I clench my jaws together, willing composure. "Nah, bro. I'm not like that." *Anymore.*

He raises an apprehensive eyebrow and motions at the faded bruising around my eye. The room is dark, but the retro disco lights that flit about illuminate me at just the right moment. "You sure?" he goads.

"Positive. And you should be glad about it, too."

"Yeah?" He squares his shoulders and shuffles closer to me. We're the same height and nearly similar in size. He puts on a dark smirk. "And why's that?"

My nostrils flare, and I press my tongue against the inside of my cheek, a sneer tugging at my lips. Clapping a gentle hand on his shoulder, I knead the muscle in a louder-than-normal timbre, I reply, "Cause I'd've fucked you up even worse for touching my girl."

The arrival of the Cupids right at that moment interrupts the disaster that almost happened next. The hockey team's entrance is boisterous, loud, and distracting.

The alcohol in my system still urges me to act on my impulse to destroy this man. I want to rip him limb from limb and watch in carnal elation as I incinerate every inch of flesh that's touched her.

Fuck. I need to get out of here before I do anything *really* stupid. I'm such a lightweight. Reaching over to grab a can of beer probably isn't the best idea, but I don't like the way I'm feeling right now, and getting just a little more inebriated will numb all that.

Will I regret what I'm doing tomorrow morning? Definitely. But it'll be worth it if I can just stop aching for a little while. Why was I so determined to go to this party, knowing she would be here? Who let me do this? I'll kill Herik for not being a better sound of reason.

It was okay to pine in isolation, where I could fill my imagination with flowery and romantic thoughts of reconciliation. But reality is torture, her reaction toward me unbearable. The destruction of my happiness is guaranteed.

I just want a reprieve from the fire that burns for—and because of—her. I chug the beer, finishing it before I reach the door. The effect it has on me is instantaneous. I wriggle my way through the crowd of people to the front lawn and plop myself onto a lonely lounge chair in the center, a little disoriented.

I'm not *drunk* drunk yet, but I'm buzzed enough to distract myself. I look at the grass and ponder the way it sways in the light winter wind, contemplate how fast the cars driving down the street are going, and create elaborate fake dialogues as I observe other people's conversations from a distance.

Halfway through a hilarious break-up scene I'm ad-libbing, she shows up.

"Are you trying to ruin my night?" Greta shouts from a distance.

My droopy head comes up immediately, my half-lidded eyes snapping open in awareness. My heart seizes in giddiness at the sight of her standing before me, towering over my seated form.

She's scowling, clearly unhappy, but for some reason, I can't process that. All I can think is that she's here, smelling like vanilla and daisies, and God, she looks so beautiful. So beautiful, my Miriam. The most beautifulest girl in all the world.

"Greta," I croon, feeling a soft, tired smile curve my mouth. The tips of my fingers tingle in a need to touch her.

"Are you... Are you drunk? What the fuck, Otis? You don't—"

Without warning, I wrap my arms around her and bring her to me, my face resting against her stomach.

She yelps and braces herself, gripping my shoulders to stay

upright.

Just like that, by her presence and proximity alone, the heartache from earlier is soothed. The demon inside me goes back into hiding.

"You're drunk," she deadpans, pushing against me.

I keep my arms around her for a moment longer before letting them drop to my sides, sputtering out a resigned sigh.

"You don't drink."

It's a simple fact that a lot of people know about me, but for some reason, her knowing makes me excited. "I do when I'm sad."

Her stony expression softens, its edges sanded. Still, there's a glint of defiance remaining in her eyes. "Is that why you were chatting up all those people? Because you were sad?"

"I was just trying to be approachable and nice. I have a bad enough rep on campus."

"And being nicer entails threatening to beat up people I dance with?"

Well, she got me there. I remain silent, which only agitates her further.

"So, let me get this straight. You're nicer now, which means you'll throw yourself at hundreds of people and flirt with them until the sun sets, but if I dance with one person, you drop the act and start acting like a territorial punk?"

Greta's remark is aimed to be scathing, critical, designed to elicit a morsel of shame, but it does the opposite. I bristle with pride, a single phrase echoing in my mind. "I didn't chat up a hundred people."

She gapes at me. "Please. That guy you were talking to when I walked in? He was practically humping your leg."

"Was he?" I feign forgetfulness, pleased that she noticed, and this riles her even further.

"And that last girl you were giving googly eyes to—was she falling every other second? Is that why she kept grabbing you?"

"She was just trying to get my attention." *Away from you.*

Greta gives me a flat look. "And groping you is how to do that? Gotcha."

I'm torn between teasing her some more and gloating at the primal possessiveness bleeding into her frosty tone and wrinkling her nose. "You jealous?" A sly smirk tugs at my lips. My leg bounces, and I ball my fists to conceal the currents of elation rattling through me.

"Jealous? Of who? Them? Please, I don't get jealous," she replies, her laugh cutting. She rolls her eyes, but her jaws clench and unclench several times, her eyes slanted in derision. Her confident disregard hints at something. It conveys more than just menial annoyance. It conveys feelings.

"Good. You'll never have a reason to be. For me, there's only you. In every iteration of my existence—in every thread of life I could experience—I hope that when I find my way to you, I'm good enough." In my somewhat intoxicated state, I can't help but pat myself on the back for being so romantic.

Greta's expression oscillates between horror, amazement, pain, and something I'm too afraid to name.

I shouldn't have said that. I came on too strong. This is the first actual conversation I'm having with her since the fight. I should simply have reassured her in a less obvious way. But I can't stop myself from baring my soul to her even more, the honesty addictive, her reactions precious. "You're so fucking beautiful right now."

"St-Stop." She shakes her head and squares her shoulders, determination pleating the skin of her forehead. I've overwhelmed her. Stepped over my bounds. And I know all that from the painful way she chokes out that one word.

"I'm sorry." I sulk and hang my head low, my chin dropping to my chest.

She emits a high-pitched groan. "Stop always saying you're sorry. Not when you're only saying it to get your way."

The pointed retort hurts. My head snaps up. I get up from my seat and loom over her.

She doesn't step away, standing her ground, her arms crossed over her chest, squeezing her breasts together.

With one glimpse of her creamy, smooth tits, I forget everything that transpired in the last minute. I wanna suck them. I wanna shove my face between them. I wanna rest my head on them and take a good long nap.

"Eyes up here, Princess." She places two fingers under my chin to wrench my focus back to her face, which is just as lovely.

After giving myself a moment to collect my thoughts, I'm back on track. I rub my mouth and release a shaky breath, my lips flapping together. Running my hand through my hair, I tilt my head and level a look at her. "Do you mean that, Greta? Honestly? Do you think I'm apologizing to get my way?"

An intense charge whirls between us. Her determination falters as she searches for the truth behind my eyes. We stand like that for a while, saying nothing, just looking, and it feels much more sensual than any position we've tested from the *kama sutra*.

With my eyes, I try to communicate to her all that I feel. Like, *really* feel. And I know she understands, that she gets it. The cruel furrow between her brows dissolves, and she opens and closes her mouth as if there's something she has to say. But just like her father, she struggles to let it out.

Then the spell is broken as a gust of blistering icy wind, reminiscent of the fading season, sways past us. She shivers, the reaction violent.

I act on instinct, shedding off my jacket and handing it to her. "Here." When she doesn't reach for it, I press it against her, the back of my hand brushing her satin skin. "Take it."

"No."

"Don't be stubborn."

"No. I'm not taking your jacket. I'm not yours." In petty dismissal, she snorts. "Why don't you give it to that other girl instead?"

This is not the time to get turned on. Jealousy is not hot, Otis. Get it together. "She wouldn't be able to pull it off the way you can."

Greta bites back a smile, obviously struggling to keep herself in check. Clearing her throat, she tilts her chin up, remarking tenaciously, "I'm not your girl."

"Okay," I lie to prevent hypothermia. Call me a saint.

She's unsatisfied with my half-hearted attempt at appeasing her. "Say it."

"Say what?" My arms are starting to grow sore.

Another tremor wracks through her, mincing up her words as her teeth chatter. "Say I'm not your girl. Say it, and I'll put it on."

I'm annoyed. Greta is rattling like a fucking maraca but trying to extract unwarranted demands from me. No wonder I'm in love with her.

Placing the jacket over one shoulder, I ignore her meager protests and push her arms through the sleeves. "Fine. You're not mine," I admit softly, defeated.

Her body visibly relaxes into my efforts, and she looks like she's about to say something, but I interrupt her.

If my dad was able to devote himself entirely to my mother with no expectations in return—and with the disapproval of their culturally divided parents to boot—I can, too. "But that doesn't mean I'm not yours. Because I am. I'm all yours. Heart, body, mind, and fucking soul—they belong to you. They now exist solely for you."

Once she's draped in my jacket, the material overwhelming her frame, I hold her to me for a second longer than I should, my front flush against her back. I swear she leans back into me, her body slotting itself against mine just like it used to, before pushing off.

She looks at me for a moment and bites down on her gum, pursing her lips. I wait for some sort of derisive comment to be hurled at me, and when none comes, my muscles slacken with relief.

Now, we're stuck in limbo, both of us wishing the other would break. No matter how much I'm willing to yield to Greta, this is one time I won't succumb. There's something to prove.

When she speaks, the ember of hope in my soul glows brighter, incandescent in its intensity, ready to be rekindled. "I didn't see your car," she says to the ground, elaborating when I don't reply immediately. "In the driveway at my parents' house, I didn't see your car."

I scratch my neck, struggling to engage in this casual conversation. "Uh, yeah. It's in the shop. Jenner dropped me off."

"Oh."

Just like that, I'm yearning again. Words I've spoken aloud so many times, but never to her, escape me, refusing to be held captive in the agony of my desires. "I miss you."

"Tell me something I don't know." The shuddered inhale she takes has me inching closer.

"You miss me."

"Otis." Not a denial. An admission of sorts.

I nearly whimper in joy at the sound of my name. I reach for her but clench my hand when I'm a fraction away from cradling her face in my palm. My voice thickens with barely contained intimacy. "Say it again." When she doesn't do it right away, I urge her again, shuffling infinitesimally closer. "Say my name again."

"Rutherford."

Though she utters my name in playful spite, I envelop hers in overwhelming adoration, emotions spilling from each syllable. "Miriam."

"Don't." She inhales and sucks on her bottom lip, her lashes fluttering. She squints intently at the scene behind me, depriving me of the warm relief that comes with her gaze.

"Don't what?" I murmur, bending my head.

"Please. Please don't."

There's so much in that short plea—angst, longing, conflict. She doesn't say what she wants from me, and I don't ask how to make it better, but that's because deep down, we know.

She leaves then, and I'm coated in equal parts misery and hope. I watch as she strides back into the house. When she disappears from sight, I plop back onto the ratty lawn chair.

Closing my eyes, I pray. *Hey, God. It's me again, ya boy, Otis. You might remember me from church a week ago. I know I said I would rather get fucked raw in the ass than sit in those pews again, but I'm willing to take it back if you would help me out. I've been trying to change and shit, and I feel like I'm making progress, but I need my girl to see this. So if you could be a homie and just, like, help me out, that would be much appreciated. I promise to try to not use your name in vain, and I'll even be good and shit. But, like, seriously. Help me. You know I don't beg much, but I'm willing to go down on my knees for this girl. Amen.*

The next morning, I get a text between sets in the middle of my workout. I don't look at it right away, my head groggy from all the drinking. I'd felt like shit when I'd woken up, and any athlete would say the perfect remedy for that is working out.

But as soon as I do get a break, chugging down bottles of water when I'm meant to be spotting Jenner, I read it.

678-999-8212
Today 9:33 AM

Hello Otis...

This is Céline Sahnoun...

Greta's mother...

I was just informed that Hillcroft Elementary is looking for volunteers for the month of February...

I'm sure you know Greta works there...

I thought I would reach out to you to see if you wanted to volunteer...

Leaning my head back, I expel an obnoxious holler of excitement. The sound reverberates throughout the room. I'm drunk on love, but that's no excuse for disrupting everyone else's workout. My teammates snap at me to shut up, and though I abide, I'm still grinning like a maniac. I look crazy, but I don't care.

My Therapy Log

JANUARY 13

First day of therapy went meh. My doctor is hot. He's got nice, juicy arms that are better than mine. But he won't tell me his workout routine, which is shady.

Herik convinced me to come to practice with him afterwards. Duger said I'm not off the team. Coach didn't look at me the entire time I was there.

Whatever. I don't care.

JANUARY 18

Second appointment. Herik is still taking me.

We talked about my childhood a bit. I made a joke about having daddy issues, but Dr. Toner didn't find it funny.

My guy needs to get laid. Too bad I'm committed to a nonexistent relationship, or I'd definitely offer to help.

JANUARY 20

Apologized to Rodney today. Toner and I set up a game plan for my approach. It was nice to have someone be all ears about my feelings.

When I finally got him to listen to my apology, he was pretty cool about it. I think the time apart during the break helped.

We didn't say much, but he did punch me in the face to make it even. It was Jenner's idea. My black eye has restored the natural order in the house.

We all played Smash afterwards. Herik and I won. We really are the best couple. I made everyone power bowls.

Best day since.

JANUARY 21

My prayers were answered. I saw Greta at 195.

She started to smile before giving me this dead look. It hurt, seeing the sparkle in her eyes fade, but at least I saw her.

If it's possible, she looks more beautiful when she hates me.

JANUARY 23

I'm a little sad today. I can't explain it. I'm just...

I miss Pawpaw.

And Dad.

I really fucking miss Dad.

JANUARY 25

Talking about Autumn was shitty. I felt misunderstood. I had a career-altering injury and what? I was just expected to be all fine and hunky-dory? I was doing the best with a really fucking shitty situation. I was a little mean, so sue me.

Toner didn't seem to get that. He pretended like he was on my side, but everything he said and did made it obvious he thinks I'm dead wrong.

He might be jacked and hot, but he's kind of a dick.

JANUARY 26

I get it now. I am the bad guy. In Autumn's story, I'm the villain. The guy she loved and cared for, who ended up being a total fucking asshole, and the entire time, she was patient and kind and understanding. I kept wondering why she stayed when I should have been wondering why I kept being an ass.

I might not have loved her, but I thought I did, yet I treated her... When everyone else avoided me, she was there. Always there. Always helping me. How had I not seen that?

How many more people have I hurt without realizing it? I'm so fucking disgusted with myself I could just...

JANUARY 26

I don't feel safe in my own head, so I'm just going to write about whatever.

Today was pretty uneventful. I played hooky from class, but I still went to practice. Coach is trying out this new coaching method, and it's fucking weird. Actually, he's just trying to be nice to us now. But it's making all of us uncomfortable. He'll start off with an insult and at the end make it a compliment or use the word "please."

"Get your head out of your fucking ass, Rodriguez... Please."

"Don't make me shove my foot through your skull and use you as a mop for my—Davidson, I would like it if you followed the play I set out."

It's so creepy. I think we would prefer being degraded or insulted. Or maybe that's just me and my kink talking.

JANUARY 27

Told Ma about Autumn and how things really went down. She cried. She said she didn't, but she turned off her camera during our video call and said she needed to do something real quick. I feel like shit. I think she called Autumn afterwards.

I cried too. She didn't raise me to be this type of person. She and Pawpaw worked so hard to make me a good man after Dad died, and I just know she might be blaming herself for how I've turned out. I'm not nice when it matters, when it's hard, and I hate that fact. But it's not her fault. She tried her best with what she had.

Fuck, it sucks being a disappointment. But I have to keep trying.

Even if I don't want to.

JANUARY 28

Today was the last day to put my name in the draft. I had a call with two recruiters about it before letting them know my decision. The other three dropped me after my outburst during that last game. The recruiters were disappointed, but they said they were looking forward to talking to me next year and that we'd be in touch.

I don't know what to say to Coach yet. Toner said I shouldn't think about that, though. We need to tackle Autumn first. One thing at a time, he keeps saying, but my head is muddled, and I can't help but think of everything all at once. I'm stressed.

Fuck. I need a smoke. Too bad Herik found my stash and is making me quit completely. He promised to tear my head apart if I ever smoked again. He's fucking pissed, given how our dads passed.

FEBRUARY 1

Autumn is dodging all my calls and texts. It's karma. I told Toner about what I did to her when she wanted closure and how she's behaving the exact same way now. He laughs a little and then apologizes when I don't crack a smile.

He won't let me give up. "It's not for her. It's for you."

FEBRUARY 2

Staked out 195 Extractions today and saw Greta. I know stalking is frowned upon (read: illegal), but I just had to see her. I don't know why. I just had to.

She was with friends, laughing. I wish I could pluck the sound from the air and stow it away for when I'm sad and need a pick-me-up.

She looked so fucking good. I miss kissing her and holding her and smelling her—especially her hair. I wonder if she changed shampoos. I remember her talking about that, how her scalp was getting dry and how she wanted to change shampoos. Then I suggested Head & Shoulders, and she threw a razor at me.

Somehow she saw me from my peep-spot. When she grabbed her vanilla latte, she actually spoke to me.

"Nice black eye."

Not the three words I really want to hear, but they're three words spoken in her voice. I'll pen this in as a W.

FEBRUARY 3

Finally talked to Autumn today. I had to wait outside the psych building all day to do it. But I did. I successfully apologized to her.

She accepted it, but told me she doesn't forgive me. Said she won't be able to forget what happened between us, and even when I made it clear that it had been me, that what happened was circumstance, she didn't budge.

It didn't go the way I wanted. There wasn't a heartfelt moment like I thought. And even if her response isn't what I wanted and I'm still angry, I'm proud of myself. Or, at least, Dr. Toner is proud, and hopefully, I'll feel that way about me soon.

Bottom line: I did it. I owned up to a mistake I made because I'm only human (again, Dr. Toner's words, not mine), but it's a mistake nonetheless. And I'm not going to let it hold me back. I'm not going to think about it all the time anymore.

I'm going to move forward. I have to.

FEBRUARY 7

Ma came up this weekend with Monica. Katia also surprised me, but she arrived Saturday instead of Friday.

They acted like the visit was impromptu, but I know it wasn't. I think Toner said something to Ma. Still, it was nice.

We did a lot of family stuff. Dinner, game boards, a (very competitive) game of badminton. It was fun. The most fun I've had in days.

When everyone went to bed Saturday night, Katia and I stayed up and talked. It was like old times. I actually missed her. Most of the night, she was trying not to talk about Autumn, but we eventually ended up on that topic. I told her what happened—the truth—and she slapped me.

And then she explained everything in the same way Toner had, but it just sounded different coming from her. Maybe my love for Katia made it sound different. I dunno. We went to bed after a closing discussion about her terrible love life.

On Sunday, Mom dragged me to church. I'd hoped she'd cancel since I needed to go to the team's chiropractor but apparently back pains aren't a good enough excuse.

In confession, I spoke my story for what seemed like the millionth time to the priest, but it was really the third.

And you know that saying, 'Third time's the charm'?

Shit's real.

FEBRUARY 8

We talked about Greta's dad today.

We discussed what caused my outburst. He says I wanted Coach's approval because that's all I ever wanted from my dad. Pawpaw supplemented, but when he died, I was left with nothing. I deny his claim entirely.

Admittedly, I was being stubborn, and Toner, for all his patience, cuts our discussion short and simply asks me if I'm ready to apologize to Coach. I say nothing.

Not because I don't want to, but because I'm scared. I've been trying to change, to curb my anger, to be nicer to everyone, not just people I like, but what if I get set off again?

Is it bad to follow my impulses? How do I control them and filter the good from the bad?

I don't want to become that person again. I don't want to hurt someone else. I think of how Greta looked at me that day and I just...

FEBRUARY 8

Sighting number three of Greta. She was with Elise, who was nice enough to wave and smile.

After seeing her, I debated running over to Coach's house and apologizing. Except she can't be the reason. She might be right now, but she can't be when it happens.

That doesn't make sense, but you know what I mean.

FEBRUARY 11

I took the night to think about it, and I might be ready to apologize to Coach. I'm a little scared, but I'm ready.

Maybe.

I think.

I'm scared.

FEBRUARY 13

Now I'm ready.

FEBRUARY 15

I'll never drink again. Especially on a school day. Woke up with a headache and threw up all over the bathroom. The house has put an alcohol ban on me because I'm acting like a "baby."

I'll power through the rest of the day. Tomorrow is Wednesday, and that's the first day of volunteering. I'm so excited to see Greta again. And to help the kids, of course.

GRETA

A FLOWER A DAY KEEPS HEARTACHE AWAY

THE BEST PART of my days are the flowers left at my desk.

Ever since their first appearance, I've come to look forward to mornings at Hillcroft Elementary. I've even created a routine. With gentle care, I pick up the flower. I touch the petals and relish in the delicate softness of it. Then I take a picture with it and send the photo to my mom and my group chat with James and Elise. Finally, I steal a petal and store it in my planner with the rest of them and await for them to identify the plant.

Today, it's a yellow flower with a black center.

the sluts + a virgin
Today 7:33 AM

[1 Image Attached]

anotha one

Today 8:12 AM

lisey

pretty i want one!!!!!!!!!!!!!!!!!!

why doesn't andres give me flowers everyday :(

james

sent the pic to my mom even tho we're fighting

im such a good friend

you're all lucky to have me

stfu james

& lisey sweetie

ur bf is broke

how tf can he afford flowers every day?????

come out of ur ivory tower & meet the plebs your highness

lisey

shut up >:(

yours is even more broke n he gets em for you

maybe if i had sex with andres he would buy me a bouquet...

james

fuck him and he'll forreal buy you who a whole damn island

lol more like continent

look the only reason mine is doing this is to try to buy my affections

little does he know i prefer things to shine in the sun not grow

james

i'd call you a shallow bitch if i wasn't still on the hunt for a sugar mama

speaking of which

elise if things don't work out with andres i'm here

i cook i clean and im really good at eating that kitty

lisey

i know tata told me

but i'm going to have to pass

thanks for thinking of me tho :)

Today 10:29 AM

james

theyre called yellow pansy

damn whats he tryna say

that u a lil pansy ass bitch???

he right

lisey

just googled the meaning &
im sobbing

"thinking of you"

he's so romantic

can you two kith and
makeup already i wanna
double date

Thinking of you. *Thinking of you.* I'm giddy, my hands trembling as I shove my phone back into my dress pocket and focus on Clementine, the devil child disguised as a blond-haired, blue-eyed angel. I do my best to give her my full attention, but my mind is still on the flower and its meaning.

What is he doing to me? What am I doing to him? I'm not so oblivious to my own feelings that I can't understand what I want, and there's no doubt I want him. So what am I doing? If I want him, and if he wants me, why am I stalling? Why am I wasting so much time?

Mom asks directly when she calls during recess. Ever the meddling matriarch, she rings every day to get a pulse on Otis and me and denies it when I call her out for being nosey, claiming she's simply checking up on her child. She claims it's a coincidence that her compulsion to check up on me happens to fall on Otis's first day of volunteering.

Today, she is calling me from my apartment, which means that on top of the Otis interrogation I'll receive, she'll also be grilling me about how messy the apartment is and how fat Raven has become.

"What are you waiting for?" she snaps after telling me for the millionth time that I need to eat more oranges because it's winter and I need vitamin C. "Talk to him. *Tu es complétement fêlè*, taking all this time."

"What are *you* waiting for?" I retaliate. "Talk to Dad."

"That's different." She sniffs indignantly. "Your father broke a

472

promise. Otis simply broke your heart."

I stop inspecting my nails to gape at no one, baffled by her idiocy. "And you think that's not a big deal?"

"Ever heard of glue? Very wonderful for mending a broken heart."

"Ever heard of forgiveness? Very good for getting over a broken promise."

Mom inhales deeply. I'm getting on her nerves and have been since I told her to peel my oranges for me while she's at my apartment because I hate the way they make my fingers smell.

"Greta, *tu me fais chier*. Continue to annoy me, and I'll take away the car," she threatens serenely. I purse my lips to keep from talking back. I hear cheers ahead of me, and I tell myself to not look or care but immediately fail.

Goose bumps crawl up my arms when I see the way Otis laughs and swings one of the kids around, pretending to wrestle the ball from his grasp. What is it about my libido and seeing men with kids? It's not like I even like children that much, but when I see Otis play or sit with them during lunch, I want to fucking jump his bones right then and there.

"Greta? Greta? Are you listening to me?"

I blink and look down, breaking the Otis spell I'd been put under. "What?" I grumble with attitude.

"Don't talk to me like that." She takes another deep breath. "I'm asking what you're waiting for. I'm getting tired."

"A feeling," I confess despite myself. But it's the truth. I can't identify or recognize it, and I'm not sure it exists, but I'm waiting for a feeling that will make everything better. It'll wash away all my anxiety. I imagine it'll change me, rearrange my spirit's tectonics.

Confessing this to Mom, however, after all this time was the wrong move, and of course, she makes that clear. "You're waiting for a feeling? *A feeling?*" She releases a loud, dry laugh.

I wince and move the phone away from my ear to keep from

going deaf.

"I'm going to slap the feelings into you if don't stop being stupid. *Feeling*? I want to shove you back into my womb."

I gape, offended by her response to my honesty.

"Don't annoy me anymore. Go fix things with him. You make me so angry. '*Feeling*'?" She pretends to belch.

"But—" I'm unable to get a word in edgewise since she's still screaming, clearly fed up.

"I don't want to hear it! You're being cruel. It's been three months since all this happened, and he's waiting for you. He gives you flowers. Flowers! I haven't received a flower since—"

"Last week," I interject before she can come up with some bogus lie to guilt me, not that she needs to. I pick at a loose thread on the hem of my dress.

"Whatever. They were roses. Your father has no original thought."

"Still flowers."

She mumbles unintelligibly before letting out one of those maternal sighs that usually precede a heartfelt life lesson. When she speaks up again, she does so in English, speaking deliberately. "My cabbage, please listen to me. Please. I know you were hurt. I know, my darling. When I think about how I walked in on you crying in your hotel room that first night in France, I wanted to rip that boy's head off. But I need you to know that love hurts, and that's normal. That's okay. That's what makes it beautiful.

"Look at Papa and me. You think this is the first time he's hurt me? No. But I love him because he always tries for me. I've hurt him, too, and I try for him."

Then why haven't you forgiven him yet? Granted, I haven't completely forgiven Dad either, but at least I talk to him like he's a human being instead of an insect. "This is different," I whisper, swallowing the burning frustration that threatens to crack my voice. "Otis and I weren't together yet. We didn't make a commitment.

And then he goes and... The things he said about Julien to dad? And remember how angry he got on the field? And his terrible apology to me? And his ex? What is all that about? I mean—"

Mom clicks her tongue in that way she does when she's overwhelmed and needs a second to think. "Hold on, Greta. Hold on. I'm... confused. These things you're listing—are you trying to say you don't want him because he makes mistakes? That you only want someone who's perfect?"

"I mean—that's not—no," I stammer. My grip on the phone tightens. I want to hang up. I'm starting to grow more unsettled, and this is not the time or place for me to be dealing with my tumultuous emotions.

"Good, because no one is perfect. No one. Not me, not Papa, not you, not even"—her voice hitches and cracks at the next name—"Julien. But that's what makes a person worth it, their imperfections and their dedication to work on themselves and be better even when they mess up. And that is something Otis has shown. He's a good person, worth caring for. He's just hurt. Like Juju but different." The comparison hits me squarely in the chest, and even though I'd realized it, I hadn't well and truly digested this fact until she bludgeoned me with it. "And maybe he might not be everything you've ever wanted"—except he kind of is, barring his flaws—"but he's working on himself, trying to be someone worthy of you."

I suck on my bottom lip. It's funny how I accept my own faults but put such a heavy emphasis on his. I don't know if that makes me a hypocrite, a coward, or a human. I'm also not sure how to come back from it and tell him he's redeemable, when I've more or less treated him as if he's not. "Dad is trying, too." My attempt at deflection fails.

"And? If you want me to forgive your father for whatever efforts he's put in, then you're more than obligated to forgive Otis, no?" When I simmer in my duplicitous guilt, she persists. "Am I wrong?"

"Fine," I mumble. I twirl the frayed string I've been fiddling with around my index finger and snap it off, the single thread cutting into my skin in a welcome rush of pain that takes my focus off the ache in my heart.

"Fine, '*I'm right and you will talk to him*' or fine, '*shut up, Mama*'?"

I scoff. "I know better than to tell you to shut up. This isn't my first rodeo, lady."

"That's right. I raised you well." She chortles. "Now, make sure you wash your kitchen towels when you get home. Oh, and call maintenance or James to set up this new electronic lock. Papa said he won't have time to stop by the apartment and do it."

Confusion furrows my brows. "What? What lock?"

"There was a package in front of your door, and I opened it. It had an electronic lock in it."

"That's actually an invasion of privacy. You do know it's illegal to open other people's packages?"

She clicks her tongue. "I'm your mother. I'll make you illegal."

I roll my eyes. "Mom, I didn't order a lock. Check the delivery address. They might have sent it to the wrong apartment." Unless… Maybe I was online shopping in my sleep again.

"420C. That's your apartment, no? I think it was a gift, darling. There's a note inside. Maybe James?"

Right away, my heart stops beating, and my breathing falters. I swallow several times to keep my voice from wavering. I don't even fight my urge to stare at Otis. "What does the note say?"

Mom asks me to wait. Static sounds over the line. All the while, I'm suspended, my insides floating, my face hot.

When she finally speaks up again, she does so at a slow pace, enunciating herself clearly. "'Let me know if you need help installing this. The code is set to 6847. Don't worry, I won't rob you.'" She tsks, and I gulp, clutching my knee to keep still. "Why is he joking about robbing you? That James… He needs to be more serious. He's too silly."

Emotions collect in my throat, and I swallow and close my eyes to contain them. Shit. When did I become so fucking sensitive? "James didn't send it to me," I respond in a faded whisper.

"Whatever. I don't care. I'm leaving now. I have an appointment to fix up my hair. I plan to look stunning tonight for our dinner with the Rosters. I'll wear Papa's favorite Cartier perfume."

I gag, her implication effortlessly killing my emotional state.

She doesn't get the hint and continues, "I'll put on his favorite dress and wear those Harry Winston diamonds he bought me last week."

"I don't want to hear this," I shrill.

One of the kids playing near me turns to look at me in distraught panic. I give a lopsided smile and wave.

Mom doesn't mind my objection, too busy rehearsing her villainess cackle. "Then, when we get home, I'm going to open some wine, play a little Françoise Hardy, and let him think we're making up before I kick him back into the garage."

I pause at the plot twist. I'm torn between relief, horror, and humor. "I've just had a very eye-opening revelation."

"Do tell."

"I've come to realize being a vindictive bitch might be a hereditary trait."

Mom snorts and jangles her keys. "Please, you haven't even seen vindictive. If I were, I would have divorced Farid already."

"But you're not going to."

A sad hush beats between us before she lets out a grunt of defeat. She might despise him right now, but her entire being still loves him. "No, I'm not. I can't."

I don't question her, knowing full well that I'll never understand the depth of their feelings. We chat some more about the art exhibit we're supposed to go to on Sunday until the bell chimes, signifying the end of recess.

"Talk to him today. Don't delay. I love you, my cherub."

When there are ten minutes left until the school day ends, I ask Mr. Marbury if I can run to the bathroom. He's a little reluctant, hating to do the end-of-class wrap-up alone, but relents when I do a little pee-pee dance like a second grader.

Except, Otis has already left for the day, Mrs. Hill informs me. I'll have to catch him tomorrow, which apparently is his last day of volunteering—a fact I did not know. From my understanding, the volunteer program is set for five weeks, and it's only been four.

I'm upset and puzzled and angry. By the time I go to bed with Raven and my new lock, I have half a mind to storm over to his house, bang on his door, and punch him in the face for giving up like that.

After a long one-sided conversation with Raven, and a cryptic analogy exchange with Lisey, I decide to approach him at recess on Friday. I'll be calm, cool, and collected as I confront him for not being more patient with me. Hopefully, he'll find my antics adorable and oh-so-Greta-like, that he'll forget I'm being entirely unreasonable.

On Friday, however, the worst thing ever happens. There I am, looking gorgeous as fuck with my makeup done, my hair styled and my outfit on point, standing in front of my desk, and there is neither a note nor a flower to greet me.

I check the drawers, the floor, and even the kid's cubbies. Nothing. There's no fucking flower waiting for me, and I would cry in frustration, the ambiguity driving me insane, but I don't want my mascara to run.

I'm barely keeping it together before recess. My mind is garbled as I try to dissect what it means. Those flowers represent his feelings, and now they're gone. Does that mean he doesn't feel for me anymore? What about the baby's breath he gave me that first day? It means everlasting love. Does he have a newfangled dictionary where the word "everlasting" doesn't actually mean *ever-lasting*? And what about that *I'm yours* confession? I know he doesn't know how I feel, but some part of me still thinks he should. He stares at me enough that he should have caught me gazing back, watching him, wanting to give in.

Recess can't come fast enough. I need a break from my kids who keep teasing me for looking so good—we're not going to talk about the creepy way in which Hillary hits on me. I'm proud of her for knowing herself so young, but the child put her hand under my skirt one too many times.

Outside, I stalk across the playground to him. He's crouched forward, his head turned toward Carter as he listens and nods to whatever the child says. I can't make out my student's face because Otis's handsome side profile obstructs him, but I see Carter's balled fists at his sides. I can't help but be concerned, the determination in my steps faltering.

Right then, they leave, making their way back into the school. Wanting to be as inconspicuous as possible, I wait for a little before following, losing track of them for a bit.

It doesn't take me long to locate the pair, as the low murmur of their voices echoes clearly in the empty, silent hall. Getting as close as I can while remaining hidden from view, I peer out from behind the corner and eavesdrop. Nothing good ever comes from eavesdropping, I know, but that doesn't stop me. Besides, Carter is my student, and I should be aware of any problems he's having.

The duo is seated on a bench in between the lockers, and I almost exclaim about how cute they are, and not just because of the size difference—Otis is a giant compared to the tiny little boy—but because they match, adorably so. Otis has on a black T-shirt and blue jeans, and Carter wears a blue T-shirt and black jeans. If I didn't know them, I could genuinely mistake them for family.

They're in the middle of a conversation when I catch up to them. Carter is looking down, his long, silky hair curtaining his face.

Otis locks his fingers together on his lap and twiddles his thumbs, waiting silently for a moment before shifting uncomfortably in his seat. "Feeling better now?"

Carter nods, mute.

"Really?"

"Y-yeah."

Otis doesn't appear to believe him and offers words of comfort. "Just remind yourself that they're jealous."

"S-s-s-sure," Carter bites out. I know that "sure." It's always accompanied by an eye roll.

"I'm serious." Otis sits up straighter. "They are. They notice that you're different from them, but they see that you're just as cool and have just as many friends. Of course they're jealous."

It takes Carter a handful of seconds to push out the personal pronoun before he can move on with his sentence. My heart beams with pride at the way he persists instead of giving up. It's been a bad speaking week for him, so he's been more mute than usual. And the fact that he's upset isn't helping either, I'm sure. "I-I'm n-no-not cool. It's okay. You don't-don't-don't have to lie."

Otis blows out an exasperated breath and closes his eyes. When he speaks, he keeps his tone soft, despite the sternness crinkling in his eyes. "If you tell yourself you're not, then you won't be. But I'm tellin' ya, C-Man, you are. Did you see how many snacks Clementine brought you for lunch? She's mean to everyone, even me. She called me an ugly, raisin-looking fart. But with you, she's so nice."

Carter lifts his chin a bit.

"And what about Faris? He's a fourth-grader, and you two are best friends. None of the other second-graders are friends with someone in fourth grade, are they?"

"We live d-d-down the road-road-road from each other."

"Yeah, and you're friends. You're cool, Carter. Really freaking cool. And if you believe that from now on, no one will ever get you down or make you feel less than what you're worth. You'll be able to talk and make friends with people and never think maybe they're doing it because they feel bad for you or because they want something from you." Otis bends forward, placing his forearms on his thighs to peer at Carter's still hidden face. A delicate smile pulls up Otis's lips, and I bite back a loud sigh at the appearance of his dimple. "But you have to believe you're good enough. You can't let others define that for you." When the kid remains unresponsive, the quarterback's voice grows more desperate. "If you start now, it'll never end. And you'll become someone you might not be proud of. So if you think you're cool—no matter what others say—then you're cool."

Carter finally raises his head to look at Otis, a brave expression on his face. My heart bleeds for the kid, familiar with his struggles to feel like he fits in.

The moment washes me with memories of Julien and all the tears he shed when he was picked on. But rather than feel sad, I'm triumphant with glee, reflecting on all the ice cream Dad bought us when I would get sent to the principal's office for beating up kids in retaliation. I might not be violent anymore, but I was a hellion when I was younger.

They chat a little more, and I listen intently, wanting to soak in every word Otis utters. It's about sports—football, specifically, because that's Carter's dream—and Otis feeds it, giving him advice, offering words of encouragement, lamenting over his experience. But then he checks his phone, and something there catches his attention.

Carter points at it. "What's that?"

"What?" Otis looks down at his device.

"That pic-pic-picture." Carter takes the liberty to tap the screen back to life then lets out a small giggle. "Is that Ms. Sa-Sahnoun"— it's a solid ten seconds before he can move on from my tongue-twister of a name—"on your phone?"

"Yeah." Otis clears his throat.

My heart flutters, and I try to think of what photo he might have on there. Is it candid? Or posed? It can't be a nude, or Carter would be horrified.

When Otis doesn't say anything and bows his head in shyness, the urge to giggle tickles me. If I were to get closer, would I see a blush on his cheeks?

"Are you two dating? C-C-Clem says you-you always stare at her during lu-lu-lunch."

"Do I?" Carter nods. Otis smiles and rubs the back of his neck, unintentionally flexing his biceps for me to admire. "I can't help it. She's so beautiful." He closes his eyes and tips back until his head sits flat against the white brick wall. "But no, we're not dating. I wish. But no."

He wishes. He wants me. Then why the fuck do I not have a flower today?

"So why do you have a picture of her? It's w-weird."

"Maybe a little, but it helps me remember what I'm working toward when I want to give up trying."

He hasn't given up. My knees almost give out. I need to stay aware and absorb the confession this wonderful kid is pulling out of Otis. I'm definitely going to give him my fruit cups for the rest of the year. Hell, I'll fill a fucking piñata with fruit cups if that's what Carter wants.

"I'm confused. Wh-what work? Don't you play football?"

The melancholy on his face cools and turns into quiet delight. Otis places his forefinger over his lips. "It's a secret."

"Tell me." Carter bounces on the bench, his eyes teeming with excitement. "I'm good at keeping sec-sec-sec-secrets."

Right then, Otis's eyes open, and despite my efforts to hide, he finds me instantly, purposefully, as if he's known I've been there all along. His gaze smolders, the smile curving his lips flattening. Those gorgeous dimples disappear as he dons a serious expression.

Rather than cower at being caught, I stand my ground, poised in anticipation, indignant.

"I'm working to show her I'm worth forgiving."

Carter asks what he needs to be forgiven for, but Otis changes the conversation. With the topic redirected, I'm no longer paying attention. I'm just staring at Otis, a mixture of conflicting emotions coagulating inside me. Soon, he tells Carter to go back to the playground without him, and once we're alone in the hallway, he turns to face me.

He just stands there and looks at me, and God, I just want to choke him. Not in a sexual way, either, but in a you're-driving-me-crazy-so-please-make-it-stop way.

Annoyed by the distance, I stomp toward him and pause three feet away. And even though I tell myself to be sweet and kind, I can't.

Because I'm angry. Not at him, but at myself for being the way that I am and biding my time so uselessly when I could have made everything better weeks ago when he first started volunteering.

"My flower." I huff, dejected and furious. "Where is it?"

"Uh..."

I don't give him time to respond. "You've given me a flower every day since you started volunteering at my school and now you stop? With no warning? I just have to walk into class and see no flower? Do you know how that makes me feel?" I'm flustered, brimming with emotions that threaten to crush me. I want him to end my misery by grabbing and kissing me. It's cowardly— irrational, really—to expect and want him to do it. He's done all he could to sway me. It's my turn now, and yet, I'm blundering it, incapable of delicately laying out the cloud of feelings wrestling inside me.

"Not flowery, I'm guessing."

"No, I don't feel flowery." I bite the inside of my cheeks to keep from smiling at the affectionate way he's gazing at me. "I feel very un-flowery. I feel"—what's the opposite of flowery?—"weedy."

"And not the high kind, I'm also guessing."

"Someone better get you onto *Jeopardy*. Your guesses are on fire." I fold my arms over my chest, hating how badly I want to put my hands on him, hold him, and sink into him until we're fused. But I can't, so I fixate on one thing. "Where is it? I want my flower." I'm seconds away from stomping my feet and throwing a tantrum like I've seen my kids do countless times. I kind of get them now.

"I don't have one for you today. I—"

"Why not?" Whatever eloquent indifference I'd planned to express crumbles. "Why don't I have a flower today? You gave me a lock, Otis. A freaking lock. But you can't get me a flower? You have no right to flower me and then suddenly deflower me." I'm overflowing with irrationality. I persist, needing him to understand just how fucked up he's making me feel. "Like, what the fuck, Otis? What the actual fuck? Are you over me? Is that it? Is that why today is your last day? Like, are you giving flowers to other people who, like, thank you for giving them flowers? Cause if you're the type of guy that gives flowers and expects something in return then—well—I—" I've had just about enough of myself, unable to take the humiliation I'm serving, and audibly snap my lips shut.

This is all my fault, I recognize. And yet, I can't attribute the blame to myself. Perhaps this is how Dad had felt. Not the same, but similar.

"Over you?" he repeats. He mouths the two words to himself again, as if their taste is foreign. He scrutinizes his shoes for a heavy moment, but when he looks at me, I'm at a loss for words. Constellations of devotion glimmer in his blue eyes, guiding me closer to him. "How can I be over you when all I want to be is a part of you?"

I dip my head and analyze his shoes, too. "If that's true, then I should have a flower today, shouldn't I?"

"You should." He shuffles closer by a fraction of a step. Two more inches, and our feet will touch.

It's my turn to hold my breath.

"I'm sorry, sweetheart."

Sweetheart. *Sweetheart.* I'm the sweetness in his heart. Lord, I think I'm going to go into cardiac arrest.

"I didn't mean to hurt you that way. I didn't even realize you cared. You never—"

"Of course I do," I all but howl. I know I should be softer, more romantic, but he makes me feel so volatile. "Am I a fucking robot?" A few months ago, the answer would have been affirmative. But being with him has changed me. Not fundamentally—I'm still me, I think—but enough that I'm out of character and I don't mind this shift.

He shakes his head, biting his lip. I can tell he's fighting a smile, and God, I want to just... I want to steal it and keep it with me. Store it in my pocket so I can let it heal my bad days. "Would it make you feel better if I tell you what flower I was going to get you if my card didn't get declined?"

Wow. Am I the biggest bitch or what?

He takes my silence as an invitation to answer. "A two-toned carnation."

"Are you taking me to prom?"

"I would have enjoyed that." He chuckles and moves a fraction of an inch closer. "I bet you drove the chaperones crazy."

My breath gradually increases. I peel my gaze from him and stare at his Adam's apple. I make a face but don't disagree. "What does it mean?"

Then he's surrounding me, overtaking my senses. He ducks his head, his cheek hovering next to mine, his lips an inch from my ear. His whisper makes me shiver. "*I cannot be without you.*" He leans back, and gone are my constellations. Gleaming in his eyes is the universe—*his* universe—and I'm in the epicenter.

"Otis—" I begin to speak because I've folded and I no longer care about whatever dumb excuses or selfish reasons I had to put this off for so long.

But he talks over me, suffocating me under the weight of his affections. "I love you, Miriam. I love you the way I've never loved anyone in my life. My Pawpaw told me you know it's love when it hurts at the end, and if that's the case, then they're going to have to find a new word to describe my feelings for you.

"I wasn't kidding when I said I'm yours. Even if you move on and forget me, you'll always have a part of me. You've filled me with something that I—I can't—it's more than just love or sex or whatever. You've changed the fabric of my chemistry. My DNA."

Disbelief widens my eyes. Whatever autonomy I had is stripped from me as he continues, a golden hue of emotion radiating from him and permeating into me, rebuilding the fabric of *my* chemistry and *my* DNA. I'm being worshiped with the manifestation of his feelings, so much so that I'm certain I've ascended.

"You're so beautiful and headstrong and funny and, yeah, you like pineapple on pizza, but you're so fucking good for me and I—I love you. I love you so much that at some points, I'm convinced I could drown the whole world with my feelings for you. What we have is nature, G. You're the moon and I'm the tides, and no matter your phases, I'm tethered by your gravity and moved by your existence. And that's all I want."

Once, I would have made fun of him for being so corny. But I've changed, and his confession is tattooed into my soul. I'm still speechless. I'm torn between dancing like a maniac and sobbing like a baby. I knew I wanted this—wanted him—but I didn't realize just how badly until his words cement on my heart.

"In summary," he whispers. "I really, really fucking love you. And I just… I'm sorry if you didn't want to hear that. I just needed you to know, flower or no flower."

I open and close my mouth like a pufferfish, urging my brain to be useful for once. I need to fucking say something. But it's useless. Every synapse I have is devoted to silently repeating his confession.

"You don't have to say anything. Not right now." He seems almost panicked.

"Why not?"

He takes a step back. My hand jerks to grab him, but it's futile. He's too far. "Cause I wanna keep hoping for a little while longer."

"Hoping?" He just looks at me, and the tsunami of his passion crashes into me again. A dull pinch coils in my ribs, and I exhale unsteadily. His request makes me sad, and a surge of self-loathing rolls through me. "Are you that sure I'm going to reject you?"

He shakes his head. "No. But there's this small doubt in my mind that tells me I'm not good enough, and it's too fucking loud, and I'm... I'm scared." Otis sucks in a big puff of air and looks away.

I clench my hands to keep from grabbing his face and forcing him to look at me.

"I'm so fucking scared of losing you that I just want to have the comfort of my imagination with me for one more day." He pauses, swallows, and finally looks at me. "Tomorrow is the Midnight Kiss for the university's seventy-fifth anniversary. Show up to Ender's Field if you feel the same way. And if you don't want me, then..." He winces.

I could tell him here and now and spare us the turmoil of such melodramatics. But there's something so beautiful about the way he smiles at me with such poignant hope, such veneration, such expectations, that I relent. I'll allow him to build a fantasy of what will happen tomorrow.

And then I'll give him an even better and much more fantastical ending.

papa sahnoun
Mon 8:40 AM

Eat breakfast before your exam.

Tues 9:16 PM

Dropped off your car.

Clean your apartment.

Healthy home is a healthy mind.

And make sure to come eat dinner at home this weekend.

Mama is sad.

Wed 10:33 AM

Mama said you have a cold.

Eat soup and orange please.

If you're not feeling any better by tomorrow go to the doctor.

Let me know if you need me.

Thu 7:21 PM

Dinner tomorrow is at Lamonte not at home.

can i order the seven course meal
i want to try it at least once

Do I look like I'm made of money?

do u want me to google ur salary
again cuz i will

No.

You get one entree and that's it.

Thu 10:11 PM

And an appetizer.

"**WAKEY-WAKEY**," **AN** angelic voice prompts. There's a delicate touch on my cheek and a lush body draped next to me.

I let out a contented sound and scooch closer to the scrumptious source of warmth. A billowy chuckle fans over my face. My mind buzzes, the edges of awareness lurking in my quasi-lucid state.

"Your alarm went off. Wake up."

Five more minutes. I'm not ready to start the day, not when there's so much ardor available for me in this dream.

"C'mon, Princess. If your dick can greet me this early, so can you."

That's such a Greta thing to say. I grunt in amusement. My Greta illusion cuddles deeper into me, and my skin prickles and tingles. My eyes, once fending off slumber, shut tighter to remain in this dream longer, resisting the trap my subconscious has set up for me. This is all too real. I don't give a fuck if I'm late for morning workouts. I'll take the verbal lashing if it means existing blissfully in this fabricated reality for a while longer.

"Please wake up. I need you to show me those pretty blue eyes. I'm in the mood for a morning swim."

She nuzzles into my neck, and my chin settles nicely atop her head. A sigh of satisfaction escapes me while I wrestle against my impulse to satisfy these demands. It's funny how even in my delusions, I desperately crave to please her.

"Rutherford," she whines, begrudged, her words dampened by the press of her mouth against my throat. "Wake up, wake up, wake up. Wake up and drown me in those feelings again."

I don't abide but simper adoringly at the plea. Nimble fingers reach up and brush over my lids and under my eyes, the magic touch tempting. Delight wracks me, the graze soft like the sweep of a butterfly's wing.

And just like that, I'm blessed. Appearing behind my closed eyes is a vivid—and quite real—vision of Greta.

She's smiling, her expression brighter than the sun's rays at high noon. The corners of her eyes crinkle. A light flush stains her cheeks. Her hair is rumpled, stray strands scattered haphazardly on her forehead. She's wearing it naturally, and I love it. I so desperately wish to brush it aside and press a kiss there.

But lethargy weighs my bones down. That's okay. I'm terrified the slightest of movements will jostle me awake. And yet, my eyes burn as though I am—as if I'm grounded in reality and not adrift in paradise.

"Rise and shine," she chants off-key.

Damn, I'm mean. I couldn't have imagined her with a prettier singing voice? Not that I'm opposed to her terrible singing. If she would let me have her, I'd cherish every dissonant iteration of *Happy Birthday* she'd sing for me.

She has one arm nestled beneath my head in a makeshift pillow, her other hand preoccupied with petting my face. I lock her into a snug hug, our bent legs slotted together.

"Miriam," I marvel.

"Hm?"

"I love you."

Dream Greta purrs against my Adam's apple, and the hand

tracing over me redirects its attention to my lips, swiping over them back and forth. "I know."

A chuckle bubbles out of me. She's cavalier, but an undercurrent of tenderness exists in her response.

"But how about you wake up and tell me that again?"

"But then you'll go away." With as much strength and care as I can muster, I roll us over and keep her bundled against me, her body caged beneath my weight.

Greta gasps. "God damn, Otis, lay off the fucking twinkies."

"Only if you let me have you for dessert every night."

She laughs, the sound winded. "Cute. Now get your fat ass up. You're crushing me."

But that isn't possible. Dream Greta doesn't need to breathe. And if she did, then why is she clinging onto me so tightly? Arms wrapped around my neck, ankles locked at the base of my spine— I'm knotted in her embrace, an escape from her clutches rendered impossible.

"Stop asking me to wake up." I rub my cheeks into her hair. The texture is so soft and smells so much like her. Even if things don't work out tonight and I'm stranded in a life without her, I hope I can conjure dreams like this again.

"What the fuck? Do you dream of us cuddling? With clothes on? Seriously? I'm actually offended by how PG you are."

She tunnels her fingers into my scalp and tugs.

A very vicious sensation shivers down my spine. This feels so fucking real. Her body. Her touch. The way she speaks. Even the way I feel. It all feels so fucking real, like I've begun to wake up and—

"Shit," I enunciate to no one in particular, skepticism seizing me. An alarm blares loudly in my head, commanding attention. Suddenly, I'm alert. I attempt to lift myself up. I blink several times, my eyes dry and my vision blurry from the sting of the cool morning air.

She's here, beneath me. It's dark, but the light from outside bleeds through the slots of my blinds, spotlighting her in translucent grey streaks. She's the epitome of peace and contentment, her chest moving with each exhale and inhale.

The smile I'd dreamed of is present on her face. She moves her hands to the front of my body, dragging them down my torso then settling them beneath my ribbed tank top. The trail of her touch on my skin is searing. Goose bumps scatter up my arms.

I'm dazed, my mouth parted in silent shock. I don't dare to blink in case it all fades away.

She doesn't blink, either. Her gaze rakes across me from left to right with a fondness that makes me feel all mushy-gushy. She sinks farther into my fluffy bedding, appearing almost whimsical.

"What are you... How did you... uh... Why are you... I'm confused."

She chuckles. "Clearly. It took forever to wake you up."

"What are you doing here? Are you—are you real? Oh. Oh, no." My stomach flips in horror. "I've finally gone crazy, haven't I?"

"*Finally?*" she sputters, focused on my inadvertent slip. "What do you mean by finally?"

I'm too busy freaking the fuck out to pacify her about my sound state of mind. Cold sweat drips down my back, my arms quiver like jelly, and the heart palpitations scare me a little. Being close to her isn't helping, and a small part of my brain—one that's very horny and very loud—gets distracted.

I'm too aware of her curves, of her cheeks, rounded and red, of the gleam in her eyes, and of fact that we're in an optimal deep-lovin' position.

Hold up. Is this a dream within a dream? If so, is this the start of a wet one?

No, it can't be. I've already established that it's real. And if this is real and Greta is really here—in my room, under me—then decency dictates that conversation should precede any booty-smooshing, imaginative or not.

As a testament to my will, I reluctantly untangle our limbs. She puts up a bit of fight, half protesting, but relents when I firmly insist.

Turning on my lights, I give myself a moment to collect myself before swiveling to face the woman that commands my happiness. I'm winded by the sight of her, the light chasing away the darkness that had previously obstructed the immaculate glory of her appearance. The left side of my chest flutters and itches, squeezing up the narrow channel of my throat to beat violently inside my neck.

"Greta." I toil to reclaim my ability to be articulate. My head grows fuzzy when her eyes go dark and she looks me up and down. The suggestive scrutiny goes straight to my dick. Any capacity I have to formulate coherent sentences—hell, even to string letters together to make words—disappears, my thoughts consumed by Greta.

Greta, Greta, Greta.

She's upright on the bed, the blankets pooling over her legs, sporting my jersey. If she's come here to kill me slowly, then she's doing a fan-fucking-tastic job at it. Seventeen isn't even my favorite number, but the way she wears it makes it the prime value of my existence.

"Otis," she jaunts airily. From her lips, my name sounds like honey, and I swallow again and again, wishing to savor the rich flavor.

Take two. "What are you doing here?"

"Sleeping."

"But why?"

You know why, dumbass. What you should have asked is how. Actually, that doesn't matter either. Breaking and entering is only a crime if it's unwanted, and this right here is definitely *not* unwanted. And it's easy to deduce why she's here, but it's not enough. What

I need is a definitive and indisputable admission. I need for her to say it.

And she does, her eyes slanted in determination and her shoulders squared in conviction. "Because I'm tired of waiting for the right moment. I'm not very patient, you know."

A codfish dressed in haughty drag could bitch-slap me across the face, and I still wouldn't be as bamboozled.

She continues despite the dumb, unhinged look I'm giving her, her delivery decisive. "I don't want to wait. I don't want to wait for the right moment—whatever the fuck that means. I don't want to wait for Midnight Kiss. I don't want to wait for a feeling. I don't want..." She falters as she clasps the sheets so tightly that her knuckles turn white. Her breathing quickens. Her eyes tear from me to memorize the patterns of my sheets, and so quietly that I have to lean forward to catch her words, she devastates me, collapsing my reality into hers, the boundaries between our worlds intertwined. "I don't want you to wait and hope for what you already have."

She then meets my eyes, the hesitation gone. Her face is luminous with—fuck—with whatever it is that makes her existence the very light of my life. She licks those pretty lips and rubs them together, likely to conjure some more courage, while I struggle to remain standing, placing a hand on the wall to maintain a somewhat vertical position.

But that proves to be too difficult as she keeps talking, mauling me with disbelief, joy, and relief. I resort to pressing my back flush against the wall.

"I like you, Otis. Like, really like you. Squeal and giggle at the thought of you, like you."

Like, she said.

It's not "love," but it's the first step. And with Greta, any semblance of feeling has been meticulously considered and weighed before expressing herself, making this sentiment all the more monumental. My knees wobble. I think I'm going to crumble.

Shatter to pieces. Fold myself over until I can fit in her pocket and she can take me everywhere she goes.

"And I know I've been a terrible vindictive bitch—a trait you can partially thank my mom for, by the way—and I've made you wait so long even after you... I'm sorry for that. So fucking sorry to have ever made you think you're not good enough or that you're not... I'm sorry.

"But I'm done. I'm done twiddling my thumbs and waiting. Because I know. I know what I want, and I was just too afraid of... I was just afraid. Of you. Of my feelings. Of how effortless it is for you to affect me. But I'm not anymore.

"I'm yours, and I have been since before you told me you loved me. Before you held me in your arms after you made me dinner and told me to go to sleep. Before—fuck, I don't even know. I don't know when I gave you a piece of myself, but I did, and I've accepted that, and there's no way in hell I'm going to wait a whole twelve hours until Midnight Kiss to tell you that. Not when you deserved to hear this months ago."

There they are, her feelings, well and true and not at all implied, laid bare for me to bask in. She's so candid about how she offers her affections, as though they're not special, as though I'm not left reeling from the force of them. Each syllable punctures my flesh and permeates my heart. Soon, I'm over-saturated, overflowing, submerged, sinking.

And I never want to break the fucking surface.

Greta has just confessed her all to me, and it would be the perfect moment to reiterate my devotions in kind—because proposing is a little too preemptive, even if I've toyed with the idea one too many lonely nights—except I can't.

She's wrecked me, altered the very paradigm of my existence. I'm already a fucking mess from dealing with months of indecisive agony, and I've just woken up, and I feel—well, I feel everything.

A sharp, piercing twist in my gut. Residual anxiety still knotting in my throat. The violent clamber of my heart in my chest, reverberating like thunder in my skull, echoing inside me until it's all I can hear. It's too much, and I have never been good at bottling things up, used to lashing out and forgetting, and I don't want to forget this, so I let it out.

I cry. I sink to the ground, face buried in my hands, and bawl like a fucking baby because there's no way. There's no way I can be this much of a fuckup and still get the girl. There's no way all that I'd wanted—all that I'd worked for—has paid off. This can't be real.

But it is. I've pinched myself seven times since she started rambling, and I'm still present, awake in my bedroom with Greta. This is real. She wants me, and I—let's just say there's snot streaming out of my nose because I'm blubbering so hard.

The more I try to stop, the more violent my sobs grow, and I'm sniveling like there's no tomorrow. I muffle the sounds behind my hands, but then she pulls me into her arms, and I bury my face in the crook of her neck. At first, Greta doesn't know what to do. She sits perfectly still and holds me awkwardly.

After a handful of seconds, she gets to work and tries to soothe me with apologies for her behavior and reassuring promises of *together*, scratching patterns into my head or rubbing circles on my back. When that doesn't work, she appeals to my love, telling me I'm hurting her by crying. I don't know what she was thinking, using such a tactic, since that only makes me cry even more because I don't want to be hurting her, but I can't help it, and *oh my fucking God*, how am I not dehydrated yet? Where the fuck are all the tears coming from?

"I need you to stop crying," she begs me at some point, her voice cracking. "I need you to stop crying so I can kiss you. I can't kiss you while you're crying."

Of course, this throws me into a whole new tailspin because *holy shit*, I finally get to kiss Greta again, and more than that, she wants to kiss me, too.

By the time I've regained control of myself, she's cradling me, her back pressed against the wall while I curl into the side of her body, the security of her arms the only thing keeping me whole.

"I really fucking missed you," I blurt between deep breaths and hiccups.

She presses a kiss to my forehead. "Tell me something I don't know." She pauses and sniffles. "But I really fucking missed you, too."

"No, you don't get it. Like, I really missed you. I was debating a career in astronomy because of you."

"Astronomy?"

I sit up and wipe away the last of my tears. In all seriousness, I announce, "Yeah. I wanted to be an astronaut because of all the space you wanted."

Suddenly, her silvery laughter fills the room. Her hands squish my cheeks as she graces me with the symphony of her amusement, the sound filling my soul, rejuvenating me.

Greta shakes her head and rolls her eyes. "You're so dramatic, Otis. So extra, I swear." But the playfulness in her demeanor turns somber. "I'm really sorry about that, by the way."

"You don't have to—"

"Stop. I'm being serious. Don't try to make me feel better. Let me—let me be the one to apologize this time, okay?"

She doesn't proceed until I nod.

"I am sorry. And not about being angry with you. But I am sorry about how long I dragged it out and how upset I got for the whole flower thing yesterday and, y'know, at the party, too. You"—the self-assurance in her eyes dampens, and a flush rises in her cheeks—"aren't perfect, but neither am I. I mean, you know that already. Maybe I'm not the easiest to handle, but you... You take me for who I am. And then you made a mistake, and I acted like it was all that mattered, but you worked to fix it, and *that's* all that matters. That's all that should have mattered. And I'm sorry for making it seem like it didn't, like you were irredeemable or whatever. We're both human, and I fucked up here. I have to apologize because you need to know that you're everything I've ever wanted in a person, in *my* person, and I'm so glad you want me and all my imperfections."

I'm fulfilled. The acknowledgment—the fact that someone noticed how hard I have been trying—overwhelms me. It's different coming from her than it is coming from Dr. Toner, Herik, Ma, or Katia. Greta has no obligation to make me feel better. Nothing is at stake for her—she can choose freely to forgive me or not. Dr. Toner gets paid. Herik is my soulmate. Ma loves her children more than life itself. And Katia still feels guilty for stealing a hundred bucks from me during her visit.

I don't know what to say. I don't know how to tell her how much her words mean to me. If I speak, I might cry again, so I show her, instead. I cup her face just as she's cupping mine and bring her face forward for a kiss.

But I end up smooching her fingers.

"Uh, hello? What do you think you're doing?"

I stare at her in surprise and clear my throat, trying to find my voice. "Kissing you. Or am I not allowed to do that yet? You said I could earlier."

"Of course you can. I want you to. But only after you wash your face, Snotty Boy."

"Wait," I say in all seriousness as we get up from the floor. She hums in attention. "How did you get into my room? Seriously."

Greta's lips twitch as she tries to suppress a smile. "Seriously?"

I nod.

"Seriously, don't worry about it."

Even though it lingers in the back of my mind, I readily follow her command, because nothing else matters but her being here.

Here with me.

WE DON'T GO to Midnight Kiss. A barrage of texts from Coach and the boys lights up my phone as the event starts, but I remain truant, my place rightfully instated at my girlfriend's side.

Instead, we go to the football stadium and park my car in front of the back entrance—just like we'd done that night after I realized I loved her—and eat burgers from Barton's, lounging cozily in the bed of my truck. This time we're prepared with ample amounts of pillows and blankets. The back window is open, and the radio softly plays Dad and Pawpaw's favorite radio station. We lie side by side. Our bodies don't touch, but the conversation we share caresses us from head to toe.

"Hey," she whispers after a prolonged moment of tranquil silence. She raises herself onto her forearm, leaning over me. A hand rests on my chest, and I focus my gaze on her. On the aquiline shape of her nose, her thick lips and perfectly full brows, and the way her light chestnut skin appears almost golden in this lighting. I'm captivated, the visual of her holding my attention so completely I forget about the masterpiece that is tonight's sky.

"Hi," I whisper back.

"Am I your girlfriend?"

My heart flutters and stalls. The grip she has on my shirt, just above the very muscle she owns so entirely, tightens. I nod, afraid to speak. The quiet happiness that dimples her cheeks anchors me. "Which means you're my boyfriend, right?"

Another nod, this one more eager. The happiness that lights her face is infectious and radiant and she shares it with a gentle peck. The touch is fleeting, but it's enough to fill me with intoxicating joy. She buries her face in the crook of my neck, still smiling, before settling the rest of her weight atop me. I tangle our legs together and wrap my arms around her, loving how she holds me like this is forever and smells like the best of dreams.

When midnight comes, we share another kiss—a midnight

kiss that's both sweet and passionate. It tastes like sparks of starlight and feels like a perfect sunset. It's the type of kiss that communicates adoration and love, replenishing the soul, no matter how deteriorated it is.

It's the only midnight kiss I'll ever want to partake in again. Football rituals be damned. I tell her this, too.

When she pulls away from me and rests her palm and chin on my chest, she whispers, "Good. Cause all your kisses are mine now, Rutherford. Midnight, dawn, noon, dusk—all mine."

I look at the sky above and thank it for this moment. I thank it for letting this relationship with Greta work when all the others hadn't. For having her settle into my life at a time when I *could* make it work. For finally letting the linearity of time, place, and person intersect to give me this moment in the present.

We remain there long enough for exhaustion to settle in our bones, our throats parched from speaking so much about nothing and everything, then decide to head back.

Yet, the second we park at her place, her tiredness dissipates. She's already hopping out like a bat straight out of hell before I can open her door, much less shift to park, earning a scornful remark from me. She's halfway up the first flight of stairs by the time I get out of my truck. Taking two steps at a time, far ahead of me, Greta turns every now and then to gripe at me for being such a slowpoke.

When we get to her door, I frown.

"What's this?" I point at the standard lock on her door. "Where's my lock?"

"I was going to have you install it." She herds me up against the door, hands behind her back.

I place my hands on her shoulders and rub up and down her arms. "Day one, and I'm already being put to work," I grumble. I'm about to gripe at her some more when I remember why I'd lagged behind. Rummaging in my pocket, I produce the delicate gift, flashing her a toothy grin. "Ta-da."

"What's this?" She tilts her head at the flower I've flourished. "A flower?"

"Not just a flower. *Your* flower." I place it behind her ear, brushing her hair away. "A two-toned carnation."

"*My* flower," she gushes. And the look Greta gives me at that moment makes me wish I'd bought the whole store.

She looks at me as if I've hung the stars in the sky. And now I get to spend however long she'll have me showing her that I would rearrange the entire galaxy for her.

Hooking her fingers into the waistband of my jeans, she draws me to her and kisses me, her nose pressing deeply into my cheek. I reach up to cradle her face, slanting her more to slot my mouth against hers, loving the way her breath accelerates when I touch her.

The kiss we share is deeper and more sensual than earlier. This one is filled with desire and longing, a precursor to more. And despite wanting that, wanting to fully immerse myself in all the sensations her gorgeous body provides, I know I shouldn't get ahead of myself when we've only just become official, so I pull away.

Greta is not happy about it, and her scowl makes that clear "That's it?"

I gently brush away stray strands of hair from her face. "What?"

"That's all I get? A kiss with a little tongue? Raven gives me hotter kisses than that."

And *I'm* the dramatic one. "I'm trying to be respectful, G."

"Respectful? Are you kidding me? You've fucked my tits and jacked off all over my face. I think we're past respectful."

"It's our first real date. Just let me be a gentleman, okay?" I lean forward and peck her scrunched nose. When I pull back, her frown drops, and a smile filled with mischief and promise curls her lips.

I should excuse myself as quickly as I can to get away from her conniving grip. Too bad I don't want to.

"You want to be a gentleman?" she whispers, wrapping her arms around my waist, and locking her fingers against the small of my back. I nod, and she yanks me forward. I steady myself against her, our bodies flush. She bites her bottom lip and sizes me up. "Alright, Princess, be a gentleman. But do you mind being one inside?"

"Inside where?" I pant when she rolls her hips against me, harder and more insistent than before.

She clamps my bottom lip between her teeth and tugs. "Inside me."

katty batty katia
Today 11:17 PM

BITTTTTTCHHHHHH

you got the girl?????

dre dre just told me

ayeeeee papi i cant believe u still have game

finally got the lady after fucking everything up

maybe theres hope for us morgans after all

> stfu
>
> and call ma
>
> she says you've been ignoring her all week

GRETA

I KNOW YOU KNOW I L-WORD YOU

OTIS IS MULTITASKING or at least trying to. We're inside my apartment, side by side on my couch, an infinitesimal gap between us. He has a one-hand feel on my thigh and the other on my pussy.

"That's my pretty kitty," he croons, nuzzling his nose against Raven's.

I do my best to ignore them but can't help but glower when my cat's purring grows louder. For the last twenty minutes, I've been relegated to my boyfriend's sidepiece because of my traitorous pet.

For a guy who claimed to be a good multitasker, he sure as shit doesn't know how to divvy his attention properly.

To add insult to injury, I'm also being provoked by my child. Whenever I glance in the feline's direction, he gloats about how he's the one getting kissies and scratchies from Otis. He even has the audacity to stick his tongue out at me.

Granted, he could simply be licking his nose, but knowing what a diva Raven is, I believe the gesture to be more calculated than a mere grooming habit.

It's only after my black tabby gives me a smug look, where his ears twitch in delight from the ass taps he receives from Otis— where are my ass taps? This is a hate crime—that I abandon them and head to the bathroom to remove my make-up.

I'm not left to my own devices for long. No sooner do I reach into the cupboard to grab my micellar water than I notice Otis studying me through the mirror.

He leans against the doorway, appearing as gorgeous as ever and obviously intrigued.

"Can I help you?" I raise my chin in indignation. It doesn't matter how horny I might be. I refuse to give the goods so easily now. To be shunned for a cat—oh, the wounds my pride has suffered.

Otis licks his lips and arches a brow. His stare travels down the length of my body, lingering on the curve of my fine, un-tapped ass, before traversing up to meet my gaze in the reflection. The corner of his mouth twitches, and lust clouds his dilated pupils, his nostrils flaring. Still in a trance, he pushes away from the doorway, but I stop him. Tutting, I hold my hand up, effectively halting his approach.

He pouts. "What? What's wrong?"

I ogle in disbelief and mock his concern. "*What's wrong*? Did you not just spend the last ten minutes ignoring me for a cat?" It doesn't matter that I love this cat more than life itself. He's still just a cat.

"Aw, don't be like that. My pretty kitty missed me. I couldn't ignore him."

"What about this pretty kitty?" I sputter, gesturing to my crotch. "She's been missing you, too, but you sure as hell ignored her."

Otis bites the insides of his cheeks, his shoulders shaking in quiet amusement. Even I swallow a chuckle at my ridiculous behavior. But I keep up the act, adoring the playful atmosphere around us. Spinning around, I rip off my shirt and toss it aside. Reaching behind, I toy with the clasp of my bra. His breathing picks up audibly. With my back still facing him, I turn to give him my cheek and smirk.

Fingering the latch, I taunt him. "Pay attention. We don't want a repeat of last time." With one hand, I effortlessly snap the hooks apart, and just like that, my tiny titillating tatas are on full display.

A second doesn't pass between the time my bra drops to the floor and Otis reaching me. Faster than light, he presses the front of his clothed body flush against the back of mine. The flat of his palm rests against my navel, and he delves his fingers into the waistband of my skirt, teasing. He skims up my torso, parting my breasts with the span of his hand, and makes his way down again. He repeats this over and over again until I say fuck it and try to take off the skirt myself, ready to get railed into the next century.

But when I go to unzip the offending article, he catches my wrist and lifts it up to his mouth. "What do you think you're doing?" he whispers into my pulse point, his mouth trailing past my elbow and to the curve of my shoulder.

"Getting naked."

"And who gave you permission to do that?" A gasp escapes me when he bites down on the junction of my neck and then sucks. He still has my wrist bound to him, his other hand tracing circles around my belly button.

"Otis." Desperation hitches my voice. I'm no longer interested in playing games. I don't care to have him work for anything. The mixture of emotions and celibacy has turned me into a monster that has only one thought in mind: Sex.

My boyfriend silences the rest of my plea with a shake of his head. Placing tentative hands on my waist, he repositions me, my back to the sink and mirror. His eyes are dark and smoldering, revealing his intentions well before he can act on them. My heart swells, and I swallow my impatience.

Pressing his cheek against mine, he breathes against my ear. Every exhalation sets my nerves on fire, and my stomach clenches in anticipation. When he finally speaks, it's low and gruff. "Do you know how badly I wanted you back?"

"Tell me."

A husky chuckle from him shakes us both. "I'll show you." Stepping back, he rips off his shirt and undoes my skirt but doesn't take it off. "I told God I'd get on my knees if I got you back."

Otis then drops to one knee and gently caresses my ankle, lifting it to set my foot on his upright thigh. His breathing is labored, and we're both silent, entranced, as he removes my fishnet stockings, tickling me as he does so, one foot at a time. He presses a kiss on the sides of my knees and ankles. With both of my feet back on the ground, he drops his other leg to kneel before me properly. The calloused pads of his fingers are feather-light against my skin, skimming up the inside of my leg until he reaches beneath my skirt. One of my hands moves to cling onto the edge of the bathroom sink while the other twists in his hair as I try to remain upright, my vertical integrity compromised by his ministrations.

He plays with the hem of my underwear, wriggling his fingers beneath the material to tease the damp seam of my folds, taunting me. He takes pity when I let out an embarrassing gurgle of desperation and bites the waistband of my thong then drags the skimpy material down my body, allowing it to pool at my feet.

I hold my breath when he kisses back up and hovers at the apex of my thighs. His breaths fan over me—inside me—and I'm blooming before he's even touched me, growing hotter and wetter. He remains out of reach, motionless, alluding to all the splendor he could lavish me in with a light brush of his mouth over me. I'm drenched, aching, seconds away from really begging.

"Now look where I'm kneeling."

Finally, he tastes me, and had he not held onto me, I would have collapsed, my legs quivering beneath the tremendous weight of gratification that bolts through me.

It's gentle at first, as always. He draws out my anticipation, tending to the pre-chorus with the same dedication he gives the hook.

He peppers butterfly kisses along my pussy, exploring the

soaking expanse with pressure so light, so brief, it's like it's not there. I twitch in agony, growing wetter. Otis notices and chuckles, his amusement rattling me. A purposeful and unexpected swipe of his tongue has me shrieking.

"I've missed getting a taste of you." He hums in approval, the curve of his smile burning into me. He places a blunt, curled finger between the valley of my folds, dragging up and down, collecting my flavor against the crook he's created. He moans when a fresh wave of arousal rushes out of me. As if I'm not stimulated enough, he's printing his name on the inside of my thigh, using my wetness to draw it there.

Otis resumes his lighthearted antics for a while, ghosting his lips over and around me, getting his kicks from my broken, desperate whimpers. I tunnel my fingers into his hair, trying to control him, but he's resistant, adamant in practicing his own form of worship on me.

It's right when I've reached the precipice of insanity, certain that I will self-destruct if he doesn't give me exactly what I want, that I'm hauled onto the sink. The ledge cuts uncomfortably into my ass, but there's no time to dwell on the discomfort when he's dived into me, devouring my pussy with such vigor and intent that my body caves and jolts forward, a scream tearing from my throat.

I welcome the onslaught of delight he delivers. He's brought my legs over his shoulders, his head clamped between them. Every erotic suck, every pointed lick, and each cautious bump against my clit is rewarded with an involuntary squeeze of my knees. It's when he incorporates his fingers, maneuvering his hands around my body to spread my pussy lips better and tap on my clit, that I concede all control to him.

The effect on me is visceral, and I'm pummeled with muted pleasure as molten heat licks up my body starting from the soles of my feet. I have no energy to keep myself upright and slant back, relaxing my neck to press my head against the cool mirror. I shove his face against me, suffocating him. He makes a wet snuffing sound, almost a protest, almost a moan.

I realize I must actually be suffocating him and loosen my grip. This causes him to growl, bite on my labia in protest, and bring my knees together to clamp tighter against his head.

His voice comes out muffled and gravelly as he commands me, squeezing the outside of my thighs in emphasis, "I want those gorgeous legs to crush my skull, or this stops."

There's no time for me to protest or inquire about his well-being because he's rubbing back into me. The entirety of his face is hidden between me, chin-and-nose settled deep in my sopping wetness, tongue slithering out, his jaw moving animatedly, doing everything in his power to break me.

He sucks the fucking soul of me, moaning every time I undulate above him, directing his movements in a certain way. He moves back to give himself space to trace the moist slit of me, fluttering the pads of his hot fingers against the slick, sensitive skin until he finds my entrance. When he pushes a finger inside, I offer no resistance, my body opening willingly to the intrusion.

He adds a second finger and fucks me feverishly, wiggling the tip of his tongue against my clit as he pistons his digits in and out, then adds another finger. "That's it. Pull me in," he encourages, his baritone raspy. He scatters a constellation of kisses along my inner thigh as he curls his fingers up to rub against a delicious bundle of nerves inside me. I sob and tighten my legs around him. He moans and latches his mouth back onto me.

When he pulls back against the tight clearance my clamped thighs afford, a string of saliva stretches between him and my pussy. He rests his cheek on my inner thigh and looks at me with adoration and amazement, his eyes glistening, making my heart thump. I feel immortal. All the while, he maintains a sensual, purposeful rhythm with his fingers.

"The expressions you make while I finger fuck you are so

beautiful. I could do this all day."

I don't have time to simper over his dirty compliment when he burrows his face back into me. I screech, like, actually screech as his teeth tug gently at my clit while his tongue assaults me, and his fingers—

"Yes!" I scream. I'm sure that by the end of this, I'll have him bald, my hold on his scalp violent.

Coiling a hand around my body, he brings his free hand to my thick lips and pinches them together, forcing the engorged nerve bundle out of its hood. He sucks loudly, his tongue lapping out to swipe horizontally against it. Every sound I make is answered by one of his own.

"You're so good to me," I say, panting when I get close. Fireworks dance in front of my eyes. The end is near, and I don't know whether I should mourn or celebrate.

"I'll be even better when I'm inside you," he croons, the pitch of his voice low. And that's all it takes. He keeps nibbling, keeps licking, keeps doing everything he can to get me there. Intense waves of heat dance beneath the surface of my skin. One more twist of his wrist, one more suck, and a circular twirl of his tongue, and I'm letting go, rewarding him with the proof of his efforts by a rush of arousal.

He's right there, taking it all in, tongue wiggling deep inside me to beckon for more. The waves of my orgasm have me contorting in pleasure. I'm sensitive, but Otis doesn't care. He still gorges on me with unmatched enthusiasm, amplifying my sobs of gratitude.

When this insatiable man is finally satisfied, when I've pleased him with my pleas to stop and tears squeeze out the corner of my eyes, he grins, looking up at me in immense satisfaction like he's the one that's finished. His face is shiny with the proof of his enthusiastic performance.

My muscles protest when I lean forward to cradle his jaw and bring him up to kiss me, relishing the taste of myself on his skin.

As I suck my juices off his nose, lips, and chin, I undo his jeans and reach into his pants to quickly grasp his hot, beating cock. He hisses at the gesture.

The feel of it—the realization that he's probably close and that's from eating me out and nothing else—wipes away the exhaustion that had once settled in me.

"Bedroom," Otis pleads, the tendons on his throat flexing to the strokes of my hand on him. I swipe my thumb over the leaking tip, smug when he grabs the wall beside us. His other hand digs into my thigh, his fingers imparting deep craters there. A blush stains the skin of his chest, neck, and face. It's adorable, especially given how close he is, the steady drips of pre-cum smearing my hands signaling his imminent release. "I wanna fuck you in the bedroom. Please."

But I'm not paying attention to him, and to be frank, I don't care. My mouth waters, the urge to fill it with his thick cock too strong to resist any longer.

"Here."

And whatever ability he has to protest is robbed when I contort my body and kiss the tip of him, dragging my tongue along his sensitive vein, my hands juggling his sac. Hand still pumping along the base of his cock, I bring him into my mouth, loving the hard, heavy heat of him, thrilled from the way he pulls back when his dick hits the back of my throat. He still tries to protest, knowing this will end too soon, needing me to stop so that doesn't happen, but he contradicts his claims with a hand on the back of my neck, helping me bob and suck the length of him, holding me deep at the base when I hollow my cheeks just right, constricting my airway with such a lovely burn.

It doesn't take long before his release detonates, exploding in my mouth. And though it's been a while since I've swallowed, I do my best to take everything he has to offer, swirling my tongue around the bulbous tip when I make my way back up, gagging all the while, a sound he's very fond of.

Then it gets to be too much for me to take and I pop off him with a gasp. His cock continues to pulse, jets of his cum streaking over my face. This goes on for a while. It's the most a guy has ever nutted on me. I'm equally horrified and impressed.

When he's finally done, he falls into me, enveloped between my legs, the dead weight of his head on my shoulder. I angle my messy face from him. Struggling a bit, I wrap my arms around his large frame and lock my hold in place by grabbing my other wrist.

"I'm going to die," Otis groans, embarrassment charring his words.

"Why? Cause you came in less than a minute?" I shouldn't find this funny, but it really is. I think this is the fastest he's ever come with me. Even faster than the "quickies" we've had.

"Give me another minute, and I'll throw myself off your patio."

I kiss his cheek. "Aw, don't be upset. I've got a good mouth on me. No one can blame you for busting so fast."

"Stop talking."

I obey for a moment, just long enough for our breathing to calm down and for him to lower his guard. "I can't wait to tell your teammates you're a two-pump chump." I snicker.

His body freezes up. "I hate you."

"YOU DONE POUTING yet?"

Otis pauses in his task of installing my new lock to glare at me. "No. I hate you, remember?"

I roll my eyes. "I have flowers and a lock that says otherwise."

Walking past him, I smack his ass. Raven, who had previously been napping but awoke to the ruckus Otis created with the power drill he brought up from his truck, glares at me for touching what he believes is his. I stick my tongue out at the cat.

I go into the kitchen and grab us both cold glasses of water. It's almost three in the morning, but the night isn't over. In order for it to be over, I've got to have my guts rearranged, and that hasn't happened yet.

Now, to get him to stop being so cranky and actually fuck me...

I wait in bed for him to finish working on my lock. I'm careful to keep my slightly damp hair off the pillow. We'd taken a quick rinse after our escapade in the bathroom, one where Otis refused to hanky-the-panky in protest of my mean behavior. That's fine, I'd asserted back. I was still sensitive and had no doubt in my mind that by the time I knocked out for the night, I'd be tucked into bed with his spent cock inside me.

Taking this alone time to reply to the plethora of texts from my friends and parents—my mom yelling at me for not returning her jewelry like I promised I would, my dad angry that my credit card statement was well over my allowance, Elise with a barrage of texts about what we did after ditching, and James asking me for my streaming service password—I hardly notice when my man walks into the bedroom. Like before, he stops at the entryway, arms up to clutch the frame above. He rests his head on his defined bicep.

I can't explain it, but this dégagé display has me instantly wet.

"Are you coming to bed?" I toss my phone aside and pat the empty space beside me to beckon him.

He doesn't move, and my left eye twitches. *Don't be aggressive, Greta. Entice him.*

Employing a different tactic, I do my best to do that cute shit I've seen Elise do to Andres when she opens her arms for him, eyes wide and bottom lip jutted out, and he fucking sprints to her. I metaphorically kick my feet in victory when I realize this ploy works on more than just six-foot-seven offensive center with a penchant for virgins.

With Otis's weight crushing me, his head pillowed by my breasts, he grumbles, "I'm still mad at you."

"Can you be mad at me and fuck me at the same time?"

He doesn't respond, and I play the bongos on his ass. The smile he's concealing burns into my skin, making its first appearance since he finished too quickly in the bathroom.

"I'm not a machine, woman! It takes time to, y'know." He grinds his boxer-covered length against me and releases a resigned sigh. Then he grunts and lifts his head up, his expression twisted in dismay. "God, I'm so upset, I don't think I'll ever get hard again."

Please don't let that be true. I'm too horny for this shit.

"Why'd you have to make me come like that? I wanted to do it inside you," he whines.

"I did too, Fordy," I say, mimicking his petulant tone. I hold his face between my hands and press a peck on his lips, hoping to assuage him before I destroy his self-esteem with honesty. "But you and I both know you weren't going to last a single stroke."

He gapes and tries to pull away from me but is unsuccessful. When he speaks, his voice is filled with torture. "You're so wrong! I could have lasted at least three! Four if you weren't so wet, and if I really put my heart and soul into it."

"Of course, you could have."

And just like that, Otis's competitive drive takes over, and he unravels himself from my hold, determined to prove his point. He reaches over to the nightstand. I'm only too eager to be dominated and kick the sheets off my feet, undoing the knot of my robe.

"Where're your condoms?" he asks over the sound of miscellaneous items clanging together inside the nightstand.

"I don't have any."

The drawer slams shut. "What the fu—why?"

"Cause I used them up on all the other guys I've been fucking." I snort to indicate sarcasm.

He doesn't register it, though, and his face turns white. "Deadass?"

Baffled that he believed me—though I can't really fault him for that, given my repertoire—I throw a pillow at him. "No, you moron! I don't have condoms cause they expired and I didn't need to buy new ones!"

"So," he begins carefully, the gears in his head turning to understand the implication of my explanation. "Should I run to the gas station and get some, just in case?"

He's asking if I'm clean. If I've fucked anyone since we were together.

"That's a joke, right?" I don't know if I want to squish his cheeks or pull his ear.

"No?" Uncertainty flashes in his eyes.

Embodying all that is good in the world and doing my best not to be myself, I take a deep breath and respond in a calm, level manner. "No, Otis, you don't need to go to the gas station. I haven't had sex with anyone since you, and I'm on birth control."

He blinks quickly. "No one?"

I shake my head.

"Not even that hockey bit—guy?"

"Nope." I'll mention the almost-could-have-would-have with the Parisian guy some other time.

"So," he whispers gutturally, swallowing as he lowers himself onto me again, "I don't need to go to the gas station?" I shake my head and his eyes widen, his lips parted. "I can hit it raw?"

I nod, my lips twitching in humor. What a great way to put it, huh?

The look that splits his face is like water on the surface of a burning star, the tumultuous exchange of energy incinerating the last vestige of my reservation in devoting myself to him. It's the final push I need to start tunneling down the chasm that is love, and though I'm falling at a gradual rate, a little frightened, I'm exhilarated by the caprice of reaching the glorious destination that waits for me at the bottom: Him.

Unable to contain this newfound feeling, I brush my fingers over his face, pushing away strands of his hair. He's gorgeous, with his high cheekbones, broad nose, and straight-edged jaw. Inside me is a light. It originates from me, but its intensity—its existence—is controlled by him.

"I adore you," I murmur, hoping he understands the importance these words hold for me. "And I want to spend the rest of forever adoring you."

The moment should have been romantic. It should have been heartfelt, reciprocated by his own amorous declaration. It was a confession that's one step ahead of *like* but still beneath *love*. Except his response comes in the form of his dick growing hard against me.

Pushing his shoulder back, I gawk in disbelief. "Did you just get a boner?"

"I can't help it." He groans, gyrating against my abdomen, his chin lowered to his chest as he loses himself in the movement. "It's such a turn-on when you're being all romantic and sweet and shit."

There's no time for me to process his words when he starts to feel me up. He wiggles his eyebrows and bends to lick my chin and lips. "You ready to get some of this McLovin?"

"That sounds like cheap dollar-menu sex from McDonald's." *Still down. Sex is sex.* I'm already rearing up to kiss him.

"I love their fish burgers," he comments between pecks. "I always get extra pickles and mayo. Shit's delicious."

"I'm more of a premium wagyu steak type of gal."

He stretches back, his expression incredulous. "You're going to break my wallet, aren't you?"

I shimmy my shoulder and wiggle my brows. "I've already told you: I'm materialistic. I've got a weakness for Chanel Nine boots and Balmains, and I'm not ashamed of it."

Shaking his head ruefully, Otis burrows into my neck and kisses the sensitive skin there before moving to the delicate wing of my collarbone and tracing it with his nose. His hand goes to my breasts, cupping them, playing with them, brushing his fingers over the nipples until they're erect. My robe falls open, and his shirt pushes up his chest.

After a quick dozen seconds in which we frantically shed our clothes, acting like they'll catch on fire if they remain on us for a second longer, we collide into each other, our limbs tangling together.

There isn't much ceremony or foreplay. There's absolutely no need for us to drag this out for long, not when we're both so desperate. The rubbing, the touching, and the whispers of devotion have served their purpose in replacing any of the erotic incentive that precedes sex.

He's effortlessly taken charge and arranged me beneath him, my mind and body ceding control to him once more. My legs are wrapped high around his waist, my fingernails digging into his back, poised for the first thrust. One of his hands grips my ass, leveraging me up to align better with him. With his other, he grabs his dick and coats himself in my dampness.

"Look at this gorgeous pussy," he murmurs, lathering himself between my folds. "Always ready. Begging for my cock. What a perfect girl you are for me."

Perfect girl. I'm dizzy from his compliment, still basking in how good it makes me feel, when he pushes in, holding himself at my entrance, waiting to be drawn in deeper naturally. A gasp escapes me, the intrusion sublime, my untried muscles flexing to welcome his massive cock. He notches in a few more inches as resistance slips away and my eyes roll back into my head. I circle my hips for more. He puts a hand on my waist to hold me still.

A smirk of glory graces his lips as he looks down to watch the way I accept him. He pulls out to stroke himself, lubricating his length with our fluids. He's quick to fix the emptiness he's created before I can miss him. Another strangled sound escapes me at the more forceful drive of his hips, giving me more.

"Damn," he bites out, his voice hoarse, laced with tormented joy. "You're a fucking vision when you take me, G."

Tossing his head back, he works in another inch, my cunt receiving him with a tight squeeze and a flood of moisture. When he opens his eyes, he's looking at me in magnificent agony.

My heart beams from how affected he is by me. From how wrecked I make him feel. "Do you like my pussy that much?" I purposefully clench around him when he fails to answer, loving how he involuntarily ruts inside me. He's almost there—so close to where the physical boundary between us blurs. My lashes flutter, and I hold my breath, enjoying the burn that tickles throughout of my body from his invasion. "Do you like how well I take that *big* cock of yours?"

The word "big" always spurns guys on. My vulgar questions serve as the final incentive for him to abandon the patient glide he'd taken up. He retreats once more, but this time, when he pushes back inside, he impales me, snapping his hip forward in a single, swift forceful thrust that jars me. Pleasure spirals between us, ripping a savage growl from him.

I feel everything as he stretches me, enveloping me in a reality dominated by him. I feel him in the back of my throat, in my stomach, and even at the nape of my neck.

Arching my hips off the bed, I gyrate into him, succumbing to the blind pleasure that comes from the stimulation and friction of his cock rubbing against every inch of my wall. He falls forward, his hands landing on either side of me. I turn my head to the side to kiss his forearm, and he purses his lips, eyes screwed shut. My nails are working hard on his back, tearing the inked skin. The muscles beneath my fingertips dance.

"So good," he moans sonorously into my ear as he stares down at me with heady eyes. "Always making me feel so good."

There's no chance for me to fully comprehend what he's said, to preen with pride from my accomplishment, when he starts to properly thrust in me, offering a languid but harsh rhythm that builds. The sudden movement ricochets me up the bed, and my head beats against the headboard. There's complete ease in the way he slips inside me, and every time he bottoms out, he takes a second and remains sheathed for a while longer, his hips circling to brush and bump against every inch of me as my nipples scrape their own little pattern against his chest. Again and again, he does this, expelling whatever ability I have to breathe each time he glides out and dives back in.

Dipping his head, he tends to my breasts, brushing his wet lips over them and capturing a nipple when he fucks into me just right and they jiggle into his receptive mouth. He draws amorous messages on them with the tip of his tongue and scrapes his teeth over the soft skin when I abandon my plans on his back to grip his ass, urging him to sink in deeper, as if he's not already bumping the hidden recess that reveals all the pleasures the universe can offer.

But then we get close. Really close. The beat of his cock synchronizes with the pulsing of my snatch, and he's dripping inside me, out of me, leaking down my ass and onto the bed. And it's at this cusp that the dynamic between us shifts and the playful dominance he's asserted turns possessive and urgent, touching where we're joined.

"Is this pussy mine?" Otis rasps.

My response is instinctual. On any other day, I wouldn't have endorsed his display of overt possession, but today, I want to be possessed by him. And he wants to possess me.

"Yes."

He marvels. The furious movement halts. He holds still within me, pinning my hips down when I try to resume our coupling. The opaque cloud of arousal around us starts to disperse, and in its gradual dissolution is a new understanding of what we are to each other. It grounds me to the occasion. In his eyes, I'm a miracle, and in mine, he's a benediction.

"Are you mine?"

"Yes."

"Louder."

"Please," I chant, drawing out the word.

He grabs my face, pinching my cheeks with one hand, forcing my eyes to snap open. He withdraws from me, and I feel the weight of him resting on my inner thigh. The emptiness is unbearable. I wriggle, desperate to fill that empty chasm he's left me with.

"I said louder," he whispers sweetly, but there's a glint of manic obsession in his eyes. "I want to hear you scream who you belong to." He grabs his cock and slots it against my entrance, pushing in but not enough to satiate me. The grip on my face tightens. "Scream louder, and if you stop, I'm going to stop, too. Got it?"

I gasp my submission. "Yes."

His formidable, strong body towering over me trembles. He gave himself to me, and now he wants me to give myself to him. And even if he knows I want him, he needs to reaffirm it, believe it, and hear it over and over again until the last ebb of doubt in his mind is cleared.

"Then tell me, darling," he directs, poised to reward me with the plunge of his cock. "Tell me who you belong to."

"You," I say at a regular volume, louder than all the whispers from before. I devastate him with my honesty, and he endorses the wreckage. He reaches deep inside, and I cling to him, certain he'll never be able to leave.

He continues this line of questioning for a while. He withdraws and asks, and I'm telling him *you, you, you*, even before he finishes speaking because I need more friction, more heat, more of him.

This goes on until I'm a mess, my responses turning breathy as the fire in my gut spreads. He's snaked his finger between my legs and plays with me, tuning my clit to a frequency that only he's familiar with, instigating sparks to ignite throughout me. And yet, it isn't enough for him.

"Louder." His hand leaves me and goes to the curve of my shoulder, gently caressing a path up my neck, his thumb pressing on my jugular, finding the erogenous buttons there. "I need you to scream louder." He's finally at my mouth, his thumb swiping against my bottom lip until he pushes it in. I suck, tasting myself when I curl my tongue all over it. He indulges in the antics for a heartbeat before he pries my jaws apart. "Please."

I surrender, every ounce of resistance stripped from me by his devotion. With whatever strength I can muster, I strain my vocal cords and become louder, so loud that the room is never offered a moment of reprieve from my cries of willing submission, the words blurring into hollow echoes.

But then it gets to be too much, and I can't speak or move. All I can do is relinquish myself to the feeling he evokes. Anticipation blooms in every crevice of my body as his hips rub in quick circles designed to accelerate my descent into mind-numbing bliss.

"One more time," he begs, his unsteady breaths billowing over me. "Scream one more time for me, and I'll give it to you." He kisses along my jaw. He's the one begging now, his command crumbling to reveal his desperation. "I'll give you everything you want. Just scream one more time. For me." He pauses and stares deep into my eyes. "Who do you belong to?"

My composure is hanging on by a thread, and yet, I'm able to sob, "You. I belong to you."

Just as he'd promised, he gives me everything I want. And it's funny, because I thought I wanted to come, but no. What I truly want are his next words.

"And I belong to you." He stills in me.

The unsuspecting confession causes my heart to tremble. I might have heard them before, but it's different now. I gasp, my eyes shooting open to marvel at him. A quiet ferocity gleams on his face as he looks down at me with such adoration, I think I might burst from the eye contact alone. He cants my hips and resumes his movements—his lovemaking—punctuating his next words with deep, steady, measured thrusts, ensuring that I feel the sincerity in his words as he mirrors them with the depth of his strokes. "I'm all yours."

There's no more talking, and for the next couple of seconds we create a steady tempo. Just like that, we let go together, his confession masterfully orchestrating a sensationally shared orgasm. Our release is hot and wet, our bodies undulating as we embrace the oblivion of pleasure surging through us.

Despite his efforts to prolong our release with shallow thrusts, I keep him there, my walls clamping tight around him so that he can't move—won't want to move—as I bear down all around, forcing him to relish this moment. Electric shocks of ecstasy tremble through me, fizzling between us, and we let out bitten-off moans, our mouths open against each other, sharing the same breaths.

When it's over, when the last tide of intense, delectable euphoria dissipates, we look at each other. He still hovers above me, resting a little more than half his weight atop me. I urge him to give me all of him, loving how solid and heavy he is. He relents, and in that moment, I feel so entirely safe and wanted and cherished that if I had the ability to bear the burden of him constantly, I would.

We're talking about getting up and cleaning ourselves, but neither of us moves. After a while, he rolls off me but remains inside, spooning me. My head is pillowed on the hard curve of his shoulder. Our soft chatter dies away after a while, and we just look at each other, reeling in the afterglow.

"Rutherford?" I whisper suddenly, my voice cracking. An inexplicable impulse washes over me, and I've never been good at fighting my impulses. My heart thrums loudly in my ears. I'm sure he can hear it—feel it.

There's something I have to say to him now, because there's no other moment that will be just as perfect.

He hums, a tepid smile curling over his lips. "Yes, Miriam?"

Giddy excitement buzzes over me. My middle name never sounded so beautiful before. When I speak again, I find that my tone has dampened in its intensity, reflecting the fear winding inside me.

"I think I'm falling in love with you."

I take his breath away, which is only fair since he's stolen a chamber of my heart. Otis swallows repeatedly and finally croaks, "Are you scared?"

I worry my bottom lip, silent. He clutches me closer, tangling our limbs. I dissolve into the shape of him, and our souls merge.

"Don't be. I'm already waiting to catch you after the fall." Pressing an endearing kiss on my forehead, he breathes against me, silently reminding me that he's *my* perfect, as if I didn't already know. I have his confession engraved into the very essence of my being. "I love you."

And though I might feel the same in some capacity, I'm still not ready to say those three precious, little words aloud to him, and choose instead to trace them onto his back.

"I know."

REMINDERS
♥

O   fall in love with my fordy

OTIS

EPILOGUE

GRETA IS NOT happy with me, and no matter what I do, I can't get her to *not* not be happy with me.

Which is to say: She big mad.

"It was a joke," I whine, trying to hold her hand. She wrenches it from my grasp and picks up the pace, walking ahead to maintain a gap between us. I slow down to get a better vantage on her swaying hips, admiring the way her ass jiggles with each angry stride she takes.

Greta's body is perfect. Her ass, her tits—oh, not to mention her fupa. Fuck, I love that fupa.

"Hurry up!" she snaps when she notices I'm lagging behind.

"Yes, ma'am." I pick up the pace and grab her hand when I reach her, stupidly adding, "It really was a joke."

Mistake number one. Greta wrenches away and practically jogs ahead. She likes distance when she's angry, just for a little while. I'm the opposite, needing reconciliation immediately.

But we're camping, which makes distance impossible. And even though I promised to respect her boundaries this morning after I said the thing that upset her, I don't, because we're almost at our final destination and I really need her to not be mad at me when we get there or it'll ruin the surprise I have.

"Jokes are supposed to be funny, Morgan," she calls over her shoulder. *Morgan.* It's what she calls me when she's mad at me. Her dad calls me Morgan. *Ick.* "Does it look like I'm funny-ing?"

I jog to catch up, careful to not trip over a branch like last time—or maybe I should trip and fall, since that had her funny-ing before. When my gait matches hers, I walk backwards, facing her, knowing damn well she'll let me topple on my ass if there's an obstacle in my way. Placing both my index fingers on the corners of her mouth to manufacture a smile from her, I chirp a playful, "Now you do!"

Mistake number two. You're on a roll, Morgan.

She stops dead in her tracks, and my pulse races. I'm supposed to be afraid right now, except I'm kind of turned on. One, her tight athletic jacket is unzipped enough to showcase those wonderful knockers of hers. And two, Greta Miriam Sahnoun is fucking delicious when she's angry, which makes antagonizing her an incentive rather than a deterrent.

"Get your hands off me before I break them."

I'm quick to retreat, placing those money-makers behind my back—not in fear but because I'm worried I might hug or squish her to me if I leave them vulnerable between us.

We stand there in complete silence for a while with her glaring at me and me looking down her top. And when she realizes the direction of my focus, she punishes me and hides the titties with a conservative zip of her top.

I shimmy my shoulders and pout. "Not the boobies."

She pushes me aside. "Boobies, booty, and pussy. You get *nada.*"

"Just because I proposed? People love proposals!"

"Not after five months of dating, and especially not when they're in the middle of sex!" Greta shrills. She heaves rapid puffs of air before shrieking in unintelligible frustration. Reaching down, she grabs a rock and hurls it at me. It's a small pebble, but her aim is way too good for someone who can't pitch a baseball.

I clutch where she's hit my shoulder. "It was a joke!" I moan. She and I need to have another conversation about using our words or I'm tattling on her to Dr. Toner.

Her face is marred with doubt, and I don't blame her. She knows I'm flat-out lying. I'd marry this girl in a heartbeat. Give me a minister and a black bear for a best man—don't tell Herik—and we're good to go.

"Get better jokes." With that, she storms onward, which is kind of silly since I'm the one who knows where we're going.

But I let her lead, giving her the time she needs to cool down, guiding her only when she deviates from the blue trail. After half an hour of silent hiking, she slows, and at forty minutes, we're walking in step. It takes only forty-five minutes for her hand to bump against mine. By hour one, we're holding hands again.

It's the fastest reconciliation we've ever had, and I'm grateful. I'm also certain she's quicker to forgive me because she knows how anxious I get when she's upset with me, especially when this weekend is meant to be nice, fun, and argument-free.

We're chatting about my upcoming season, this Monday marking the last day of July and the dawn of our final year in college. She says she wants to come to my game, but I tell her it's okay, that she doesn't need to. She insists, but the grip she has on my hand is tight, blood-restricting.

We haven't talked about what we're going to do after college, but it doesn't matter. We don't really need to, not when I'd follow her to the ends of the world, making the trip a million times if I knew I could keep her as mine.

Even if we have to go about our relationship long-distance, I'll be by her side every chance I get. And that's if I get into the league. If I don't end up playing professionally, I'll just get a job in her city as a data scientist or some shit like that. That's what people do, right? Put their degree to actual use?

"What is this?" Greta asks when we've arrived at our destination, pointing at the tree that has her brother's name carved into it. I'd hardly noticed we'd arrived, paying attention to her detailed analysis of the sociological and feminist brilliance that is the movie *Mean Girls*. And to think, I thought it was a vapid chick flick.

Technically, this camping trip was meant to be a family one. Though I'd been asked to come, I'd accepted the invitation with reservation, not ready to spend a whole weekend with her dad, my coach. Getting through a dinner with him is hard enough, what with his insistence on inquiring about our sex life and warning me against doing anything bad to his precious girl.

If only he knew how much his precious girl liked all the bad stuff.

But this Wednesday, Coach Sahnoun had received a call from family back home in Algeria about his brother being hospitalized, and him and Mrs. Sahnoun departed that night, chartering a private jet to get there as soon as possible. Greta would have joined them had she not signed up for summer classes—I bet she regrets taking college more seriously—and had a final on Monday.

They hadn't wanted to cancel the camping trip, though, so they insisted that I go with Greta instead. And that's when I learned about the meaning behind the getaway. She'd mentioned it that first night.

It was Julien's birthday gift before he passed away. That year, Greta was going to graduate from high school, and since his birthday coincided with the day, the family would take a celebration trip to a national park and hike, something her younger brother had always wanted to do but never could because of the intense football training regimen he had.

They'd pushed it off long enough, her parents explained. It had to happen, and since I was Greta's other half, it was appropriate for me to accompany her.

Releasing Greta's hand, I set my backpack down and then reach in to grab the sweater I've secretly been carrying all weekend, just for this moment. Her dad explained its importance and adamantly dropped it off at my house on their way to the airport.

"That is the tree your parents and I bought for"—I pause and grunt as I try to yank the article of clothing from where I'd stowed it in the bottom of the pack—"your brother. In memory of him and whatnot." I don't mention that it was my idea. Now is not the time to show her how considerate and amazing I am. God, I'm such a great boyfriend sometimes.

Greta stands there stunned, and a few tugs later, I have the hideously knit jumper out. She looks at it, mesmerized. Mrs. Sahnoun had explained that it was a sweater Greta made Julien for Christmas when she was eight. Her little brother had loved it and worn it until the threads were bare. And when he couldn't put it on anymore, he cuddled with it at night as a nappie blanket.

With a successful harumph, I march over to the Julien Francis Sahnoun tree, neatly fold the wool top, and place it at the base of the trunk. I feel a little uncomfortable saying something, so I just wave at him, shoving my hands in my pocket like an idiot when I realize it might have been a little dumb to wave at something that can't wave back.

When I turn back to look at her, I smile. And instead of wearing a look of panic, she wears an expression I've never seen on her before.

But it doesn't fail to make my pulse race, giddy excitement jumping in my veins. My girl is so pretty.

"Otis?" she whispers, her voice drowned out by the sound of water rushing through the stream beneath us on this cliffside.

"What's up, ma?"

"I've got this feeling."

That's a weird thing to announce. "Like a sneeze, but better?"

"No, it's..." She doesn't finish her sentence. Allowing the

ambiguity to dangle in front of me, she instead rummages through her backpack to procure a thin white Kleenex. She hands it to me.

"What is this?" I inspect it, unsure if it's what I think it is. I mean, it is a tissue. It's just so fucking random that she's handing it to me.

"A tissue."

"I'm not blind. I'm asking what it's for. Do you want us to—I know we had sex this morning, but that was in a tent. I'm not about to fuck bare ass in the open wilderness. A beaver could come out and bite my dick off."

Her eye twitches, but I see her visibly swallow a snarky retort. She might be hot angry, but patient Greta is downright the sexiest thing I've ever witnessed. Actually, second sexiest. Dominant Greta definitely tops all.

"Remember how you told me you'd be needing a tissue or two if I were to ever say *something* to you."

Realization crashes into me before she finishes speaking and my heart seizes. The look had been different because she finally feels different.

Oh, God. Oh, I think I might throw up or faint or scream or cry. There's no time for me to prepare myself, not mentally, physically, or emotionally.

Nothing in the world could have fortified me against the force of her confession. The words I speak to her every night, which I've never expected to hear back but always held out hope to receive one day, are expelled all at once, and I'm bludgeoned by the truth and utter satisfaction in them.

"I love you."

They say the best way to traverse life is to learn from others' mistakes. And if you're not able to do that, at least learn from your own. Sounds logical, right?

But not for me. I don't do either. I thought I knew how I would react at this moment. I've imagined it many times. But I was wrong.

Because instead of crying like a little bitch like I told her I would that one night months ago, I twist the Kleenex into a makeshift ring and drop down on one knee. "Marry me."

This morning, she'd kicked me off her when I'd moaned a passionate proposal in the throes of an orgasm. This time, when she kicks me to rebuke the sincere proposal I offer, I fall back and land on an ant pile beside her brother.

It's not the beavers I should have been worried about. It's the ants crawling up my shorts and biting my dick.

But it's still worth it. Greta will always be worth it.

REMINDERS
all that matters

O   convince G to marry me

ACKNOWLEDGMENT

Being concise has never been my forte, but I'll try and make this as short as possible.

To my beta readers who had to look at this book before it was fleshed out: I'm eternally grateful for your help. Without every single one of their unique inputs, the book would not be what it is today—which is to say, it would be much worse. I could write a dissertation about how grateful I am to each and every one of you guys, but I'll just list the names, since I promised to keep this short: Sassa, Arzum, Julia, Kimmy, Kerry, Tash, Julia, Nahia, Chris, Lucia. Thank you guys, from the bottom of my heart.

To my editors. Kate, you line edited the fuck out of this book and I genuinely believe if there's any good in it, it came only from your suggestions and work. Brooke, you are an angel sent straight from the heavens. The fact that you accepted my last minute proofread request makes you just about the best person to exist.

To the readers who were willing to pick up my book and give it a chance, whether you completed it or DNFed after the first four chapters, I'm still thankful to you guys.

Finally, to Steph. You encouraged me and lifted me up when I was at my lowest. You consoled me when I cried and doubted myself entirely. You celebrated and believed in me. You are so amazing, and I have to believe your friendship is a gift from the cosmos because no one on this Earth can be this amazing and perfect. You're the reason this book happened. Love ya, hottie.

And Elma, if you're reading this: I love you. Don't tell mom.

LANGUAGE GLOSSARY
FRENCH, SPANISH AND KABYLE

Greta and Otis are both multi-cultural, with Greta having a French and Algerian (Kabyle) background, and Otis having a Spanish one. A special thank you to Chris for helping me with the Spanish (**S**), Nahia for the French (**F**) and Ruki for the Kabyle (**K**). Not every word/phrase that is non-English will be translated given how common they might be.

COMMON/REOCCURING WORDS AND PHRASES
(**F**) *Mon chat*
My kitty (darling)
(**K**) *Jedi/Setti*
Granddad/Grandmother
(**K**) *Lo siento, mijo/mi amor*
I'm sorry, son/my love

CHAPTER 1
(**F**) *Le désir de l'interdit*
Forbidden fruit is the sweetest

CHAPTER 6
(**F**) *merci beaucoup*
Thank you very much

CHAPTER 9

(**F**) *Maman! Papa! Je suis la.*

Mom! Dad! I'm here.

(**F**) *Dégage. Je suis claqué.*

Piss off. I'm exhausted.

(**F**) *Où est Papa?*

Where is dad?

(**F**) *Ici*

(He's) here

(**F**) *Trés bien*

Good

(**F**) *Recule*

Step back

(**F**) *L'espace vital tu connais?*

Do you know vital (personal) space?

(**F**) *Coucou*

Hi (slang)

(**K**) *Shnou bghiitii*

What do you want?

CHAPTER 10

(**F**) *C'était quoi ce bruit?*

What was that noise?

(**F**) *A table*

We're eating

CHAPTER 19

(**F**) *Tu vois ce que je veux dire?*

You know what I mean?

(**F**) *C'est bizarre, non?*

Weird, isn't it?

CHAPTER 22

(**S**) *Su papa.*

Your dad

(**S**) *Tes ves gringo. No sacaste herencia mía. Qué vergünza.*

You are so white. You have none of my heritage. It's a shame.

(**S**) *Pero su nombre es—Me revienta! Me vuelve loca! Ai!*

But your name—It annoys me! It drives me crazy! Aye!

(**S**) *Comportate*

Behave

(**S**) *Mal agradecida*

Ungrateful

CHAPTER 23

(**F**) *Tu es chiant*

You're a pain in the ass

(**F**) *Laisse tomber*

Never mind

CHAPTER 27

(**F**) *Va te faire foutre*

Go fuck yourself

(**F**) *Au revoir, blaireua*

Bye, badger (slang insult)

CHAPTER 29

(**F**) *Je vais teur ton pere*

I'm going to kill your father

(**F**) *Comment peut-il continuer à me briser le coeur comme ça?*

How can he keep breaking my heart like this?

CHAPTER 30

(S) *Bendición*

Blessing (a greeting between children and their parents/grandparents)

(S) *Ay, como si te importara tu familia, niña malcriada. Vete, ya!*

As if you cared about your family, (you) spoiled girl. Go away!

(S) *Pasa algo? Te duele la rodilla?*

Did something happen? Does your knee hurt?

(S) *Por qué estas triste?*

Then why are you sad?

(S) *Mi amor, háblame. Quiero—*

My dear, talk to me. I want—

(S) *Ay, hueles horrible*

You smell horrible

(S) *No puedo más*

I can't take it anymore

(S) *No me contestes*

Do not argue with me

(S) *Esto [...] Sé que no quieres hablar conmigo, pero no me importa! [...] Llego a casa y te enuentro durmiendo, o si no, estás mirando las estrellas. [...] y a veces te escucho llorar! [...] Me estás lastimando. Yo—No puedo más, Otis. Soy tu mamá y*

This [...] I know you don't want to talk to me but I don't care! [...] I come home and find you asleep, or looking at the stars. [...] and I hear you crying! [...] You are hurting me, I—I can't take it anymore, Otis. I'm your mother and

(S) *No me malinterprete*

Don't misunderstand me

(S) *Soy seria*

I'm serious

CHAPTER 31

(F) *Tinquilète je gère*

Don't worry, I can handle it

(F) *Fille irresponsable et sale*

You're irresponsible and (a) dirty (girl)

(K) *Ya tafla*

You girl

CHAPTER 33

(**F**) *Tu es complétement félè*

You are completely crazy

(**F**) *Tu me fais chier*

You are pissing me off

Made in United States
North Haven, CT
27 December 2023